HEMLOCK

ALSO BY MELISSA FALIVENO

Tomboyland: Essays

HEMLOCK

Nature held me close and seemed to find no fault with me.

—Leslie Feinberg

Oh, come and shake me till I'm dry
Oh, come to me and kill the night off

—Scott Hutchison, Frightened Rabbit

For my parents

HEMLOCK

A NOVEL

MELISSA Faliveno

LITTLE, BROWN AND COMPANY

New York Boston London

Copyright © 2026 by Melissa Faliveno

Hachette Book Group supports the right to free expression and the value of copyright. The purpose of copyright is to encourage writers and artists to produce the creative works that enrich our culture.

The scanning, uploading, and distribution of this book without permission is a theft of the author's intellectual property. If you would like permission to use material from the book (other than for review purposes), please contact permissions@hbgusa.com. Thank you for your support of the author's rights.

Little, Brown and Company
Hachette Book Group
1290 Avenue of the Americas, New York, NY 10104
littlebrown.com

First Edition: January 2026

Little, Brown and Company is a division of Hachette Book Group, Inc. The Little, Brown name and logo are trademarks of Hachette Book Group, Inc.

The publisher is not responsible for websites (or their content) that are not owned by the publisher.

The Hachette Speakers Bureau provides a wide range of authors for speaking events. To find out more, go to hachettespeakersbureau.com or email hachettespeakers@hbgusa.com.

Little, Brown and Company books may be purchased in bulk for business, educational, or promotional use. For information, please contact your local bookseller or the Hachette Book Group Special Markets Department at special.markets@hbgusa.com.

Excerpts on p. vii: *Stone Butch Blues* by Leslie Feinberg. Used with the permission of the estate of Leslie Feinberg. "I Wish I Was Sober" by Scott Hutchison (Frightened Rabbit), courtesy of Domino Publishing Company Limited. Excerpt on p. 254: T. S. Eliot, "East Coker," from *Four Quartets*, Harcourt, Brace and Co., 1943.

ISBN 9780316588195
LCCN 2025935322

10 9 8 7 6 5 4 3 2 1

MRQ-T

Printed in Canada

One

✧✧✧✧✧✧✧✧✧✧✧

SHE ARRIVED AT the cabin at night. It wasn't late, but here in the woods, in the springtime—in the far northern part of this far northern state, in this far northern country—the light left early and the dark stayed long. It was nearly pitch-black as she drove the long gravel road that cut through the trees like she was taught: slowly, her eyes scanning ditch to ditch in a figure eight for deer. She flipped on her high beams, the light cast out before her like a torch, but still had trouble seeing. She had forgotten how dark it got, this deep in the woods.

She knew she was close. She could feel it by the narrowing of the road, by the trees bending in—the bright skeletons of birch curling across the path, their bare branches reaching like arms, stark white against a black curtain of pine. The car crawled down the rutted path, too low to the ground for this kind of terrain, tires crunching over downed branches and pine cones, gravel spraying its belly like buckshot.

And then she saw it, like a beacon in the dark: the small metal sign on a low metal post, hammered long ago into the ground, a fire number blazed in white paint against red. No one in the woods had addresses or mailboxes, and there was no post office here. Mail could be sent to the grocery store in town, some fifteen miles away, where an old woman behind the counter served as de facto postmistress. But most people rarely checked, and the mail piled up, the bills turning yellow to pink, the letters from home getting more frantic and then less frequent, until the old woman behind the counter eventually threw everything away. For most people who found themselves here, and especially for those who stayed, part of the point was to disappear.

The cabin was a small place, made of hand-laid pine, that sat far back from the road in a clearing, surrounded on all sides by deep forest. She turned down the gravel drive and watched it emerge before her, materializing like a ghost from the shadows. It was smaller than she remembered. In her dreams, where it turned up often, it was huge—a hulking, looming thing with endless doors and hallways, walls that seemed to breathe; a maze of passages that changed shape and stretched on forever, into nothing. In reality, it was a normal little house, with four normal walls, a normal little porch and a chimney. It sat, unassuming, on a small slope of lawn, tucked safe inside that circle of trees. It almost looked inviting.

She parked the car but kept the engine running, the headlights casting a strange yellow glow around the house. She sat for a moment, watching it, waiting for something but not knowing what. For a figure to appear in the window, a pale hand drawing back the curtain? For the building to take a great breath, its pine-board bones expanding, filling its cavernous lungs, then sighing back into the shape of a house? Ridiculous thoughts, but there they were, unbidden in her brain. And then came another, ringing bright and clear as if someone had said it aloud: There was still time to turn back. To leave this place and never return.

She shook the thought from her head. Hopped out of the car and jogged to the shed, a large winter-faded outbuilding that served as garage, workshop, and storage unit some fifty feet from the cabin. She pulled on the heavy door, shouldering into it as it cracked up and then open.

Inside, the smell of rot. A squirrel or a mouse had probably crawled inside and died over the winter. Her stomach curled at the smell, sick and sweet. She pulled the string on a bare bulb that hung from the ceiling, but nothing happened. She squinted into the dark. At the back wall, she could make out the shape of the woodpile, a solid cord of maple and birch stacked high and neat, an axe leaning against it. The night was cold, and it would stay cold for a while, but with all this firewood she'd be set, depending on how long she stayed.

She scanned the shadows, spotted a small fishing boat with an outboard motor, covered in a tarp. And beside it, what she'd most hoped to find: her father's Chevy S-10, a late-'80s model, cherry red and perfect. She opened the door, found keys in the ignition, and turned. It sputtered for a second then roared to life. She smiled. At least she wouldn't have to drive her tiny foreign car while she was here. Nothing would make her stand out more. She jogged back to the car and cut the engine, grabbed her bags and stepped out into the night.

The darkness was a solid thing, the silence loud. It rushed through her ears like wind, leaving a high-pitched ringing in its wake. She'd developed tinnitus in the city, but the constant din could usually drown it out. Here, the sound was sharp. And beneath it, from out of the silence came a symphony: crickets and peepers and tree frogs, singing into the night. She stood in the clearing, closed her eyes, and listened. She breathed deep, swallowing the cool night air. It tasted clean and sweet, like water. She opened her eyes again. A sliver of moon peeked through the trees and cast a pale light, carving a path through tall grass to the cabin. She followed it.

A fake rock on the porch housed a spare key, as it always had. She pried open the plastic by feel, fumbled to find the lock. She turned the key and pushed the door open, then stood on the threshold. A chill passed through her body. *Like a goose walked over my grave,* her grandmother used to say. She flipped the switch on the wall by the door, but no light came.

"Shit," she said, aloud, to no one. She'd forgotten about the breakers. She'd have to go to the basement to turn them on, bring the cabin back to life. She hoped the pipes hadn't frozen, as they often did when the place sat empty through winter. She'd forgotten about the problem of arriving at night, in the dark, after the place had been closed up so long. She hadn't, it occurred to her then, thought at all about the implications of coming here like this, of being a woman alone in the woods. She hadn't considered being afraid.

She stepped inside. The place smelled musty and strange, like it belonged to someone else. Beneath the dust and damp, that same sweet suggestion of rot. Like something had lived and died in the walls. She left the door open, let a small slant of moonlight pour in. Her eyes began adjusting to the dark, and the place took shape before her. Not much had changed. It was a small space, a living room with a fireplace and a kitchen, a short hallway that led to two small bedrooms and a bath. And a door that led to the basement. The furniture was the same—same old couch and rocking chair, same old kitchen table. It had all been in her parents' house once, in the town where she grew up, several hours south of here. The furniture had made its way to the cabin over the years, piece by piece, as her parents had pared down and planned, eventually, to retire here. It was a plan, like so many, that never came to pass.

She closed the door behind her. It clicked, and she was left again in darkness. She carried her bags down the hall, running her hand along the wall. She thought of the hallways in her dreams, then shook the thought away. She chose the bedroom that had once been hers, though her parents' room was bigger. She wouldn't be able to go in there yet, not for a while.

She dropped her bags, then walked back down the hall. She stood outside the basement door, grabbed the knob and turned. It was locked. People rarely locked their doors up here, so it was strange that this one should be—from the inside, no less, and from upstairs; as if to keep whatever was down there out. She turned the lock, her heart beating fast. She imagined an animal—a raccoon or opossum, maybe even a mother bear and her cubs—having gotten in over the winter and living down there. It happened sometimes. She imagined yellow eyes in the dark, a growl and a hiss, claws and teeth. She imagined some-thing far worse could be waiting.

Among the things for which her home state was famous—beer, cheese, freezing games of football in the snow—was a long and storied tradition of serial killers. From those who made national news for eating their victims or making skin suits and furniture from their flesh, who terrorized entire generations only to be memorialized decades later in some bad true-crime docuseries; to those who got far less publicity, who kidnapped women and took them to remote northern woods like these. Like one story when she was a kid, about a college girl who'd been abducted after a night out and held captive in an abandoned cabin much like this one, not far from here. By the time the girl's body was discovered she'd been dead for weeks, and the man who killed her was never found. The story became, as such stories do, part of local lore—like Bigfoot and UFO sightings and the Paulding Light, a mysterious glowing orb that hovered above the train tracks just across the border. It became part of the mythology of the place, told around campfires in the summer. *And that's what happens when girls go out alone,* they'd say, flames casting shadows across grave faces. *Girls who wear short skirts and drink too much and ask for trouble. And that man—that monster—is still up here somewhere, roaming the woods and waiting.* When she was a girl, she'd been fascinated by these stories, with this gruesome history of her home state. It had all seemed so far away from her then, some safe distance that could never be crossed. But now she was here, and she was alone, and it all felt much closer.

She stood at the basement door and shivered, tried to stop her stupid brain from cycling through every horror it could summon. She fished her phone out of her pocket. The battery was in the red, but she flipped on the flashlight. She took a breath and opened the door.

The stairs were steep, thin planks of pine with no risers that creaked under her feet as she stepped slowly down, the small circle of electric light illuminating each step and nothing more. She reached the cement floor and stopped, then jogged to the breaker box. She felt like a kid, running to the cellar in her grandmother's farmhouse for a jar of pickles, heart slamming wildly in her chest. She tried to shake the fear, but it was no use. She'd watched enough horror movies to know that a woman going down to the basement by herself, in the dark, was a recipe for certain, brutal death.

She found the breaker box and opened it, then flipped the two switches marked with Scotch tape. *Septic, electric,* the handwriting scrawled in Sharpie. The cabin hummed to life. She flipped the light switch on the wall. Still nothing. Some bulbs would need to be changed, but she wouldn't worry about that yet. For now, she sprinted back to the stairs and then up them, slamming the basement door behind her. She locked it, leaned against it, her pulse beating hard in her throat. She flipped a switch on the wall and the hallway flooded with light. She exhaled, realized she'd been holding her breath. Everything was fine. She was fine. There was no one here. No monsters, no bears, no bad men lurking in the dark.

She walked around the cabin, turning on lights, opening taps, the pipes moaning and sputtering till the rust-colored well water ran clear. A thick layer of dust covered the counters. She surveyed the floors, found piles of dead flies along the baseboards. She cracked open the cabinets, their seals long stuck, found nothing inside but mouse droppings and an ancient box of tea. She plugged in the old yellow refrigerator, and it groaned on. She pulled back the curtains, and more dead flies fell from their folds. She opened the patio door and stepped out onto the porch, the light of the cabin burning behind her.

She looked up at the sky through the circle of trees, a spray of stars unlike anything she could see in the city. She listened to the crickets and peepers and frogs. Somewhere, not far away, the yip of a coyote, then a collective howl from its pack, a circle of hunters in the distance, echoing in the night. There were no monsters here—only the woods, and whatever lived within them. It was just her and the wilderness, deep and dark.

Two

◇◇◇◇◇◇◇◇◇◇◇◇

IT WASN'T SO much that Sam decided to leave. It was more like the leaving had been decided for her; that some external force had compelled her to go, then carried her all those miles. She packed two bags, threw them in the back of her '95 Mazda—her grand-father, a General Motors man who worked the line his whole life, no doubt rolling in his grave—and, not looking back as she shifted into fifth on the Brooklyn-Queens Expressway, pretty much vanished.

She left at night, the streets of New York and the tunnel and turnpike oddly empty, though it wasn't that late. She drove west, through New Jersey and Pennsylvania, across that endless stretch of I-80, skirting Lake Erie and heading halfway through Ohio, where she pulled over at a truck stop not long before dawn and slept until the sun rose over the Sunoco sign. She pressed on through Indiana, past the thick green stink of Gary, and into Chicago, the traffic at midday not bad but not good either, then north across the state line. Through Beloit and Monroe, where her grandparents had both worked in factories, and where her mother had too; then on through Janesville, past the burnt-out husk of the GM plant, where her grandfather had assembled chassis for over forty years, before things got bad and GM went bust and everyone, including her grandfather, had lost their pensions. He died a few years later, just before he'd planned to retire, leaving her grandmother broke and alone with a new set of suitcases. They'd never been out of the state, had planned to drive across the country, maybe get on a plane for the first time, cross an ocean and see the world.

She passed the exit for her hometown as the sun began to set again, and stepped on the gas. She wasn't ready to go back there yet, wasn't sure if she would ever be. She skirted the capital city, its lakes and rivers shimmering in the dusk, and drove north.

Even as darkness fell, she knew the way by heart. The small handful of turns had been imprinted on her body before she ever knew the names of the roads. She knew exactly where, just north of Mosinee, the smell from the paper plant, fishy and thick, would blow in through the windows. She knew the very moment when the long stretches of farmland turned, in a blink, to pine. She knew the billboards, weathered to white, advertising divorce lawyers and Adult Megastores and the World's Largest Cheese Emporium, reminders that abortion stops a beating heart and God is watching. She knew the crumbling bunker that had once been a military armory, a hulking cement mass now swallowed by weeds.

She stopped only so often, to stretch her legs and refill her coffee, hitting the same gas stations she knew from her youth, the same glowing signs like lighthouses in the middle of land-locked nowhere. She bought dusty bags of beef jerky and Sour Patch Kids to keep her mouth busy, wanting badly for a cig-arette instead. She promised herself she wouldn't buy a pack until Wausau, but only made it as far as Portage. She bought Newports, a brand she hated, the smell bringing back bad memories—the kind that worked its way into your clothes, into the carpet, and stayed. She'd bummed American Spirits from her friends in New York and occasionally bought a pack, though she never called herself a smoker. But Newports had been her mother's brand, and her grandmother's before her, and when she spotted the teal-and-white package behind the counter it had called to her. And anyway, they'd passed everything else down, so it felt right. The best way she knew to pay homage to the women who raised her.

"To the line," she said, aloud to the night, outside a crumbling Mobil station near the prison where Jeffrey Dahmer had been locked up and then murdered. She slipped the plastic off the pack and tossed it in the bin between pumps, slid a cigarette between two fingers and raised it in silent salute. Above her, the fluorescent lights flickered and then blinked out, like the streetlights always seemed to back in Brooklyn whenever she passed beneath them.

In the car, she smoked with the windows down, the menthol making her lips go numb. She passed the exit to Plainfield, where Ed Gein had made his famous lamps and leggings of women's skin. She turned the radio up, the Allman Brothers singing through blown out speakers about gypsies and freight trains and crossroads. She sang along, even as the signal faltered and fuzzed, flicking ash at the blackened highway that disappeared behind her.

She hadn't been home in years. She wasn't sure how long. She wasn't even sure she could call it home anymore, or if it had ever really been. Still, driving these empty roads at night, the roads she knew so well, it was as if she'd never left. She felt a tug of something—nostalgia, probably; regret, almost certainly;

longing, maybe most of all, for something she'd never really had. For the hope of what might have been, had things been different. Whatever it was, she knew one thing for sure: No matter how far she ran, this place always called her back.

She woke in the morning, sunlight slanting through the bedroom window. She was tired, and her head was cloudy. Her back and neck ached. She hadn't slept well, despite the exhaustion of a twenty-hour drive. She rarely slept well, but it had been worse than usual. She had heard things in the night—crunches and cracks in the woods, in the walls, each new sound making her bolt upright in bed in the dark, until she'd given up and turned on the bedside lamp like she had when she was a kid, afraid of monsters and convinced the light could save her. She'd slept in brief bright fits after that, strange dreams weaving in and out of her half-conscious mind, lamplight casting shadows on the pine-log walls.

She rubbed her eyes and sat up, the bedsheets crinkling. She'd found a set in the closet the night before, still in their plastic packaging. They were white and stiff and smelled like chemicals, like they'd never been used. There was an old, patterned afghan spread across the bed, its colors bold and gaudy, that she was pretty sure one of the many great-aunts she didn't know had made. She yawned and stretched and popped her neck, brushed a dead fly off the sheets. She grabbed her glasses off the nightstand and put them on, noticed a spiderweb stretched behind the lamp. It was large and intricate, like it had taken a long time to make and had been there a long time too. At its center, a fly carcass entombed in webbing, and a fat black spider beside it.

She couldn't tell what time it was. The light outside was

bright, but mornings in the woods were weird like that—it could be six or nine or noon, the tall pines bending up around her, the sun already high. The light and the trees played tricks.

The bedroom window was open and the cool spring air blew in, sending the still-bare branches of maple and birch tapping against the walls. Soon those trees would be blooming, but for now, she could still feel winter. This far north, the cold held on as long as it could. She kicked off the blanket and sheets and shivered. It had been so long since she'd been in this place, in this room, where she had spent so much time as a girl, the morning sun making the honey-colored pine walls glow. She could almost smell the coffee brewing, the bacon sizzling in the cast-iron skillet. Her father had always gotten up early to make breakfast.

He had built the cabin himself. It took him years, making the long drive from their hometown on weekends, after long weeks of work, sometimes with the family in tow but more often alone. With the help of some local friends, old guys who bartered labor to get by up here, where there were very few jobs, he sawed and sanded and shellacked the pine, then laid each log by hand. He installed the windows and roof, built the porch and stained it. For a long time, there was no running water or power, but he eventually had electricity and a septic system installed. No internet, never, and barely any cell service, if you picked up a signal at all. There were some modern conveniences her father wouldn't allow, and if they could have lived completely off the grid, they would have. Up here, miles deep into the woods, with very few people around, it was as close as you could get.

He'd named the cabin Hemlock, after one of his favorite varieties of pine that grew in this stretch of forest. People always named their cabins here, as if each place had its own personality, its own little life. He carved a sign out of a piece of driftwood, and they painted it together and mounted it above the door.

"If you make something," he told Sam, when the work was done and the sign was hung, "if you love something, you've got to give it a name."

That the tree—tall and tender and shade-giving—shared a name with a creeping plant full of deadly poison was something Sam thought of sometimes, but never said aloud. Her father liked the sound of it, and Sam did too.

She got out of bed, pulled on a sweater and long johns. She made coffee, then sat on the porch and drank it black, her hands wrapped around a mug that said I FISH THEREFORE I AM, her father's old favorite. Steam curled up into cold spring air that sliced into her lungs. She liked the sharpness of it. Around her, the circle of trees was dense, despite the season. The forest was made mostly of conifers and evergreens—cedar and spruce and hemlock, white pine and balsam fir—and dotted among them the deciduous hardwoods, maple and birch and basswood and oak, their branches still bare. Beyond the property lines, the deep woods of state land stretched for miles, all the way to the border. It was a region known as the Northern Highlands, part of the Chequamegon-Nicolet National Forest. Also known as the boreal forest, the Taiga, or snow forest. It was a place of many names. To the locals, though, it was known only as the Northwoods.

It was quiet—nothing but birdsong and light wind in the trees. The kind of quiet that had once brought her calm. But now, after her many years in the city, having grown so accustomed to the traffic and lights and life, the quiet made her uneasy. But she was grateful for the solitude and the space, the unpolluted air. She said a little prayer of thanks. Not to God, exactly, but to a power beyond herself. It was a practice that still made her itch, but she was working on it. She listened to squirrels and chipmunks running through the leaves. She wondered what else might be out there. The thought sent a shudder down her spine. But she took another sip of coffee, shook the feeling away. She watched too many horror movies, read too much Stephen King. She didn't have time to be afraid. There was too much work to do.

This was the plan: She would spend a few weeks fixing the place up, doing the things her father had been unable to do. She'd get the cabin in shape and then sell it. It would go fast, this little place in the woods, on several acres of land with a lake just down the road. With some work, it would even be cozy. And Sam didn't mind the work. She liked the physicality of it, after spending so many years in an office, hunched at a desk, her eyes bad and neck bent from craning toward a computer screen. She was looking forward to a little exercise, a little sweat, to spending some time in the sun and fresh air and getting strong again.

The work, she hoped, would also keep her from dealing with other things—things she had tried hard to forget, but that lived in the walls and the trees up here. The things she knew, somehow, were coming. She could feel it in her bones, the way her mother swore she could feel a storm, long before the wind had shifted and the sky turned dark.

Her parents had let the property go. The deck was in bad shape, its paint peeling, the pine boards weathered to white, a few of them rotting. A typical winter in the woods saw more than a hundred inches of snow, and the deck bore the brunt of it. It was the first task on a long list of things to do, and a big one: she'd pull up and replace the bad boards, then strip and restain the whole thing. The roof could use some patching too, but she'd let a professional do that. The kitchen sink had a leak, and the basement and garage, both packed with her parents' stuff, would need to be cleared. The lawn was overgrown with weeds, and she planned to pull them. Maybe plant some wildflowers in their place. She stood on the deck and made the list in her head.

After her mother had gotten bad, but before she was gone, Sam's father tried to keep the place up. He weeded and mowed and plowed, cleaned the gutters of leaves and snow, climbing a rusted extension ladder to the roof. Sam hated that he did this, in the middle of nowhere, with no neighbors and cell service so spotty, the nearest emergency room over an hour away. She begged him to hire some help. But money was tight, had always been tight.

Her father had worked odd jobs his whole life, often several at a time. For the past decade he'd been working at the Cenex, a combination gas station–farm store in their hometown, hauling lumber to the trucks of his friends, selling cigarettes and lotto tickets and plastic fifths of whiskey from behind the counter, his hands cramping as he rang up his neighbors' vices—none of which he ever touched himself—and slid them into brown paper bags. The last time Sam had seen her father, a year or so ago, he looked like a man of eighty rather than sixty-five.

Sam's mother had disappeared a few years before. Her parents had been at the cabin for a week that fall to watch the colors change. They thought it might do her mother some good. But one morning she went for a walk and never came home. That was it—one second she was there and the next she was gone, as if the woods had swallowed her whole.

For a while, of course, they looked for her. There was a search, and a reward no one could afford to pay. Sam came back from New York to help, trudging through the woods with her father for days, and then weeks, starting at dawn and searching until the sun fell and the air got cold. Sometimes they would go back to the cabin at dusk, eat a quick dinner of hot dogs or tomato soup and warm up their hands, then put on another layer and head back out, flashlights flickering through the forest, illuminating nothing but shadows and their breath against the night, catching the fast red flash of animal eyes, still and silent in the dark.

But then October turned to November. The leaves fell, and then the first snow. The lake began to freeze over. Eventually all the folks from town—most of them lifers, some of them tourists who hoped to get close to some kind of action, who probably listened to murder podcasts and thought they might solve a crime, who were up north for their kids' fall break and would soon leave, forgetting all about the missing woman in the woods—stopped showing up. The search parties thinned out. The cops—if you could even call the county patrol that—were no help at all. No one could find a trace of her. What they knew, the only thing they knew, was that she'd gone for a walk in the woods and never returned. She had, quite simply, vanished.

After the search—after the panic and fear and desperation had mostly passed, and after the hope had too; after the sharp sting and swell of grief had subsided into a low and steady current, leaving Sam and her father to settle into a numb and silent haze—she thought her father might be okay. That he might even be better off on his own, without someone to worry about the way he had worried about her. That the whole thing might offer him a new beginning. Sam went back to New York, and she thought maybe he'd go somewhere warm, where there was no more winter. Maybe Florida or Arizona or Palm Springs. Or maybe, like he always dreamed, he'd finally see the world.

Instead, he seemed to recede from it. His body got smaller, a once robust frame looking increasingly thin. His black hair went white. His back was stooped. His skin, which had always been a deep olive, turned pale. The light in his green eyes went dark.

Sam called him more often after her mother left, or was taken, or disappeared, or died—she never knew what words to use, and they rarely talked about it anyway—and invited him to come visit her in Brooklyn.

"You can stay with us," she said more than once.

"I don't want to be a burden," he said.

"Dad, you're never a burden. Come stay as long as you'd like. You can crash on our couch and see the city. You can show me all your old haunts, we can go to a game."

"Maybe," he said, a quick glint of possibility in his voice that faded fast.

Sam's father had grown up in the Bronx, in a large and loud Italian family, and for a stretch of years had worked in the city repairing vending machines in hospitals and office buildings, taking the train to a Yankees game whenever he could score tickets—usually scalped, often slipped into his shirt pocket as an under-the-table payment by the guys he worked for.

When Sam was young, her father told stories about those guys. *Wiseguys*, he called them—guys with names like Tiny and Sal and Little T, Bobby the Eye and Paulie the Hook.

"Did he really have a hook?" a young Sam once asked, wide-eyed, dreams already haunted by the hook-handed man.

"Nah," her father said with a laugh, tousling her hair. "Threw a helluva punch, though."

Back then, Sam had never been to New York. In her father's stories, it seemed to her a world away—massive, teeming, scary. A place where you could get lost and never be found. Sam was sure her father had a lifetime of stories he'd never told her. He had seen some shit, she knew, but never said much about it. He was one of those guys who grew up poor in the city and dreamed of getting out—to escape the crowds and the noise and a cramped apartment full of people to open space, clean air and quiet. Where he might have a little patch of land and a place to call his own. The cabin was supposed to be that for him—his refuge, a place that was his, a place that would keep his family safe.

He never took her up on coming to stay, and he never went back to the cabin. He couldn't go back, he said. It was where he and Sam's mother were meant to spend the rest of their days, and where her mother had been happiest. It was also where, he and Sam both understood without saying it, she had finally, and fully, given in to whatever demons had possessed her for so long—where she finally let go of her tenuous grip on reality, and dissolved into the darkness of her mind. It seemed, sometimes, Sam's father said, not just that the woods had taken her, but that she wanted to be taken. He couldn't bear to go back.

So Sam went back for him. It was the one thing she could do. She'd fix the place up and then sell it, get her father some money to retire on, to move somewhere else and start over. He'd be okay, she told him. They'd both be okay. They'd stop searching for her in every crowd; they'd take the missing-person website down. It was stupid to have one anyway—barely anyone had Wi-Fi in the woods, and even if you did, there was rarely a connection. So they'd stop looking. They'd stop hoping she'd come back. They'd move on with their lives, and everything would be okay. Sam forced herself to believe it, for both of them.

She thought of this on the first day, in the morning, as she made her list of things to do. She thought of it later as she washed the deck, prepping it for refinishing. She went at it with a home-made solution of water and bleach—most chemical cleaners, her dad had taught her, could poison plants and animals—and used a deck brush to scrub it clean. She rinsed it with a garden hose, sunlight catching the water and creating a rainbow, and sub-merged her head under the stream. She tried not to think about any of it, tried not to think at all, just let the work carry her into a methodical lull. The sky was clear and the sun was high, and it was warm for spring. She was sweating through her shirt. Her arms and back began to ache. She felt out of shape, but she liked the work. It was work her father had taught her to do, that they once did together—silent, sweating, and focused. Afterward, happy.

She surveyed her work. The deck was clean. The next step would be to pull up and replace the rotting boards—she'd spot-ted several more that needed to go, now that they were clean. She noted the black patches, pressed her fingers into the soft parts of the wood. She'd save that for another day.

She took off her T-shirt and tossed it on the railing, wearing a sports bra and cutoff shorts, and ran her head under the hose again. She felt exposed, her pale stomach showing, even though no one could possibly see her. There was no one around for miles. Still, she had the distinct feeling she was being watched. She always did, up here, especially after her mother disappeared. She swallowed hard, her throat gone dry. She was thirsty.

She drank from the hose, the well water clean and cold, and tried to shake the feeling. She closed her eyes. She was fine. It was only the first of what would be a long stretch of days, and weeks, and more work than she had imagined, but she was ready to feel strong again, capable and sure like she had back home but never had in New York.

You've gotten soft, she'd tell herself sometimes, standing in front of the bathroom mirror in her Brooklyn apartment, flicking the flab under her arms, pounding a fist into the flesh of her thigh until a dark bruise bloomed, scratching her fingernails across the skin of her stomach. It was an old habit, from a long time past, which reared up once in a while—like some dark spirit inside her that lay dormant for long stretches of time, making itself known like a ghost in the house it haunted, knocking a book off a shelf, flickering the lights—as if to remind her it was still there, still inside her; that it possessed her and would never leave.

Now, here in the woods, in the sun, her muscles ached in a way they hadn't in a long time. It was a good kind of pain—the kind that made her feel a little closer to the place, and the people, she came from. The kind of pain that meant something being torn down in order to build something better. The kind of pain that meant transformation.

She stood on the porch her father had built, shirt off and sweating and alone. And this, she knew—just like her father, and like her mother too—was all she ever wanted.

Three

◇◇◇◇◇◇◇◇◇◇◇◇

IT STARTED WITH a beer. Just one beer, on a warm night, not long after she arrived. She hadn't planned it. She told herself this. It was as if the place had planned it for her, had willed it into being. That it was written in the stars, or maybe the trees. That it was always meant to be.

She found the six-pack in the basement. Its vintage uncertain, the bottles thick with dust. She discovered it as she surveyed the small cement workroom, packed with tools and garden supplies, trying to decide what she might get rid of and what she might keep.

It was sitting on the damp concrete floor, tucked in shadow beneath the workbench. She hadn't seen it before, though she'd been in this room several times since arriving, looking for tools and birdseed and shrink-wrapped packages of suet. It just appeared one day, she would swear it, inexplicable and ominous—like the Necronomicon, she thought, compelling some innocent teenager to open the obviously evil thing and start turning pages, chanting the words inside. She should ignore it. She knew this. You never open the book of the dead. You don't even touch the thing. You leave it the fuck alone, pretend you never saw it. But here she was, pulling the six-pack from out of the shadows anyway. She looked at it, chewing the inside of her cheek, then slid a single glass bottle from its little cardboard holster and held it aloft. She turned it in the light of the bare bulb that hung from the ceiling. A shaft of dust slanted in the air around it, creating a strange kind of halo. She ran a thumb over the dark-brown glass, leaving a trail in the dust. She licked her lips.

She brought the six-pack upstairs, planning at first to dump it all out. It was probably skunked anyway. But then she watched her hand slide it into the fridge, and it was some other hand, moving beyond her. *What harm could it do?* she found herself thinking. Maybe she even deserved it. After putting in so many hours of work, her back and arms and body sore. She told herself this time would be different. She told herself she'd be all right.

That evening, she sat on the porch at dusk, cold bottle in hand. She listened to the birds. Watched the hummers dive past, then land, strangely still, on the feeders she'd filled with sugar water like her mother had taught her, letting it cool on the kitchen counter before carefully filling the bright-red vessels, their little plastic drinking spouts shaped like tiny yellow flowers.

She took the first long drink and watched the squirrels, perched on a plastic trough in the yard that sat on a sawed-off tree stump. The trough was filled with corn for the deer—another habit of her mother's, one she knew wasn't good for the ecosystem up here but that she carried on anyway. She knew her mother would have wanted her to.

She took another drink and then drained the bottle, her body settling into a buzz. It felt good, on that spring evening, winding down from the day. The sun dipped below the tree line, the forest around her breathing and alive, and she felt alive too. For the first time in a very long while, she felt happy.

But then one beer turned, as it does, to two, and in a couple of days the six-pack was gone. There was nothing else in the cabin, but for a few dusty two-liters of club soda and tonic in a back cabinet, and an ice bucket for entertaining, though her parents never entertained—least of all up here, in the middle of nowhere, in this cabin in the woods.

And so she drove to town, some fifteen miles of back roads, to the combination gas station–grocery store. *Just a six-pack,* she'd thought as she grabbed it, eschewing the cheap stuff for a high-octane IPA, but as the cooler door snapped closed, she found herself pressing on into the spirits aisle. An appropriate name, she thought, as if the aisle were full of ghosts.

Like most grocery stores in this part of the state, Hal's had very little produce, cheap nonperishables of suspect vintage, and a very decent liquor section. She walked past the wilted lettuce and bruised apples and stale bags of white bread to the far back aisle, past a long metal rack of bad wine and wine-product, mostly Smoking Loon merlot, which was not actually merlot but a heinous red blend sold for three bucks a pop at every grocery store and gas station in the state. She made her way to the brown liquors, the kind she liked best, past the huge plastic handles of Korbel brandy, a state favorite, and on to the bourbon. She ran her fingers along the glass, tracing the cool, smooth curves of the bottles, the amber liquid inside them glowing in the fluorescent light of the store.

She stopped, realizing as if for the first time where she was and what she was doing, and turned to leave. Then she turned around again, facing the bottles head-on. She picked up her brand from back in Brooklyn and a rush of adrenaline spiked to her brain. Her vision began to spark at the edges, then faded fast to black. She stood in the aisle, momentarily blind, heart beating behind her eyes. It was a thing that used to happen to her all the time, but it had been a while. She felt her hand reach out to grab a metal shelf, holding herself up. And then—nothing. A vast black void in space and time. She had no idea where she went when it happened, or what was happening at all. She had no idea how long it lasted. She knew only that everything, including herself, had been swept away, like chalk erased on a blackboard. There one minute and gone the next, a brief disappearing act of her own.

And then, eventually, the metal shelves and humming cooler and flickering fluorescent lights slowly rematerialized. She blinked, and shook her head, and let go of the shelf she was holding. The bottle of bourbon was still in her hand. She walked back down the aisle. The old woman at the register didn't raise an eyebrow. She had no idea, of course. Or maybe she knew too well. Sam watched the woman slide the bourbon into a brown paper bag and thought of the first sip, the moment that always felt like waking up. Like her brain had been zapped back to life after a long sleep. Like her heart had been shocked back to beating after death, her whole body buzzing. She took her whiskey neat, two or three fingers in a rocks glass, and there was no greater anticipation than that first pour—before the veil dropped and numbness took over, before her brain fogged up and she fell into the wide open mouth of oblivion. She liked that part too, the oblivion, but second only to the first sip. This, to her, was sublime. It was the closest she'd ever felt to God.

Until arriving in the woods, she hadn't had a drink in ten months. She should have stopped sooner—years earlier, like on her twenty-sixth birthday, when she'd gotten into a fight at a bar in Brooklyn and spent two nights in Central Booking. The fight was with a man, who was drunk and stupid and loud, and when she clocked him in the jaw with a right hook it felt good.

Don't stop at the target. She'd heard her uncles' voices in her head as she swung, one of the many lessons they'd taught her. *When your fist hits his face, keep going. Follow through.*

Her knuckles had hurt for days, but it had been worth it. Fighting, and being thrown in jail, was something that happened to women back home, to the women in her family, to the women who had been her friends, who wore cropped white tank tops and days-old eyeliner, tramp stamps and tribal tattoos fading to blue on their backs. It did not happen to the women she knew in New York, the kind she pretended to be. But sometimes that old self came swinging back. It had landed her in all sorts of bad spots back home—strangers' beds and basements, too many bathroom floors to count; a park bench at the edge of town, a man with gray hair buckling up his belt; a stint in the emergency room, where she'd come to after a blackout to find a doctor sewing up her wrists, the cuts running lengthwise like she meant it.

"The ol' devil rum," her grandmother had called it, shaking her head and smiling, two teeth missing, swearing off the stuff as sin even as she sipped her Diet Coke laced with whiskey, a daily ritual she thought was a secret but everyone knew full well. "It'll tell you things."

When Sam found herself curled on a bench in that small, hot cell full of women downtown—some muttering to themselves, some shouting, some curled into shivering balls like her, sweating out whatever poison was pumping through their own veins—she promised herself she was done. And she had been, for a while.

But eventually she came back, just like she always had. Just like everyone in her family always had. Making promises to themselves, to everyone else, but never once sticking to them. Sometimes drying out just long enough for a kernel of hope to pop in the people they loved, even though anyone who's ever loved a drunk knows that having hope is the most hopeless thing.

Ten months ago, though, she swore it off for good. And she meant it this time. She'd been crossing off the days on the calendar, relishing each thick black X she drew in Sharpie, holding tight to the promise of a year.

Here in the woods, back in this state she had once sworn off too, she tried not to think about the way it had snuck back, so swiftly, into her skin, then settled in—like a vampire she welcomed through the door, like a demon she'd summoned herself. It set up camp in her spine, in her chest, in the back of her throat. Just a tickle at first, like spit swallowed wrong, then threatening to choke her. A monster that grew fast and strong as she fed it.

She told herself, at first, that she was stronger than it was; that she was safe from the knowledge—creeping around her brain, a whisper in her ear—that she was alone, that no one was watching, that no one would ever know.

Now, so soon after arriving, she found herself back at the beginning, all those black X's erased. She woke each day in bed to the sound of a woodpecker banging against the maple outside her window, to the sun, already high and bright, and her head ached. Her memory was a fog; she kept forgetting where she was. Each morning, she felt the old familiar waves of nausea run through her, and alongside them waves of shame. And each morning she said, "Enough."

But by afternoon, as the sun fell below the tree line, the thirst always returned. Whether she wanted to feel empty or full, she wasn't sure. Either way, it was never enough.

"Just a beer," she'd say to herself, pulling a bottle from the fridge and popping the cap with her grandmother's church key, which she carried on a ring clipped to her beltloop. And then: that blissful little crack and hiss like Pavlov's bell, and she the slavering dog.

"Just this one."

She said it aloud, in the cabin's small kitchen, repeating it as she sat down on the porch, as if making a promise to the trees and the squirrels, to the birds and the crickets and peepers. To anyone who would listen, and maybe hold her to it. Most of all, she said it to herself. Sometimes she said it with conviction. Sometimes she said it like a prayer. Sometimes, at least until cracking a second beer, or pouring herself two fingers of bourbon—tilting the glass in the low evening light, watching the legs of the liquid climb and fall in long slow sine waves, letting the sweet poison work its way into her blood—she believed it.

Four

◇◇◇◇◇◇◇◇◇◇◇◇

"HOW LONG WILL you be gone?" Stephen asked.

Sam was packing, stuffing a large hiking backpack with clothes for every season. She never knew what kind of weather she was going to find in the woods, but knew she'd be gone long enough to see at least one season change. She brought shorts and wool socks, flannel shirts and tank tops, a winter hat and gloves, sunscreen and running shoes and a swimsuit.

"Just a couple weeks," she said, stuffing an oversized wool sweater into the bag, one of her father's that he had given her a few Christmases back, the last time she'd been home, because she never packed warm enough clothes when she went back in the winter. A couple of weeks would be good—just enough time to fix the place up. She wasn't planning to stay long.

"That seems like a conservative estimate," Stephen said, folding one of her T-shirts. He folded wrong, his creases always crooked, and she had to refold her clothes whenever he did laundry. Sam had worked retail jobs at discount clothing stores when she was younger, and she was fastidious about folding.

She'd been called obsessive more than once. She'd always been that way, lining up figurines on her dresser when she was a kid, making sure everything was in order. Since her mom disappeared, the habit had gotten worse. She'd taken to reorganizing the medicine cabinet, the junk drawer, the books, making sure their spines were aligned. Each morning she'd adjust the objects on her desk and nightstand until they met in symmetrical lines. She nudged kitchen chairs to ensure the legs formed right angles with the tile. Her father was like this too—they clawed at control wherever they could find it.

But she let Stephen help her now, resisting the urge to refold. She let him feel useful. He finished folding the shirt, then placed it on the pile. The cat jumped up on the bed and crawled into Sam's bag, as she always did when Sam was packing. She started purring, rubbing her cheeks against the straps and buckles, looking up at Sam.

"I can't take you, sweet face," she said. "I'm sorry." She was always better at apologizing to the cat than to Stephen. Better at showing her affection, too.

"I love you," she said, to the cat, to the man. "I'll be back soon."

Sam plucked the cat from the bag and pressed her to her chest. The cat, who they'd named Monster, rubbed her face against Sam's chin. The cat was black, with bright-green eyes. They'd adopted her together, on Thanksgiving Day several years before, but she had always been more Sam's cat than Stephen's. They called her Sam's familiar.

She set the cat back down, and she curled up inside one of Sam's sweatshirts, a little Garfield purring beneath the fabric. Stephen laughed and Sam did too, and she felt a stab of guilt, a slow creep of panic. This was her little family, and she loved them. She didn't want to leave.

"Maybe you could come?" she said, rolling up a pair of socks, not looking at Stephen.

"You know I can't," he said, letting the air spill out in a sigh. He looked at her, his eyes a little pleading, and she knew he wanted to, though they both knew he couldn't. She'd taken an unpaid leave from work, and he had a school year to finish.

"I know," she said. "I'm sorry."

"It's okay," he said. "I wish I could come."

"I wish you could too," she said, "and bring the Monster with you. We could hole up in the woods together and never come back."

"That does sound good," he said, but gave her a quick sideways look as he said it, setting another badly folded shirt atop the stack. She had worn a black T-shirt and jeans pretty much exclusively her entire adult life, except when she was at work, when she wore the same five button-downs every week. She had given away all the skirts and dresses gathering dust in her closet—relics of the past, things she wore when she was young, when she was trying to be something she was not and would never be.

"Can you imagine?" she said. "If we just left? Together? Got the fuck out and never came back?"

"I have imagined it," he said. "In fact, I've imagined it so thoroughly I've made a spreadsheet. You should see it. It's beautiful."

Sam laughed. Stephen loved spreadsheets and made them for everything. Color coded and exceptional, it was how he made sense of things. Sam joked that seeing Excel math made her disassociate. Stephen joked that he would put it in Google Sheets instead. It was something she loved about him more deeply than she could articulate.

They talked about leaving all the time. They'd both lived in New York for fifteen years, since their early twenties. For a while, Sam had liked her life in the city. She had a job at a magazine, and liked the work she did: exacting and precise, there was a right and a wrong, an answer to every question. It was her job to fix things, to find the broken parts and put them back together, make each story better. She loved the feeling of making something—of sitting in the office late in the evenings at each issue's close, then holding the finished product in her hands. She felt like she was part of something solid, something she could touch, something stable and predictable. A kind of order, she supposed, in a life that had seen very little of it.

But outside the office, she often felt like she was pretending. At cocktail receptions and fundraisers she attended for work, she felt like a fraud. She met rich people whose only job seemed to be attending such parties, and the well-groomed young artists and writers born to them, kids Sam's age who never had to worry about debt or what came next.

You have no idea where I come from, she found herself thinking sometimes, as she stood around a gallery, on her third glass of free wine, talking to some famous poet or finance person or wealthy donor. *You have no idea who I am.*

In recent years, it had become a kind of mantra. She repeated it in her head, sometimes even whispered it aloud, mouthing the words like song lyrics on her walk from the train to the office downtown, past so many people in expensive suits. Back home, when she was young, Sam didn't think much about money. Most of her family and friends lived in apartments and duplexes and trailer parks, but her parents had owned a house. It was small, but it was theirs. They worked hard—physical jobs that would bend their backs with age—to give her the kind of life they'd never known. She knew she was lucky, that to not think too much about money was a privilege.

But in New York, she thought about it all the time. It was impossible not to. It existed on the surface of everything, and it ran deeper. It was inherent, inherited, something that lived in your blood. It came in the form of education and family lines, the way you spoke and the way you held your body at parties. What you did for work, if you worked at all. Sam was hired at thirty-two thousand a year and had to bartend at night to make rent. Everything about her gave her away: her old blazers from H&M, her hesitation over which fork to use at gala dinners, when she dropped a *g* from a word in conversation. When she turned down invitations to fancy restaurants and bars, knowing she couldn't afford her share. She had never felt so broke.

"Living in the city is so hard," her boss would say, talking about his kids' private-school tuition or his summer house on Shelter Island, and Sam would have the sudden and specific urge to pick the stapler off his desk and throw it as hard as she could at his clean, Waspy face.

The city did that to you. It made you love and hate in equal parts. You loved all the things the city could afford—its museums and restaurants and music and art, its lights and life and possibility. But that word, *afford*, was key. It was a place that made you want. And want became a way of life; it became fuel, like food. You never stopped being hungry. To exist this way had begun to make Sam itch. It made her want to peel off her skin, unzip the thin carapace in which she lived, step out of it and start over once again.

Sam and Stephen had lived together for nearly a decade. He took care of her, a thing that still shocked her after so many years. She'd wake up and find him next to her, in their little Brooklyn apartment, and she would feel like she was hovering outside her body, watching someone else's life. He'd get up and make coffee, then bring her a mug and a book in bed. It was strange, that someone could treat her in such a way, and, so far, hadn't left. They'd lie in bed on Sunday mornings, the cat curled at their feet, and she'd look at her little family and think, *This is someone else's life.*

Sam had dated a lot of shitty men. Drunk men, bad men. Some had hit her, shoved her, held her too hard. One had thrown a plate at her head, the porcelain shattering across her skull and leaving a small white scar in the shape of a claw on her temple. And this, she thought, when a bruise bloomed on her stomach, when she wore long sleeves to cover up the red stamp of finger- prints on her wrist, was exactly what she deserved. She certainly didn't deserve a nice man, the kind of man who was stable and dependable, whose last intention would be to harm her.

Stephen was the kind of man who moved easily through the world. He was handsome and charming, half Cuban and half a bunch of other stuff, and talked to the neighbors in fluent Span- ish. The guys who played dominoes on the sidewalk called him Papi, and the women in the laundromat did too. As they did their laundry on Saturdays, he'd translate the telenovela play- ing on the TV above the washers, whispering giddily about who was sleeping with whose wife, who had killed whom in a jeal- ous rage. Sam both admired and envied the way Stephen seemed to fit wherever he went, from gallery to bodega, while she felt increasingly like she belonged nowhere.

They lived in a tiny, rent-stabilized apartment, a vinyl-sided six-family in Greenpoint where the stove rarely worked and the water was never hot. But their neighborhood was tree-lined and quiet. They knew their neighbors, and the annual summer block party felt like a family reunion. Things were changing, though. The trees were cut down and old buildings razed, making way for hideous cement condos with empty retail space on street level, where beloved family-run shops and restaurants used to be, and which would eventually become CBD dog treat dispensaries or upscale clothing boutiques selling $200 shirts that smelled of sandalwood. They still walked the twelve blocks to the Associated, and the last remaining fruit stand, while watching an increasing number of Amazon and Instacart trucks deliver groceries to the faceless strangers inside slate-gray towers around them. There was constant construction, the sound of jackhammers and pile-drivers composing the soundtrack to their days, the Polish and Puerto Rican families pushed from apartments they'd lived in for generations, replaced by trust-fund kids who worked in marketing and called themselves "creatives." Now Sam and Stephen couldn't walk down the street without feeling implicated in this mess, hating their new neighbors and missing the trees, the sun blacked out by massive cement monoliths that soared to the sky.

When they first met, Sam was renting a cheap room in a railroad apartment a few blocks away that had been turned, less than legally, into a three-bedroom. What should have been a door was a moving blanket tacked to molding, and she had to walk through her roommates' bedrooms to get to the bathroom. They'd gotten bedbugs twice, and Sam had worn turtlenecks to work in the summer to hide the bites on her neck. Her commute to Manhattan was made of three trains, packed with pukers, flashers, frottagers, proselytizers, and fidgety people she knew not to look in the eye. But she found the subway miraculous. She could go anywhere, shoot miles underground and see something new every time. She took the train to the Lower East Side and the Village, to Flushing and the Rockaways. She went to the Met on Friday nights when admission was free, stayed until they kicked her out.

She knew nothing about art, but it didn't matter. She could just stand in front of a painting and look, and no one would notice her.

She had come to New York to be a writer. Or at least that's what she told people. It was a thing that seemed like a pipe dream, that would have made her grandparents, had they still been alive, press their lips together in a thin straight line. She doubted she would ever make it, but a professor once told her she had promise, and New York seemed a place made of promises. It was a place you went if you had a dream, and it felt like she should have one. More than anything, though, she wanted to escape. To disappear and start over. New York was a place for that too. So she bought a box of white Christmas lights at the dollar store and strung them in her window. And on nights she wasn't working, she wrote. She was alone, and she was happy. She hadn't planned on meeting anyone, especially not a man.

Sam had dated both women and men, and if there had been a video to the Replacements' "Androgynous," one of her favorite songs, she might have been the star. She had short dark hair, buzzed at the sides and neck; a small chest and straight line of a waist; olive skin and dark hair on her arms. She was often mistaken for a man, regularly got called Sir in restaurants, watched women do double takes in bathrooms, and more than once had been told she was in the wrong line or locker room. When she was younger this had bothered her, but as she got older she had settled more into herself. She wasn't easily decipherable, and she was mostly okay with that. It was only when people made a big deal of it that she wished to crawl inside herself and disappear.

Before Stephen, she had been in love only once, with a woman. She never snuck out of the woman's house at dawn, hungover and ashamed, like most of the men she slept with. For the first time in her life, she had wanted to stay. But the woman had broken her heart. She wasn't gay, she told Sam, the last time they spoke.

"I'm not sure I am either," Sam had said. "I don't really know what I am."

And it hadn't really mattered. Sam didn't have the words for what they were, or what she was, but she didn't care. Some long-sealed well of understanding had opened up in her. All she knew was that she loved this woman and wanted to be loved back. It was the first time she felt such a thing, and it was a long time ago. When she met Stephen, she felt it again. She allowed herself to feel it, let it wash over her like a whiskey buzz, all warmth and swell inside her skin, filling her whole body up. It reminded her of what she once felt in church—a feeling that kept bringing her back, long after she stopped believing. For the first time in a long time, she had allowed herself to feel hopeful. Like something good might finally come her way.

Five

<figure>◇◇◇◇◇◇◇◇◇◇◇◇</figure>

WHEN THE DEER first spoke to her, she was sure she was hallucinating. She'd seen things before, visions appearing and then
vanishing like dreams. In the house where she grew up, in a dark
corner, she once saw an old woman curled in a rocking chair.
When she switched on the light, there was no woman, but the
chair was rocking. More than once, she saw a figure disappearing into the guest room, a cold burst of air passing over her skin
like a breath. As she got older, the visions almost always came
when she'd been drinking. Once she saw a man in the road, stepping out of the corn, as she drove home from a dive bar outside
town. It was a place she frequented in college, far away from
campus where the bartenders never carded and no one knew
her name, where she could drink as much as she wanted and get
into her car without someone insisting on taking her keys. She
had swerved that night to miss the man, then spun out and skid-
ded to a stop, tires screeching. When she looked in the rearview
mirror, there was no one behind her. She got out of the car and
called out, but heard only crickets, the car's clicking engine, the

echo of her own voice in the night. She stepped off the shoulder and into the corn, green and summer-high, certain at any second the man would jump out, attack her, something. But there was no man. There was nothing. Just her and the silence, the endless rows of corn.

The deer was different. It was a doe, a young mother with her ribs sticking out, skinny from winter and very real. She'd been coming to the yard each morning, just after dawn, and again each evening at dusk, to eat from the feeder Sam filled. She knew she wasn't supposed to feed the deer—chronic wasting disease was still a problem, and it was technically illegal here. She'd made a critical mistake a few days before, when she drove to the hardware store in town to buy a bag of corn. The bags were stacked on flats outside, next to a freezer where musky and northern and largemouth bass were kept on display, part of a summer-long contest to see who could snag the biggest fish. The winner, announced in August at the annual Musky Fest on Main Street, received a gift certificate to the local bar. Sam had looked at the fish, scaled and hideous, their sharp bottom teeth curling up in gnarly underbites, creating insane-looking grins across their frozen fish faces. She'd gone inside the shop to pay, a bell jingling above the door.

"Hi there," the woman behind the counter said. "What can I do you for?"

"Hi," Sam said. "Just a bag of cracked corn, please."

The woman—older but not old, hair graying at the temples, with stern but not unkind eyes—looked at Sam, clearly an out-of-towner in her black clothes, the opposite of the loose-fitting light colors locals wore. Sam watched the woman take in the strange shape of her, ready to be misgendered or worse. But the woman only raised an eyebrow above her glasses.

"Whuddya feeding?" she asked.

"Um," Sam said, stretching out the sound of it. She knew she should lie, had never had trouble lying, but for some reason she told the truth.

"Deer," she said.

The woman nodded once, turned to the register and rang her up.

"You want whole corn," she said, the antique register dinging. "That'll be twelve fifty."

Sam handed the woman a twenty, and the woman counted back the change.

"And next time someone asks," the woman said, looking at Sam, one corner of her mouth curling up, "you say squirrels."

Sam had smiled, and thanked her, embarrassed but grateful for the kindness. She walked outside, the bell jingling again, and threw the fifty-pound bag of corn over her shoulder and into the truck, the fish smiling their sick grins behind her as she drove back into the woods.

When the deer spoke to her, she was sitting on the porch at dusk, drinking a beer. She'd had a productive day. That morning she'd been weeding—pulling up yards of a stick-like vine, an invasive species that was taking over the forest, reaching beneath the soil and strangling the native plants. She'd begun cleaning the garage out too, had packed several black contractor bags with rusted-out tools and trash. She'd thrown the load in her father's truck and taken it to the dump—or transfer station, as they called it—in the next town over. When she got back to the cabin, the sun was dipping in the late-afternoon sky. Her back and arms were sore, her hands raw from the weeding despite wearing a pair of her mother's old gardening gloves. She swept up the garage, then decided she deserved a beer. By the time the doe showed up, she was on her third.

She read a book while she drank, some old thriller she'd found on the shelf, and listened to the wind in the trees. It always sounded like water, like a lake or a river or rain, some liquid body moving through the forest. It was a sound she'd discovered had a name—*psithurism*—from the Greek, she'd written down in the small notebook she carried, *to whisper.* It was a sound here that never seemed to stop, even when there was no wind. Just a steady, gentle rushing—of air, energy, life. It gave Sam a feeling that the trees were breathing; that they stood around her like sentinels, keeping watch, protecting her from whatever dangers might be lurking beyond them.

She thought of this as the doe made her way down the hill on the western side of the property, emerging tentatively from the tree line and into the clearing.

Sam heard her coming before she saw her, the soft crunch of hooves on dead leaves. The doe had been coming to the yard this way for a few days, since Sam first brought home the corn and filled the feeder. It had taken her a while to adjust to the sound of the doe's footsteps in the woods, afraid at first it might be a bear or a wolf or worse, but she came to recognize the footfalls of the deer, and of the squirrels, of the chipmunks and the birds digging for bugs on the forest floor. Every sound was amplified, the sound much larger than its source—especially as evening fell, as the sky turned to soft pink haze and the woods went dark, when you couldn't see what was out there.

She sat still as the doe approached, holding her breath, afraid of scaring her away. The doe edged into the yard and stood still, ears twitching, tail flicking, haunches shuddering. She crept to the feeder, a plastic trough Sam kept on a sawed-off tree trunk, where her mother had kept it before her. The doe bobbed her head low, then snapped it back up every few seconds, listening for predators, ready to flee. When she was sure she was safe, or at least safe enough, she dropped her head into the corn and ate. She knew Sam was there, just a few feet away, and stopped every few seconds to watch her while she chewed. Sam, in turn, watched the doe—saw her jaw move in slow circles, heard the crunch of the corn, her teeth cracking into it, the sound echoing through the trees. The doe swallowed, and for a moment she kept her eyes on Sam, unblinking. Sam did the same. The doe dropped her head into the feeder again and took another bite.

Sam brought the beer to her lips and took a drink. That's when she heard the voice.

"I've been watching you," the doe said.

Sam froze, the bottle still aloft. She stared at the doe in silence, wondering if she'd imagined it. Maybe the beer was playing tricks, as it had so many times before. Maybe, after the long day's work, she had sat down in the sun and fallen asleep. Maybe she was dreaming.

But no—there was the wind in the trees, on her skin, there was the book and the bottle in her hands. There was the doe, her eyes looking straight into Sam's.

She swallowed the beer, then set the bottle down, and found herself speaking back.

"Oh yeah?" she said, her voice seeming to exist outside itself. "Well, I've been watching you too."

"You're alone," the doe said.

"So are you," Sam said.

"Not for long," the doe said. And Sam knew it was true. Soon, she imagined, the doe would start showing up with a fawn, a small fuzzy reddish-brown thing with stick legs that stumbled when it walked, who would quickly grow into a young doe. A daughter. They would take turns at the feeder, one trotting away to stand guard while the other ate, dancing on and on like that until they were full.

"I won't be alone forever either," Sam said. The words were slow and thick on her lips. "I'll be going home soon."

"Good," the doe said. "You don't belong here."

Sam felt a pang of defensiveness. "Maybe I do," she said.

"Maybe someday," the doe said. "In another life. But right now, you have a different life to get back to. You can't stay here."

Sam didn't know who this deer thought she was. She felt indignant then, ready for a fight. Alcohol did this to her, a fact she always forgot when it was happening. She could go from zero to murderous in an instant, and all that mattered was the red-hot veil of rage that fell over her eyes, a darkness she could rarely see into when she was sober. She would wrestle this deer if she could catch her, throttle her furry little throat.

"Whatever," she said, resisting the urge to hurl her bottle at the doe, taking a drink instead.

The doe looked at her, cocked her head, and for a moment said nothing. Sam could have sworn then that she smiled—tight-lipped and wry, a look her grandmother used to give her.

"Better be careful," the doe said at last. "There are things up here that will hurt you. Things that will hunt you. Things out in the woods that are waiting."

Sam brought the bottle to her lips again, though it was empty. The doe paused, and stared Sam down, her black eyes unblinking.

"Something is coming," the doe continued. Her eyes had gone cold, her voice grave. Sam could have sworn it got deeper, louder, that it echoed in the trees.

"You won't know when it will come," the doe said, her voice like a sudden storm cloud looming, threatening to break. "But it's getting close. It will be here soon."

Sam set her bottle down on the table. She shivered. Evening was falling, and the wind had shifted. Soon it would be dark.

The doe stood still and silent, looking at Sam. Then she flicked her tail. The storm seemed to pass.

"You should stop drinking too," she said, the light back in her voice. Then she buried her muzzle back into the corn and chewed, the crunching loud and sharp and a little funny, filling the sky with sound. Her mouth worked its methodical circles, her eyes blank, just like a deer and not some mysterious woodland oracle.

She swallowed and stared at Sam a few seconds more. Then her ear twitched, and a long shudder ran down her spine to her skinny haunches, and she sprang away into the woods, leaving Sam alone in the dying light of day.

Six

◇◇◇◇◇◇◇◇◇◇

THERE WAS A knock on the door. It was morning, rainy and cool, the kind of spring drizzle that settled in your bones and set you to shivering. She was working in the basement, boxes and bags of tools and trash on all sides like the moat around a castle. She stopped when she heard the knock, stood still and listened.

Another knock, then a series of them—loud and firm, making the screen door rattle.

"Hello?" A voice rang out. A man's voice, deep and booming. Sam remembered she'd left the door open to air the place out. Whoever it was could walk right in.

"Anyone home?" The voice sounded friendly enough, but Sam had long ago stopped trusting friendly-seeming men.

She waited to hear the screen door swing open on its hinges then slam against the frame, to hear footsteps inside the house. She waited, and hoped instead to hear the crunch of gravel under boots as the man walked back down the drive. But the footsteps didn't come. The man didn't enter, but he also didn't leave.

"I'm a neighbor," the voice called out. "From down the road."

Sam let the air out of her lungs, her fear replaced with anger. *Don't be a fucking coward,* she thought. *This is my house.*

She wiped her hands on her jeans, then curled them into fists—a reflex, old and knee-jerk, ready to fight. She walked up the stairs and saw him at the door: a large man, white and ruddy-faced, like most of the men up here, burly and bearded with a mass of red-brown hair curling around his ears. He wore a buffalo-check flannel shirt, paint-stained blue jeans and work boots, his belly big and taut. He wasn't old and wasn't young. He was grinning.

"Well hey there!" he said, bringing up one large paw in a wave through the screen door. "I'm Danny. Just wanted to stop by and introduce myself."

Sam stopped a few feet before the door but didn't open it.

"Hi," she said, her voice low, resisting the urge to pitch it up a notch, hide inside the friendly, more feminine voice she'd learned long ago; a voice used to disarm, to accommodate, to assure whatever man she was talking to that she was small, weaker than him, not a threat.

"Nice to meet you," she said, making no movement toward the door.

His smile faltered—fast as a flash, but Sam caught it—then wound back up into a grin.

"Thought I'd bring you some firewood," he said, motioning to a bound stack beside him. "Figured you might need it."

"I have plenty," Sam said, her voice a straight line. "I chop my own wood."

"Okay, very cool, I gotcha," the man said, putting up both hands as if in surrender, still smiling. "Just the ol' Northwoods cup of sugar, you know?"

Sam nodded. It was a thing up here, she knew that. An old way of welcoming newcomers. Not least those from the city, who might not have an axe or know how to use it.

"Thanks," she said, the hard edge of her voice softening a little. "I appreciate it."

"You got it," the man said. He glanced down at the door handle, as if willing Sam to open it. But she'd seen enough vampire movies—and had met as many mortal men—to know better.

"It was nice to meet you," she said, a finality to it. His smile fell again, and his brow crunched in. Sam's eyes fell to the man's hip. He had a pistol tucked in his belt. She looked back up, and their eyes met through the screen. Sam knew he'd seen her see it. She smiled, knowing it was her best defense.

"I'd invite you in, but it's a real mess in here," she said, code-switching to country, another tool she used sometimes, spreading her lips into a smile. "Kinda in the middle of it."

"Hey, no problemo," the man said, his vowels stretched long. It was an accent that sounded inherently nice, which was part of what made it dangerous. "Like I said, just wanted to say hi, meet the new neighbor. I'm Danny, like I said."

"Sam," she said, the old Midwestern manners snaking back up of their own volition. She immediately regretted giving this stranger her name, though she suspected he already knew it.

"Well, hey there, Sam," the man said. "Sure is nice to meet ya, and to have a pretty new face up here."

She needed to swallow but refused to do it, not wanting to show any sign of fear. She kept the smile plastered to her face.

"Thanks for the wood," she pushed the sound out. "See you 'round."

The man stood still for a second, a dark look passing over his eyes. It reminded Sam of the way lakes turned color just before a storm, going blue to gray to black. Then the man smiled again, sun breaking back through the clouds.

"You need anything, just holler," he said. "Or, you know, if you ever wanna have a beer sometime. I'm right down the road. Few lots down, place on the corner."

Sam knew the place. She passed it whenever she went for a run, on every walk to the lake. It was an old cabin, deep in the forest and far from the road, its walls gone gray after too many winters. Its porch had collapsed, probably from a snowstorm years ago, its boards caved in on themselves. She had no idea anyone lived there. She assumed it had been abandoned, like so many properties up here, lost to time or the weather or the death of those who built them, kids who moved far away and never came home.

"Thanks," Sam said.

"You betcha." The man nodded. He turned to go, then pivoted back to face her.

"Sam," he said. He smiled again, but this time what Sam saw in his eyes was unmistakable. It was a hollow look, faraway. She'd seen it before.

"And consider that invite open," he said.

"Will do," she said.

"Alrighty," he said, still smiling. "You take good care now. It can get dangerous up here, 'specially for a lady like you, all alone."

Sam stiffened at the word *lady*, at the mention of being alone. The man brought his hand back up in a wave, then turned and walked slowly down the porch steps. His boots—big, brown, caked in mud—crunched down the path. He turned and waved once more, as Sam pulled the door closed and locked it. She pressed her back against it, closed her eyes and willed her pulse to slow. She looked at the clock on the wall. It was almost noon. She looked at the fridge, and she swore the thing was glowing, a bright humming beacon in the darkness of the day. She swallowed, at last, her throat clicking. She needed a drink.

Seven

<small>◇◇◇◇◇◇◇◇◇◇</small>

IN HER FATHER'S cherry-red S-10, she drove with the windows down. The day was warm, and she was heading to town for supplies. The town was called Boundary Pass, a name Sam had always found a bit funny—like whoever named the place couldn't decide whether it was the edge of nowhere or whatever lies beyond it. Maybe it was both. As you entered town from Highway M, a weathered sign read WELCOME TO BOUNDARY PASS: WHERE CIVILIZATION ENDS AND THE NORTHWOODS BEGIN. POPULATION: UNINCORPORATED. This too made Sam smirk, a cynical city look she tried to keep tamped down up here. If a town possessed no people, was it really a town? If a tree falls in the woods and no one hears it, does it make a sound?

Smiling to herself, she pulled into a parking spot outside the hardware store, alongside a row of boarded-up shops. Even though it was nearly summer, Main Street was mostly empty. Main Street was not technically named Main Street—it was called so locally, but was, in fact, a short nameless stretch of Highway B that housed two bars, a diner, a bait and tackle shop, the combination gas station–grocery store that had no sign but was known as Hal's, and the hardware store. There were no houses or apartments—everyone in the Northwoods, whether lifers or weekenders or vacationers, lived miles outside town, as deep in the forest as they could get. But Main Street had once been a bustling place, especially in the summer. The empty storefronts had housed gift shops, restaurants, and a café, whose espresso machine was still a thing of wonder at the turn of the century. For a good long stretch in the eighties and nineties, there was even an art gallery, filled with paintings and pottery, jewelry and weavings and woodwork made by local artists. There were festivals every season, bringing tourists from all over the state. It was once a destination, a place teeming with life.

Over the past decade, all that life had vanished. Like so many Northwoods towns, tourism had taken a bad hit in the recession, when people lost their jobs and had to sell their cabins or could no longer afford family trips to lakeside lodges. Most of the lodges closed down too, except for the one on Lynx Lake, which had somehow held on. The town never really recovered, and many of the storefronts still had handwritten For Sale signs stuck with yellowed tape to the windows, making the once-lively Main Street look more like a ghost town.

Sam had grown up coming to this place, at least once every season with her parents, but she still felt like an outsider. She always felt like she was being watched, even when the streets were empty. She felt heads turn and necks crane whenever she walked into a place and whenever she left it, felt the trail of eyes behind her wherever she went. In a place where the term *city slicker* was tossed as an insult and a Chicagoan was worst of all, Sam could only imagine the level of disdain she might receive if she admitted to living in New York, not least as someone whose body was marked with a question. So she told only one version of the truth if anyone asked—that she was from a small town down south—and kept it at that.

She sat in the truck and looked at her phone. She had a few bars of service—a small miracle—and called her dad. He rarely answered when she called, but this time he picked up.

"Hey kiddo," he said. He never called her anything else. "How's it going Up Nort?"

Sam smiled. Her father had never really become Midwestern; he still had a trace of that East Coast swagger, in the black leather jacket he wore and the musical lilt of the Italian-American pidgin he'd grown up speaking, but he had been slipping, chameleon-like, into the upper-Midwestern accent for so long it had stuck. It was good to hear his voice.

"Hey Dad," she said. "It's good. I'm about to start on the deck. And I'm going to fix the sink if it kills me."

"It might," he said. "I've been battling that thing for years."

Sam laughed, and her father did too. It had been a while since she'd heard him laugh.

"How's the weather?" he asked. That perennial Midwestern question, and her father's love language across the distance— words that really meant *How are things where you are?* and *Are you safe?* or *Do you need anything?* and *I miss you.*

"It's good," she said. "Sunny and clear today. Chilly in the morning and warming up by afternoon. Cool again at night, light breeze." The meteorological inflection coming back to her like a doctor tapping her knee.

"Perfect," he said.

"Yeah," she said. "Wish you were here."

She immediately regretted saying it. Not because she didn't mean it, but because she knew it would bring up a whole mess of feelings he didn't want to have.

"Me too," he said, and they left it at that.

She asked him for tips on the deck and the sink, even though she didn't really need them—she'd watched a few YouTube videos on her phone in the library parking lot, the only place up here she could reliably get Wi-Fi, and felt like she had a pretty good handle on it. But she wanted him to feel useful. And sometimes, after a childhood spent growing up too fast and mostly taking care of herself, she simply longed for some advice from her dad.

She thought of him alone in his house, a few hours south—not far, in Midwestern miles, but somehow a world away. She'd briefly considered making the drive down to see him, but she couldn't go back there. A long time ago she had promised herself she never would, and it was a promise she intended to keep. He still lived in the same house she grew up in, which was just as haunted for her as the cabin was for him. They were both haunted by the same things, but they shouldered their hauntings as they did everything else: alone. They never talked about it. Instead, they talked about the weather and sinks and stain types and ailments—practical things, tangible things; issues that could be named and diagnosed, problems that could be solved. They could talk for a long time about such things and clammed up at anything resembling a feeling.

"That should do it," he eventually said. "Don't forget the flex tape. That's the trick." It was the third time he'd reminded her.

"Got it," Sam said. "Thanks, Dad."

"Thanks for fixing up the place," he said, then paused. "It means a lot."

"No problem," she said, squinting out the window into the sun, searching for a quick change in subject. "The truck is running like a charm, by the way."

"Oh, good," he said, light in his voice. "Get her speed up on the highway, give her a good workout."

"I will," she promised. She wanted to say more—about how much she missed him, about all the ways he and her mom had been on her mind. But she swallowed it all.

"Okay," she said. "I should run before the store closes."

"Okay, kiddo," her father said. "Love you."

"Love you too," she said.

She ended the call, pulled the bill of her baseball cap down over her eyes, and headed into the hardware store. The bell jangled above the door, and the same woman who'd sold her the corn was there again, hunched over a crossword puzzle at the counter. She gave a nod as Sam walked in, without looking up. Two men hung out by the fishing section, ostensibly looking at lures but clearly just killing time. Sam caught a glimpse of them—camo, trucker caps, the permanent circle of tobacco tins in the breast pockets of their shirts—and their eyes met hers. Their faces folded in, dark and unkind. She looked away but felt their eyes on her as she made her way down the aisle.

There was, rather inexplicably, a birdcage in the back of the store, a green-and-yellow parakeet singing inside it, rattling its wings against the metal bars.

"Hello," she said softly to the bird.

"Hello," it called back, then whistled at her. Sam smiled. She found what she needed: the flex tape and a can of stain, a new roller and detail brush.

"See you later," she said to the bird.

"Later!" it chirped.

She turned back toward the counter, sure to avoid looking at the men, who she knew were still looking at her. The older woman set her crossword down and rang Sam up.

"So," she said, eyes on the register, one bony finger pecking out the numbers on the ancient machine. "How's the squirrels?"

For a second Sam stopped, remembering the doe. *That was a dream, right?* she thought. *Just a dream and nothing more.*

She shook off the feeling and laughed, a little sheepishly.

"Glad to be fed," she said. "And a bit less skinny." The woman nodded, that same barely perceptible smile curling up one side of her mouth.

"Say hi to 'em for me," the woman said with a wink, handing Sam her change.

"Will do," Sam said. "Thanks."

The woman nodded, and Sam walked to the door, paper bag in hand, feeling the eyes of the men following behind her. She glanced at a newspaper in a rack by the door, realized it was Friday. She'd lost track of the days, wasn't exactly sure how long she'd been here. A week, maybe more. Outside, the sun was low in the late-afternoon sky.

Not too early for dinner, she thought. But what she really wanted was a drink.

She stopped at a place called Goocher's, a divey little lodge on a lake, known for the best Friday fish fry in town. It was early-bird hour, just before five. She could still get a seat, and drinks—which were already dirt cheap—were two dollars off.

She took an empty stool at the bar. Above it, a window looked out onto the lake, which sparkled in the late-afternoon sun, just beginning to set over a long line of evergreens. The bartender passed her a laminated menu.

"Getcha a drink?" she asked. She could have been twenty-five or forty, with dyed-blond hair and dark roots, a few tattoos on her arms whose black ink was going blue. She had the voice of a smoker, and yellowed teeth to match. But she smiled at Sam, and her smile lines were deep.

"Brandy old-fashioned," Sam said. When in Rome.

"You got it," the bartender said. She spun away, grabbed a clean rocks glass and tossed in a cube of sugar. With a few expert flicks of the wrist she added the bitters, before muddling two cherries and an orange slice at the bottom of the glass. Her pour of rail brandy was generous, adding a second shot after the stopper clicked. She topped it off with a splash of soda and three more cherries on a red plastic spear. It was a drink that would horrify New Yorkers, but it was a tradition out here that bordered on the religious.

"Cheers," the bartender said, setting the drink down. Sam wrapped her fingers around the glass, then held it up to the light. The sunset reflected off the lake, and a dusky glow filled the room. The deep auburn of the brandy and cherries caught the light and turned the liquid to amber, seeming to set it ablaze. Sam thought for a moment of being suspended there, a fly caught forever in all that warmth.

"Cheers," she said aloud, though the bartender had already turned away.

She brought the glass to her lips and drank. Her whole body seemed to unlock. The tension she always carried—in her shoulders, her jaw, her temples—fell away.

The bar began to fill up, and by five thirty the place was packed. An older man with white hair and the purplish-red nose of a professional drinker pulled out the stool next to her.

"Anyone sitting here, buddy?" he asked.

"Nope," she said, taking a drink. Her glass was nearly empty.

"Oh," he said, doing a double take when she spoke. It was a look, and a sequence of events, she knew well: that of a man who had mistaken her for a man, and then realized she was not, in fact, a man. That she was a woman, or at least something like it. What happened next could go one of two ways, and neither was great. She braced herself and waited, watched him size her up out of the corner of her eye. She could almost see the calculus inside his brain, the data unspooling as he wondered and wagered about her body. Then he sat down, and ordered a pint of Miller Lite.

"So," he said, "on your own tonight?" A friendly enough question on the surface, but her hackles stayed up just the same.

"Family's back home," she said, the response instinctual. "Just taking a little time to myself." She drained her drink and kept her eyes on the glass, rattled the ice around.

"Ah ha," the man said, drumming the bar with thick fingers. "I gotcha."

The bartender slapped down a coaster and a pint in front of him.

"'Nother one?" she asked Sam.

"Please," Sam said, and the bartender nodded, and Sam watched her flip up a clean glass, her hands working fast, and in a flash she was back, setting another drink down.

"Thanks," Sam said, and smiled. She took a sip and it was sweet, and very strong. The buzz was kicking in now—that glorious turning down, smoothing out, a slow softness settling in. Her brain a lake and she in a canoe, gliding across it.

Beside her, the man took a long pull from his pint. He was watching a baseball game on the TV above the bar, or at least pretending to.

"Yep," he said, looking at the TV. "Gotta get away from the old ball and chain."

"Something like that," Sam said. She knew how to talk to men like this. She'd had a lot of practice. In high school she wait-ressed at a pub in her hometown, where she'd get hit on by her classmates' dads on Saturday nights, and then see them with their families at church on Sunday. In college she bartended at a sports bar near campus, a place frequented by ruddy-faced alumni who still called girls "coeds"—the kind of men who considered themselves "good men" and "family men," but who, after dark, and a few drinks, showed their true selves: what Sam thought of then as things that crawled. Slick, fat slugs that slith-ered among the girls, their beer bellies pressed against tight cot-ton polo shirts. Back then, when she had long hair and presented in a far more feminine way, they'd grab her ass as she passed with a tray of drinks, press their meaty paws against her bare thigh. And she would grit her teeth and smile because she knew if she was friendly—and better yet if she flirted—this sludge of a man might stuff a twenty in her pocket. Sam had worked to pay her way through college and needed all the help she could get. So she touched the men right back, let their fingers linger on the strip of exposed flesh where her T-shirt met shorts. She'd bump her hip against them before pulling away and stealthily wiping off their residue with her apron, touching the twenty in her pocket and telling herself it was worth it.

Most men, Sam knew, were like this. Even the good liberal men she knew in New York, like the kind she worked for, were the same. The kind of men who told themselves they weren't like the monsters they read about in the news, but who dangled their power over the women who worked for them like it was something they too might obtain, if they just worked for it hard enough and stayed in line. This white-haired man at the bar was no different. She clinked her glass against his and he looked at her full-on for the first time. She could see him wondering what might lie beneath her shirt, below the waist of her jeans. He licked his lips, and Sam had the sudden desire to slam her glass against the bar until it shattered, then stab him in the throat with it. Watch his blood beat and sputter from his jugular as he struggled for breath.

Instead, she asked the bartender for her tab. The woman brought over the bill along with a red plastic basket of perch for the man, and it was only then Sam realized she'd forgotten to eat. But by then the buzz had staved off her hunger, had filled her up in other ways.

She paid the bill, then raised the dregs of her drink and downed it.

"To family," she said, and the man grunted beside her, tearing into his fish, his hands covered in grease. As she got up to leave, Sam caught the bartender's eye. She gave Sam a nod, the subtle kind of code that says *I see you,* and Sam nodded back, seeing her too.

She walked out of the bar and into the night, the brandy keeping her warm against the chill, keeping her from thinking too hard about the man at the bar, or the men at the hardware store, or the man who had shown up at her door—about any number of men who might be up in these woods, watching her now, the light of the bar disappearing behind her as she stepped out into darkness, alone.

Eight

◇◇◇◇◇◇◇◇◇◇

THE FIRST TIME it happened, she was afraid. The fear was physical, born in her body like some ghastly thing, a creature that dwelt in her blood and bones, attempting to claw its way out. In the days and weeks to follow, when she would try to remember the feeling and there was little left to hold onto—only thin ribbons of memory, fluttering in the wind as she tried to grab them—she would find there was no other way to describe it. It was a terror that lived inside her.

She woke up in the woods. Her body was not her own. She found herself existing outside it, above it, watching it move on the ground below her as she hovered somewhere far away, perched like a bird on a high branch in the trees.

She watched her body wake up on the forest floor, atop a bed of moss and leaves and pine straw. She watched in this way for a moment—a stretch of time that could have been a second or an eternity—separated from herself and suspended there, until she felt the dampness of the ground work its way into her skin. The chill hit her then, and she felt herself shiver, a violent wave of cold racking her body, calling her back inside her skin. And then she was on the ground, inside herself, and she was freezing.

She was somewhere strange, in a part of the woods she didn't recognize. Somewhere far from the cabin and the places she knew. The trees were denser, and the light was different—the earth and air were darker, the forest bending in. The smell was different too—the loam of the ground was richer, sweeter. She could smell the dirt beneath the leaves, beneath things dead and downed, and it all smelled remarkably alive.

It was early morning, sometime before dawn, and the small slash of sky through the trees was still a deep black-blue. She could see stars. She was barefoot, wore only jeans and a T-shirt. She'd never been so cold.

She stood up and shivered, looked around her in all directions. She had no idea how she'd gotten here, or where she'd been before. She tried to reach down the dark corridor of her memory, but found nothing. She closed her eyes, and a flash of something came to her—a shard of an image, brief and sharp. A memory much farther away, too far to fully grasp. Small hands reflected in a mirror. A child's hands, maybe, but with hair on the knuckles. She could feel the hair, thick and coarse and dark, one finger smoothing it down. She kept her eyes closed, tried to see the image more clearly. But as quickly as it came, it was gone. She opened her eyes again, looked down at her hands. They were smooth and hairless, but for the fine soft down on her fingers that had always been there, so light it was barely visible.

The circle of sky beyond the trees was just beginning to brighten, the first suggestion of sunrise streaking in. She followed the light, hoping she'd find her way home.

She walked for what must have been miles, shaking the

whole way, unable to get the trembling in her limbs to stop. She clenched her teeth, her jaw bolted tight, trying to still the chatter of her teeth. Her skin was pale purple and yellowish white—the colors of frostbite, she thought, and dead bodies washed ashore. She tried to shake the thought from her head. Around her, the forest was waking up. The crickets fading to birdsong, the first of the day's cicadas. She heard a crack in the woods behind her and began walking faster. Another crack, and then she ran, leaping over downed branches and rocks, as fast as numb feet could carry her. At last, as if by some miracle, she broke through the tree line and into the clearing. And there was the cabin, its porch light still burning, as if she had never left.

She ran toward it, bounding up the broken stairs. The door was open. She stepped inside, breathing hard. She closed the door behind her and locked it. She stood for a moment in the silence, the cabin still dark in the predawn. She waited and listened. When she was sure she was alone, she peeled off her dew-damp clothes and stepped into the shower, turned the water as hot as it could go, scalding her flesh back into feeling.

She stood in the steam until the shivering stopped, until the heat seared through her. She watched her skin turn red. She wanted to burn away the fear—to force it from her body like a lit match to a tick. Watch it unburrow itself from her flesh and flee, and then get washed away, spiraling down the drain until it was gone, returned to whatever hell it had come from.

Nine

◇◇◇◇◇◇◇◇◇◇

"YOU'RE NOT LEAVING me, right?" Stephen asked. Sam was carrying her backpack down the stairwell of their apartment building. It was a narrow passage, always dark, the lightbulb on the ceiling perpetually burned out. The yellow linoleum was cracked, the wood banister missing some slats. The radiator on the landing hissed. He was behind her, carrying a cooler of sandwiches and snacks he'd packed for the drive. It was a long drive, and he loved to feed her, and always fed her too much. She stopped at the landing and turned to face him.

"What do you mean?" she asked, dropping her bag on the floor. He stopped on the stairs above her and looked at the ground, where a chunk of linoleum was missing from a step. She followed his eyes there. The metal lip of the step was cracked too, making the narrow stairs treacherous, not least to their older neighbors. The whole place, it seemed, was crumbling.

At the top of the stairs, the cat cried and scratched at their apartment door.

"I mean," he said, "you're not going to, like, disappear into the woods and never come back, right?"

"That's crazy," she said.

"Is it?" he said. He was still holding the cooler, and he suddenly looked so small to Sam, like a kid heading to the school bus with his lunch. She could see the little boy he'd once been, before he'd become this man. She felt a surge of affection then, wanted to go to him and hold him and never let him go. Instead, she stayed still on the landing, and he stayed on the stairs, some absurdly dramatic Brooklyn tableau.

"Stephen—" she started.

"It's not crazy," he said.

She knew what he meant. He knew her well.

There was part of Sam—a big part—that only wanted Stephen. He saw her, and loved her, and would do anything for her. He would go anywhere she needed to go, put her first, build a life around her. On her good days, it sounded nice. She felt lulled by the promise of it, and by the lesson that had been ingrained in her early, despite her best efforts to shake it: If you found a good man, you kept him. He would keep you safe.

The truth was that she wasn't sure what scared her more: the possibility that this man might one day leave her, as she believed everyone eventually did, or that he might actually stay.

"I'm coming back," she said. "I'll be home before you know it."

"Okay," he said, letting out a long breath as if he'd been holding it. "I believe you."

Sam stood still for a moment, letting his words hang suspended in the air around them with the dust. For a second, she was suspended there too, considering this idea of *belief*—of his belief in her, of believing in anyone other than yourself. Of trusting in them, having faith in them. Of knowing they won't let you down.

Growing up in a family of drunks, you learn a few things. First, everyone has the ability to let you down, and probably will. You can't count on anyone but yourself. Second, you are bad. You were born bad, or turned bad, and either way everything gone bad is somehow your fault. At first, you try to be good. So good you might fix things. So good you might control things. So good you might orchestrate entire days, entire lives, with your own small hands—like learning to command the weather, shift a storm cell from its course. But you learn pretty quickly that the weather is volatile, and you have no control over anything. So you stop trying to be so good. You lean instead into the bad, which you believe is written in your blood. You carry that belief with you, like the Saint Christopher medallion you wear around your neck, let it guide you and protect you.

The third lesson is that everyone lies. To other people and especially to themselves. You learn how to lie, too—how to keep secrets, your own and others, and how to keep them well. You learn, above all, how to hide.

And this will lead you to the fourth and final lesson, which is perhaps the most important lesson of all: There's more than one way to disappear.

Sam was good at disappearing. She was good at hiding, and she was very good at lying. So good she'd forget she was doing it. So good she often fooled herself. She'd learned from the best. Sam's mother, like her grandmother, drank in secret. The secrecy itself was something of an art—a family practice, passed down and perfected. When Sam and her father began to suspect, her mother became a master. She no longer kept the whiskey in the kitchen cabinet; she hid it in the linen closet, behind the towels, instead. Later, she poured it into shampoo bottles and kept them beneath the bathroom sink. Later still—when Sam, obsessed with searching for her mother's stash, inevitably found each new hiding place and dumped the bottles out—her mother began to skip spirits entirely, in favor of Listerine. She would disappear into the bathroom and reappear again: slower, then stumbling; slurring then silent then gone. The empty plastic bottles filled the recycling bin, dregs of bright-blue astringent pooled at the bottom.

Sam was a teenager when the feeling crawled inside her chest and stayed. At school, she'd count down the minutes until she had to go home. Turning her key in the door, her heart would beat so fast she thought she might pass out. So fast she thought she was dying. She was terrified of what she might find. Would her mother be silent and swaying over the stove, stirring a pot in slow motion with a long wooden spoon? Would she find her fallen at the bottom of the stairs, her body bent at odd angles, the laundry spilled around her? Would she find even worse?

Sometimes Sam would watch, as if in a movie, as her body passed through the front door and moved across the kitchen, to kiss her mother on one hot, red cheek. Sometimes she would ask what was wrong. Sometimes she would say she was sorry, though she never knew what for. Sometimes she would scream. But always, she was met with silence. Once, enraged by the silence, Sam had shoved her mother against the wall, and she had fallen to the ground in a small, soundless heap. Sam had stood over her mother's body and looked at her trembling hands, horrified by what she had done. At the same time, she felt a valve unscrew inside her, the pressure in her chest released.

They had never spoken of it, but what was born in Sam that day stayed coiled inside her forever. It came out sometimes, an eruption of violence so otherworldly it terrified everyone around her. She punched walls and people, tore at the flesh of lovers who tried to contain her. She shattered dishes, threw books across the room. She screamed until her throat went raw, the sound animal and wild.

But most of the time, she stayed quiet. She kept the feeling—what she began to think of as a monster that lived inside her—tucked down deep in her guts. Whenever it tried to claw its way out, she mostly turned it on herself, leaving marks in places no one could see.

Of her mother's secret, she never told a soul. Eventually she stopped asking what was wrong. Eventually she stopped talking altogether. Her father never said anything either; whether unable or unwilling, or some combination, Sam never knew. And so the three of them continued this way, in silence—a small family sitting around a dinner table, taking the shape of any other family, forks scraping against plates, saying nothing at all.

Sam and Stephen walked out of the apartment and into the north Brooklyn dusk. The sky over the Pulaski Bridge was streaked in orange and pink, the evening traffic a slow and steady hum. The streetlights began to flicker on, one by one. It was getting late, and Sam was anxious to get on the road. She had a long way to go.

She put her bags in the trunk, and Stephen set the cooler on the passenger seat. They stood on the sidewalk and he hugged her, and with his face in her shoulder he said goodbye. She knew that when she got into the car and drove away, she would see him in the rearview mirror, standing on the curb and waving. She would wave back, and they would keep waving that way as she drove down the street, until she turned the corner and was gone.

But for a moment, they stood on the sidewalk holding each other, neither of them ready to let go.

"I'll be back soon," she said. And when she said it, she believed it.

Ten

◇◇◇◇◇◇◇◇◇◇◇

THE DAYS WERE passing quickly. There was something about the woods in spring—the way the canopy of trees closed in against the sky, which only stayed light for a while—that made time feel slippery, a fluid thing that dissolved as fast as it appeared. Sam had read somewhere, in one of her mother's books, maybe, that this bending inward of the trees was an evolutionary tactic, a kind of paradox, to limit the sunlight—it made the trees grow taller, live longer. A little darkness, the trees knew, could make you stronger.

Sam spent most days without speaking. Sometimes she talked to herself while she worked. Sometimes, if she could get a signal on the radio in the kitchen, she sang along to whatever classic rock station she could get. Sometimes she talked to the hummingbirds, who would hover and dart at the feeder, so aggressive for such small creatures. Or to the pileated woodpecker, who banged his beak against the tin chimney each day at dawn and dusk, a springtime mating ritual whose echo rattled the fireplace, and sounded to Sam like someone slamming a fist at a metal door, yelling to be let in.

"Haven't found anyone yet?" she said one day, and the woodpecker stopped pecking for a second and cocked his little red crest at her, before getting back to the business of looking for a mate. She talked to the squirrels and chipmunks too, who came to feed at the same trough as the doe, scrambling inside its thick plastic walls, sending kernels flying.

"Save some for the rest of us," she said, and for a moment they stopped digging, cheeks stuffed full, considering her, before plunging back into the corn, like Scrooge McDuck diving into his pool of coins.

Some mornings, sitting outside on the porch with her coffee, she talked to the trees. She thanked them for keeping her safe. They stood around her, pillars of maple and birch, blue spruce and pine, creating that clearing of sky, a halo of sunlight or stars, encircling her like a protective wall. They sighed in the wind. She whispered her thanks aloud.

But most of the time she was quiet. She went days without saying a word. Sometimes she couldn't remember the last thing she said, or to whom. The woman at the market, maybe, who had asked Sam if she would like to join the rewards club.

"Might as well," Sam had said, writing down her phone number on the form.

The cashier looked at her number, the same one she'd had since college, a small memento she kept from home. "You from the city?"

Sam hesitated, unsure of what to say. She could have told this woman her story—that she had once lived in that city, the one the woman meant, the capital city in the far southern part of this state, but had left, without warning, waving goodbye to the only home she had ever known. That for a long time she had lived much farther away, in a much bigger city—the one that everyone there referred to, obnoxiously, as the City, with a capital C, because they couldn't possibly imagine other cities might exist—but that she still didn't know quite where to call home.

"Yep," was all she said.

"The big city," the woman said, shaking her head and bagging up the coffee and milk, apples and beer.

"Yeah," was all that Sam said.

"You have a good one now," the cashier said.

"You too," Sam said.

And that might have been the last thing—before she threw the plastic bags into the truck and drove off again, past the boarded-up shops and ice-cream parlor and minigolf course and back into the woods, where the cell service faltered and then failed, where the radio stations flickered in and out like the afternoon sunlight through the trees.

On this day, when the deer spoke again and Sam spoke back, she had been pulling up rotten deck boards. She used a hammer to pull out the nails, a crowbar to pry up the wood. The boards were soft and pulpy, and they fell apart in her hands, revealing a deep, black rot within the wood. She got about halfway through and could have kept working—there were still a few hours of daylight left—but she was tired. She cracked a beer instead. She sat on the porch with another detective novel from her mother's shelf, the sweat of the day's work cooling on her skin. She noticed the lines of muscle on her forearms, more distinct than they had been. Hard calluses dotted her palms, and when she made a fist her grip felt more sure.

"You're getting stronger," the doe said.

Sam looked up to see the animal before her, standing at the feeder. She hadn't heard her arrive; it was as if she had just materialized in the yard. The doe's body looked different too—her ribs no longer jutting out like a jail cell at her sides, but fortified now by muscle. Her coat was thicker, a more lustrous shade of reddish brown, speckled with white.

"You are too," Sam said. It was the first thing she'd said aloud in days, and the sound of her own voice shocked her almost as much as the doe's, almost as much as the fact of the animal speaking, the silence around her shattered.

"Thanks to you," the doe said, a crooked grin spreading over a huge mouthful of corn, kernels spilling from her lips.

Do deer even have lips? Sam thought ridiculously. She tipped her bottle toward the doe, a drinker's salute, then took a pull. The doe chewed, swallowed, cocked her head.

"Now if only you'd put that bottle away," she said. "Think of all you might do."

"Please," Sam said. "Don't start. I'm fine. It's fine. Work hard, play hard, you know?"

"Sure do," the doe said, her muzzle twisting up in what was, without question, a look of irony. Sam laughed.

"Right," she said. "Have you ever actually had fun in your entire life?"

"Hard to have fun when your whole job is to survive," the doe said. "And the world does everything in its power to prevent that."

"Fair point," Sam said.

"Plus," the doe went on, "what's so fun about getting shellacked to the point you can't do shit, let alone remember what day it is?"

"What *isn't* fun about it?" Sam said, wondering what day it was. Monday? Thursday? Who could know. "Anyway, time is a construct."

"Fair point," the doe said. "But still. Sometimes life can slip away. Sometimes it slips so far beyond your grasp it never comes back. You'll just wake up one day and not know where you are, or who you are. And that'll be the end of that."

The light had dimmed from the doe's voice, replaced by a familiar sound—like a church hymn landing on a minor chord, a strange and sudden transition that hung in the air as the note rang out, unresolved and ominous, making the hair on her arms stand up straight.

My little werewolf, her mother had teased, whenever it happened. And she could see them sitting together in the chapel, shivering in wooden pews, a mother rubbing her daughter's bare arms.

Sam set her beer on the table and rubbed her own bare arms, smoothing the hair back down.

"Damn," she said. "Buzz kill."

"Better to kill the buzz than the brain cells!" the doe said, her voice lilting absurdly like some '90s PSA about saying no to drugs. "Hold on to however many of those you've got left, babe."

By the time Sam's mother disappeared, there was little left of her mind but madness. She talked to herself, and the animals, and the trees, barely ever to Sam or her father. She stopped going to the grocery store, refused to drive. She grew increasingly paranoid, convinced that people were watching through the TV, listening through her phone. She got rid of both, then tore out every cable from the house, leaving holes in the plaster. She cycled from suspicion to silence, then to something beyond recognition, something neither Sam nor her father could understand. Coming up to the cabin for a while, getting a little peace and quiet, had been her father's best guess at how to make things better. But it only got worse. The isolation closed in, and she only got quieter. She went days without saying a word, standing at the edge of the woods, looking into the trees. Sometimes she whispered, sometimes she sang—a low chanting sound, not words exactly but a melody of sorts—and sometimes her body swayed along with the trees, with the wind, to what seemed like music only she could hear. The last time Sam had seen her, this was the version she saw. It was as if her mother had become someone, something, else.

"*Annny*way," the doe said, the singsong chirp still in her voice. "Enjoy your evening!"

Her tail twitched, and she chewed maniacally at her side, then bounded off into the woods. Sam sat in stunned silence as the sky turned orange and pink. It would be dark soon.

I'm going fucking crazy, she thought.

She knew she should tell Stephen about the doe, about the drinking. But she couldn't stomach the thought of it. His disappointment, his concern. That she'd let him down, again. This was her cross to bear, and she'd bear it alone.

That night, she poured out the rest of the beer. She watched the golden ale swirl down the drain, where it would disappear into the sludge of the septic system. She dumped the bourbon too. She wouldn't let it happen to her. She wouldn't lose her mind. She'd beat this inheritance, this curse, break the cycle the women before her couldn't.

She remembered the first time she tried to quit, when her hands shook so badly she could barely make drinks at the bar. She'd only lasted a few days then, starting again during a particularly bad shift, when she lost some tips after dropping a drink, and said *Fuck it* and took a shot of whiskey, and her hands stopped shaking.

"She's back!" one of her regulars had yelled, and she felt the burn in her chest, like her heart was on fire. She took a second shot, and a third, and it washed over her like a wave, covered her like a quilt, wrapped her in a great swell of warmth. And she spun between tables, steady and sure and light on her feet. She stuffed tips in her pocket, turned the music up loud, and let herself be swallowed by the sounds of the bar—that cacophonous, glorious choir, a whole drunken congregation of voices rising up into the night.

This time, she made it a little longer. A week or so, maybe more. She tried keeping track at first, like she had back in Brooklyn, white-knuckling it through each day, drawing imaginary black *X*'s on an imaginary calendar. She kept herself busy with the deck, cleaning out the garage, taking trips to the dump and crossing things off her list, fueled by coffee and the last few cigarettes in her pack. But the days were fading into each other, time seeming to slip out of her grasp.

At some point, she must have gone back to the store. She must have bought another six-pack. But she couldn't remember going. She couldn't remember driving to town, or leaving the cabin at all. And yet, here were the bottles in the fridge again, as if she'd never poured them out. Or, as if they had just rematerialized there one day, long-necked and cold and calling.

She pulled one out, held it in her hand. She marveled at the smooth curve of brown glass, cool against her palm, wondering how it got there. When she was younger, she blacked out all the time. There were whole days that vanished and never came back. Her friends would tell stories about what she'd done the night before, and they'd laugh as they told them. Sometimes, a few flashes would come back to her, like scenes from a movie. But usually the stories were just that: stories, told by someone else, or sewn together by a group, and it was like hearing another person's life narrated aloud. It was never her in these stories, it seemed, but some other person, some shadow self, like a ghost who only came out at night. She couldn't remember much of her life back then. There was a vast black hole where her memory should have been, and it mostly stayed dark forever. It was as if, in those stretches of time, she hadn't existed at all.

But she remembered snapshots sometimes, like the last threads of a dream upon waking, like lines of poetry or characters from novels she'd read—the kind of stories that stayed with her, that made her want to tell her own. And now she stood outside at dusk, a half-empty bottle in her hand that she didn't remember opening. She walked down the porch stairs, skipping the broken step, and headed toward the woods. She moved, it seemed, not of her own volition, but at the command of something else. Like an imaginary string pulling her up like a puppet, then dragging her forward, her little cotton feet trailing the grass. Like she'd been summoned.

She stopped at the edge of the woods and listened. She thought she could hear something, deep within the trees. A kind of whisper, something like music. She remembered her mother, standing at the woods just like this—the last time Sam had seen her, not long before she vanished—whispering some secret convocation, humming some silent hymn.

Sam always believed that her mother had killed herself. It was the only explanation that made any sense. That she had walked into the woods one day, taking a shortcut to the lake—she always knew the shortcuts, preferred blazing her own path through the trees to taking the road. That she reached the shore, filled her pockets with rocks like some Midwestern Virginia Woolf, then walked into the water. Or maybe it wasn't so intentional, or anything so romantic. Maybe, more likely, she got drunk and went for a swim and drowned. But they had dragged the lake, just before the freeze, and never found a body.

Even so, Sam often imagined her mother might still be down there, decomposing on the sandy floor, her flesh having been eaten by bottom-feeders. She thought of fishermen in winter carving a hole in the ice, popping up their shacks around it, a case of beer in the snow and whiskey-laced coffee in thermoses, their lines in the frigid water, and reeling in a part of her. She thought of the lake thawing each spring, a body washing to shore.

Now, she stood at the edge of the woods, wondering if her mother might be somewhere else. If she was out there in the forest, alive or not, and waiting. It was a ridiculous thought—superstitious and maybe insane. But she couldn't help but think it. She thought of the afterlife, of spirits and ghosts and hauntings, the kind of thing her mother believed in. She thought of God, in whom they had both once believed. She wished, now, that she believed in anything.

Something came back to her then, the night falling fast around her, as she raised the beer to her lips. Something she read in an English class once, or maybe it was philosophy. She had hated philosophy, or at least the people who took those classes—pretentious, well-spoken assholes who got off on making her, a Pell Grant kid still seeking the words and ideas she didn't yet have, feel like an idiot. She remembered so little of her college classes. She was usually hungover, or still drunk, when she went at all. And yet here it was anyway, surging up in her brain unbidden—a flash of a memory, and she pulled it out of nowhere, a rabbit in her hand when she hadn't even realized she was reaching into the hat. By some miracle, she could see herself studying at a wooden desk, a carrel in the library, hunched over a book, underlining a passage, dog-earing a page. *The God-shaped hole.* She saw her hand writing the words in the margins, pencil lead pressing into paper, so she wouldn't forget: *the void in one's heart or body or soul that can only be filled by God.* A bottomless abyss, massive and endless, a gaping thing made of longing so vast that one will do anything to fill it. With something—anything—to feel less empty.

Eleven

◇◇◇◇◇◇◇◇◇◇◇

SAM HAD TRIED most of her adult life to forget the place she'd
come from. It was a small town, several hours south of the cabin,
surrounded not by forest but farmland. A blue-collar place,
made up mostly of white, Protestant families that had been there
for generations, whose kids took over the farm, whose kin never
lived more than twenty minutes away. Close enough to gather
for Sunday dinner and football games on Friday nights, those
days in the fall more hallowed than the Sabbath.

In her hometown, the high school boys were kings. Sam
had both hated and envied those boys: for the way they moved
through the world, free and easy, bouncing on the balls of their
feet, unaware of the way their bodies were beheld, or how much
space they took up. Rather than shrinking—pressing themselves
against lockers, counting calories and going without lunch,
trying to be as small as possible—they only got bigger. They
ate and ate, animals made only of appetite, devouring everything. They got taller and stronger. They were big and loud and

reckless and mean. They were heroes. Even when they got drunk after football games, got girls pregnant in their pickup trucks, then crashed those trucks into cornfields. Even when they were escorted home by the cops, their names making the paper not for the laws they broke but the records. They never missed a game. After church on Sunday, people would drink from paper cups of burnt coffee and whisper stories from the Friday before, passing them around like an offering plate. They'd shake their heads and laugh and say *Boys will be boys.*

Sam longed to possess this kind of power—to take up space, to do no wrong in the eyes of the town—rather than existing, as she did, under constant scrutiny for every curve that bloomed, every mistake she made, for all the ways she stood out.

Sam and her parents were outsiders. No matter how hard they tried to be part of the place, going to church and football games, community service fundraisers and PTA meetings, they never fit in. The cabin, far away in the Northwoods, was their place of escape. Where they could get away and not be seen. Wherever she went, Sam had always stuck out. Where the kids she'd grown up with had fair hair and smooth skin that turned the color of honey in summer, their bright-blond heads like spun gold, Sam was swarthy skinned with a dark, frizzy mop of hair. Thick black hair covered her arms and legs too, long before the other girls began sprouting their own brand of barely visible down. Sam's mother bought her a bottle of Nair when she was ten, but it never worked. So she started shaving instead, both her legs and arms, even when the hair busted back through by late afternoon, her own full-body five-o'clock shadow. Even though she knew the harder she fought it the stronger it would grow back.

But it wasn't just that she didn't look like the other girls. It was that she looked, and often felt, unlike a girl at all.

She was in college the first time a stranger asked her what she was. A girl with tight curls and light skin turned to Sam and asked the question as they stood on a curb at a red light, waiting to cross the street. Sam didn't know what to say, or even what exactly was being asked. She opened her mouth but stood there silent, looking at the stranger, who shrugged as the lights changed, then crossed the street and walked away.

In a way, it was a question she'd been asked, and had been asking, her whole life.

What are you?

The answer, whatever it was, seemed to go beyond the surface of her skin. She suspected it was something deeper—something strange and inexplicable, maybe unspeakable, that lived inside her.

"That girl is feral," a friend's mother once said to another, as a young Sam played with a group of girls at a birthday party. The mothers stood on a patio while their daughters, no more than seven years old, ran around the yard. They wore dresses, and ribbons in their hair, while Sam wore jeans torn at the knees, covered in mud, her dark hair tangled. The mothers thought Sam couldn't hear, but her ears had always been sharp—tuned like antennae to a whisper, a breath, each silence that might be a threat.

"Something wild in her," the mother had said. "Something animal." The other mother had nodded, and Sam was never invited to play there again.

On the school bus, the boys made guttural, growling noises when Sam got on, snarling and spitting as she walked down the aisle. They called her a beast, and a monster, and they spat when they said it. More than once, she stepped off the bus with a wad of saliva in her hair. The bus driver, an old man with kind eyes, looked at her in the mirror and smiled. As she fought back tears, he'd tell her not to mind those boys.

"It's 'cause they like you," he'd say with a wink.

But when she got off the bus, she would run to the girls' bathroom to wash the spit from her hair. She would look at herself in the mirror. What she saw was a nose too large for its face, thick black eyebrows reaching dangerously close to one another across her brow. She saw the hair on her arms, coming in sharp from the morning's shave, skin that glowed a sickly green in the flickering fluorescent light. What she saw, without question, was ugly.

Maybe I am a beast, she thought. *Maybe I'm a monster.*

She thought about those boys on the bus, and knew it was impossible they liked her. Desire, she would learn, could be a dangerous thing, but what those boys possessed came from a different place entirely—uncertainty, and the rage born of it, a threat far greater. Maybe better to be a monster, then. At least a monster could fight back.

Sam had always tried her best to be good. To be a *good girl*—in the eyes of her family, of God, of the town—to do as she'd been told good girls do. She sang in the church choir, went to Sunday school, never missed a service. She wore dresses though she hated them, their high collars and cinched waists making her sweat in the pews, tights making her legs itch. She shook people's hands during fellowship, saying *Christ be with you* and *Thanks be to God.* Near the turn of the century, when the fervor of purity culture had reached its zenith, she joined the cultish youth group like all the good kids did. She took vows to stay pure, wore a silver band with a Jesus fish on her ring finger—promising herself to God, promising that she would be good.

But no matter how hard she tried, people talked. She caught

the ladies at church scowling, and she heard what they said, their sibilant hisses like the serpents in the Bible, but she, somehow, the snake. They said they didn't want their daughters hanging around her, and certainly not their sons. There was just a look about her, they said. And no, she hadn't done anything wrong—not really, not yet. They just had a feeling. She would grow up to be one of *those* girls, the kind with sin written all over her. No good, a bad seed. The kind of girl that had the devil in her.

Sam eventually grew out of her ugly phase. She was never exactly pretty, but she could walk through the halls of the high school without being hassled. And as her body bloomed, she did her best to become what she knew she was supposed to be. She wore tight shirts and short skirts and too much makeup, plucked her eyebrows and straightened her hair. She went to parties and shotgunned beers, let boys in pickup trucks run their hands up her thigh, spinning the ring on her finger as they did it, never asking them to stop, even when she wanted them to.

Later, after she left—after she took off the ring and drove away for good—she stopped caring so much what her hometown thought of her. Far away from where she'd come from, and what she'd once tried to be, she began to feel more at home in herself. But as hard as she tried to forget that place, sometimes she remembered. She remembered what the boys had called her. She remembered what the mothers had said. She remembered now, standing at the edge of the woods, empty bottle in her hand. She wondered what might be out there, and what might happen if she stepped out there too. Because no matter how far you run, she knew—no matter how hard you try to shed your old skin and become something else—the place you come from stays with you. It always calls you back. And sometimes, when you hear stories about yourself early enough, and long enough, they work their way into your skin. They live inside your still-growing bones and run in your blood. They become a part of you.

Twelve

◇◇◇◇◇◇◇◇◇◇◇◇

ONE AFTERNOON, SHE heard footsteps. She was outside, planting irises she'd dug up from the ditch. The flower beds her mother had planted, alongside the cabin, were dotted with the tiny green heads of ferns and hostas, perennials just starting to make their way back. Sam had cleared the thistles and mulched the beds. She'd planted the irises on the east side, and would plant more on the south side next. Her mother would have loved them.

She stood up and peeled off her gloves, wet and heavy with dirt, and lifted the hem of her T-shirt to wipe the sweat from her face. That's when she heard the sound—footsteps crunching up the gravel drive.

From around the side of the cabin, a figure approached. Sam thought of the man who brought the wood, the man with the gun. *Danny.* She clenched her fist around the spade.

But it was not a man. It was a woman. Older, in her late fifties or early sixties. She smiled and waved. Sam felt her grip loosen around the wooden handle, dropped the spade to the ground.

The woman had sun-leathered skin and long hair that was

mostly gray, but for a few streaks of black, pulled back into a low ponytail. She wore work boots, khakis, and a light denim shirt. Light colors, Sam had learned, to better spot the ticks that latched on to the cuffs of pants and burrowed into socks. She'd picked two off her ankles with tweezers that morning, cursing her dark clothes, the little bloodsuckers already having latched on.

"Hello," the woman said, extending her hand. Her skin was freckled. She looked strong.

"Hi," Sam said, and her voice cracked. The adrenaline was fading, but the remnants were still there. She realized she was hot, and thirsty.

"I'm Lou-Ann," the woman said.

"Sam."

"Pleased to meet you," Lou-Ann said. They shook, and the woman's grip was firm. It was a grip that had worked, with calluses and short nails and permanent crescents of dirt beneath them. She looked like she could have built houses, or diesel engines, or fixed cars or something.

"You new up here?" Lou-Ann said.

"Not really," Sam said. "Kind of. This was my parents' place. But, uh," she stammered, not sure what to say, "I'm taking care of it for them."

"Ah," Lou-Ann said. "That's nice of you. I'm sure they appreciate it."

"Yeah," Sam said, not sure why she had the sudden desire to tell this stranger the truth, that her parents were both gone, in their own ways, that she was here trying to figure out what to do with this place, with her life.

"Do you want to come in?" Sam said. "Want a drink or something?"

"Got some tea?" Lou-Ann said.

"Sure," Sam said.

"Don't go to any trouble," Lou-Ann said. But Sam said it was no trouble, and led the woman to the porch. She pulled open the screen door, and the woman stepped inside. She was the only other person who had been inside the cabin since Sam arrived. Sam was self-conscious, unsure about the space. Was it clean? She hadn't cleaned. She surveyed the one-room living area and kitchen. There were empty bottles on the counter, mugs stained with thick rings of coffee, a half-eaten apple. If you looked close enough, you could see a line of small black ants marching along the baseboard toward the fridge.

"Have a seat," Sam said, and Lou-Ann sat on the couch. Sam turned her back to the woman and threw the browning apple in the bucket of food scraps she took out into the woods each night. It was filled mostly with coffee grounds, eggshells, and apple cores. Sam didn't eat much else. She scrounged around in the cabinets for tea. She wasn't a tea drinker but her mother always kept some around. She spotted the ancient box of Bigelow on a far back shelf; behind it was an even more ancient-looking plastic tub of Country Time Lemonade, which Sam was sure had solidified into one sour clump and might even be teeming with ants.

She fished out two bags of tea and set the kettle to boiling. She wished she was drinking a beer instead but banished the thought from her brain.

"So, you live around here?" Sam asked.

"Oh yeah," Lou-Ann said. "Been up here my whole life." She was silent for a few beats. "Shit," she said then, "time passes."

Sam laughed, a quick percussive sound. She couldn't remember the last time she'd laughed. Stephen made her laugh all the time. Without him, she tended to get too serious.

"Sure does," she said, slipping the tea bags into two small mugs. She wrapped the tags around the handle of each cup, like the woman she once loved had taught her. That had been more than a decade ago, but Sam could still see the morning clear as day, standing in the woman's kitchen, sunlight slanting in through sheer curtains, making the bright-yellow walls even brighter. The two of them leaning against the counter in tank tops and underwear, no bras and bare feet. She felt the sharp pang of missing, both the woman and Stephen, a past that seemed somehow simpler, though it had never really been. The kettle whistled and Sam flicked off the burner, poured the water into the mugs.

"Milk?" she asked.

"Black is fine," Lou-Ann said.

Sam handed the woman a mug, then sat across from her in an old armchair, next to the fireplace she hadn't used since she arrived. There were logs stacked next to it, a wicker basket of kindling and newspaper and a lighter, a tableau her dad had always prepared, ever ready to burn.

"Hemlock, huh?" Lou-Ann asked, her hands wrapped around her mug.

"Oh," Sam said. "Yeah. My dad named it."

"Good name," Lou-Ann said with a nod. "Good tree. In trouble, though."

"Yeah," Sam said again. She'd read an article in the local paper, if you could call it that. It was really just a monthly half-fold newsletter, put out by some lifers down in Lakeland, composed of stories and op-eds about festivals and forest preservation efforts, highway cleanups and bingo nights, each old lodge that closed and new bar that opened, two wildly controversial proposals to pave the roads and install a cell tower. They gave the paper away for free at the grocery store, and her dad always got a copy when he drove to town. There were several years' worth stacked by the fireplace, and it was in one such issue that she'd read about the tree's threatened status. "I heard about that."

"Interesting, too," Lou-Ann said. "Old growth. Been here a long time. Strong but vulnerable. They tell a good story, the trees."

Sam nodded, thinking about all the trees they'd watched wither, some invasive insect sucking the sap from their needles or tunneling into their bark and feeding on their phloem until they fell. How her father eventually had to cut them down, and how she'd cried each time. She thought about the trees that had somehow held on.

"Course," Lou-Ann said, one eyebrow raised, "there's lots of stories in that name, aren't there? The other kind of hemlock grows here too, you know."

Sam nodded. She did know.

"You can find it in ditches, at the edge of the woods," Lou-Ann went on. "Little white flowers. Looks harmless, even pretty. Like baby's breath or Queen Anne's lace, carrot flowers."

Sam knew this, too. Her mother taught her to identify it, alongside poison ivy and sumac and oak.

"You ever read *Macbeth*?" Lou-Ann asked.

"Sure," Sam said. It was one of her favorites. She loved an ill-fated protagonist, a haunted antihero. She saw a flash of memory then—the three witches on a stage, stirring a cauldron. Steam rising up. A theater in the woods at night, whip-poor-wills and crickets. A place she went with her parents once, when she was young. She remembered it felt like magic.

"*Root of hemlock, digg'd i' the dark*," Lou-Ann recited. "Drunk in ancient Greece to off yourself, too. It's what Socrates drank, when he was sentenced to death."

"Huh," Sam said, her mind still on the stage. "I don't think I knew that."

"I like stories," Lou-Ann said. "And I love a word that means more than one thing."

Sam nodded absently, still thinking of the witches. There was something else crackling at the edge of her mind, flashing on the periphery like the aura of a migraine, hazy and fractured and strange. Sick greenish skin, black fingernails. Dark eyes ringed in coal. A sound, too—like a moan, a ghostly wail. But before she could grasp the image, it was gone.

"So," Lou-Ann said, "what's your story?"

"My story?" Sam said, willing herself back into the room. "Not sure I have much of one."

"Honey, everyone has a story."

"Maybe, but mine is pretty boring."

"Oh, I doubt that," Lou-Ann said. She took a sip of tea and looked around the room. "Nice place you got here. How long your parents had it?"

Sam followed the woman's gaze, looking around the room. The furniture was old and worn. Maybe she could find some newer stuff, sweeten the sale. There was a Goodwill in the nearest city, which was really just a town, an hour south. But she looked at the pine-log walls her father had cut and sanded and lacquered, the pine-board floors he'd laid himself. It was a nice place, despite the broken things. Good bones. Once she fixed it up, it would be beautiful again. She felt a pang of something then. This place was her family's, and she didn't have much of a family left. Maybe she didn't want to let it go.

"My dad built it about twenty-five years ago," she said. "Planned on moving up here full time, but that didn't really pan out."

Lou-Ann nodded. Sam sipped her tea and grimaced. She'd left the bag in too long, and it was bitter. She'd never liked tea, only ever drank it because people around her did.

"But this is your first time back in a while," Lou-Ann said. It wasn't a question.

Sam choked the liquid down. "That easy to tell?"

"Don't have a lick of the accent," Lou-Ann said. And it was true. When she moved to New York, Sam had stripped herself of the long vowels and clipped words of her homeland, the dropped g's and *ain't*s and *I seen*s, taught herself to speak from her throat instead of her nose. It was a hick accent, that blue-collar Midwestern lilt she'd come from, and like many things from her past, she'd worked hard to kick it.

"You got me," Sam said. "Left a long time ago. I live in New York now."

"New York!" Lou-Ann said, slapping her thigh. "What took you out there?"

"You know, I thought I knew once. But to be honest, I have no fucking idea."

Lou-Ann laughed. "You couldn't pay me to live there. Back when I was a kid, maybe. I went once, in the eighties. Lot different then, I suspect. I liked it. Too many people, though. And the noise—you'd think those assholes were paid to honk their horns."

"Yeah," Sam said. "It's pretty awful."

"But kind of its own magic too though, right?"

"Definitely," Sam said.

"Actually, went out on a motorcycle, if you can believe it," Lou-Ann said.

"No way."

"Way. Had a sweet ride back in the day. A little Softail. Rode her a thousand miles out. Wanted to see the ocean. Thought maybe I'd stay a while, then work my way down the coast. Get away from all this, start something new."

"Sounds familiar," Sam said. "Still have the bike?"

"Nah," Lou-Ann said. "Had to sell it. Things were tight. 'Bout broke my damn heart."

"I'm sorry," Sam said.

"Ah," Lou-Ann said, waving her hand. "It's fine. Too old for a bike these days."

"I don't know about that," Sam said. She held her cup in both hands, looked down at the steam. "I take it you didn't stay long."

"In New York? Nah. A month or so. Met some folks, did some drugs, saw some things. To be honest I don't remember a whole lot but a bunch of bright lights and blur. In a different life, maybe I could have stayed. But I had to come back. My family is here. Home is here."

"I get that," Sam said.

"So how long you been out there?"

"Too long."

"But you're here now."

"Just for a while."

"Mmm," Lou-Ann hummed. She set her tea on the side table and picked up a small wooden duck, hand-carved by a local artist who sold them at the annual craft fair in town. Sam's mother had collected them.

"You could always stay," Lou-Ann said, turning the duck over in her palm.

"I've thought about it," Sam said. She realized, as she said it, how content she felt—how safe—with this stranger. Over the years, Sam had turned further inward, away from the world, preferring her own company to anyone else's. It was shocking, now, to feel so comfortable with this woman, to share these parts of herself. She felt like she could tell her anything.

"So?" Lou-Ann set the duck down and looked at Sam.

"I've got a job back there," Sam said, the warmth from the tea working its way into her hands. "And, you know, people."

"Ah," Lou-Ann said. "You got someone who loves you?"

Sam nodded. "Yeah. I guess I do."

"Well," Lou-Ann said, slapping both hands on her knees. "You gotta hold on to that."

Rising to her feet, Lou-Ann reminded Sam of her grandmother. Of her mother, too. Without warning Sam was hit with a wave of grief, the quiet kind that catches in your chest, pulls at you. She missed them both, wished she could call them, wished they were here—that they were all sitting at the kitchen table, drinking coffee, talking like they used to.

"Welp, better be off," Lou-Ann said. "Just wanted to say hi, meet the new neighbor."

"Oh," Sam said, setting down her mug and standing up. "You could stick around a while, if you'd like? Thinking of grilling a steak tonight. Or we could have a drink?" She couldn't believe she was inviting this woman to stay.

"Don't drink, sorry to report," Lou-Ann said, holding up her empty mug. "Bona fide teetotaler these days. Or *tea*-totaler, if you will." She grinned.

"Oh," Sam said, forcing a laugh. "Yeah. I don't really either."

They looked at each other, and Sam caught a flash of recognition in Lou-Ann's eyes.

"Rain check on dinner?" Lou-Ann said, and handed Sam her mug.

"Sure," Sam said. "I'm not sure how much longer I'll be here, though."

"I'll check in next week," Lou-Ann said.

"You have a number you want to leave, or—" Sam started.

"Just a land line," Lou-Ann said. "No cell phone. No TV, no internet. Rots the brain."

"That's true," Sam said, fishing a piece of scrap paper and a pen out of the junk drawer. The woman scrawled a number down.

"And honestly, sometimes I keep the phone off the hook," Lou-Ann said with a grin. "But I'll stop over next week. Maybe Friday? If you're here, you're here. We could go out for fish fry. And if not, well," she said, and looked at Sam as she opened the door, "nice to meet you."

"Likewise," Sam said. "Nice to have someone to talk to up here."

"Yeah. But it gets old quick," Lou-Ann said with a wink. "Be seeing you."

"See you," Sam said, following the woman outside, still holding the cup in her hands. She watched the woman step slowly off the porch, then walk down the gravel drive. She listened to the woman's footsteps fade until there was nothing left but silence, and the sound of birds singing, and the wind in the trees, which always sounded like rain.

Thirteen

◇◇◇◇◇◇◇◇◇◇◇

THE NEXT TIME it happened, she was not afraid. She awoke in the woods once again, just before dawn, and waited for the fear to come. It was still dark, so deep in the forest, but the first threads of light were beginning to break above the trees. Soon the sun would rise, and the circle of night sky between the pines would be burned away, replaced first by pale yellow, then a clear and brilliant blue. Soon the birds would burst into song, the forest filling up like a choir. But for now, the song still belonged to the night—to the crickets and frogs, the hoot of the barred owl. The fear never came.

It was just above freezing. She wore no clothes, no shoes. She understood it was cold—knew it by the frost on the ground, the earth still half-frozen; by the smell in the air, pure and clean and electric. But she didn't feel it. She felt, instead, somehow warm—felt the blood in her veins, her heart in her chest, her pulse quick and loud and light. She pressed her fingers to the hollow of her throat. Her skin was warm too, nearly hot.

She held her hands in front of her, turned them over, front then back in slow motion. She inspected her arms and legs, long muscled limbs that seemed foreign and new, as if they belonged to someone else. The hair on her body was thick and dark, reminding her of the newly seeded grass she'd known as a kid, which seemed to sprout up overnight, the product of a garden hose and Miracle-Gro in a suburban backyard. She liked the way it felt, covering her body like a coat.

She remembered this feeling, somehow. From what or when, she didn't know. She only knew that it felt familiar. She felt safe inside it.

She didn't know where she was, in which particular stretch of forest. She had to be pretty far out, way into state land. It was a strange place and still, somehow, she felt she knew it. Felt certain she had been here before.

She stretched, and stood, and looked to the sky. Her senses seemed sharper, she could swear it. The predawn light too bright, the sounds of the forest too loud, the cool air on her skin like the pricks of a thousand pine needles, like a jump in the lake after first thaw. Her whole body hummed. She pressed her toes into cold earth, half-frozen leaves beneath bare feet. She was surrounded on all sides by trees—Scotch pine and blue spruce and fir; poplar and maple and birch, their white-bark branches just beginning to bud. She inhaled deep, took in the sweet scent of evergreen, the damp of dirt and tamped-down leaves. The air alive with spring and the suggestion, not far off, of water. She took it in, let it fill her lungs. She drank it.

Around her, morning seeped in slowly. The birds began to sing. Sparrows swooped from branches, squirrels leapt through the leaves then scrambled out of sight. Somewhere in the distance, a woodpecker banged its head against a dead tree, its hollowed-out trunk a casualty of winter or some kind of borer, an insect made of hunger that ate trees alive.

This was a place of trees, both living and dead, of animals and insects and all things wild. It was a place of darkness, where shadows fell fast and ran long, where anything might live beyond the reach of sunlight. It was a place of beasts, and of monsters. It was not a place of men. Or, if it was, then perhaps it was the kind of men who lurked in these shadows—their own brand of beast, stalking their prey.

This knowledge should have frightened her. Instead, she felt a strange kind of calm—like she belonged to this place, to this darkness, to these trees. Like nothing could hurt her here. Like she had been gone a long time and finally returned. Or, maybe, like she'd been here all along.

Above her, the pines stretched up and then in, enclosing her beneath them. It was a trick of the eye, from this vantage point on the ground, that the trees appeared to bend so far in. In reality they stood much straighter, shooting toward the sky. But from here, it looked like they were reaching for one another. And sometimes, when the wind kicked up and a summer storm rushed in, they did bend so far in they touched, huddled together against the rain.

Some days, this closing in frightened her. She swore that the trees were trying to trap her, to keep her, that they would never let her go. On those days, she thought about getting back in the car and driving east, returning to New York, where, paradoxically, she sometimes felt a little less trapped, a little more free.

But on this day, on this early morning in the woods, the trees enveloped her and it felt like being held. She wanted to be kept there forever.

She looked for her shoes, for her clothes, but they were nowhere to be found. She walked north, bare feet on cold ground, knowing somehow which way to go. Her fingers and toes were numb, but she didn't mind. She walked a long time, sure on her feet against the cold. When she got to the clearing, the cabin breaking into view, the sun was rising. There was a deer at the feeder. She wasn't sure if it was the same deer as before, the one who had spoken. She stopped at the edge of the woods and watched the deer eat. It looked up, once, and stared at her, one ear flicking. It blinked, then lowered its head again to the trough.

Just a normal deer, she thought. *Just a normal, everyday, non-talking deer. Just as it's always been.*

She shivered. The cold morning air seemed to hit her for the first time then, and she made her way across the yard, up the porch steps and to the door. She stepped lightly, her feet making no sound. She heard everything else so loudly—the birdsong, the crunching of the corn, all of it in stereo. And there were her boots, lined up neatly outside the door.

She stood on the porch, let the morning air prickle her skin. She tried to recall the night before, but her memory was blank. She watched the maples sway in the breeze. It would get warmer soon, and there would be thunderstorms at night. The mosquitoes and black flies would hatch. But for now she was safe. She loved springtime in the woods, in all its volatility. The temperature dropping and soaring, all the new life buzzing, the constant threat of storms—either thunder or snow, it could go either way. It was a time when, after a long and brutal winter, everything was coming back to life, and anything could happen.

She stepped inside the cabin. It was dark. On the counter, in a narrow slant of light, she saw an empty bottle of bourbon, a rocks glass still sticky with the dregs of it. She'd apparently kept the party going when she got home, though she had no memory of it. She was tired, but she was not hungover. This too seemed impossible.

She walked down the dark hallway and crawled into bed. She slept for hours, deep and hard, better than she'd slept since she'd arrived. She woke again in late afternoon, as the sun was falling behind the trees, the pink glow of dusk settling in.

Fourteen

◇◇◇◇◇◇◇◇◇◇

"YOU'RE DOING IT wrong," the doe said.

Sam was working in the south flower bed, in front of the cabin. She'd dug up more ditch irises and was pressing them into the soil. She stopped and turned, and there was the doe, standing at the feeder. The animal worked her mouth in that slow circular rhythm, like a cow grinding its cud. She looked at Sam while she chewed.

"What?" Sam asked, annoyed more at herself for responding than by the doe's tone, which she found to be more than a little condescending. She was hungover, and tired, and didn't have time for the doe's shit today.

"The irises," the doe said, corn tumbling from her mouth.

"Don't talk with your mouth full," Sam snapped. If the doe had eyebrows, she might have raised one. But she closed her mouth and kept chewing big, exaggerated chews, then swallowed big too, making a whole show of it. Sam rolled her eyes.

"As I was saying," the doe said. "The roots should be shallow.

You see how they run perpendicular to the plant? They need to be just below the surface, so the sun can get them."

Sam inspected her work, pawed gently at the dirt where she'd buried the irises, then looked back at the doe.

"How do you know so much about plants?" she asked, pulling off her gloves. She sat in a squat and her quads were burning, but she didn't stand up. She didn't want to spook the doe. She looked at the creature curiously then, her irritation turning to something softer.

"I studied botany," the doe said with a wink.

"Did you just wink at me? Can you even wink?"

The doe didn't respond, only lowered her head back into the trough. Her comic timing was perfect.

"You're funny," Sam said.

"Tip your waitress," the doe mumbled through a mouthful of corn. Then she grinned maniacally, kernels spilling everywhere. Sam appreciated her commitment to the bit. She shook her head, and looked back at the irises. They did look kind of deep. She remembered her mother telling her something about roots like these, that it was best they were buried shallow so the sun could soak through the soil. Sam's mother had loved irises, and they had planted the wild ones together one summer when Sam was young, digging them up from the roadside early one morning, working quickly and giggling and swatting at mosquitoes like thieves. Her mother had loved to plant things, like her mother before her. Back at home she'd had a garden, grew flowers and vegetables, and they planted and weeded together, their skin freckled from the sun. When Sam left home her mother stopped planting much, let the garden turn to weed.

Gloves off, she dug her fingers back into the earth, gently

pushing up the plants by the roots and packing them in again, loosely, a little higher up in the soil.

"Better," the doe said.

"How can you even see this far?" Sam asked. The trough was at least thirty feet away.

"Good eyes," the doe said.

"Could have fooled me," Sam said. "How come you and your people are always diving into the road in the dark then, just as cars are passing?"

"It's genetic," the doe said. "We come from a long line of folks killed by pickup trucks and SUVs. Increasingly some hybrids. You might call it generational trauma. Some might say we head toward those lights like it's fate, some kind of collective destiny, following in the footsteps of our forebears. But our vision is solid."

"Huh," Sam said absently, and continued to press her fingers in the soil.

"And we're not people," the doe said.

"What?" Sam stopped digging, looked up at the doe.

"You called us people. But we're not like you. We might jump in front of cars, but your kind destroys itself in a whole different way."

"Right," Sam said.

"You destroy everything else you touch, too," the doe said, her voice having lost its humor. "Including us."

The doe looked out into the forest and Sam followed her gaze. It was dense and dark and old as far as Sam was concerned, but it was mostly new growth—a product of the logging industry at the turn of the century, all the lumberjacks that worked up here.

"Right again," Sam said.

"Those will bloom next month," the doe said, nodding toward the irises. Then she turned back toward the woods, whatever strange universe she came from.

"Wait, really?" Sam asked as the doe walked away. "I figured it would be a year."

Sam never had much luck growing anything. Her mother and grandmother had taught her some things, but she never quite developed the knack. She always ended up killing the herbs and tomato plants she attempted to grow on her fire escape. She had even killed some succulents, which she was told was nearly impossible. Growing things, and keeping them alive, was one thing she hadn't inherited.

The leaves of the irises were pert and green, and Sam wondered whether their flowers would be purple or white, if they ever bloomed at all.

"You'll see," the doe said, not looking back. And then she trotted away on spindly legs, disappearing into the woods without a sound.

Fifteen

◇◇◇◇◇◇◇◇◇◇

"I THINK I might be losing my shit," Sam said.

The connection was bad, as usual. When she'd first arrived, she tried to call Stephen every day, but the calls always dropped, and when they connected the signal was spotty, creating an underwater effect that sounded like they were both drowning. She had two bars now but knew it wouldn't last.

"What do you mean?" Stephen asked. It was a Saturday morning, which she'd learned when he picked up, and he was home in Brooklyn doing chores, making himself some kind of kale and quinoa concoction that would last him the week. Stephen did most of the cleaning and cooking and had introduced her to foods like kale and quinoa, the latter of which she had no idea how to pronounce when she first encountered it. She'd said *"Kwih-no-ah?"* aloud in the grocery store, and Stephen had laughed; it wasn't a cruel laugh, but it still sent heat to Sam's cheeks. But she appreciated that Stephen took these tasks upon himself. Where Sam came from, even women of her own generation still did the cooking and cleaning, even when they had jobs and dreams of their own. Even when, like their mothers and grandmothers before them, the work became a kind of cancer—the exhaustion settling into their bones, resentment spreading in their blood. Sam had refused this tradition. Left to her own devices, she was prone to PBJs and macaroni and cheese, a stovetop covered in grease. So Stephen kept her fed and the kitchen clean, one of the best ways he knew to take care of her.

She hesitated now, unsure of whether to tell him. Of what exactly to tell him. It would sound crazy. It *was* crazy. It was absolutely batshit, and she was afraid to say it aloud. But she felt the desire to tell him, to pull the slackened thread between them tight. To kick the old instinct to keep everything a secret and be honest for once in her fucking life.

She cracked her knuckles, inspected her nails, picked dirt from beneath them. Then she spoke.

"This is going to sound absolutely insane," she said. There was a short delay on the line, and she heard the echo of her own voice.

"Try me," he said. She could hear pans banging around in the background, kitchen cabinet doors and drawers closing, and she felt suddenly, painfully, homesick.

"So," she said, attempting to pop her knuckles again, though they silently refused, "this doe has been talking to me?"

She said it as a question. For a second or two, there was silence.

"A doe," he said. It wasn't a question.

"A doe," Sam said. "A deer. A female deer."

Stephen laughed, breaking the tension, and Sam laughed too.

"What's she saying?" he asked.

"Weird things. Today she told me how to plant irises."

"Today—" Stephen began. "How long has this been going on?"

"A while," Sam said. "She's talked to me a few times now."

He cleared his throat, a subtle sound he was trying to hide, but she heard it. "And she tells you how to plant things."

"Well, today she did. She said this thing I remember my mom telling me a long time ago. When we used to plant flowers together. About roots. That you have to plant them shallow, so the sun can get in."

"Well, that certainly feels ripe with metaphor."

"Yeah," Sam said, forcing a tiny laugh through her nose. It was a sound she and Stephen called *the gala laugh*—the kind of fake laugh deployed at fancy parties to make whatever boring person you were talking to believe that talking to them didn't make you want to die.

"Did you just give me the gala laugh?"

"No!" she said, then smiled. "Yes. I'm sorry. It was actually funny."

"Fine," he said, fake hurt, trying to keep things light, to not let on how concerned he was. "So did you, like, actually hear words coming out of her mouth?"

"I did. I literally saw her mouth move. She talks while she eats, and spits corn all over the yard."

"Rude," Stephen said.

"Such an animal," Sam said. They both laughed for real then, and she felt a little more at ease, less like she was admitting to something that could have her committed.

"Are you sure you weren't dreaming?" Stephen asked.

"Pretty sure," Sam said.

"Because it sounds a lot like a dream. Maybe a waking dream?"

"I was wide awake."

"I know but, like, that does happen. Like a hallucination. Have you been sleeping?"

"It was so real, though," she said, ignoring the question. She hadn't been sleeping. Not well, anyway. And the more she drank, the worse her sleep got. She remembered, then, waking up in the woods. She had forgotten, somehow, the memory of it slipping away like a dream. But it came back to her now, or at least the feeling of it: her bare skin in the cold, the sharp sound of the forest. The deep sleep that came after. Had it happened more than once? She couldn't remember. She decided not to tell him this.

"I was standing there, or squatting there, in the garden, in the sun. And the doe was talking. I heard her voice, I saw her mouth move, and she had this look on her face. This wry kind of look." Sam stopped for a second. "Like she really *saw* me."

"Huh," Stephen said, a few beats of silence ringing out. "What did her voice sound like?"

"It was low," Sam said. "Like mine. A little raspy. Like she could have been a smoker."

"Hmm."

"What?"

"Just that—" Stephen said, and the connection wavered, and he sounded like he was underwater again. The call would drop soon, Sam knew, and this would be the last of his voice she'd hear today. Once the connection cut out it rarely came back until the next day. Most days, somewhat inexplicably, she'd get service in the morning, then nothing all day, then full bars again right around sunset. After dark, nothing. Just an ominous SOS where the bars used to be. She wished, now, that she could stay on the phone with him all day, and all night, take the phone with her to bed and let his voice send her off to sleep. Better yet, she wished he was there, to curl his body around her, keep her wrapped tight in the warm cocoon of him.

On the other end, his voice crackled back to life.

"Maybe this is dumb," he said, pausing, leaving a low hum in the space between his words, "or, like, too Freudian or whatever. But it kind of sounds like your mom."

"Oh," she said softly. "Oh, shit. Yeah."

The hum cut out sharply, and there was silence.

"Stephen?" she said. "Are you there?"

But there was nothing. No crackle or waves, only a dead line.

"Stephen? Can you hear me?"

She called to him again, but he was gone. On the screen, his name was still there, the green orb of connection still live. But she was calling out to nothing, across a dark abyss of data, like the quarries she used to party in as a teenager. She'd stand on the ledge of a rock face, calling out to her friends on the other side, a vast black chasm between them, waiting for the echo of her own voice, then an answer. She'd stand there, on the rock's sharp edge, look down into the void and think about jumping, until a friend called back. But this time, there was no response. Only the echo of her own voice, and no one on the other end.

On the days Sam talked to Stephen, she didn't need a drink. Or, at least, the need didn't feel so present. Maybe it was guilt—when she talked to him, she felt the secrecy of it, which felt like betrayal. Which *was* betrayal. She wanted to tell him but didn't know how. For the past ten months, he had been so supportive of her sobriety. He had even stopped drinking too.

"In solidarity," he said. But he had grown somewhat attached to sobriety, and found it came easy. He was better at sticking to things than she was.

Sam had never gone to an AA meeting. At the suggestion of a

friend, she'd been to a few Al-Anon meetings, where she sat in a circle of metal chairs meant for the family and friends of addicts, many of whom were addicts themselves and hadn't admitted it yet. Sometimes Stephen went with her, though no one in his family had been addicted to anything. Sam found this mystifying. What must it be like, Sam wondered, to grow up in a family where people didn't drink, or just drank socially, like normal human beings? Who never drank until they fell down, or threw up, punched walls or each other? Who never drank in secret?

For a while, back in Brooklyn, she'd gone to the Al-Anon meetings every week. The first time she went, the shock of recognition in the stories she heard—about fathers and mothers and siblings and lovers—left her stumbling out the door. The people in those meetings often spoke about God. It made Sam uncomfortable on her best days, and pissed her off on her worst. She met a woman at the meetings named Mary, and they got coffee together sometimes. They talked about the higher power stuff, the idea of letting go of the illusion of control. When Sam told Mary she no longer believed in God, Mary told Sam a higher power didn't need to be God, or at least not the version she'd been taught growing up. It didn't need to be the bearded white dude in the sky, she said. It could be the universe, energy, whatever.

"Could it be trees?" Sam had asked one night. It was a joke, kind of. They were at a diner in Greenpoint, their usual spot, where they ordered coffee and apple pie with vanilla ice cream.

"Trees?" Mary asked, as the waitress delivered the pie.

"Trees," Sam said. "They're, like, the closest thing I have to God."

She thought about a story she'd heard growing up, in her little Scandinavian town. The Old Norse legend of Yggdrasil, a massive, sacred ash tree around which the gods convened. A site of both worship and terror. That seemed about right.

"Not too many trees around here," Mary said with a laugh.

"True," Sam said, thinking about the sad state of her neighborhood, the sugar maple in front of her apartment that had just been cut down. Greenpoint was not, in fact, very green.

"But sure," Mary said with a shrug, taking a bite of pie. "It can be trees."

Back then, Sam found herself walking every now and again into the arched doorway of Trinity Church, on Broadway, during her lunch break. Just a few years earlier she had hung out there with the Occupy Wall Street crowds, shouting about dismantling the system, a thing she'd believed could happen then. It was just up the street from her office, and there was a Pret A Manger on every block, where she would buy a ten-dollar sandwich when she'd been too tired or hungover to pack a lunch, or when her cupboards were bare because she was broke. Falafel wraps and egg salad peppered her credit card bill, which grew and grew.

When she walked into Trinity for the first time, she did it as if compelled by some other force. She walked into the cool dark of it, the smell of incense and hymnals and musty upholstered pews hitting her in a crush. She crossed herself out of habit and sat down in the back, looked up at the altar, the crucifix, the candles, the sun coming in through stained glass. She kept coming back, sometimes in the mornings before work. Even though she no longer believed in God, she missed church sometimes. Missed the ritual of it, the safety of it. The feeling of being protected, less alone. She missed the Eucharist on her tongue, the wine in her throat. She missed confession, being held in that small dark box, casting off her sins and being forgiven. It was harder to be afraid of the world, and of yourself, when you had something to believe in.

She would sit in the back row of Trinity and try to pray. She tried at first to pray to God, but it all felt wrong. So she tried the trees instead. She used the Latin to address them, which at least felt a little more right, and not so different from mass.

"Dear *Acer saccharum*," she would say to herself. Dear sugar maple. Like the one that had been cut down. Sometimes she whispered it aloud, just enough so the trees could hear.

"Dear *Betulacea*." She loved the sound of that one best. Dear birch.

She'd talk to the trees as if to God.

"Forgive me, *Quercus*, for I have sinned."

It was ridiculous, praying to an oak. But it was all ridiculous, the whole idea of prayer. It was absurd to talk to that bearded man in the sky, or some saint of lost souls or lost causes, or a tree, and believe they were listening. To ask them to save you.

Now, at the cabin, she stood in the clearing at the base of a birch. The buds on its branches were just beginning to bloom. She thought of Yggdrasil again, and recalled another part of the story. That it was known as the gallows tree, as Odin had hung himself there—a suicide meant to access knowledge of the universe. She remembered something else, too: four harts, or male deer, lived inside the tree. They ate from its branches, and the dew from the leaves pooled in their antlers, forming the rivers and the sea.

In front of the birch, she knelt. She did it without thinking, like some old power pulling her to the ground. Bent in the position of submission, a position she once swore she'd never take again, she thought maybe the woods could be her church.

Maybe I can talk to the trees, she thought, *and maybe they'll listen. And maybe I can listen back—for the wind in their branches, like water, like breath—and I'll know they're saying something. I'll know they hear me.*

She pressed her fingers into the earth, wanting to be absorbed by it, swallowed whole by the dirt and the loam and held there. She thought of the root systems below the surface—that vast, intricate network of signal and song, lines of communication bearing messages of warning and care. A sick tree in need of more nutrients, a predator nearby. She wished she could be part of their system. That she could talk, and the roots would listen—that they might send help her way, maybe even save her. She thought she might as well try. Bare knees against the ground, the wind rising up in the trees, she prayed.

Sixteen

❖❖❖❖❖❖❖

SHE DID THE work. Every day, one day at a time, she chipped away at her list, crossing things off, getting things done. She felt good about her progress. When she was finished, she would go back to New York, to Stephen, to their apartment and their cat. Maybe she'd go back to her job, or maybe she'd find a new one. She needed a change anyway. Maybe she'd finally finish the novel she'd been working on for years. Either way, she'd go back to her life, and it would continue like normal. They'd stay a while longer, then maybe they'd move somewhere else, make a fresh start in a new place, maybe even buy a little house—where they couldn't be kicked out, where the land couldn't be dug up and developed. Where their home would be theirs.

This was the plan, and she was sticking to it.

But the days slipped by, and they turned into weeks. One morning over coffee, she looked at the calendar on her phone and found that nearly a month had passed. She'd left sometime in April, and now it was mid-May. She couldn't make sense of it. Time had somehow vanished, and she still had so much to do.

She wasn't ready to go back. More than that, she wasn't sure if she *wanted* to go back. Sometimes, in the golden morning glow of her little back room, or just before she fell asleep at night—the boreal chorus frog singing, its song like a finger over a fine-tooth comb; the wind in the trees outside her open window—she knew she wanted to stay. It was so peaceful here. She could think, and she didn't have to deal with other people. She was responsible to no one. She could do whatever she wanted, and no one would know.

Did she miss Stephen? She told herself she did. She missed, in any case, the idea of him, and their life together—their fuzzy little Monster, their cozy apartment, Sunday mornings in bed. There were things about the city she missed too: walking to the bodega for milk, to the park on a Saturday, to the pub on their block for dinner, to watch a baseball game over nachos and Cokes. She missed her neighbors, those who had managed to stay amidst all the development, the little community that was holding on together.

But here in the woods, it felt like she was returning to herself— to the parts of her that she'd always felt separated from in the city. Here in the woods, she felt whole. For the first time in a long time, she felt like she was home.

That evening, around the time cell reception typically failed, she called Stephen. Despite a single flickering bar of service, the call went through easily. She was almost disappointed, hoping to have an excuse not to say what she needed to.

"Hi," he said.

"Hi," she said.

"How's it going out there, woodswoman?"

"It's good," she said. "Really good. But there's still so much I need to do."

"Okay," he said. "How much?"

"A lot," she said. "I still have to finish the deck and fix the sink. And sell the boat, and take a bunch of shit to Goodwill, and figure out what to do with the stuff I want to keep. If there's anything worth keeping."

"Okay," Stephen said again. "That's a lot. Do you need me to come?"

"I can't ask you to do that."

"Sam, you can. I'm happy to. It would be easier if you had help."

"Yeah, but work, and the cat—" she said, hearing herself make excuses.

"I can get some time off, and we can board the cat. Or I'll just bring her with."

"She would love it here," Sam said, despite herself.

"She would absolutely go after a squirrel and get lost and never come back."

"She'd get eaten by a bear in like two seconds." They laughed. Their cat was afraid of everything. She often slipped out their door, but never got farther than the landing before freezing in terror, then fleeing back to the safety of their apartment.

For a moment, Sam considered the idea. It would be nice to have them here. Her funny little family. But another feeling crept in. She felt a wall go up around her, and around this place, around the life she had here. It was hers, and she didn't want to share it.

"That's so much to ask," she said, instead of all the things she was thinking.

"It's not," Stephen said. "This is important. I can take a leave. I want to help."

"What about the plants?" she asked, grasping now, though

116

she did have a ridiculous number of houseplants, all of which required varying amounts of water and light. She could barely keep them alive, and Stephen's green thumb was worse than hers.

"We can get the neighbors to water them," he said.

"They'll die," Sam said. She heard petulance in her voice, hated herself for it.

"Look," Stephen said. "Do you not want me to come? If you don't, just say it."

"No," Sam said, "it's not that. It just—seems like a lot."

"It's not a lot for me," Stephen said. "But maybe it is for you."

There was a beat of silence on the line.

"Hello?" Sam called into it, worried that the call had dropped.

"I'm here," Stephen said. "I'm still here."

"Okay," Sam said. "I thought for a second—"

"I'm here," Stephen said again, his voice harder. "I'm always here. And when you figure out what you want, I'll still be here."

"Stephen—" Sam started.

"I should go," he said. "I've got work to do."

"Okay," Sam said.

"Talk to you later," Stephen said.

"Wait," Sam said. "Just wait a second. Please."

She was standing on the porch, the spot that got the best reception. Sometimes, while she was on the phone with him, she'd walk down to the basement, willing the connection to fail. Sometimes she just didn't feel like talking. But now she didn't want to get off the phone. She wanted to hear his voice, to feel him there with her. To hold onto him as long as she could.

"I want you here," she said. "I miss you."

"I miss you," he said. "But I'm not sure I believe you miss me."

"I do," Sam said. "It's just weird here. It's hard. I find myself thinking about stuff I don't think I had room, or bandwidth, or whatever, to think about before. Maybe I was too busy, or maybe there was just too much noise. Or maybe I just didn't allow myself to think about it."

"Like what?" he said.

"I don't know," she said. "Life. Death. The meaning of this experiment called humanity. Little things." It was an attempt at a joke, but he didn't laugh. She kept talking to fill the silence.

"I've been thinking about my parents. About my mom. About all the things she chose and didn't. I've been thinking about my dad, too. How they both disappeared in their own ways. And I'm scared I'm going to do the same thing. And I'll look up one day and be old and think, 'What did I do with this life?' If I even make it that far."

"So, what, you're having a midlife crisis?" Stephen asked. It was his turn at a joke, but it came out sounding mean.

"I'm only thirty-eight," she said.

"Your grandparents died in their seventies," he said.

"Good point," she said. "I don't know. Maybe? But it's not like I'm going to have an affair with some young buck or buy a sports car."

"No," he said, "it'll be a woman and a motorcycle."

She laughed. "You know me so well."

"Sam, I get it. You're going through a lot. And I just want to help you through it. I don't want you to do it alone. This shit is stressful. And right now, you're alone in the woods and I can't help but think this isn't a good situation for you to be in."

He paused. She stayed quiet, heard him screwing up the nerve to say something. After a decade together, she knew what the sound of his silences meant. That a certain intake of breath meant he was figuring out how to say something he was afraid to say.

"I feel like it's a dangerous place for you," he said. "Surrounded by all your parents' things, their life, your mom's disappearance—"

"What could possibly be dangerous about it?" Sam broke in.

"Sam," he said.

"What?" she asked. Her body had gone tense.

"Are you—have you been drinking?"

"What?" she said. It was a sharp sound, all hurt and disbelief. How real it sounded. Her ability to lie with such ease shocked her sometimes. "How could you even ask me that?"

"Sam, I know you. I know the sound of your voice. I know what you sound like sober, and I know what you sound like when you've been drinking. I literally know what you sound like when you've had a single beer. And a few days ago, when we talked, I heard it."

Sam was silent. He was right, of course. But everything inside her told her to deny it, to lie, to tell him he was crazy. Like she was told her whole life—that she was imagining things, that she was making things up—so often she believed it. The impulse to do the same to Stephen rose up in her chest and coiled around her neck, like a snake she wore draped around her body. It had a voice, and she heard it.

Lie, it said. *Lie to him.*

She could feel the voice inside her skin, telling her to hide, to fight or to fly. She couldn't fess up. It was too much of a betrayal. It would mean, above all else, that she had failed. Not just to stay sober, but to keep the promise she'd made.

After Sam's grandmother died, her mother had gotten worse. Every time Sam called, her mother was drunk on the phone. Every time she went home to visit, her mother was drunk when she walked in the door. Her sober mother—the mother

Sam loved, the mother she longed for—never returned. So Sam stopped calling, and she stopped going home. Sam's grandmother had disappeared the same way. After her husband died, the old woman—who had once loved to talk, who was quick with a joke and laughed easily—got quiet, sipping her whiskey-laced can of Diet Coke and saying nothing, disappearing a little more each day until she was finally gone for good.

Where Sam came from, you didn't talk about hard things. You didn't talk about the bills that piled up and just kept coming. You didn't talk about pain—at least not the emotional kind, those wounds that go far deeper than skin. You could talk about physical pain all day—about the ailments and injuries that bent your back, required meds and surgeries you couldn't afford. It was as if the physical pain became a proxy for that deeper kind—the kind you kept tucked away, shoved so far down in your guts that it bubbled up like acid and lived in your chest, a permanent companion you carried around with you like heartburn. No matter where you went, there it was, coiled under your rib cage, ready to burst free. But you knew to never let it.

So you drank instead. To numb the clawing of it, like a cat at a closed door, begging to get out. Some people Sam knew dealt in different ways—gambling and weed, oxy and heroin and meth. But in her family, it had always been booze. The drug that, in a state where you could rack up five DUIs before losing your license, always got a pass. The devil they knew so well.

Sam had finally made a promise to herself. And for ten months, she'd stuck to it. She wouldn't live this way, and she wouldn't die this way either. She would break the cycle, end the line. This disease, she swore, would die with her.

But the thing was, drinking wasn't just a disease. It wasn't just sorry and struggle and sadness, wasn't just a sick mess. It was also a love affair. Deep and consuming, the kind of love Sam had read about when she was a girl, the kind she watched in Disney movies, wearing out the tapes in their puffy VHS cases. The kind she longed for as a teenager, listening to love songs as she drove out past the cornfields at night. The kind of love that might take her somewhere, that might save her, that would never leave.

She tried to think of Stephen this way. She wanted to believe that if she just tried hard enough, if she worked hard enough, was *good* enough, he could be this love. That she might love him forever. But when she thought about alcohol—when she thought of all the people in her life who shared the same affliction, or affection; the same desire and ecstasy and misery; the kind of love that always called you back, even though you knew it was bad for you, even though you knew better; the kind of love that showed up at your door in the rain, sad and sorry and begging to be forgiven, that you always let back in; the kind of love that conquered, the kind of love that killed—she knew, like she had always known, that it was the love of her life.

"Sam?" Stephen's voice called to her from the other side of whatever boundary she'd just crossed, reaching across the chasm that stretched between them. "Are you there?"

I'm here, she wanted to say. *Come find me.* But she said nothing. The thing inside her tightened its grip. She was terrified to speak, that what would come out would be a lie.

"Sam," Stephen said again. "I'm not mad. I'm just worried."

At last she choked out some words. "I should go."

"Sam," Stephen said. "Please. Stay on the phone."

"I need to go," she said.

"Okay," Stephen said. "Okay. I love you, okay? No matter what. I love you."

"Yeah," she said. "Okay."

He was about to tell her he loved her again. He was about to say something sweeping, something honest and true. He was about to tell her that no matter what she was going through, however badly she had fucked up, he was there, he loved her, he would help her get through it. He would stay, like he always had. He was about to say everything she always wanted to hear.

But she hung up before he could say it. She turned off her phone and threw it in a drawer. Then she walked out of the cabin and toward the woods, the blue night folding in around her.

Seventeen

◇◇◇◇◇◇◇◇◇◇◇

THE SUN WAS rising over the lake, the water still as glass. She was lying on a small strip of beach, at the water's edge, her skin slick with sand. Barefoot and shirtless, shoes and sweater in a pile beside her, jeans rolled up to the knees. The lake water, weedy and green, licked her toes. It was cold, but she didn't seem to notice.

What she did notice were her legs, covered in leeches. They'd attached themselves to her ankles and calves, little outlines of blood around their fat black bodies. She didn't freak out, like she would have in the past. She hated leeches. She'd been somewhat traumatized as a kid, playing in a lake like this one with her cousins, when they emerged from the water covered in them. They had peeled off their swimsuits and torn the fat, slimy things off each other's backs, pulled them from between their legs and toes, screaming the whole time. In retrospect, it was kind of funny. But it haunted her just the same.

Now, she sat up on the sand and inspected the creatures attached to her skin, grown plump with her blood. She marveled at their tenacity, how tightly and thoroughly they had bound themselves to her body. She peeled them off slowly, leaving small blooms of bruises on her skin, like the hickies that drunk boys in high school had left on her neck, her throat throbbing as their saliva dried. She'd tried to cover them up with concealer, but that only made it worse. And still, she'd go to school after some weekend party, feeling not humiliated but claimed, her heart beating hard in that hot purple spot, reminding her that, at least for a night, she'd been wanted.

She set the leeches back down at the water's edge, foam pooling around their bodies atop the sand. After pulling more than a dozen of the slick things from her skin, she stood on the shore, feeling her pulse in each bruise the leeches had left. She smiled.

The morning sun began to crest the trees, the mourning doves singing their long, lonely songs. She tried to remember how she got here, but her mind drew a blank. Had she been drinking the night before? She didn't think so. She remembered talking to Stephen on the phone, but after that, nothing. A dead line, a long black hallway in her mind. She wasn't hungover, no sick acid in her esophagus, no sweet fuzz on her tongue. She felt strangely fine. She even felt good. She stretched, reached her arms toward the sky, and looked around her. She knew exactly where she was, though she'd never been here before.

The beach was a secret spot, which her dad's friend Irv, a retired ex-military guy who'd lost a finger in a wood splitter, told her about one day at the grocery store. They'd run into each other at the beer cooler, and Sam had pretended she was on her way to the deli.

"It's top secret," Irv had said, holding his basket of cured meat, milk, and bread. He had brought his half-finger to his lips. "No one knows about it, so you can't tell no one either."

Sam had caught herself looking at the finger, then snapped her gaze back up to meet his.

"You got it," she had said with a nod. "Where do I find it?"

He gave directions in a whisper, glancing over his shoulder with a conspiratorial wink.

"Used to be a boy scout camp," he said. "Back in the day. Now it's empty, all overgrown. But when you get there, you'll see these big old stones—that's how you know. Used to be the entrance to the camp. Won't look like nothing, but when you see those stones, that's it. Walk in between the stones and head into the woods. The trees'll be thick, and there won't be much of a path, and you'll think, 'Is this it?' And that's it. Just keep on walking. And then *bam,* the trees'll break and there the lake'll be, all white sand around it."

Now, she stood on the shore, looking out at the water, her feet in that white sand. She tried again to remember getting here. Tried to conjure the stones, the path, the dense trail of trees. But where memory should have been there was only a dark expanse, in which anything could have happened. This should have frightened her, but it didn't. Instead, she looked out at the still water and felt just as calm.

The morning was quiet, but for the finches and chickadees and longspurs singing, the occasional warble of a redstart, the echo of a woodpecker rat-tatting at the hollow column of a dying oak. There was a community dock, an old rickety thing with sagging boards, its ancient metal posts covered in rust and algae. She imagined the ghosts of the boys who spent their summers here at camp, running down this dock and jumping, their bare chests gold in the sun, screaming into the air and being suspended there, the lake twinkling beneath them, before cannonballing into the water. She remembered running and jumping and swimming too, in lakes just like this one, her shirt off like the boys, until the adults started telling her she needed a proper swimsuit for a girl.

She stepped onto the dock, and looked down at her own bare chest. Her breasts seemed to have gotten smaller, her pectoral muscles more defined. She flexed, and pressed her fingers there, liked the firmness she felt. All the work, and not a lot of eating, seemed to have sheared some of her away, carving out something harder beneath the flesh she once wore. She liked what she saw. Liked the cool morning air on her skin, open and unbound.

She looked across the water. The lake was bordered by evergreens, and pale white birch trees sticking out among them like bones. A small handful of cabins—big lakefront A-frames owned mostly by rich Chicagoans—peeked through the trees. A few private docks dotted the shore, fishing boats and canoes and pontoons tied to their posts. The water was so still it mirrored the clouds and trees like a painting, but for a ripple of a mayfly, the occasional bluegill breaking the surface.

Way out toward the western shore, two loons called to one another, their sad songs echoing up over the trees. Of all the wildlife here, Sam loved loons the most, so lonely-sounding, particularly in the dead of night, when she could hear them most clearly, calling out across the distance, singing to one another—forlorn and desperate, a little mad with longing.

She watched these two come together, then float along the surface in synchrony, their bodies choreographed. She thought of the female, who later that summer would appear with a baby on her back, a tiny fuzzy thing that rode along with her as they fished, the mother teaching her child how to spot dinner underwater, teaching her how to swim. Sam was pretty sure she didn't want kids, but seeing the baby loons on the backs of their mothers, a strange kind of grief pitched up inside her that made her think of drowning.

Whenever she tried to tell someone about this feeling, they never seemed to get it. Maybe she didn't quite get it herself. Maybe she was just never good at articulating her grief. And anyway, people always assumed their grief was the heaviest; whatever small losses other people carried could never compare to their own. It was one of the deepest flaws of humankind, she thought, the inability to see other humans as capable of being as complicated as oneself.

Stephen wanted children. At least, he wanted them more than Sam did. She knew this, had known it for a long time. She knew it even more than Stephen did. This was one of the problems with dating men. They all wanted to be fathers. Or, at least, they wanted to see themselves in a child, watch it grow into a person who looked like them, who shared their sense of humor and curly hair. They wanted to see their line continued without having to do any of the hard work, like carrying or labor or keeping a kid alive with their body. Even though Sam and Stephen had talked about a future without children, she knew he would wake up one day and see his friends having kids, start to wonder about things like duty and purpose. He might see himself as less than other men. He'd look at himself, and his aging parents, and the undefined void of his future, and he would be terrified of finding himself alone.

And maybe this was why she left. Maybe she knew that someday Stephen would realize he'd made a mistake. He'd leave her and find some other, younger woman, fertile and wide-hipped and hungry for a baby. She remembered what her high school biology teacher had always said—*Love 'em and leave 'em!*—the Darwinian impulse of every man to spread his seed as far and wide as possible, to make little versions of himself wherever he went, a trail of females in his wake, left alone to care for the children he'd made. It was a joke, kind of—something her teacher, and all the boys in her class, thought was hilarious, sent them high-fiving each other in the classroom. But Sam knew even then that her teacher had meant it, that the boys had too.

Sam had hated that teacher, hated all the boys in her class. She hated that this behavior was so excused in men it was a joke. That she, born female, was expected to stick around, to stay in one place. To have and raise children, build a home and keep it, never leave it. She had always seen herself, in many ways, more like a man than a woman. And she had never wanted to be the kind of woman she so often saw—barefoot and pregnant, stretched and expanded and overtaken by a creature that would burst forth from her body like that scene in *Alien*, destroying its host in order to live. The kind of woman with kids crawling around her, clinging to her breasts, their sticky hands all over her skin, vomit crusted to her shirt: always in need, never letting go, leaving their mother depleted, her body an empty vessel made to serve. She never wanted to be the one who stayed, who was stuck, while whatever man had done this to her was allowed to leave. To go off to work, rarely help at home, eventually have an affair and leave for good. She'd seen it so many times. So she'd promised herself she would never be left. She would never stay anywhere long, would always be the one to leave.

Sam stood on the dock and watched the loons, feeling the ghost of a fuzzy little version of herself on her back. She felt her bare chest getting warmer as the sun got higher, and she wondered what it meant to be a woman, or at least a body with a uterus and ovaries, who chose not to use them. She wondered what it meant to be born, to live in this world without doing the one thing women are constantly told is their reason for being. She was a feminist, and had still never found an answer. She had learned early that any woman who puts herself first was selfish at best, and at worst some kind of monster. So deeply had the understanding been buried inside her that, like weeding, when she tried to pull up the plant by the roots, she was left with only leaves and a handful of dirt, the entire system still buried beneath the soil.

She plucked her clothes from the sand, put her shirt back on but carried her shoes, and walked the road toward home. The gravel and sand dug into her feet. She felt a bite on her wrist, a quick sharp sting—most likely a no-see-um, the invisible biting midges that swarmed the woods unseen—and scratched it. She watched red lines from her fingernails streak down her flesh, over a series of white scars. She ran a thumb over the scar tissue and remembered the night she almost left for good. The memory was hazy, a tapestry of vignettes whose edges were blurred. She remembered the tub, the water up to her chin, billowing around her like a pink blanket. She remembered steam on the mirror, a blue towel on the rack, white and black tile. What she remembered most was not pain, but the warmth of the water as it held her, the pink of it turning red. And, at last, the feeling of relief, like exhaling after a lifetime of holding her breath. Sometimes she thought of that night and longed for that feeling again. The release, the letting go. To sink into those waters once again, and slip under this time. She'd worked hard over the years to fight this feeling. But sometimes it came back, as old ghosts do.

She shook the thought away and kept walking, the bruises on her legs from the leeches beginning to throb. She turned up the drive to the cabin, the branches of birch trees bending over the path, opening up like a passageway in the woods. It was then she felt a presence. There was no car in the driveway, no one she could see. But she felt it. Someone, or something, was here. She'd become attuned to the silence, in its many shapes and forms. She knew the various contours of quiet, and what lived inside each of them.

She stopped, midway up the path, and waited. She listened to her own breath, to the wind in the trees, the forest breathing alongside her. The sound itself a living thing.

She didn't hear footsteps. No one called out. But she was certain someone was there. It could have been Irv, who stopped by every few days to get something from the garage, which he shared with her father in exchange for plowing the driveway and clearing downed branches when her father wasn't there. He stored a snowmobile there in the summer, a small fishing boat in the winter, swapping them out as the seasons came and went. He might have been there now, tooling around. He never told her when he was coming over; he'd just show up. She would head out to the garage with a bag of empties, to throw them in a pile for the dump, and she'd find him there with his tools out, fixing something.

"Hey Irv," she'd say.

"Oh hey, Sam," he'd call out, as if having forgotten she was there. He didn't need to come by as often as he did, and she knew he was checking in on her.

Sam walked toward the garage and opened the door. It was dark inside. Irv wasn't there. She walked back out into the light, the sun too bright after the dark of the garage. She waited.

She wasn't scared so much as on guard, her ears pricked up like an animal's. This place was hers, and it was hers to protect. She'd never felt this way before, so protective of a place, of anything at all.

"Hello?" she called out.

Silence.

"Anyone there?"

Silence still. She crept to the porch, climbed the stairs slowly. The door was open. She could have left it that way, but she couldn't remember. She heard a crack in the woods and stopped, her heart beating fast. Two squirrels darted out of the trees, chasing each other around the clearing.

It's fine, she thought. *Everything's fine.*

She opened the screen door and it creaked on its hinges.

This thing needs some WD-40, she thought.

The screen door slammed as she walked inside. In the dim gauze of early morning, the cabin was still dark. It took a few seconds for her eyes to adjust. It was only then that she saw the figure, looming in the black mouth of the hallway. She wasn't alone.

Eighteen

◇◇◇◇◇◇◇◇◇◇

"HELLO," A VOICE said, and the figure stepped out of the shadows.

"Jesus," Sam said, dropping her shoes.

"Didn't mean to scare you." The body emerged into the light. It was Lou-Ann.

"What—" Sam started. "What are you doing here?"

"Well," Lou-Ann said, "I came over to see you, and the door was open, so I came inside. When it became pretty clear you weren't here, I thought I'd wait."

She stood in the kitchen, holding a cup in her hands. "I made some tea, you want some?"

"Make yourself at home," Sam said, her voice sharp.

"I'm sorry," Lou-Ann said. "Should I go?"

The older woman carried her cup to the sink and Sam stayed by the door, waiting for her pulse to slow. Was it Friday? Had it been a week? She was sure it had only been a couple of days since she'd last seen this woman. She shook her head.

"No," she said finally. "Stay. You just freaked me out a little."

"I'm sorry about that, hon," Lou-Ann said. "I wasn't thinking.

Up here we just walk into each other's houses sometimes. I suppose that's a little strange."

"Yeah," Sam said, shaking off the last of the shock. She walked to the kitchen and grabbed a cup from the dish rack. There was still a coffee ring inside it. She tore open a tea bag and poured some still-hot water from the kettle into her cup, then topped off Lou-Ann's. They carried their cups to the living room and sat down.

"I'm glad you came over," Sam said finally. "I think I was starting to feel a little lonely."

"I thought you might be," Lou-Ann said. She held the mug to her lips but didn't drink. "So, Sam—is that short for Samantha?"

"Yeah," Sam said. She took a sip of her tea and grimaced, set the cup back down. "But I've always kind of hated that name. It's such a girl's name, you know? Like the American Girl doll." Her grandmother had given her the doll when she was young, the brown hair and nametag, SAMANTHA, making Sam's stomach turn. She'd buried the doll beneath a pile of stuffed animals, displayed it only when her grandmother came to visit.

"I hear you," Lou-Ann said. "Never did like the *Ann* part of my name much. Too girly. Tried to go by different things, at different times in my life, but they never seemed to stick. I guess I've always felt attached to my name, in the end, even if it doesn't quite fit. Like it's something my parents gave me that I actually want to hold on to."

"I get that," Sam said.

"Holds both sides of me too," Lou-Ann said. "The masculine and the feminine. The hard and the soft. Folks would be a lot better off if they embraced both."

"I obviously agree," Sam said, gesturing at her own body. They both laughed.

"I was such a tomboy growing up," Lou-Ann said. "Always off with the boys playing baseball, running around in the woods. My mother called me an animal, said good girls didn't play with boys, didn't roll around in the mud and fight like I did."

"Sounds familiar," Sam said. "My parents didn't care, though. They weren't around much. Which meant I got in some trouble." She cracked a sideways smile.

"That sounds familiar too," Lou-Ann said. "I knew I liked you."

Sam liked Lou-Ann too, and was glad to know she was up here. Sam had felt sure, when she'd first arrived, that she wanted to spend the entire time alone. Even Irv's little unexpected visits irritated her sometimes. With people constantly on top of her in New York, she'd been looking forward to some solitude. But she liked having this woman around.

"So what do you do up here?" Sam asked.

"Oh, odd jobs here and there," Lou-Ann said. "Help folks out with their trucks and boats sometimes, plow in winter for the part-timers. Clear the roofs, break up the ice, make sure the gutters don't collapse. Run the heat every so often, get the hot water running so the pipes don't freeze. I like to think of myself as a keeper of sorts, a caretaker of the empty houses."

Sam nodded. The preserve was populated now mostly by retirees, snowbirds who came up in the summer and fall. The wealthier ones flew south for the winter, closing up their cabins in mid-October, after peak color, and didn't come back till June. The winters were unpredictable, with the snow often starting by Halloween and not letting up until May, temperatures staying in the negative double digits for weeks at a time. The people who stayed year-round had generators and knew how to survive if the power went out. But even for them, winter was isolating. It could get brutal.

Lou-Ann sipped from her cup.

"Sometimes I fill in over at the Torches," she said. "Tend bar."

Sam knew the casino. It was owned and operated by the Lac du Flambeau Band of Lake Superior Chippewa, and her parents had gone sometimes, way back before things got bad, when they used to take her grandmother to the cabin. She had a thing for the slots and was good too. Sam remembered the three of them coming back to the cabin those nights, smelling of beer and cigarettes, loose and laughing.

"Used to work there full-time," Lou-Ann continued. "Now I just cover shifts once in a while. My family's been working there for years, a few generations now."

"So you're—" Sam started, then stuttered, unsure of which word to use and feeling stupid for saying anything in the first place.

"Ojibwe? Yeah," Lou-Ann said with a smirk. "Half, anyway. My mother was Irish Catholic."

"Same," Sam said. "I mean my mom, the Irish Catholic part."

"What about the rest of you?" Lou-Ann asked.

Sam shrugged. "My dad's Italian, but the other side of my mom's family is a mystery."

Lou-Ann nodded. "A little mystery is a good thing," she said, raising an eyebrow. "Means you could be anything."

"True," Sam said, fiddling with her cup. "So how's the casino faring these days?"

"Oh, fine," Lou-Ann said. "Two things you can count on are people's love of booze and gambling. But it's no place to get sober, or stay that way."

"Ah," Sam said, a ripple of warmth crawling up her neck.

"That's why I left. My brothers weren't happy about it. I was a good bartender. Made good money, brought in a lot of regulars. Those old blue-hairs loved me."

"I bet," Sam said, smiling. "I used to bartend too, and man I made some cash."

"Best paying job I ever had," Lou-Ann said. "All you gotta do is make a strong drink and flirt, and not go home with any of them assholes."

"I made that mistake once or twice," Sam said, tapping her fingers on her mug.

"Honey, who hasn't?" Lou-Ann said with a laugh. "When I was young, some of those men—" She shook her head. "Well. They promised you things. Said they'd take you places. Threw their money around like they were God's gift." She shook her head again and smiled. "But they were just drunks with a thing for Indian girls. And a girl like me, who had drunks for parents, drunks for brothers, well"—she paused, shrugged—"sometimes you believed them."

"I hear you," Sam said.

"So I screwed a few of 'em, one got me pregnant. Had to sneak over the border to take care of that, since I couldn't do it here. Drove all night through Duluth and into Thunder Bay myself. And no chance that man was gonna cover it. Fact, he disappeared straightaway when I told him I was knocked up."

"Of course he did," Sam said. It had happened to her once too. She wanted to say so but couldn't find the words.

"Course he did," Lou-Ann repeated. "So after that, well. Got pretty blue. Not because of the baby so much but because I was sick of my life. I wanted to do something. Go to college. See the world. I'd never been farther than the border, and Ontario ain't much different than here."

Sam sat for a minute in silence. She thought of her grandparents, who never left the state.

"Anyway, I gave up men when I gave up drinking," Lou-Ann

said. "Two best decisions of my life." She laughed, and Sam did too.

"Seems wise," she said.

"Hell yeah," Lou-Ann said.

"So where would you go?" Sam asked. "If you could see the world."

"Oh, I don't know," Lou-Ann said, smiling, drawing out the sound. "Spain, maybe. Italy. Those places always sounded nice to me. Warm. I'd go to those beaches and just sit there all day, reading my books. Or maybe Central America. Guatemala or Venezuela. I like their food."

"You should come visit me," Sam said. "In New York." The words tumbled out of her mouth before she knew they were coming. "There's a great arepa spot near my apartment. And a lot of Italian and Spanish food—we could eat our way through the city, make it a world tour."

"Ha!" Lou-Ann said. "That sounds pretty good, honey, but I think that ship has sailed."

"Why? Make it a road trip. Stay with me. You can see the sky-line from my roof."

Sam wasn't sure why she was asking this stranger to visit. She hated hosting people in New York. There was no space, every-thing cramped. But Lou-Ann waved her hand anyway.

"Nah. The only roofs I get up on anymore are these here, to clear the snow. Much lower to the ground. Don't got the travel bug anymore," she said. "I like it here. My home's here. I like the trees and the lakes and the quiet."

"I get that," Sam said. "I like it here too."

Sam studied Lou-Ann. She was tall and strong. *Built like a barn*, as Sam's grandmother used to say. *Thick-skinned*, *big-boned*, any number of things Sam and the women in her family had been called, things they often called themselves. But Sam found Lou-Ann striking, and strangely familiar. Sam's grandmother had always claimed, somewhat suspiciously, that there was Native blood in their line. Chippewa or Ho-Chunk, most likely. She also claimed they were Jewish, but she said it in a whisper, like it was some kind of secret. A cousin had once spit into a tube and discovered they had roots in the Middle East or Mediterranean. *Cyprus or Lebanon,* she'd said one year at Christmas. *The Levant,* she'd said at the next. She'd said it with the overconfident sniff of someone who had only just learned what the Levant was, and their grandmother had nodded sagely, as if it were common knowledge. The truth was that no one knew anything for sure, and while it was also true that Sam was not what people in her hometown called "the good kind of white," she also knew enough about white people claiming cultures that weren't theirs to claim nothing at all. And anyway, she took everything her family said—not least that bored and box-wine-swilling cousin, and especially her grandmother—with a massive grain of salt. Sam was never sure if her grandmother was telling stories or the truth, and was never totally sure if she, or anyone else in the family, knew the difference.

By the end, her grandmother's mind had deteriorated so fully she talked crazy. She saw things. She knew things. Heard them whispered to her in the wind. She, like Sam's mother, was convinced she was being watched. She talked about Big Brother like it was some guy she knew, believed elections were rigged and billionaires staged riots, that we would all be nuked someday.

The thing was, none of it seemed that crazy to Sam. The world was on fire, the president was a madman, everyone's phone was actually listening to them, and the Earth was going to be swallowed by the ocean at any minute, or the ozone would burn up first. Her uncles had built bunkers, stocked them with canned goods and guns, and this seemed increasingly smart to Sam.

But sometimes she wondered if this, too, was her own brain damage talking. None of it seemed crazy, but then no one who loses their mind knows that's what's happening to them. Even the nightmares feel real.

She swallowed the rest of her tea. It had gone cold and terribly bitter. Her temples were starting to pound. Maybe she had been drinking last night.

"I'll be right back," she said to Lou-Ann. She got up and walked to the bathroom, shut the door. She looked at herself in the mirror, which was smudged with fingerprints and flecked with bits of food from flossing. She really needed to clean.

She looked like shit. Like she hadn't slept in weeks. She always had circles under her eyes, but they were much darker now—thick rings of purple that gave her a certain undead quality. Her skin was dark from the sun, but a sickly green had worked its way to the surface. She opened the medicine cabinet and tapped two Excedrin into her palm. She ducked her head under the faucet, filled her mouth with cold water, and swallowed the pills down.

"You're a mess," she said aloud to her reflection. She left the tap running and splashed cold water on her face.

"You all right?" Lou-Ann asked as Sam walked back out. The older woman was standing by the door, holding the empty mug in her hands.

"Oh yeah," Sam said, "I'm fine. Just a little worn out."

She thought of the rotting boards on the porch. She'd pulled up most of them, but still had a few to go. Then she would replace them. The day before—or maybe it had been a few days before—she'd gone to the lumber mill and bought a dozen five-quarter boards. On the drive home the truck had filled with the sweet scent of fresh-cut pine and sawdust.

"Why don't I take you out for dinner tonight?" Lou-Ann said. "It's Friday, and Goocher's has fresh-caught walleye."

"It's Friday already?" Sam asked, rubbing the back of her neck, digging her thumbs into the knots that lived there.

"Yes, indeedy," Lou-Ann said.

"That keeps happening," Sam said. She tried to laugh, but she was getting worried. About losing the days, how time kept slipping away. The idea of leaving the house tonight and sitting in a roomful of strangers sounded like hell, but a basket of beer-battered fish sounded divine. Her stomach growled.

"That does sound good," Sam said.

"I'll drive," Lou-Ann said. "Pick you up at six?"

People ate early up north, and even six was a little late for fish fry. The regulars showed up around five to put their names in, get a few drinks at the bar before being seated. Sam loved this ritual, that part of the deal was to get drunk, and no one judged how many old-fashioneds you had before dinner, or how many beers you had with it, or that you drove home afterward. She felt a little flint in her chest, thinking about a cocktail, and then another—when her body would fill with warm light, and that roomful of strangers would become friends.

"Perfect," Sam said. "See you then."

"*Miigwech,*" Lou-Ann said, holding up her empty mug. "Thanks for the tea."

"Anytime," Sam said. She took the cup from Lou-Ann and opened the screen door. She was hit with a sudden feeling of déjà vu, certain she'd been here before, in this very moment. She closed her eyes, tried to shake the feeling, but it felt like she was watching herself in a dream.

Lou-Ann stepped out onto the porch, nodding at the gaps where the rotten boards used to be. From this angle, the whole thing looked like a mouth full of missing teeth.

"Need an extra hand with this?" she asked.

"Thanks," Sam said, trying to hold it together. "But I'm good. Getting there, anyway."

"If you ever need any help, all you need to do is ask."

Sam nodded and waved as Lou-Ann walked away. She held the empty cup in trembling hands, unsure whether she was awake or dreaming. She listened to the crunch of footsteps on gravel, the sound fading until it was gone completely.

Nineteen

SHE WANTED A drink. It was four o'clock, two hours until Lou-Ann would pick her up. They'd go to dinner, maybe sit at the bar and eat, and she'd do it without a beer, without an old-fashioned while she waited for her food, letting the sweet buzz settle in on an empty stomach. She didn't want to drink in front of her new friend. She didn't want to drink at all. But the thought of sitting at a bar and not drinking made the collar of her shirt feel tight. Her skin was clammy. Her vision began to fade out of focus, like the shutter of a camera lens closing. She sat down at the kitchen table, closed her eyes, and tried to breathe like a therapist had once taught her. In for five, hold for five, out for five. She opened her eyes.

Just one beer. That's all she wanted. A little something to ease the tension in her temples, her shoulders, her jaw. To turn it all down a notch, like the volume on a radio. She got up and opened the fridge, eyed the six-pack on the bottom shelf, its bottles cold and waiting. There were five left. She closed the door, rubbed her jaw. She'd been clenching her teeth, grinding them at night. She paced around the living room, went down to the basement to check the dehumidifier. It was full, so she dumped out the bucket in the yard. She went back upstairs. She stood in the middle of the kitchen, lifting a finger absently to her lips. She chewed a hangnail, tore off the skin. A sharp and sudden pain. It was an awful habit. She was always picking and biting at her cuticles until they bled, the site of the wound warm and throbbing. Sucking on the bloody finger, she opened the fridge again. She stood there, cool electric light pouring into the room. She imagined that first sip, how perfect it would be. That cold carbonation on her tongue, that rush of blood to the brain.

She swallowed. Shut the door. Kept her fingers wrapped around the handle.

She heard a rustling outside, through the patio screen. It was the doe, standing at the feeder, looking straight at her.

She let go of the handle, walked out onto the porch.

"What are you doing?" the doe asked. She had a tone, and Sam was immediately annoyed.

"What do you mean?"

"I *mean*," the doe said wryly, "what are you *doing*?"

"Nothing."

"Hmm."

"What do you mean, *hmm*?"

"Why do you keep asking what I mean?"

"Because I don't know what you mean," Sam said. "And you're clearly implying something."

"I'm not *implying* anything," the doe said.

"Fucking Midwestern passive-aggressive bullshit," Sam said.

The doe looked at her, eyes narrowed. "I am *not* passive-aggressive. I'm pretty sure you know *exactly* what I mean."

She bent her head into the feeder. Sam could hear the crunching of corn from where she stood, the sound of it amplified, reverberating in her bones. Her whole body a clenched fist. She wanted a beer. She wanted a smoke. She had a few cigarettes left in her pack. But she felt increasingly like it was wrong to smoke up here. The air was too clean. She longed for something, anything, to turn all this feeling down. Instead, she just stood there and felt it, irritable and angry. She watched the doe, who seemed to be getting thicker as spring pressed on.

"Getting your fill I see," she muttered. The doe looked up, still chewing. The crunching was deafening now. Sam winced.

"Is that a crack at my weight?" the doe asked.

"Not at all," Sam said. Now she was being passive-aggressive.

"You try living in the woods for an entire winter and surviving," the doe said, "and then come find me when you're presented with an entire trough of corn every day." She bent down and kept eating. Sam felt herself soften. She couldn't help but like this bitch. She reminded Sam of all the women she liked most—smart, funny, a little mean. Sam sat down in a deck chair, a cracked plastic thing that threatened to collapse under her.

"So," the doe said, looking up from her dinner, "you never actually told me what you were doing."

"Nothing," Sam said again, letting a long sigh escape her lips, resigned to pass the time with the shit-talking deer. She leaned back in her chair. "I'm doing absolutely nothing at all."

"I see that."

"I mean, I'm trying to figure out what I'm doing, I guess," Sam said.

"I can tell you what you're doing," the doe said.

"Shoot."

"You're sitting alone in the woods talking to a deer."

"This has occurred to me, thanks," Sam said.

"Has it?" the doe asked. She was looking curiously at Sam and had stopped chewing.

"I mean, I guess I'm probably losing my mind," Sam said.

"Or maybe you're just finding it."

Sam laughed. The sound seemed to carry much farther than it had before.

"Yeah, maybe you're right," she said.

They sat still, looking at each other. The wind blew through the leaves, silvery in late-afternoon light. Sam closed her eyes and inhaled deeply, trying to take as much air into her lungs as she could. Sometimes she forgot what clean air tasted like—sweet, crisp, like honey or apples. Sometimes, in New York, she forgot to breathe. Sometimes she wondered if she'd been holding her breath for years.

"So when are you going home?" the doe asked.

Sam opened her eyes.

"I don't know," she said with a sigh. She really needed a drink. *I'd give my goddamn soul for just a glass of beer,* she thought, summoning Jack Nicholson at the empty bar in *The Shining,* just before the devilish bartender appears.

"Maybe you should dump the rest of that beer out," the doe said, as if reading Sam's mind. *"Again."*

Sam huffed, like a hog or a cat or some kind of trapped animal.

"You can't tell me what to do," Sam said. "You're not my mother." Her voice was stupid and petulant, and she cringed at the sound of it.

"Nope," the doe said. "Your mother is gone. And she couldn't tell you what to do either. She didn't even know what to do herself."

Sam didn't know why this deer insisted on talking so much shit, but suddenly it struck her as very funny. She laughed.

"Is this some kind of tough love thing?" she asked. "A woodland intervention? Because it's not going to work."

The doe shrugged. Sam was sure of it.

"The bourbon too, while you're at it," the doe said. "Pour that shit down the drain."

"That's perfectly good booze that I paid good money for," Sam said.

"Yeah, well, it's killing you," the doe said, then bent her head back in the trough and ate.

"Maybe that corn is killing you," Sam said. "Maybe it'll make you fat and slow and you'll end up getting shot because you can't run away. Or you'll get sick, contract chronic wasting disease and give it to everyone else."

The doe kept eating. Sam immediately regretted what she said.

"Sorry," she said. The doe looked up from the trough and swallowed.

"If the corn is killing me, then you're the murderer. You're the one who keeps buying this shit, even though you know you shouldn't. You're the one who fills this trough every day."

Sam said nothing. The doe took another bite and chewed.

"You're the agent in this," she said, kernels spilling from her lips. "You call the shots. And you can change things if you want to."

"I wish you'd just say what you mean rather than speaking in parables, like some forest prophet who emerges at dawn and dusk each day to judge me, but never directly. Just always speaking in, like, harbinger code."

The doe laughed. "Harbinger—I like that," she said. "Maybe I am a harbinger."

"Well if the harbinger so pleases, could she be a bit more specific about what she's trying to portend?"

"Listen," the doe said. "You're not an idiot. You know what I'm saying. And all I'm saying is, if you're doing something that might kill me, you have the power to stop."

"So you want me to stop feeding you?"

"Not at all."

"Then I should keep doing it."

"You should do what feels right."

Sam laughed again, but it was a bitter sound. "I honestly have no idea what that even means. What *feels right* even feels like. I don't feel right or wrong. I feel nothing, all the time. I feed you because you're hungry. And because my mom fed you, and she would want me to feed you too. She wanted me to take care of you."

"But are you?"

"Am I what?"

"Taking care of me."

Sam considered the question. What did it mean to care for someone anyway? She knew what it meant on the surface—food, shelter, aspirin and soup when someone was sick. When she was little, it meant being sung to in the bathtub and tucked in at night, read to from the same books over and over, kissed on the forehead. A bedroom door kept open a crack, a nightlight. But wasn't care also a sense of safety? And wasn't part of safety also stability, permanence? The belief that you wouldn't be left, that the people who were supposed to take care of you wouldn't disappear, one way or another? This, she knew—beyond the boundaries of a house, four walls and a roof—was where safety really resided. It was a house she never lived in. She had never known what it felt like to be that kind of safe, or to make someone else feel that way. She did know, however, what enabling looked like. It looked like giving things to people that kill them, and it looked a lot like looking away.

"I don't know," Sam said. "You seem happy, and well fed. And alive. I like that."

"Mmm hmm," the doe said, all attitude.

"And I guess I like having you around, even though you're a real asshole sometimes."

"Aha!" the doe said. "So there's the rub. You like having me around."

"Sure, I guess so."

"So maybe feeding me is more about the company, and less about taking care of me. Maybe it's actually about you. Maybe it gives you something to feel good about. Or maybe you're just afraid of *not* having me around. Maybe you're afraid of being alone."

"Jesus Christ," Sam said. "So what, I'm just a total narcissist?"

"Honey, we all are," the doe said. "Anyone who claims otherwise is full of shit."

"Yeah, okay, I suppose that's true."

"But it's also human nature," the doe said. "Animal nature too. Most of us, anyway. We're in it for ourselves, but we're social creatures. We form bonds. And sometimes those bonds are bad for us. Some ties are better severed. Sometimes you have to cut someone loose in order for them to survive, for you to survive. All you can do is hope they come back someday."

"What are you, some kind of sage?" Sam asked.

"Harbinger, sage—I'm whatever you need me to be."

The doe bent her head back down into the corn. The sun was dipping past the tree line, and Lou-Ann would be here soon.

"So you gonna grab that beer or what?" the doe said, looking up, crunching away, kernels spilling from her mouth. "You've still got time."

Sam ejected another sharp sound, not quite a laugh.

"No, actually," she said. "For your information, I have a date. With a person."

"Ooh, a *date*," the doe said, batting her lashes. She did a little dance, her front hooves kicking up. Sam rubbed her eyes. Then the doe jerked fast, biting her tail and scratching her haunches with her teeth.

"Fucking mosquitoes," she said, giving her whole body a shake. Her tail kept twitching.

"They suck," Sam said.

"You're funny," the doe said, scratching. "Well, I'm off. Thanks for the grub. Have a good time tonight, and lay off the hard shit."

"Thanks," Sam said. "I will."

She closed her eyes, and when she opened them again the doe was gone. Where she had just been standing, a circle of corn lay scattered in the grass.

Twenty

AT SIX ON the dot, a '90s-era Subaru pulled up the drive, dark green and rusted out at the wheel wells. Lou-Ann kept the engine running.

"Heya," she called out the open window. "You ready?"

"Coming!" Sam called, pulling on her boots. She locked the door and jogged out to the car.

"Still locking your door, huh?" Lou-Ann said.

"Yeah," Sam said. "Stopped for a while but started to get a little spooked. You can take the girl out of New York and all."

"No one's breaking in up here," Lou-Ann said, pulling the car slowly down the drive, gravel crunching under the tires. "Though some crazy old ladies might show up unannounced."

Sam laughed. "Gotta watch out for them."

"Bears too, I suppose."

"That too."

Black bears did have a habit of breaking into cabins. There were stories all over town one summer about a mother bear breaking in through screen doors, getting into people's pantries.

150

Sam had been up north that summer with her parents, and one morning just before dawn her dad had knocked softly on her bedroom door.

"Sam," he had whispered. "Wake up."

She'd shot up in bed, freaked to find her father standing in the doorway in his long johns.

"What is it?" she said, throwing off the blankets, terrified something had happened to her mother. But her dad was smiling.

"Come here," he said, then slipped away into the darkness.

Sam stumbled into the hallway, bare feet freezing against the hardwood floors. It was around the same time of year, in late spring, and the morning was cold. Her father crept down the hallway and she followed, in silence, to the kitchen. He stopped at the sink, pressed a finger to his lips, and pointed out the window. Out in the backyard, a bird feeder that had been hanging from a birch tree lay shattered on the ground. Next to it, legs splayed out in front of her like a child, a large black bear sat on the ground, eating the seed. She pulled pawfuls to her mouth, the seed spilling down the front of her, like a kid learning to eat with their hands. Sam and her dad stood in the silence of morning, hands over their mouths and giggling, watching the black bear eat. When she'd had her fill, she stood up slowly, then ambled back up the hill into the woods. Sam and her father had looked at each other and cracked up. Then he made a pot of coffee, and they sat together at the table and drank it as the sun came up. They would find seed and tiny splinters from the feeder in the yard all summer long.

In the car, Sam and Lou-Ann sat in silence while they drove. Sam rolled her window down, watched the trees pass in a blur of brown and green, listened to the tires kick up gravel behind them. Lou-Ann clicked the radio on, and Tom Petty crackled in through the speakers.

"I love this song," Sam said, turning up the dial like she did when she was younger, driving these roads on her own, screaming at the top of her lungs and dreaming of leaving—imagining a horizon not of farmland or forest, but of skyscrapers and sea.

"You would," Lou-Ann said with a grin. Then she turned the volume up even more. They picked up speed as they hit the highway and sang along together.

Sam felt good, out here on the road, in this woman's car. For the moment, she felt safe. She'd gotten so used to existing on a slow wave of worry, caution that crested into panic, wary of what other humans wanted from her, what they would take if given the chance. And at the heart of it the small knot of knowledge, growing harder each day, that in the end, we were all on our own. Even at home, with Stephen, in the moments she felt like she had a partner, that they were a team, the feeling always crept back in. Over time, she had let the weight of it press down on her, had forgotten what lightness felt like. Now, she found herself singing along to a song she loved, with this new friend beside her, the wind whipping in, the sun falling behind the pines. Maybe, she thought, she could be happy here.

"I've never seen so many trucks in my life," Sam said as they pulled into the parking lot, which was really just a giant patch of gravel and grass, carved out and surrounded, like most places in these parts, in a circle of spruce and pine. Lou-Ann laughed.

"Men up here and their trucks," Lou-Ann said, pulling her old Forester—tiny and squat by comparison—into one of the unmarked spaces, tight between a Ford F-150 and a Dodge Ram.

Sam opened the door gingerly, careful not to ding the Ford, and squeezed out sideways between the cars. The trucks were huge.

"They've grown a lot since I was last here," she said, craning her neck up at the long row of gleaming monstrosities, with hemi engines and names like Big Horn and King Ranch, thinking fondly of her dad's little S-10. "These things must get like ten miles to the gallon."

"If you're lucky," Lou-Ann said with a grunt. "Big toys for small boys." She hooked her keys to her belt loop with an old carabiner. It was a pretty gay move, what Sam's friends back in Brooklyn called a signifier. It was how Sam wore her keys too. She felt a little more comfortable walking into a place like Goocher's beside Lou-Ann. Where she normally made herself seem softer, more feminine in places like this, beside Lou-Ann she let her butch side loose. She walked with a swagger.

Their boots crunched on gravel as they wove between trucks toward the bar. The screen door banged open, and a pair of large men burst out, their faces beet-red, a burst of purple veins in their noses. The drunk's dead giveaway, a signifier all its own—one Sam had seen her whole life, one she was afraid she might wake up to find on her own face someday.

"Ladies," one of the men said, then elbowed his friend. "Or is it gentlemen?"

The men laughed, too loud, their teeth blackened from chew.

"Ladies," Lou-Ann said, tipping her baseball cap to them as they passed. One of them spun on his heel, his dumb mouth hanging open as Sam and Lou-Ann slipped past them.

"Fuckin' good ol' boys," Sam said.

"Drunks too," Lou-Ann said, and spat into the dirt. Sam remembered a time, in New York, when, without thinking, she'd spat on the sidewalk as a well-dressed woman passed by.

The woman made a loud show of disgust, and shame had radiated through Sam's body. It was an old habit, and a dead-on tell about where she came from. Here, she smiled at Lou-Ann and spat too, then held the door open.

"Ladies first," she said.

"Well that puts us in a pickle, don't it?" Lou-Ann said with a wink, stepping into the dark bar. Sam laughed, and followed, the door banging behind them.

The bar was dimly lit, with knockoff Tiffany lamps suspended from the ceiling, neon Miller and Leinenkugel and Stroh's signs on the walls. A row of mounted bucks looked down from the wood panels, their antlers sharp, trophies of the owners and regulars. The same bartender that had been here before was working, and she nodded as Sam and Lou-Ann sat down at the bar. Sam looked at the faded blue-black ink on the woman's arm as she wiped down the counter, trying to decipher the script that wove between flowers.

"Hey Lou-Ann," the bartender said. "What'll it be?"

"Good to see you, Tiff," Lou-Ann said. "Diet Coke for me."

On the ride over, Sam hadn't thought about a drink. A small miracle. But sitting at the bar was a different story. She considered the chalkboard draft list, would kill for a beer.

"Just a club soda and lime," she said, a red-hot thread crawling up her neck.

"You got it," the bartender said.

"The most boring drink on the planet," Sam said as the bartender spun away.

"Hey," Lou-Ann said, "people up here would be better off if they ordered that boring drink more often."

Sam glanced around, watched a waitress carry a tray of old-fashioneds to a table. Watched the faces of the old men and women at the table light up. *The happiest hour,* Sam and her friends used to say. She swallowed, a dry clicking sound.

"Do you ever miss it?" she asked, still looking at the table of eager drinkers.

"Hell no," Lou-Ann said. "Turns out I like being alive in this world a lot more than being dead in it."

Sam nodded, but said nothing. The bartender with the tattoos set her club soda down.

"To living," Lou-Ann said, raising her pint of Diet Coke.

"Sure," Sam said, raising her own glass. "But it's bad luck to toast with water."

"Not if you're sober," Lou-Ann said. They clinked their glasses together then knocked them on the bar. Sam took a drink.

"Ahh, nothing like fizzy water to really unwind," she said.

"I take it you miss it," Lou-Ann said.

There was so much Sam missed. She missed sitting at bars like these, talking to people around her, slowly fading out. She missed the softness and haze as it fell like a curtain, the slow buzz that warmed its way up her spine, that sat at the base of her skull and stayed there, then spread over her body. It was a feeling like floating down the big river in a black rubber inner tube as a kid, tied with rope to her mother and aunts and cousins, a cooler next to them in its own tube, from which the adults pulled cans of MGD and she and her cousins cans of pop. Blissed out in the summer sun, warm and happy.

She missed the darkness of a dive, like blackout curtains blocking out the day, and stepping back out into the night. She missed the bar-time streets of Brooklyn, trotting down cement steps to the subway, standing on the platform and waiting for the train, then taking a seat with headphones on, surrounded by strangers, her whole body humming. And emerging from those tunnels again, walking home beneath the warm haze of streetlamps, alongside street sweepers, past everyone else resurfacing from underground like happy rats, full and unafraid. It was then that she felt most connected to the 8 million people living in New York City, like they were all in this shit together. She missed, in the end, how it all made her feel less alone.

Sitting at the bar, she could have admitted this missing to Lou-Ann. She could have admitted that the missing had broken her open—that it had led her back, as it always did. That she was struggling, now, to hold on. She wanted to tell her. Longed to let go of the weight of it.

"Not really," she said instead. She studied the plastic menu in her hands, but the words all blurred together. She felt Lou-Ann looking at her.

"The walleye's good," Lou-Ann said, "but the perch is where it's at."

Sam tried to get her eyes to focus, to force the words into recognizable shapes. She loved a Friday fish fry—the glorious pile of fat and starch they'd set down before you, three or four huge pieces of fish, caught fresh from the lake that day. Fries, coleslaw, brown bread and butter. Every time she ordered it, she was sure she couldn't possibly finish her plate. But she always did.

"Lake perch it is then," she said, setting her menu down. She laced her fingers together on the bar, then pulled them apart. She fiddled with her glass, already sweating and ice melting. Sam was sweating too. She felt a familiar tingle in her scalp.

"You all right?" Lou-Ann asked.

"I'm fine."

"Don't look so fine."

Her skin was cold and damp, and little dots and squiggles of light were speckling across her sight line. The room felt like it was breathing, a hot mouth closing around her, swallowing her. She glanced over her shoulder and spotted a man sitting alone in the back corner of the dining room. Large, red beard, flannel. He looked at her and grinned, and it was a sick grin full of sharp teeth. She closed her eyes, and when she opened them again, he was gone.

"Just a little hot in here," Sam said, peeling off her hoodie and hanging it on her chair. Lou-Ann studied her, brow knitted tight. She flagged the bartender.

"Two orders of the lake perch," she said.

"You got it," the bartender said.

"Let's get something in that stomach," Lou-Ann said. "That'll help."

Sam watched the bartender put the order into the computer, a remarkably old-looking POS system she recognized from her own days behind the counter—what she and her coworkers lovingly referred to as the Piece of Shit. She had loved bartending. There was a camaraderie in those jobs she'd never had anywhere else. And there was a kind of power in making drinks, in giving people what would make them feel good. She mixed a good drink and could talk to anyone back then, had regulars come in just for her. She'd make their drinks then lean against the counter, listen to them talk about their jobs, complain about their wives, brag about the ten-pointer they'd nailed. She liked talking to the hunters, who sometimes came in with their sons—ten or twelve, out for the first time—and ordered them a short glass of beer. They could do that back then. She'd served her fair share of beer to children.

"Start 'em early!" the men would say, slapping their sons on the back, sending their small bodies lurching toward the bar. "Put a little hair on your chest, make you a man."

Now, she watched the bartender muddle fruit and sugar in an

assembly line of rocks glasses and the desire was like starvation. The ice in the glass and the shot stopper clicked, and the sounds banged in Sam's head like gunshots. The bartender pierced the cherries with the little red spears and she might as well have been stabbing Sam directly in the heart.

"You sure you're all right?" Lou-Ann asked, sipping her Coke.

"I'm fine," Sam said again, her voice a brick wall.

"Okay," Lou-Ann said. "But you can talk to me if you need to." She paused, looked at Sam. "There's a meeting up here, at this old church in the woods, if you ever want to go."

"I don't do meetings," Sam said fast, refusing to look at Lou-Ann. "And I don't do church. I hate that shit."

"Hey, I get it," Lou-Ann said. "I spent a long time hating it too. But that shit can help."

"I don't need help," Sam said. She'd heard those words before. "Sorry," she added quickly, trying to soften up. "It's just been a long day."

"No problem," Lou-Ann said. "But listen. I've been there. For so long I thought I could do it on my own. I got so many stories of being alone up here, fighting that shit, going crazy, no one else around. Stories that would make your guts roll to hear 'em. Damn lucky I survived."

Lou-Ann paused. "I'm not here to tell you what to do. But I am here."

Like a magician, the bartender appeared before Sam could respond. She set the plates down on the bar, flopped a stack of paper napkins before them.

"Enjoy," she said, then whisked herself away.

"Bounty," Lou-Ann said, tucking a napkin in her shirt with a grin. Sam laughed a little, despite herself.

"What, no napkins in shirts back in the big city?" Lou-Ann asked, a fork in one fist like a king ready to feast.

Sam shook her head, then tucked a napkin into her collar. "Fuck the big city," she said.

They dug into their food like the doe at the trough. Sam was ravenous. She hadn't known how hungry she'd been, had forgotten how hunger worked its way into you, despite your best efforts to staunch it. How it could lie dormant for a while and then come to life, fighting with the first bite for more, a body screaming to be fed.

"This is so fucking good," she said, her mouth full, dunking a piece of fish into a ramekin of tartar sauce and stuffing more into her mouth. The batter was light and crisp and golden, the trace amounts of beer used to make it just a suggestion of what had once been. She shoveled a heap of slaw into her mouth, then buttered a piece of bread with a pad of foil-wrapped Land O'Lakes butter and wolfed that down too.

"You eat like a teenage boy," Lou-Ann said, laughing.

Sam chewed a giant mouthful and swallowed hard. "Not usually," she said. When she was a kid, she would eat her own lunch and then polish off her friends'—their hot-lunch trays left mostly full, she'd devour half-eaten hot dogs and hamburgers and squares of gelatinous pizza, wash it down with a second chocolate milk. She did eat like a boy back then, something her friends—most of whom were obsessed with being skinny—never stopped telling her. This was before she began silencing her own hunger, fighting against her growing body, battling the hips and breasts that bloomed, insisting on making her something she didn't want to be.

"But this is glorious," she added, her mouth still full.

"This place is so ass-backward in so many ways," Lou-Ann said, dipping a handful of fries into ketchup. "But fish they do right."

They cleaned their plates, talking very little while they ate, sticking to safe things like the weather, the lodge down the road that was for sale, the bald eagles nesting in the dead birch tree on McCullough, the old man who had taken to firing a shotgun into the sky three times every night at 1 a.m., like he was calling out to someone in his own kind of Morse code, waiting for return fire through the trees.

They didn't talk about the harder things, which hung in the air between them. With the food as a buffer, they sat at the bar in the middle of nowhere—a packed house around them eating and drinking and laughing, forks and knives scraping on plates, glasses clinking, ice rattling around in tumblers—and did as people in the Northwoods do: they ate, and they talked about things that somehow made a life, but had nothing to do with living.

Twenty-One

SAM HAD DISAPPEARED before. Once, when she and Stephen had been living together a few years, she went out to get groceries and didn't come back. She passed the market and got on the G instead. She headed south, got off at Hoyt-Schermerhorn and got on the A, then took it to the end of the line. She hadn't planned on doing it. Later, she wouldn't be able to explain it. It had just sort of happened. She didn't bring her phone. At Brighton Beach, she rolled up her jeans and took off her shoes, despite knowing better. She walked in the sand, dodging trash and broken bottles and probably more than one hypodermic needle. It was summertime, and the tide came in and covered her feet, the waves lapping against her ankles. She imagined Stephen at home, calling her phone and finding it in the kitchen, then heading out to look for her. Maybe she went to the park, he might have thought. Maybe she stopped in the bookstore or was digging through crates of used vinyl in one of their favorite record shops. When he didn't find her there, he would have checked the bars—their old haunts, places they used to go after work and on weekends, spending whole Saturdays getting slowly drunk in a sunny spot by the window.

Back then, she was trying to get sober and failing. She'd quit the job at the bar and that had helped, but she'd go a few weeks without a drink, and then one bad day at the office and she'd slip, start over again. She didn't tell Stephen how much she struggled, but she suspected he knew. That he'd been checking the levels of bottles in their apartment, before eventually pouring everything down the kitchen sink one night—while she listened from the next room, simultaneously panicked and relieved. She suspected that he was afraid in the same way she had been afraid growing up: that one day he'd come home and find her obliterated, or worse. That he wasn't just afraid of her slipping; but afraid, in the end, of her. She'd once promised herself she would never make another person afraid like she had been afraid. And now here she was.

At Brighton Beach, she didn't drink. She sat down in the sand and looked at the ocean—a thing still incomprehensible to her then, both terrifying and thrilling in its vastness. Sam was never one to think deeply about what she wanted, or what she had; she lived day to day, trying not to dwell on the past or hope too hard for the future. She was certain that anything she allowed herself to want, or feel grateful for, would be taken away. But on the beach, she thought about Stephen. The only person with whom she had ever imagined a future.

They had met at a bar, her favorite neighborhood spot in Greenpoint and a place long gone now, run by friends who comped Sam drinks and fed her fries when she'd had too many. She came in a lot back then, by herself, on her way home from work. The night she met Stephen, she was sitting at the bar, working on two fingers of bourbon, half-reading some book she was covering for work. A novel, probably, and not a great one, but one the industry was freaking out about. She mostly hated the industry by then, and she wasn't writing anything herself. She'd seen too clearly inside the machine, knew how it worked and who ran it, who got paid and who didn't, who was fucking whom and which new darling debut author was secretly some rich guy's kid (most of them, it turned out). On her best days, she felt ambivalent about the whole endeavor; on her worst she felt sick, with a vague desire to burn it all down.

She tossed the book on the bar, with a loud and involuntary sigh.

"That bad, huh?" The voice came from two seats down. She looked over and saw him: he was handsome, with curly dark hair and salt-and-pepper stubble on his jaw.

"Terrible," she said, taking a sip of her whiskey. "One of the best books of the year."

He laughed and smiled. He had one dimple on his left cheek. His teeth were a little crooked, and his smile lines were deep. She found herself smiling back.

"I'm going to wager you work in publishing or something," he said.

"Magazine editor," she said. "Books are my beat."

"Ah, so you're a tastemaker."

"Really I just sniff out the taste, then pretend to share it."

"Criticism at its finest."

"I'm pretty sure there's no such thing as criticism anymore," she said. "I honestly don't know what's good or bad, just who people like and who they don't."

"Sounds rough," he said, his fingers wrapped around a pint glass.

"I mean, not really. It's a job. I'm just kinda sick of it."

"How long have you been doing it?"

"Almost ten years," she said.

"Damn," he said. "That's a long time to be anywhere."

"You're telling me."

"I'm Stephen."

"Hi, Stephen." She held a hand across the empty chair between them. "I'm Sam."

They shook hands, and his shake was firm—not soft like so many men insisted on being with women. She liked that too.

She learned he was a high school teacher from Florida who liked to paint. They compared their blue-collar upbringings, complete with trucks, guns, bonfires, and grandmothers who could shoot and pan-fry squirrels.

"They actually do taste like chicken," Stephen said, and Sam laughed.

"They actually do," she said, and raised her glass.

When he raised his glass to hers, and then to his lips, she felt the tug of desire, and something else—a feeling she'd rarely had in New York, if she'd ever had it at all: as if she could be seen, and known, for real. As if she might see and know someone too.

Above the bar, one television screen played a Mets game, and the fans watching were a chorus of groans. The other was showing *Terminator 2* with the sound off. Sam drained the last of her glass and clinked the ice around. She dumped a cube in her mouth and sucked on it.

"So," she said, "how does it feel to care about what you do?"

"What, teaching?" he said. "Mostly I'm just exhausted all the time."

"Still," she said, "it's important work."

"Books are important too," he said.

"They are, absolutely. But media companies, not so much. I'm always like one bad quarter away from getting the axe."

"That must be stressful."

"It used to be. Now I wonder sometimes if I'm secretly hoping for it. Like, just lay me off and let me go do something else with my life."

"You don't have to wait, you know."

"For what?"

"Something else. Sometimes you just need to take a leap. Make a change."

She felt a bristle of irritation. "Thanks," she said, crunching down on the ice cube. "But not everyone has a safety net."

"I'm sorry," he said, putting up an apologetic hand. "I totally just mansplained how to live your life. That's not cool."

"It's okay," she said, with a shrug, the defensiveness passing. "You're right. I've been doing this job for years, and just waiting for—something. Anything, I guess. To change. Sometimes I definitely fantasize about just cutting ties and taking off. No warning, nothing. Just pick up and go. It's a cliché I guess but I feel it."

"That's what I did," he said. "I thought I'd stay in Florida forever. I thought it was what I wanted. I liked my life there. I had a good job and good friends and family, a nice girlfriend. And then one day I was like, *Wait, this is not what I want at all.* So I left. Started over. New city, new job, new life. No safety net."

Sam nodded. "I guess I did too. Not so long ago, actually. I forget sometimes that I did that. That I could do it again."

"I'm a firm believer in the seven-year rebirth," Stephen said. "Saturn returning or whatever. The occasional molting. Shedding the skin, seeing what new animal emerges."

Sam drummed her fingers on her empty glass. His glass was empty too.

"Staying for another round?" he asked.

"I am now," she said, and flagged down the bartender, who knew her well. He poured Sam another bourbon—three fingers this time—and refilled Stephen's beer. He shot Sam a smile and a shrug as if to say, *He seems fine.*

Sam slid into the empty chair between them, felt the heat of his body next to hers.

"To change," Stephen said, raising his glass.

"To new beginnings," she said. They clinked their glasses, then raised them to their lips and drank.

At Brighton Beach, a few years later, Sam sat alone in the sand and watched the sunset. Then she took the long train ride home. She walked up the three flights of stairs to their apartment and unlocked the door. She found Stephen sitting at the kitchen table, a thing made of cheap pine they'd bought at IKEA one summer, along with four chairs, a set of bookshelves, a nightstand, and a desk they'd schlepped by train all the way from Red Hook in the heat. The cat was curled up on the table next to him, atop an open *New Yorker.* They both looked up when she entered. Stephen's hair was a mess, and there were dark circles under his eyes. She stood in the doorway, looking at him. He looked at her, unmoving in his chair, searching for some kind of answer. She walked over to him, knelt on the linoleum floor, and wrapped her arms around his waist. She put her head in his lap and held him, promised she would never leave him again.

Twenty-Two

◇◇◇◇◇◇◇◇◇◇

THE TRANSFORMATION BEGAN slowly. At first, it was barely perceptible. The hair on her arms looked a little darker. But it was dark to begin with—far darker than Stephen's, a fact about which she often felt self-conscious—so it took a while to notice. She usually let her leg hair grow long in the winter, and then on some occasion—a trip to the beach in summer, a work trip with a hotel pool, even just a day at the gym—she'd shave in a panic, return to the shape of *feminine* again.

In the woods, she hadn't shaved at all. Her leg hair was thick and dark and long. It had always been much darker and coarser than her arm hair, which, over time, had grown lighter and more fine. She was spending so much time in the sun, working outside, and usually it got even lighter in the sun. But now, somehow, the reddish-brown highlights were gone, giving way to black. It was thicker and longer too, more like the hair on her legs. She didn't understand it but knew it to be true. When she looked at her limbs, they seemed to belong to someone else.

There were other changes too. She stopped bleeding, was one thing. She'd gotten her period when she first arrived but hadn't bled again since, though it had certainly been over a month. She kept expecting the pain to come, searing through her abdomen out of nowhere, as it had since she was thirteen. But the pain never came.

The extra flesh she had always carried in her belly and thighs fell away. The slight curve of her hips seemed to have been carved away too. One day, getting out of the shower, she noticed new definition in her abdominal muscles—slight and small and unequivocally there. She chalked it up to all the work she'd been doing, weeding and planting and tearing up boards, hauling fifty-pound bags of corn from the hardware store to the truck bed, contractor bags of her parents' stuff tossed over her shoulder. But she'd never had abs before, even when she was in the best shape of her life. She'd tried so hard when she was younger, but always assumed her body, which carried the soft stomach of her maternal line, wasn't built for it. And here it was, the beginnings of a six-pack, ridged across her midsection. She looked in the mirror and marveled. New muscles were blooming elsewhere too—her quads and calves more defined, that new ripple in her forearm, a solidness in her shoulders and chest. Her jawline and cheekbones were more distinct—the roundness in her face gone entirely, as if someone had chiseled it away, leaving only the hard, square lines that lived beneath it. Her breasts kept shrinking too. They had always been on the small side, but a solid B cup. Now she was at most an A, her chest almost completely flat. She could go without a bra, let her T-shirts hang freely against her chest, the fabric rippling against bare skin in the breeze. It was a feeling she'd always wanted, forever cursing her breasts and the bras that held them. Finally, she felt free.

But none of this seemed that strange. She spent most mornings going on long runs in the woods, or swimming in the lake, or paddling the network of channels in Irv's canoe. She spent full days working outside. She was getting stronger. Her body felt pared down, distilled to its solid center, like the apples she gnawed throughout the day, whose cores she had begun to eat too, seeds and all. When she stood in the mirror, she liked what she saw.

But there were other, weirder things. Things she couldn't explain. Her eyes changed color. She was sure of it. At first it seemed a trick of the light, but she was certain now. Their usual hazel had turned more distinctly green. Some days they looked bright, the color of her cat's eyes, and some days they looked darker—so dark, in fact, they appeared almost black. *Doll's eyes*, she thought, looking at herself in the bathroom mirror on one such day, reciting the line from *Jaws* in her head with a demented grin.

Her senses had gotten even sharper. So sharp it seemed impossible. She could hear things deep in the forest, knew someone was coming to the door long before they arrived. She could hear the snap of a twig with all the windows closed, hear the oar of a canoe dipping into the lake, though she was nowhere near the shore. One day, after many days alone, Lou-Ann dropped by for a visit. When she said hello, Sam heard a strange voice emerge from her own throat. It was deeper than usual. She'd always had a deep voice, but as she spoke to Lou-Ann that day, it sounded like someone else was speaking. She felt like a ventriloquist, or perhaps the dummy, heard the words coming off her lips but they didn't sound like her own. And at the same time, somehow, the voice was familiar.

And then, one morning, she stepped out of the shower.

The bathroom was filled with steam, and she wiped the mirror above the sink. Her vision was sharper, no need for the glasses or contacts she'd worn since she was a kid. In the small circle of glass, she noticed them—a few short hairs, sprouting from the center of her chest. She looked closer, found a few more. She ran her fingers over the hairs. They were coarse, almost sharp. She inspected her neck, and found several more, bursting from her skin just above her trachea. There was a shadow across her jawline too—slight but definitely there. She'd always had a fine layer of fuzz on her jaw, barely visible, which she'd never had to touch with a razor. But that downy softness had given way to something darker, and much more visible. She'd often find a few rogue hairs on her body, springing out of a mole, that one stray thing that grew with irritating regularity from her chin. And certainly the line of black above her upper lip she'd been fighting her whole life.

But she'd never had hair on her neck before, and certainly not on her chest. It was strange, and foreign, and she dug around in her Dopp kit to find the tweezers. But as she stood there, holding the sharp metal tool ready to pluck, she looked at her reflection in the still-fogged mirror. She dropped the tweezers back into the bag. She ran her fingers over the new hairs again, feeling the bristle in her skin. She remembered that day in middle school, inspecting herself in the bathroom mirror, cleaning the spit out of her hair.

Why not be a monster? she had thought back then. *Why not a beast?*

Now, she looked at herself in the mirror again. Without thinking, she growled. It was a low, guttural sound that creaked from her lungs and off her lips. It was a sound she knew, that she'd made before. She didn't know when. But it felt familiar in her throat, curling up from her guts and out of her mouth. She imagined herself in a movie, like *An American Werewolf in London,* traipsing across the foggy moors, snarling with each step, stalking her prey. She wiped the steam from the mirror and smiled at the thought, showing her teeth.

Twenty-Three

ONE AFTERNOON, THE sky turned dark. The sun had been out all morning, and Sam had pulled up the last of the rotten boards. Then she replaced them, cutting the new boards to size and drilling them down. She didn't notice any rot in the joists, and the screws seemed to go in firm. The new boards gleamed bright against the faded wintry gray of the old. She carried the rotten boards to the woodpile—they were soft, but they would still burn.

By the time she finished, it was late afternoon. She stood on the deck and surveyed her work. She felt good, like she was finally getting things done. The clouds were building, climbing up into great bubbling towers above the trees. It looked like they were breathing. The wind picked up, and she marveled at the trees as they swayed. They were so strong, meant to withstand so much. Even the oldest branches were limber. That word itself, *limber*, sharing the name of a particular pine—always bending and never breaking. Her mother had taught her that.

The sun was gone and the air was cooler. But it was humid too, so thick it felt like a membrane, like you could slice it open

172

with a kitchen knife. The wind shifted in the trees, boughs bending toward the ground, like the big green palm fronds they used to wave in church on Palm Sunday.

She wanted a beer. There was nothing better than standing on a porch with a beer, watching a storm roll in. But she hadn't had a drink in a couple of days, and the fridge was empty. She tried to shake the want away. She looked back to the sky, watched the dark gray mass turn a subtle shade of green. There was an electricity to the air, and it sent a long, slow shiver down her spine. The temperature was dropping, and what had just felt like a summer day had turned to chill. It smelled like rain, but nothing was falling yet. There was only the wind, a warning of things to come.

She went inside and put on a sweater. She went down to the basement and found a kerosene lamp. There was enough fluid inside the vessel—its hand-blown glass once clear, now cloudy and yellowed with years—to last several hours. Back upstairs, she dug around the junk drawer until she found a lighter and a box of matches. Her mother had kept a few candles throughout the cabin, most of them half burned. She found a flashlight and a camp lantern; they both flicked on, but the light was low. There were no spare batteries to be found. She gathered her supplies on the counter, tucked the lighter in her pocket.

Outside, the wind sent a rush of sound through the trees. She couldn't tell if it was raining yet or not; the sound was growing from that of a creek to a river. Either way, it would be here soon. Another gust of wind, and the lights flickered. She closed the windows but kept the screen door open. She stepped back onto the porch, and waited for the storm to come.

*　　*　　*

She woke on the couch to a great explosion of thunder—the kind so loud it shakes the ground, so deep and elemental you feel it in your bones. The kind that sounds like an animal, growling and lowing, the kind you swear is alive. It was night. The lamps had all gone dark, the low hum of the fridge gone silent. The power was out.

The darkness was total. No moon or stars, not a shred of light. Just a solid black expanse of nothing, a darkness like obliteration. She felt her body dissolve into it.

The night had turned cold. A flash of lightning illuminated the room, the trees outside. And then the light was gone again, leaving the imprinted images of the trees on the backs of her eyes. Rain pounded the roof, battered the pressed-tin chimney like gunfire. There was a low roll of thunder and the wind moaned, that wild and living sound.

She stood up, stayed still in the dark. The cabin didn't have a generator, and the power company was fifty miles away. It would be hours before someone would be sent out to fix whatever line had gone down. An outage could last days, sometimes even a week or more.

She waited for another flash of lightning. They were coming faster now, the storm getting closer. Soon it would be on top of her. She imagined a tree coming down, crashing through the roof. She imagined things much worse.

A flash of white light, and on the table by the couch, an empty whiskey glass. She hadn't been drinking, had she? She swore she hadn't, couldn't have been. She had poured everything out. Another flash, and the pile of supplies on the counter. She stepped slowly through the dark, making her way to the kitchen. The thunder was a low and constant roll between crashes. The lightning came faster, capturing the trees like a flashbulb, and it seemed in that trick of light like their branches were frozen in place, though in reality they were bending and blowing in the wind, which came in through the chimney like a wail. What if there was a tornado, and it struck the cabin? They rarely got tornadoes up here—*too many lakes,* the lifers said, these old legends of the land, told and retold to make children less afraid, like no mythic monster of weather could get them here, where the trees closed around you like walls. But there had been tornadoes, and this was the season for it, as spring turned to summer and the weather got wild. The only truth about the weather here was that anything could happen.

She lit the kerosene lamp and carried it to the door. She'd left it open a crack, and there was rain coming in through the screen. She closed the door and locked it, looked out through the glass. The table on the porch was overturned, the plastic chairs blown away. She would find them scattered in the yard in the morning. She stood at the door and watched the storm light up the woods. The rain was coming in sheets, slamming sideways against the windows. Maybe it was hail. She carried the lamp to the fireplace. She crouched on the floor, opened the flue, and the sound of the storm opened up with it. It howled.

She crumpled newspaper and laid kindling atop it, then built a pyramid of logs. She lit the paper and flames licked up the chimney. The wood took hold and blazed. She turned off the lamp to save kerosene, then sat in the chair by the window. In the firelight, she saw the empty glass on the table. She picked up the book she'd been reading—some ripped-from-the-headlines crime story she'd found on her mother's shelf, about a serial killer who raped and murdered and dismembered single women in a small rural town and kept their butchered bodies in his basement—but set it back down. A chill sent her body shivering, despite the warmth of the fire. She looked from one dark corner of the cabin to another, down the hall, scanning the shadows. Her eyes came to rest on the basement door.

The firelight danced across the walls, and the shadows seemed to change shape, morphing into monsters, into men, into all the sinister things that dwell in the dark. It was true she read too many books like these, had seen every heinous episode of *Law & Order: SVU*. But the possibility of evil, the promise of certain lurking terror, had worked its way into her bones and she knew it like she had once known God. It was the reason she still slept with a nightlight sometimes—to burn the shadows away, trick herself into thinking the light could save her.

She got up, threw another log on the fire, crouched by its warmth. The rain kept coming. The thunder a snarl, the lightning a strobe. Her heart was hammering along with the storm, her head hazy and thick. She looked at the glass on the table again, couldn't for the life of her remember pouring a drink. She swore the house was clean. She curled back up in the chair, lightning and thunder crashing in an almost-rhythm, an erratic drumbeat. Outside, she watched the trees bend in slow motion in the strobe light, ready for one fast flash to illuminate whatever was out there—something in the woods or closer, just outside the cabin walls or maybe even within them, crouched in a corner, waiting.

Out of the dark, she heard a sound. It was one of those late-night sounds, the kind where you can never quite tell if it's real or a dream, the last lingering fragments of a nightmare. She bolted upright in bed. When had she gone to bed? She couldn't remember. She remembered the fire, the whiskey glass. Sitting in the chair by the window. But now she was here, and she had heard a sound, and she knew it was real.

She held her breath. Heard her own pulse, her heart beating in her temples. The storm had let up, leaving a humming kind of nothing in its wake. A few flashes of lightning, several minutes apart, held on, beating silently against the night. No more thunder, no more rain. Just wind in the trees, a buzzing in her ears.

She sat on the edge of the bed and listened. All she heard was the buzzing, fading a little more each second as sleep slipped away. No crickets or peepers, those usual nighttime sounds. Only silence.

She tried to recall the sound. A screech of some kind, high and loud, and a crash—and then, she remembered—something being dragged through the woods.

And footsteps. She heard them now, slow and unmistakable, in the trees. Whenever she walked through the woods, the sound of her own footsteps crunching on dead leaves echoed for what felt like miles. Out there, the sound was amplified. Even the smallest animal could sound like a man. She heard the footsteps again.

She clicked the switch on the bedside lamp. Still nothing.

Light does something to ears tuned to the dark, and she longed for the clarity of it, for the sound falling away, replaced by the hum of electricity. She took a breath and held it, then let it out slow, her pulse in her throat.

She wished she had a gun. Her uncles were always offering one—a rifle or pistol, a .22, something small and light she knew how to handle. *You might need it,* they'd told her. *For protection. A girl like you out there on your own.* She always refused, laughing at the offers and making jokes about gun nuts. But now she cursed herself for saying no.

She was cold. Felt the hair on her arms and legs standing up. Like antennae, picking up the sound. She got out of bed and stood by the window, looked out into the blackness of night.

Probably just a deer, she thought. Maybe the screech was an owl, the kind that sounds like a woman screaming at night. The crash was a branch coming down in the storm. Everything had an explanation. There was nothing to be afraid of.

But what was the dragging?

She moved away from the window and felt her way to the dresser. She pulled out fleece pants and a pair of wool socks, picked a sweater off the floor. She opened the bedroom door and felt her way down the hall, running a hand along the wall. The fire had died, but for a few glowing embers. She found the kitchen sink and poured a glass of water from the tap, grateful for what remained in the pressure tank but knowing this could be the last of it for a while. She let her eyes adjust to the dark. She looked out the window and waited.

No footsteps. Not another sound. Only the wind, whistling in the chimney. She was freezing. Wrapping her arms around herself, she stood silent and still.

Then, in a flash of lightning, she saw it: a figure, at the edge of the tree line. Standing upright. Not animal, but man.

The lightning blinked out and the dark returned. She could still see the shape, the silhouette, imprinted on her retinas. A person, standing in the woods.

Maybe it had been a trick of the light. Maybe she was hallucinating. But no, she had seen it. She was sure. Someone—or something—had been there.

No more lightning came. Darkness surrounded her. She grabbed the camp lantern and switched it on. She checked the door and the windows—all locked. She carried the lantern down the hall to her room, closed the door and locked it, then crawled into bed. She checked her phone, but it was dead. Pulled the covers up to her neck, tried to hold still. A circle of dim light from the lantern glowed on the ceiling. She was shivering, even under the covers, in her sweats and socks. She swallowed, the sound of it massive, filling up the room. The whole world might have heard. She felt her heart, her whole body, beating. She couldn't move.

She switched off the lantern, wanting to preserve the batteries. She lay there in the dark, stock-still with fear, thinking of who, or what, might be out there.

She didn't sleep again until the first ribbons of light came in through the window, when the sky above the trees turned from black to gray. When all that was left of the storm were branches in the yard and droplets of water, falling from the leaves.

Twenty-Four

◇◇◇◇◇◇◇◇◇◇

LATE-MORNING LIGHT POURED in through the windows, bathing the pine-board bedroom in gold. At some point, she must have fallen back to sleep. In the daytime, there was nothing frightening about the woods. It was quiet and calm, enveloping her in light. As she kicked off the blankets, the terror of the night felt like a dream, some small shred of something in the back of her brain slipping away. She was safe, she was alive, she was fine.

She got up and opened the window. The storm had passed and the sky was clear. The crisp morning air drifted in, the smell of wet leaves and pine sap and moss. She walked to the kitchen and tried the switch. Light flooded the room, the power miraculously back on.

That was fast, she thought. She made a pot of coffee, opened the patio door, and stepped outside. She righted the table, collected the chairs from the yard. One small tree had come down, and was splayed across the drive. She'd have to clear it in order to get out. A few more branches were scattered around the property. The trough was overturned, and the bird feeders had fallen. She'd have to refill those too. But the birds were singing. A woodpecker tapped at a maple. There was no more wind; the forest was still.

I can't believe I was afraid of this, she thought.

The imagination, she knew, was a powerful thing. The eyes played tricks. There had been nothing out there, no man in the woods. She laughed at herself for being so afraid.

Sitting on the porch, she took a sip from her father's mug, warming her hands. She felt the insistent beat of a headache, but the coffee was helping. She rolled her neck, closed her eyes, and opened them again. That's when she noticed the footprints. Human footprints, in mud. The shape of bare feet cast in wet earth, stuck to the deck.

"What the fuck?" she said aloud.

She set down the mug. She stood and followed the prints to the door. She walked back inside, looked at the floor. More muddy tracks, leading from the door to the kitchen and down the hall. She followed, the footprints leading to her bedroom, all the way to her bed.

Her heart pounded. Someone had been here last night, inside the cabin. Someone had stood over her bed while she slept, and watched her. She remembered the figure in the woods, the silhouette in lightning. She felt dizzy. She sat down on the bed, put her head between her knees. She looked at her feet, saw they were covered in mud.

"What the *fuck*," she said again.

She ran a finger along the dirt, caked on her shins, flecked up the backs of her calves and knees, as if she'd been running. She picked at it and watched it fall off her skin in clumps. How had she not noticed before? She got up and followed the footprints back outside. She stood on the porch and picked up her father's old mug—I FISH THEREFORE I AM—the coffee having gone cold. She tried not to think of the footprints, or the mud, or the questions that banged around in her brain. She tried her best to shut them out, to silence them, tried thinking about fishing instead. It was an old trick, the place she went in her head when she was a girl, an image she returned to when she couldn't sleep. It was something her mother had taught her, a long time ago, as she sat on the edge of Sam's bed, running a hand through her daughter's hair.

Think about the place you're happiest, her mother had said, her voice a whisper. *Focus on that image. Let it carry you to sleep.*

She had thought then, as she did now, about the little fishing boat, out on the lake before dawn. The low putter of a small outboard motor gliding slow across the lake, slicing the water into wings. Her father cutting the motor and they'd coast, the water still as glass, the morning silent and cool and calm. They'd bait their hooks with night crawlers, slick fat bodies they pulled from a Styrofoam cup filled with soil. She'd wrap her small fingers around the still-living, wriggling thing, piercing its body in the middle, wrapping it around the metal hook twice to keep it secure. She had once been horrified by this process, and made her father bait the hook for her. But he started insisting she do it herself.

If you're going to kill a fish, you have to be okay killing the worm too, he'd said. *Circle of life, kiddo.*

She wiped the dirt on her jeans and they cast their lines into the lake. And there they sat, for hours, trawling the reedy shoreline, waiting for a bite. Her father always brought a tall metal thermos of coffee and let her take sips—she liked the taste of it even then, dark and bitter and black. They'd coast to another spot, a thick patch of lily pads, where they might have better luck. Their lines would go taut, they'd reel in bluegill or bass or perch, throw the flopping bodies in a cooler of ice. When the coffee was gone and the cooler was full, Sam's father would coax the motor back to life and they'd set off toward the cabin, the morning sun on their backs.

Now, she sat on the porch and closed her eyes, saw herself in the boat—a girl of eight or nine, afraid of nothing. The boat rocking gently on the lake, the first pink ribbons of sunrise. She saw the ducks and loons and bald eagles, the dragonflies skimming the surface of the water, carving shimmering V's in their wake. She saw her father, guiding them home, where her mother would be waiting with a fresh pot of coffee and pancakes. She saw the night crawler, squirming in her hands, and the tiny bloom of blood in its body as she pierced it with the hook.

Twenty-Five

<small>◇◇◇◇◇◇◇◇◇◇◇◇</small>

LATER THAT MORNING, she chopped up the fallen tree. Using her father's chainsaw, she cut off the branches and sliced them into kindling, then made a series of clean cuts through the trunk. It was white pine, and the blade sliced easy through the soft wood, the smell of it wintry and sweet. The high whine of the saw searing up through the trees. Then she got to splitting. She hefted the axe over her head, squared her feet and swung. The blade landed dead center of the log, sending a fissure through its heart. She pried it out and swung again until the log split in two, then did it again into quarters. She worked this way for hours, lost in the rhythm of hefting and swinging, sending blade through tree. Her back and shoulders ached, but she worked until it was done. Then she carried it all to the garage, stacked each piece neatly atop the woodpile. She touched the bark, and the bright sapwood beneath. She touched the heartwood, that dead center, which still felt so alive. She said a little prayer for the tree, thanking it for the warmth it would bring.

Afterward, she took a shower, scraping the remaining dirt from her shins. She watched the mud run down the tub in small rivers, then get washed away. She got dressed, then she drove to town. She parked the truck outside a boarded-up gift shop that had once sold Northwoods-themed T-shirts. She cut the engine and walked into the hardware store, the bell jingling above the door. It was Saturday, she was pretty sure, and the place was quiet. No men by the fishing lures. The parakeet chirped from its cage. She said hello to the bird, and the bird said hello back. She grabbed what she needed and walked to the counter. Behind it, reading a copy of *People,* was a girl. Not the older woman who was usually there, but a younger woman. She looked up from the magazine and smiled.

She was pretty. Late twenties or early thirties, dark blond hair and honey-colored skin. Freckles across her nose and cheeks, a gap between her front teeth.

"Hey there," the girl said, tossing down the magazine. She wore a faded T-shirt and jeans, a leather bracelet on one wrist. "Find everything you need?"

Sam's stomach did a flip.

"Yep, all set," she said.

"What're you fixing?" the girl asked as she rang the items up.

"Sink," Sam said. It was more a croak, a sad little squeak.

"Sounds fun," the girl said. She was smiling, a big crooked grin like she had a secret she was barely keeping, that sliver of a gap between her front teeth, the soft pink suggestion of a tongue pressed behind it. Something about a gap-toothed girl always made Sam's knees a little weak. She fished around her pocket, pulled out a ten, handed it to the girl. For a second, Sam's index finger brushed the girl's open palm. She noticed short, unpainted nails, a surefire signifier in other parts of the country, but less certain up here. For a second the girl held Sam's gaze, then Sam broke free of it.

"Yeah," she managed. The girl opened the register, an ancient thing that made a loud ding each time the drawer popped open, and handed Sam her change. Their fingers touched again, and Sam thought she might actually die.

"Need any help?" the girl asked.

"What?" Sam asked, stuffing the change back in her pocket. She was in desperate need of water. *What the fuck is wrong with me?* she thought.

"Do you need any help," the girl said again, enunciating one slow word at a time, as if talking to a child. It was a statement, not a question. "With the sink."

"Oh," Sam said, letting out a stupid belch of a laugh. "No, thanks, I can handle it."

"I'm sure you can," the girl said. And was that flirtation in her voice? Sam hadn't flirted with anyone in ages, and if she'd been flirted with she hadn't noticed. She was so out of practice. And anyway, there couldn't possibly be any young, queer women in the woods. Not a chance.

"What I meant was," the girl said, tucking a strand of hair behind her ear, "do you want some company?"

"Oh," Sam said again. "Um…" she trailed off, adjusted her baseball cap, scratched her forehead, a nervous tick.

"You know," the girl pressed. "An extra set of hands?" She raised one eyebrow, and now Sam was sure of it. This pretty girl at the hardware store was flirting with her.

"Uh," Sam grunted, speechless and stupid, dropping her hands awkwardly at her sides.

Is that literally all you can say, you idiot? she thought, desperately clanging around in her brain for more than one syllable. *Speak! Make words! Be a human!*

"That's okay," she eked out. "I'm good."

The girl looked at Sam and nodded once, the tiny curve of a smirk twisting up one side of her lips. And leaping off that smirk and into Sam's skin was the spark of a feeling, sudden but sure, something she hadn't felt in a very long time. A pinging back and forth of energies. Inexplicable but undeniable: physical, tangible, like you could catch hold of it.

Sam swallowed again, horrified by the sound of it, loud and wet.

"Well," the girl said with a shrug, picking her magazine back up, "if you change your mind, you know where to find me."

"Sure," Sam said. "Thanks."

She turned to leave, then turned back.

"I'm Sam, by the way."

"I know who you are," the girl said, looking up from her magazine. "Mike and Victoria's kid, right?"

"Yeah," Sam said, shocked by the sound of her parents' names. She couldn't remember the last time she heard them spoken aloud. Her mother always went by Vic, the shorter and less feminine version of her name, like Sam. She wondered if this girl knew about her mom. She suspected so. People kept to themselves up here, but it was still a small town, and word traveled fast. The story of a woman disappearing in the woods and never found—like the town's very own episode of *Unsolved Mysteries*—would have worked its way into the fabric of the place by now, taking on its own mythology, becoming part of the lore.

Sometimes, she could almost hear someone whispering around a fire, *when the moon is full and the sky is clear, you can still see her, the Ghost Woman of the Northwoods, singing strange songs in the trees, wandering through the forest at night.*

Sam shook her head and grabbed a free paper off the rack, awkwardly killing time.

"So," she said, clearing her throat, "you new here?"

"Nah," the girl said. "Not really. My mom works here, but I take her shifts sometimes."

"Cool," Sam said, arguably the least cool thing that had ever come out of her mouth.

The girl set her magazine down and studied Sam, cocking her head a little. Sam was lingering, and they both knew it.

"You sure you don't want some help?" the girl said.

"No thanks," Sam said. "I work better alone." And then, without thinking, the words just came. "But maybe we could grab a drink sometime?"

The girl smiled. "Sure," she said. "I'd like that. Gets lonely up here, doesn't it?"

"It does," Sam said.

She immediately regretted the invitation, the opening, but her stomach flipped around anyway. The girl tore off a page from a receipt pad and wrote down her number. She folded the paper in half, then reached across the counter. Sam stepped toward her and held out her hand, and the girl pressed the paper into her palm, letting her fingers hover there for a second. The touch made Sam's heart hammer in her chest.

"Call me sometime," the girl said, looking at Sam. "If you can get a signal."

"I'll do that," Sam said, and felt a small shred of swagger slip into her voice.

She unfolded the receipt paper, saw the name *Gina* scrawled over a number. Sam folded it up and put it in her pocket, and the girl returned to her magazine.

"See ya," Sam said. "Gina." And the girl gave a nod but didn't look back up.

Sam pushed open the door, the bell above her jingling. She stepped out into the sun and felt the warmth on her face. Her heart was beating hard, the familiar warmth of thrill and guilt spreading in her chest. She got into the truck and saw herself in the rearview mirror. She pulled the brim of her hat down low. She was smiling.

Twenty-Six

<><><><><><><><>

SHE FIXED THE sink in record time. She felt capable and good, like she was finally getting things done. She went for a run, her energy seeming endless, her legs and lungs strong. She felt like she could run forever and never get tired. She ran her favorite loop, a narrow trail through a dense stretch of woods she had blazed herself. Soon she wouldn't be able to do this route; the forest would be too thick, full of mosquitoes and black flies and ticks. But for now, the path was clear. She ran for miles. When she got to the lake, she kicked off her sneakers and peeled off her clothes. She walked the length of the dock and jumped in.

It was a shared landing, and usually there were a few fishermen around, but today it was empty. She swam out to the middle of the lake and treaded water, the sandy bottom some thirty feet below her. She heard a loon cry, and then another. She spotted the mother, with two babies at her side. Sam treaded in quiet circles, careful not to ripple the water too much. The loons glided past. Sam held her breath, stayed as still as possible. When they were a safe distance away, she swam back to shore. She sat on the dock, letting the sun dry her skin.

She put on her clothes and shoes, then walked back toward the cabin. This time she took the road. It was a bright afternoon, sunny and warm, and the air smelled like lilacs. She heard squirrels and chipmunks and birds in the trees, a light wind in the leaves.

She heard a gunshot in the distance. A second, then a third. The sound was loud, and close. It was a rifle, or a shotgun, though it wasn't hunting season. She stood still for a second, waiting for another shot, heard only silence. She kept walking.

And then she heard something else. Footsteps, behind her. She stopped, turned around, and listened. Nothing. Probably just a squirrel, she thought, or maybe a deer, whose footfalls always sound heavier in the silence of the woods.

She pressed on, picking up her pace, a slow crawl in her skin. She tried to shake it off. But she heard it again—unmistakable now, footsteps behind her. She remembered the night of the storm, the man she was sure she'd seen. She stopped again and turned.

"Hello?" she called, but was met only with birdsong, the wind in leaves. She shook her head, walked faster. The footsteps followed. She was sure she heard them, sure they were getting closer. She started to jog. Her legs were rubber from the run. Her sneakers crunching on gravel, she pushed herself forward. The footsteps still behind her.

She turned as she jogged, saw nothing. But she heard it, something or someone closing in. She ran faster, her lungs beginning to burn. She wouldn't be able to last much longer, but she ran as fast as her legs would carry her.

She wasn't far now. Less than a mile. When she turned the

next corner, she would be on her road. But she heard whatever was behind her get closer—so close, she was sure, it could lunge. That it might reach out a hand, or a claw, and have her. Her legs were on fire, but she pushed past the pain.

She closed in on the final turn, desperate to see the homestretch. She'd kick it into high gear, make the last leg a sprint. But when she turned the corner, she didn't recognize the road. The trees bent too low. There were no ditch irises dotting the path. Did she take a wrong turn? It seemed impossible. She knew the way by heart. But here she was, in unfamiliar terrain, the birch trees still bare, branches bending toward her like fingers, like bones, like ghosts. She ran as hard as she could, the cool spring air bringing tears to her eyes, stinging and blurring her vision. A black fly circled her head.

No way, she thought. *Not yet. They haven't hatched yet.* But there it was, a fat black fly, buzzing around her neck. Then one fly turned to two, then more, and before she knew it there was a swarm, a small cyclone of black buzzing around her as she ran. This couldn't be happening. It was still too early for flies. But here they were, and they were biting her neck, and she slapped frantically at her face as she ran. The swarm got thicker, the flies drawn to her sweat. She felt her body slowing down—from the flies, from the burning in her legs and chest. She tried to push, but her lungs were out of air. The footsteps were still there, following close.

She'd had dreams like this her whole life. A recurring nightmare she'd had since she was a girl. She was running in the woods, and something was chasing her, and she ran until she couldn't run anymore, her legs giving out beneath her or getting stuck in some swampy mire of earth, holding her still and struggling just as whatever followed fell upon her. And now it was here. It was happening. The dream was real, and she was living it.

She was lost. The flies circled her head, biting and blinding. The footsteps were closer.

I'm going to die. The words played over in her head, a record stuck and skipping, the same words she'd heard in her dreams. *I'm going to die out here.*

Her breath turned ragged; her muscles screamed. Pain seared her lungs and throat. She kept running, her legs made of rubber, the flies in her eyes, in her mouth, slamming against her sweat-slicked neck. She took another turn, then another. She didn't know where she was going. She only knew she couldn't stop.

And then, at last, she saw it. The fire number, that bright-red beacon. In one last burst, she flew toward it, pushing her body beyond its limits, her sneakers slapping gravel. She ran as fast as she could, no longer feeling the pain—if only she could touch that small metal sign, she would be safe. Like that game she and the neighbor kids played on summer nights. What was it called?

"Ghost in the graveyard," she said aloud, her voice a rasp, her vision sparking around her, threatening to go black.

When she reached the fire sign, her legs gave out. She fell to the ground at the foot of the driveway. Small sharp rocks dug into her knees. Her lungs wheezing, gasping for air. She closed her eyes and waited for whatever was coming.

But nothing came. Only silence again, the wind in the trees.

She opened her eyes, crawled to her feet. There were rocks torn into her palms and knees. She was bleeding. She looked behind her, turned in a circle, looking into the woods on all sides. But there was nothing. No man or creature closing in. No black flies. Just her and the forest.

She stumbled to the cabin, breathing hard. When she got to the porch, climbing the stairs on wobbly legs, she saw something by the door. A bundle of wood, tied together with twine. Crouching, thighs burning, she saw a small note on lined paper, tucked beneath the knot.

Hi neighbor, it said. *A little something to help keep you warm.*

She turned around, looked behind her, back down the path toward the road. She looked into the woods. She stood still for a moment, and her heart was a kick drum. Her lungs were still burning, but she could no longer feel the pain. Only her pulse.

There was no one there. But she knew that the man—the one who called himself Danny—had been here. She could smell him—stale smoke and dirty clothes, the musk of a man who hadn't showered in a while. The suggestion of Old Spice. He had been on this porch, while she was gone. His scent hung in the air, sharp and present. How clearly she knew it. She'd always had a good nose—could smell the remnants of food in a kitchen for days after a meal had been cooked, was sensitive to scented lotions and perfumes. But this was different. She could smell every inch of this man, every contour of flesh and dirt. It was like he was standing right in front of her. Like she could lick the air and taste him.

And hadn't this bundle been here before? She could swear she had taken it to the garage, stacked it with the rest of the wood. And here it was again, the same bundle; or was it another? Maybe she had dreamed it all—the firewood, the man. But here it was regardless, proof that someone had been here, a note tucked beneath the twine, wrapped tight around the wood, the edges of the logs roughly hewn. It wasn't the work of a log splitter, something every lifer had up here. This work had been done by hand.

She shivered, but what she felt was no longer fear. Another feeling was taking over. It was as if someone was running the tips of their fingers up the length of her spine, along the back of her neck. Every hair on her body stood on end, her hackles raised. She clenched her jaw, curled her hands into fists.

She left the bundle on the porch and stepped inside. She stood for a moment, listening for movement. Her ears twitched. It was dark inside the cabin, but outside the sun was bright. It was a perfect spring day. She closed the door and locked it, closed the windows too. She stood in the shadows, silent and still. Muscles taut, ready to fight. Ready to tear whatever or whoever had been here, whatever was following her, apart. The sweat began to dry on her skin, settling into a chill.

Twenty-Seven

◇◇◇◇◇◇◇◇◇◇

EVEN IN THE daytime, the basement was dark. A small shaft of late-afternoon light filtered in through a single ground-level half-window, casting shadows in the unfinished rooms. There was old furniture, a ratty couch, a chair and ottoman, a cheap coffee table gathering dust, creating a strange kind of living room for ghosts. Like that fucked-up scene in *The Shining*, where all the skeletons gather for a dinner party. She laughed a little, but it was a nervous laugh. With a notebook in hand, she tagged all the furniture for Goodwill.

She stepped into the storage room, windowless and black. She pulled the chain that dangled from the ceiling and the bare bulb flickered to life. The storage room was packed with tools, gardening stuff, outdoor gear, and patio furniture. She added to her list. What she would get rid of, and what she would keep. She wouldn't keep much.

The cement floor sloped a little, creating a strange tilting sensation. At the center of the floor, a drain wore a permanent ring, the water having seeped up through the ground as snow melted.

She usually liked being in this room, this workspace where she felt close to her parents. But today she hated it. She hated the ghost of her father, at his workbench. She hated the opened bags of soil and garden tools, as if the ghost of her mother was preparing to plant. What she hated most of all was the man-sized suit of rubber hanging in the corner. The waders just hung there, limp and lifeless, like a body without insides. It was usually kind of funny, but today it creeped Sam out. She thought of the six-pack materializing beneath the bench. She thought of the bundle of wood, the man on her porch. The footsteps behind her, the figure in the trees. She felt disoriented, the room around her off balance. She shivered.

"Maybe I've done enough today," she said aloud, pulling the chain and walking fast out of the room, bounding up the stairs. Slamming the basement door behind her, locking it.

It was almost four. Too early for dinner, though Sam wasn't hungry. She opened the fridge and peered inside. There were three beers left. She closed the door.

She stuffed her hands in her pockets and found the folded receipt, damp with sweat. She unfolded it and mouthed the name, *Gina,* then considered the number. It was just seven digits—everyone had the same area code up here—scrawled fast in black ink that had smudged a little. Sam folded the paper and put it back in her pocket. She went to the fridge again and opened it, imagined the cold beer in her throat, which was still raw from running. Imagined it washing away the fear that crawled in her skin. She closed the door. Pulled the paper from her pocket again and dialed the number.

"That was fast," the voice said on the other line.

"How'd you know it was me?" Sam asked. The connection was miraculously clear.

"I just knew."

"Anyway, it's been"—Sam looked at the clock on the wall—"a very respectable six hours."

Gina laughed. It was a good laugh, solid and real, and it made Sam laugh too.

"Busy tonight?" Sam asked.

"Nope," Gina said. "Shift ends at six. Meet you at the Beer Bar?"

Sam knew she shouldn't go to a bar, that she shouldn't drink with this girl.

"Sounds great," she said anyway. A beer or two wouldn't kill her. She could be good. "See you then."

She hung up. She had over an hour. She paced around the kitchen.

One beer beforehand can't hurt. She grabbed a bottle from the fridge, popped the top with her grandmother's church key, and stepped out onto the porch. The beer was cold and perfect. She hadn't eaten since breakfast, a bowl of cereal, and the beer went straight to her brain. That quick sharp buzz and then the slow, lovely hum, and Sam felt her insides settle. A warmth bloomed in her neck, the knots in her shoulders loosened. She took another drink. For a second, a flash of guilt rushed through her. She took another drink, shoved it away.

The table was speckled with bird shit. *I'll clean it tomorrow,* she thought, and took another drink.

When she looked up, the doe was there, standing at the feeder, watching her.

"What," Sam said. The sound was sharp. She felt her body twist back up into fight mode. She didn't have time for this deer's shit today.

"Nothing," the doe said. But she kept looking at Sam. It was a hard look, steely and impenetrable. She held it for a stretch of time that could have been a few seconds or an eternity. Then she shook her head.

"Nothing at all."

The doe lowered her head into the trough and ate, and all Sam heard was teeth breaking corn, echoing through the trees.

Twenty-Eight

◇◇◇◇◇◇◇◇◇◇◇

SHE WISHED SHE could tell someone about the light. It was six o'clock, late spring, a cloudless day. The evergreens were tall and alive, towering to the sky. The hardwoods were still blooming, and would soon be bursting with green. And the sun: the way it beat through the trees, golden and warm, a dappled pulse against her face as she drove. Flickering between branches, the lake—shimmering and still in the early-evening sun, the water like glass, reflecting the trees. A painting, a photograph, something caught and kept suspended forever, perfect and lasting.

She drove with the windows down, that warm glow of dusk filling up the truck. The beer had helped this feeling, head humming and happy, but mostly it was the light.

She passed some kids on ATVs, tearing down the trail that ran alongside the road. The four-wheelers turned to snowmobiles in the winter, kids and retirees traveling in packs, bar-hopping from town to town. There were accidents every winter, people Ski-Dooing drunk and crossing the highway without looking, getting T-boned by a truck or a coal train; vacationers from the suburbs going out on the ice too soon, before the lakes were fully frozen—like those college kids from Evanston in the eighties, or the bachelor party in the nineties, who went out drinking on the lake when the ice was thin. At the bar, there was an unlabeled plastic pickle jug that served as a kitty—regulars bet each winter how many out-of-towners would die. Whoever bet closest got the jug and a free fish fry.

Now, Sam watched these boys—they couldn't have been more than thirteen—tearing along the road, bouncing up and down on their ATVs. One of them looked over and screamed something at her, then zoomed ahead of her.

"I'm not racing, you idiot," she said aloud, but felt her foot fall harder on the pedal anyway, heard the truck's engine roar, and she was struck by the sudden desire to push this machine as hard as it could go, scream into the wind as she flew down the empty road. She thought better of it, lifted her foot off the gas, and watched the kids fly ahead of her.

She pulled into the gravel lot and cut the engine. She took off her hat and ran a hand through her hair, mussed it up just enough. She hadn't washed it in a while, and it was hitting peak butch shag. She smiled in the rearview, liked what she saw: masculine and strong, jawline sharp, sun on her face.

She heard a motorcycle pull up next to her. The Beer Bar was an official hangout for Harley guys. A slim figure—black jeans, black leather boots, jean jacket—kicked the stand into place and pulled off their helmet. A cascade of dirty-blond hair fell out, and Sam found herself looking straight at Gina.

It'll be a woman and a motorcycle, Sam thought, recalling Stephen's words. *Of course.*

The bike was a beauty, a Honda Hawk from the eighties, black and chrome with a bright-blue tank, an orange stripe down the side. Small and compact, it stood out among the Harleys. Sam stepped out of the truck, her own boots hitting the dirt, and Gina stood with her helmet tucked under her arm, pressed against the curve of her waist, lips cocked in a grin.

"Like it?" she said.

"Love it," Sam said.

"Know how to ride?" Gina asked.

"Nope," Sam said. "But I'd love to learn."

"Maybe I'll teach you someday," Gina said. Then she winked.

Who is this woman? Sam thought. *And what is she doing here?*

"Should we head in? I'm dying for a beer."

Sam smiled and motioned toward the bar. "After you."

"Such a gentleman," Gina said, the grin still spread across her lips.

"I try," Sam said, smiling big too. She realized she was giddy.

They walked up the wooden steps to the porch that surrounded the bar, pine planks creaking beneath their boots. The front door creaked too. Inside was a quintessential Northwoods dive bar, old and stale and smoky. Smoking had been banned in bars for years, but no one up here cared. The smell lived permanently in the carpeted floors, in the wood-paneled walls. The smell reminded Sam of home. They walked to the bar and pulled out two stools, their red vinyl upholstery cracked, yellow fluff billowing out. They sat down, and when Sam put her elbows on the bar, they stuck.

"Great place," she said.

"The best," Gina said.

The draft list was scrawled on a chalkboard—four dollars a

pint, three since it was happy hour. Bottles were two bucks. Sam laughed.

"Sometimes I forget I'm not in New York anymore and beers aren't ten dollars."

"It's dangerous here," Gina said, inspecting a sticky plastic menu.

Sam grabbed a menu too, hands nervous, eyeing the burgers and brats, fried fish and chicken strips. The bartender—a young woman with sandy-blond hair and blue eyeliner that looked a few days old—took their order. Two beers and a basket of cheese curds. It was good to be home.

"So, where did you come from?" Sam asked.

Gina laughed. "Plover."

"I mean, what are you doing here?"

The bartender threw down two coasters and set the beers on top.

"Cheers," Sam said, and lifted her bottle. Gina clinked the neck of her bottle against Sam's. They knocked them on the bar and drank. The long pull of liquid, light and cold, rushed down Sam's throat like a cool rain.

"Well," Gina said, setting her beer down, "after college I went out west for a while. Found a place in Oakland. Got a job out there at a tech startup, and liked it okay, and ended up staying a few years."

She paused, took another pull from her beer.

"Then my mom got sick."

Sam nodded, holding her bottle by the neck and spinning it slowly atop the bar.

"My dad died when I was young," Gina said, "so I came back."

"Siblings?" Sam asked.

"One," Gina said. "A sister down south. But she doesn't come up here much. She's—well, we don't talk much these days."

"Sorry," Sam said.

"It's okay," Gina shrugged. "You?"

"Nope," Sam said. "Lonely only."

Gina laughed. "Well, you've got a friend now."

Sam smiled, felt the blood rush to her cheeks. "I didn't have many of those, growing up."

"Oh, I had tons," Gina said. "But I still felt alone most of the time. I didn't really figure myself out until I got to the Bay Area. Which is of course a total cliché but it's true. It was expensive as hell, though. And I missed home. The quiet, the trees, bars like these." She smiled, took a drink. "And cheese curds, obviously," she added, as the bartender plopped the red plastic basket in front of them. The oil was already soaking through the red-and-white checked paper. "There's something deeply offensive about vegan cheese, which is all anyone ate out there."

"Criminal," Sam said, and they laughed.

"And anyway," Gina said, "pretty much everyone at the startup got laid off. Except the higher-ups, of course. A bunch of my friends were unemployed for months, and eventually had to move out of the city. So I dodged that particular bullet."

Sam thought of all her friends in New York who'd been laid off too. It was a total scam to live in such a city, to finally land a job and trick yourself into thinking that if you just work hard enough, if you always hustle and never rest, you'll make it. In the Northwoods, there was no such thing as hustle.

"So how long have you been up here?" Sam asked.

"Few years," Gina said. "Mom moved here a long time ago, after Dad died, built a little cabin on Teal Lake. She has a guest room, so I moved in with her. She's worked at the hardware store ever since, but it's been rough on her lately. She hasn't been doing well. So I took some of her shifts, picked up a few other odd jobs around town. I work on Fridays at Manny's over in Presque Isle, fill in at the gas station a few nights a week. For a while I thought I'd do some freelance work, coding or web design, but the demand for it up here is—not great."

They laughed. No one had Wi-Fi in the woods.

"I feel like most businesses up here don't even have websites," Sam said.

"They definitely don't. Some have Facebook pages they update once a year, but that's about it. Some folks still don't use the internet at all. It's a totally different world."

Sam loved that about this place, so far off the grid it was like being back in time. She had deleted all the apps on her phone when she'd first arrived, and with no email to check and no social media to scroll, she had felt a tension lift from her shoulders, as if the fiddlehead fern of her spine had begun to unfurl. Now she barely looked at her phone, kept it dead in a drawer for days at a time. She dipped a cheese curd in the plastic ramekin of ranch, then popped it into her mouth. The salt, the crunch, the oil, the melted cheese hit her tongue and she let out a completely involuntary moan. Gina laughed.

"So good," Sam said, her mouth full. She swallowed, then wiped her mouth with a napkin, leaving a kiss of grease on brown paper.

"So good," Gina agreed, stuffing a curd in her mouth. "Fat fried in fat dipped in fat. Truly a gift from God."

They both laughed, then stuffed more fried cheese in their mouths.

"Do you like it here?" Sam asked, licking grease off her lips. "Are you happy?"

"Happy is a funny word," Gina said. "But I think I am. I thought I'd be bored as hell, get cabin fever, go a little crazy. And I do miss my friends a ton. It was like I finally found my people, you know?"

"I do," Sam said.

"And there's"—Gina began, waving her hand across the bar, gesturing discreetly at the clientele—"a certain *lack* of my people up here."

"I know what you mean," Sam said.

Gina smiled at Sam. "It's been a while since someone has known what I mean."

Sam smiled back, then looked around the bar, wondered what it might be like to live up here full time, in this place where no other bodies looked like hers. Where everyone seemed to fit neatly into normal categories. Where Sam felt increasingly like her body was becoming both more indecipherable and, somehow, more like itself.

"Can I ask you something?" Gina said, looking at Sam.

"Shoot," Sam said.

"Do you, like, prefer a certain pronoun or anything?"

Sam laughed. "Can you read minds or something?"

"Maybe," Gina said, raising an eyebrow. "My mom always said I had a sixth sense."

"Mine too!" Sam said. "I think she wanted to believe I was special, or like, mystical, or something. She was like that. But I'm most definitely not." She took a sip of her beer, procrastinating. "Anyway, I don't really have a preference, I guess. People ask me that a lot, and I think the honest answer is—I don't really know. Some days I feel like a woman, and some days I don't. Maybe I've always felt that way. But lately it's been different. I've been feeling like something else—like something that doesn't have a name."

She laughed at herself, but it was a nervous sound. She took another pull from her beer. "I guess that's as far as I've gotten."

"That's plenty far," Gina said. "Anyway, it doesn't matter. I'm glad you're here."

Sam smiled. She picked at the label on her beer bottle, peeling the damp paper back from one corner. She hated talking about her body, and gender, and all of it. She'd rather never have to think about it, to pass through the world unseen, like some amorphous ghost in the wilderness. But with Gina she didn't really mind. It felt safer, somehow.

"I'm glad you're here too," she said.

"It does get hard up here sometimes," Gina said. "It can be lonely. But I really do love it. The solitude, the slowness. Mom and I have a little garden. And I kind of love the hardware store. Getting better with tools, talking with people, helping them out. It's simple, but it feels good, at the end of the day. Like I've done something useful."

Sam nodded, continuing to pick at the beer label, rolling it between her fingers, little wet beads piling on the bar.

"My dad," Gina went on, "before he died, he was a contractor. He could build anything, fix anything. Knew how everything worked, how to make it work better. It was like a superpower. I always wanted to be like that. And honestly, I hated working in an office."

"Me too," Sam said. "I don't think humans are made for that shit."

"Amen," Gina asked. "What do you do?"

"I'm an editor. Or was, anyway. I worked at a magazine."

"Fancy," Gina said.

"I don't know," Sam said. "To be honest it always felt like some strange kind of dream, that I ended up in New York. In this office, in Manhattan. There were days I would look up from my desk, and I'd look out the window at all the other high-rises and think, *How the hell did this happen?* And it was good, for a while. Until it wasn't, I guess."

"I get that," Gina said. "Do you think you'd go back?"

Sam shrugged. "I don't know. Maybe. I liked the work, being part of something, making something with other people. But now that I've been gone for a while, I don't know. I really like working outside, by myself, no bosses. I like doing things with my hands."

"I'll bet you do," Gina said, wiggling her eyebrows. Sam laughed and looked away.

"Yeah," she said, wanting to flirt but thinking of Stephen, telling herself she'd be good. She kept fiddling with her bottle. "I really do like fixing things, learning how to build shit. I'd like to get better at it too."

"Luckily you now have a friend at the hardware store who can hook you up," Gina said, elbowing Sam in the side. She let her arm linger against Sam's for a second. "Speaking of which, how'd it go with the sink?"

"Fucking nailed it," Sam said, grinning.

"Hell yeah you did," Gina said, and they clinked their bottles and drained their beers.

Sam felt the buzz settle into her skin. She felt the heat of Gina's bare arm just a few inches from hers, felt the blush from the beer rising up her neck and into her cheeks, felt herself dissolve into the warmth. She teetered on the edge she knew so well. On one side, solid ground; on the other, a gaping chasm. That long fall into oblivion. She should stay on the good side. The side of light. She shouldn't cross the threshold. But she was pulled by the dark, always had been. She looked around the bar, suddenly self-conscious. She felt like she was being watched. She looked at the men, one by one. They all seemed to look the same. White and bearded and ruddy-faced, they began to melt together, becoming one pulsing mass of man.

And then she saw him. She was sure of it this time. The stranger, the neighbor—Danny—in the back corner of the room. He sat alone at a table with a beer, biting into a burger. The juice ran red down his chin. He looked at her, blood pooling at the corners of his mouth, and grinned. His teeth were red too. His eyes were black. She looked away, then turned back to Gina.

"Hey," Gina said, putting a hand on Sam's arm. "You okay?"

"Yeah," Sam said, forcing a fake laugh from her lips. "Yeah. Just thought I saw a ghost."

Gina looked at her, brows knit together. "'Nother round?"

"Fuck yes," Sam said. As Gina ordered, Sam glanced back to the far corner of the bar. The man was gone. The table was empty. She swallowed, shook her head, and turned back to the bar. Before her, a fresh cold bottle of beer had appeared. She took a drink, trying to drown the image of the man from her mind.

They stayed for hours, for a third round and a fourth. The bartender bought shots of rail whiskey, and the three of them drank together. Sam felt warm and happy and numb. The drunker she got, the longer she wanted to stay. She wanted a fifth and sixth beer, a seventh, enough to obliterate her brain and allow her to do something stupid. To have something to blame.

She knew, as they talked—Gina sliding her stool closer to Sam's as the bar got louder; as their bare arms brushed against one another; as Gina leaned in so close to Sam she could feel her breath on her skin—that she shouldn't be here. That she was making a mistake. What she was doing wasn't fair. To Stephen, to herself. But she swallowed the knowledge, choked it down further with each beer. Let it live in her guts, where she preferred to keep such things. They would surface in the morning, the bile bitter and sharp in her throat. But for now, she tried not to think too hard. She tried not to think at all, let the beer and the bad music from the jukebox and the smell of stale liquor and fry grease and this beautiful woman's eyes hold her.

"One more?" Gina asked.

The girl could hold her liquor. Far better, Sam knew, than she could these days. She remembered that phrase—*hold her liquor*—as a badge of pride, mostly given to girls and women by boys and men; a thing that, where she came from, was something to strive for: a way to make those boys, and those men, respect you. It was a badge Sam wore with pride too, back when she believed it was actually respect. Before she understood it was something more sinister.

But Sam said yes, because she always said yes. She had learned early that to turn down the offer of one more, to say no, was to call it, to quit, to say you couldn't roll, that you were weak. And anyway, she wanted one more. She always wanted more.

"Why not," Sam said. And it wasn't a question. She couldn't remember if this was six or seven. She'd lost count. As Gina ordered the beers, Sam slid off her stool and stepped over to the jukebox, careful not to stumble. The lights from the neon beer signs swam around her. She fished in her pocket for a quarter, plugged the machine. She pressed the big white buttons and watched the 45s flip. She knew where she was going. B18, Patsy Cline, "Crazy." One of her father's old favorites. The music started to play, and she swayed at the machine, closing her eyes, letting the sound wash over her. And there it was, the oblivion. Best feeling in the world.

Then she felt two hands slip around her from behind. Soft hands but strong, wrapped around her waist. They swayed together, in front of the jukebox, and Sam hummed along.

"We could probably get killed up here for this," Gina whispered, her face against Sam's neck. They were about the same height, and they fit together perfectly.

"Mmm hmm," Sam said, and Gina was right. There were men in this place who would hate them, maybe even hurt them, but she was drunk enough not to care.

"Luckily," Gina went on, her lips brushing Sam's neck, "everyone probably just thinks we're two gal pals, having ourselves a girls' night out."

"Probably." Sam laughed, and she moved her hands from the jukebox and placed them on top of Gina's. Gina pressed herself against Sam's lower back. That long, low boil just below her stomach. That crushing weight of want. It had been so long since she'd felt it. She wanted, very badly, to spin Gina around and push her against the jukebox. To press her body into Gina's, leading with her hips. She wanted to kiss her. Wanted Gina's tongue on hers. Wanted to feel the heat of her, taste her, drink her down. She wanted to devour her.

The song ended, and in that beat of silence the whole bar might have heard her heart.

"We should probably get back to those beers," she said, swallowing hard, and Gina nodded, letting her hands linger on Sam's hips for a second more before letting go.

They stumbled back to the bar and finished their beers. Sam drained hers in two long pulls, glancing around fast, sure everyone was staring.

"Is it hot in here or what?" she asked, and they laughed. They felt the eyes of the men at the bar. But they didn't look at the men. They just kept looking at each other. They couldn't stop smiling, grinning so big their cheeks hurt. Sam got the check.

They walked outside, still smiling, feeling eyes follow them as they left. The night was cool and clear and filled with stars. The peepers were singing, and they stood on the porch and listened, their shoulders barely touching, looking up at the sky. They could see the Milky Way, and a thin green slash of the Northern Lights. *Aurora borealis,* Sam thought, hearing the name on her mother's lips, and remembering a night like this, a long time ago, when they'd taken a walk in the woods in the dark, to the lake, to see it. They'd stood on the dock, bent their necks to the sky. The greens and purples and blues swirling around in the night, dancing in the dark.

What is it? a young Sam had asked.

It's magic, her mother had said. *There's magic everywhere, if you look for it.* And Sam had looked at the lights and believed it. Later, she would learn the science behind the phenomenon, about particles from the sun slamming into the atmosphere of the Earth, about the magnetic fields protecting it. That such beauty could be borne of violence. That maybe magic could be too.

"I should get home," Sam said at last, still looking at the stars, watching them swim.

"Yeah," Gina said, "probably a good idea."

They looked at each other, their faces close. Sam's head, the stars, spinning.

"That was fun though," she said.

"It was," Gina said. "It's not often I meet someone up here who feels so—familiar."

Sam nodded, her head moving in slow motion, the night following after.

"See you again?" Sam asked.

"Definitely," Gina said.

They stood still for a moment more, thinking of other possibilities, where else the night might take them. Sam's heart beat fast, her body a live wire.

"Till then," Gina said. She stepped off the porch, hopped on her bike, and kicked it into a growl. Sam got into the truck and pulled the door closed. The windows were still down, which in any other place would have been crazy. She started the engine, gave herself two fast slaps to the face, a futile attempt to rattle herself into sobriety. Then she leaned out the window and watched Gina put her helmet on, blond hair falling down her back.

"You make that look good," Sam yelled over the sound of the engines.

"I know," Gina yelled back. Then she revved the engine and roared away. As Sam watched her disappear, she could still feel Gina's hands on her waist, the ghost of lips on her neck. She felt it as she drove the long road home, closing one eye to focus on the lines, the old trick she learned in high school, keeping both hands on the wheel. She felt it as she drove the dense wooded path and down the gravel drive. She felt it as she stepped out into the night, drinking the sweet air. She felt it as she lay down in the grass, looking up at the sky through the circle of trees. As she closed her eyes and listened to the night, she felt it.

Twenty-Nine

SHE WASN'T SURE when the dreams began. She'd always had trouble sleeping, but in the woods it had gotten worse. She would lie awake in bed, looking at the dream catcher in the window. Her mother had hung one in each bedroom. Her mother was far more spiritual, and superstitious, than Sam ever was, sensed things Sam never could. Ghosts and spirits and energies that lived in dark places—some of them good, some of them not. Sam's mother, like her mother before her, believed in omens and signs: Sam learned early the bad luck that would come of broken mirrors, of walking beneath ladders, of killing a spider or opening an umbrella indoors. If her nose itched, someone was thinking of her. Every cardinal that appeared at a window was the spirit of someone gone. In the last few years before she disappeared, Sam's mother was sure every cardinal was her own dead mother, come to say hello. And every dream—every nightmare—was a message.

Mostly, Sam ignored it. She rolled her eyes, said she didn't believe. She did, however, just like her mother, adopt only black cats, those witchy companions they referred to as familiars. In

New York, her Monster would follow her around, ride on her shoulder, and deposit dead mice at the foot of her bed, mangled and pulpy and sometimes only skeletons, their bones picked clean. It freaked Sam out, but her mother said it was an act of love.

She's bringing you presents, she'd say. *Like the crows will too, if you let them.*

But something about the dream catchers soothed Sam. When she was a kid, her mother hung one in her bedroom. *To keep the bad dreams away,* she said, tucking Sam in and kissing her forehead before turning out the light.

At first, the dreams were just that—dreams. A little weird, a little intangible, uncanny images dissolving as soon as she woke. But then they got weirder, and more frightening; something sinister lived at the edges when she tried to grasp them. She woke unsettled, and the feeling stayed with her all day. In her cabin bedroom, she touched the feathers that dangled from the dream catcher and asked it for protection. But the dreams only got worse, and no longer slipped away upon waking, but remained lodged in her brain. Sometimes she screamed herself awake in the dark, terrifying images beating bright against the backs of her eyelids in time with her pulse.

In these dreams—these nightmares—she was running in the woods. She was barefoot. Sometimes there was blood. There was fur and teeth and breath on her neck. A sound behind her, guttural and low, following her, circling her, as she fled through the forest. Something menacing, something violent, all around her.

She ran and ran, trying to go faster, but the woods always slowed her down. She got caught in branches, her ankles snared in vines. She got stuck in mud, her feet immobile as she sank. Or she would suddenly, simply, freeze. She would try to move her legs, lashing against some invisible force that held her, rendering her helpless against whatever was coming. And just as the snarling thing closed in, just as it lunged, she would wake up.

She'd been having the same dream, or some variation of it, every night for weeks. And then, one night, it changed. She was still running in the woods. She was still barefoot. There was still the same strange animal sound. But this time, the sound wasn't coming from behind or around her. It seemed to come from within her. And as she ran, she no longer felt fear. No desperation, no panic or terror of whatever was closing in. Instead, she felt sure and steady on her feet, bounding through the forest quick and light, dodging branches and brambles, leaping over roots, never slowing, never stuck. It was as if she wasn't running at all but flying, skimming the surface of the earth with nothing in her way.

A few paces ahead of her, something ran. She could hear its breath, smell its sweat, taste its blood on her lips. A quick sharp stab at the back of her jaw. She chased it. And as she closed in, she felt something open up in her chest—something alive and churning. It seemed to grow stronger the closer she got. Around her, the woods seemed to open too, the trees stretching out and up until they were giants, reaching and growing and breathing beside her, guiding her, clearing a path as she ran.

She found herself in the woods. It was still dark, but almost morning. She remembered coming home from the bar, lying down in the grass in the clearing near the fire pit, not far from the feeder. She remembered her hands behind her head, watching the stars. Looking up at the sky, and the circle of trees—the way they looked in the moonlight, the black silhouettes of leaves and the sky swimming. And the stars, a thick slash across the black. Spotting the Big Dipper, the Little Dipper, Orion's Belt, the only constellations she knew.

She remembered the night air, sweet and cold, keeping her eyes open to combat the spinning. She remembered thinking of her parents, out by the fire, their faces the color of a sunset by the light of the flames. She remembered thinking of her mother, who always built the fire and used a big stick, usually a fallen branch from a nearby oak, to stoke it. She remembered how her mother taught her to build fires too: which woods burned best (birch), how to identify if a log or a branch was too damp to burn (if it felt soft in your hands, if it smoked when lit). She remembered thinking of the three of them curled up in camp chairs around the fire, her mother with a tall plastic cup of something that smelled like gasoline, that Sam thought she might pour on the fire to make the flames reach the sky.

After that, she remembered nothing. Like all the times before, she had no idea how she'd gotten here, so far out in the woods. She sat up and looked around, no idea where she was. She didn't recognize this part of the forest. But she was not afraid.

She cracked her back and neck. The ground was wet with dew; damp leaves stuck to her skin. She did not feel cold.

Maybe I have frostbite, she thought, checking her fingers to see if they'd gone yellow or white, the way her one middle finger tended to turn when she got too cold. But she wasn't cold at all. Her skin was somehow warm.

She pressed her hands to the earth, and a word came to her. *Understory.* She'd read it in a book somewhere. The small trees and plants that grow in the dark, upon the forest floor, far below the canopy. Farther down, dead leaves and pine needles, mushrooms beneath rotting logs. There were creatures who died there, who became part of the soil. And there were creatures who fed there, who ate the dead and dying in order to survive. And the understory grew from all of it, out of the light, far beyond the reach of the sun. She whispered the word to herself, and thought of things that live in the light, and things that live in the dark. How whole worlds and realities can exist in things unspoken and unseen. How there's a story told aloud, in the open, above the surface of things, and there's a story beneath it, that one must look much harder to find.

She stood up and walked through the trees. She followed a deer trail, knowing somehow it would lead her home. The sun had not yet risen, the sky a pale blue-green. Her neck was stiff; her back ached. There was a tear in the knee of her jeans and a large gash beneath it, blood and dirt caked around it. Her mouth was dry and her lips were chapped. There was a sick, sweet smell in her nose, a thrum in her stomach. Her pulse was elevated. Pain stabbed in her temples and behind her eyes; it crouched in the base of her skull. She was probably still drunk, and the hangover was going to be bad.

She followed the deer trail for a mile, maybe more. At last she emerged at the edge of the woods, the sky a little lighter and the cabin dark. The truck was diagonal in the driveway, the windows still open. The feeder was tipped over, and lay on the ground on its side, a few kernels of corn scattered in the grass. Sam rubbed her temples and took a few deep breaths, tried to slow her heart. This was what she hated most about hangovers: along with the nausea, the headache, the numbness in her fingers, it was the way her heart pounded so hard in her chest, sporadic and fast, like a warning.

And with it, shame—disgust digging itself into her skin like a chigger or a tick, burrowing its way into her blood. It sliced through her now, sharp and sick. It worked its way up from her stomach to her esophagus in a thin stream of acid, and she heaved in the grass. A thread of yellow bile was all that came out, and then another. She thought of poison, her body working so hard to expel what she had put into it herself. She knelt on the ground and let it come, let it rack her body in shuddering waves. When it was over, tears stung the corners of her eyes. She clenched her fingers into fists and writhed in the grass. Her stomach kept spasming, even after it was emptied. She pulled her knees to her chest, wrapped her arms around them, curling her body into a ball. She hated herself, hated who she was. She hated her mother for giving this to her. She hated her grandmother for giving it to them both. She hated whoever came before, whoever had forged this birthright in their blood.

What kind of inheritance is this? she thought. *Is this all you had to give me?*

She wished she could take it all away, rewind to a time before this was her life, her legacy, before this thing had been born so fully inside her, deep and rooted and essential, like the elements below the surface of the earth. Before the desire had worked its way in. Before she had ever felt the longing for obliteration, the desire to destroy herself.

She curled up tighter in the grass, wanting to disappear completely. She thought of the wasting disease, which took the deer slowly, making them skeletal and gaunt, then stumble, zombie-like, when they walked. Their heads hung low, disoriented and swaying, dying on their feet. The way they gave it to each other, a disease that killed whole families, whole communities, and never stopped. She lay in the grass and closed her eyes.

When she opened them, the doe was standing before her, a few feet away, at the overturned feeder. She looked at Sam. It was not a cruel look. Sam could hear the doe breathing, saw the air puff from her nose in small quick clouds. She had never been this close. While just a few weeks ago the doe had looked pale and thin, she was now thick and hale. Her fur was darker and more supple, as if she'd grown a new coat. Her eyes were bright, her legs strong. Sam saw the muscles in her haunches, the soft fur of her ears. She wanted to touch the doe, hold her, be held.

The doe stepped closer. So close Sam could feel her breath. Then her front legs folded beneath her, gentle and slow. Her hind legs followed, until her body knelt in the grass. The doe sat beside Sam as the sun came up, saying nothing, and for the first time in a very long time, Sam slept soundly.

When she woke up, the sun was high and bright. The doe was gone, but there were birds all around her, singing in the trees. She heard the song of a finch, the trill of a sparrow. She heard the hummingbirds buzz around the feeders she'd rehung after the storm. She heard their chirps, high and fast, as they fought for position at the perch and then landed, silent and still.

The birds sounded wrong. Their songs were too loud, shrill and piercing. The trees, too, were too green, the sun too bright. She closed her eyes against it.

Must be the hangover, she thought, though somewhat miraculously her head didn't hurt. But the sounds were so sharp, the light nearly blinding. It was like she was seeing with different eyes, hearing with new ears. She heard the squirrels running through the woods, too far away, heard the patter of their feet as they flitted up the trees. She heard the buzz of gnats and dragonflies. She could hear the whole forest, all the way to the lake.

She could hear the fish jump. She could hear below the surface of the water—the musky and northern as they swam through the blue-black depths. She heard the motors of fishing boats like they were right in front of her, a pickup truck rumbling down the road ten miles away. Hypothermia, she knew, could cause hallucinations. She should get inside.

Her ear twitched, and she swatted a mosquito away. She sat up and shielded her eyes from the sun. The trough was still toppled over, and she was surrounded by a circle of corn. She put the trough back on the stump, told herself she'd refill it later. For now, she needed water and coffee and a shower. She walked up the porch stairs, paint peeling and two steps split. She still had to fix those, still had so much to do. What had she even done? She'd been here weeks now, a month or more. She didn't know how long. Time seemed to have stood still, or moved without her, her body on another plane—conscious only to the cycles of sun and moon, the sounds of the forest.

I should call Lou-Ann, she thought.

She walked inside the cabin, dust suspended in sunlight. The place was a mess. A frying pan crusted with eggs in the sink. Sour milk, old coffee grounds, the smell of something rotten. A pile of mail she'd picked up at the grocery store, the envelopes still sealed. She opened the windows. Then she opened the fridge, grabbed the last bottles of beer. She popped them open and poured them down the sink. She gathered the last of the whiskey, half drunk, and dumped it down the drain in the basement. The sickly sweet smell worked its way into her throat as she poured. She gagged, watched the liquid swirl down the drain, staining the concrete around it. It couldn't be good for the septic. She tossed the bottles into a contractor bag, the piercing crash of glass. She tied the bag and carried it to the garage. She'd have to go to the dump today. Keep the ants away, get rid of the smell.

Back inside, sticky and sore, she turned the shower on and took off her clothes. She looked in the mirror and found three large tick bites on her belly, perfect little bullseyes dotting her skin. She told herself to find a doctor, get a Lyme test. Then she stepped into the shower, turned the water as hot as it would go. She stood beneath it, letting her flesh turn red. She washed her face and body with an old bar of Dial, her father's soap, a sliver worn down to a thin yellow crescent. She washed her hair with her mother's raspberry-scented shampoo. Her hair was getting shaggy, falling down her neck. Chemical berries filled the room.

She opened her eyes underwater and saw a spider scuttling up the plastic shower curtain. Her vision was perfect. She blinked the water out of her eyes, studied the shower tiles, could see the moldy grout between them. She watched the spider, could see the hair on its legs as it crawled across the curtain. It was a wolf spider, and in the past this would have scared her—she had always been afraid of spiders, even the harmless ones—but today she didn't mind. She closed her eyes as it crawled through the steam.

She turned off the shower and toweled herself dry, wiped a circle in the mirror and inspected her body. It was thinner than it had been, but her muscles were roped and lean. The hair on her arms and legs was thick, and a few more patches had sprouted on her chest. Her reflection should have been a blur, but she could see it sharp and clear, the steam swirling thick in the pale bathroom light. She pressed three fingers into the tick bites, wondering if they'd gotten their fill.

A flash of something glinted in her periphery—like light off a shard of glass, or metal. A sick smile in a mirror, a mouth full of teeth. Sharp and long as fangs. Those hands again, covered in fur. And something else: where fingernails should have been, there were claws.

And then, as fast as the image had come, it was gone. She looked at herself in the mirror, slowly opened her mouth. No fangs, normal teeth. She looked at her hands, and they were normal too. No fur, no claws. But on her belly, the tick bites were still there.

She heard a tap against the window, looked up at the sound. And there she saw it, clear as day: a cardinal, a female, perched on the window ledge, peering inside. She cocked her head, tapped her beak against the glass, and looked right at Sam.

"Hi Grandma," Sam said. The bird cocked her head once more, then flew away.

Thirty

◇◇◇◇◇◇◇◇◇◇◇

THAT AFTERNOON, SHE stripped the deck. She did it by hand, using the paint scraper and hand sander her father always used. Crouched on all fours, she sanded and scraped, watching layers of old stain curl up in spirals, polishing the pale pine boards beneath. It took hours, the sun beating down on her back and neck. She knew she would burn.

She had a headache, and could smell the alcohol sweating out of her skin. It made her stomach clench, but it also felt like the punishment she deserved. She sweated and scraped, her fingers numb, her whole body pulsing with pain. She wore cutoff shorts, and her bare knees wore deep indentations from the wood. She took only a few short breaks, just enough to down a glass of well water and then another, eat an apple that had been browning on the counter. Then she got back to work.

It was early evening when she finished the job. She kicked off her sneakers and stood on the smooth raw boards in bare feet. She closed her eyes and stretched, reaching her arms to the sky and pressing her feet into the wood. She felt something soft beneath her toes. She knelt down and pressed two fingers into a board. They sank. She pressed harder, and her fingers went deeper, revealing a black cavity of rot gaping up at her.

"Shit," she said. She was sure she had found all the rotten boards. She'd been careful. She pressed her fingers once more into the wood. It was warm and damp—*like the insides of an animal,* she thought inexplicably. She inspected the deck, making sure she hadn't missed any others. But everything else looked solid. Somehow she had missed this one. She still had a few five-quarters in the garage and would replace the bad board tomorrow.

She inspected the black residue of rot on her fingers, then wiped her hands on her shorts. She went inside to make herself a sandwich. The bread was stale and dotted with mold, so she opened a can of tuna and ate it plain, with a fork, straight from the can. She was starving, and finished it in a few bites, her teeth tearing into the flesh of the fish.

She plugged in her phone and found three missed calls. One was from Gina, and Sam's guts lurched. She wasn't sure if it was excitement or regret, or some combination. The other two calls were from Stephen. This made her guts lurch too, and she was certain of the cause. She hadn't done anything wrong, not really—not like in her past life, when she'd cheated on people without a thought—but she also hadn't been good. She wanted, so badly, to be good. It was what she had always wanted, ever since she was a girl. Since she'd first learned to believe she was bad.

He had left messages—funny and sweet, as he walked home from work, as he made himself dinner. He told stories about the neighbors—how the old Polish man downstairs, a 9/11 first responder who lived alone and went through several bottles of vodka a week, had been yelling again; how someone in the building was cooking a pot roast, and would it be weird if he knocked on their door and asked to join them? He put the phone up to the cat, who meowed into the receiver.

"Monster says hi," he said. "And also come home. Also feed her."

Sam laughed. She wasn't sure if he had forgiven her since their last conversation, for not coming home. But he was trying. She longed, in that moment, to go home, the feeling a clenched fist in her chest. She missed him, and the cat, and their little life. She was happy here, sort of. But things were getting bad. If she didn't stop now, she'd be in trouble. She called him back.

"Hey," he said. The connection was miraculously clear.

"Hey yourself," she said. "How are you?"

"I'm okay. Didn't get that pot roast, though."

"There's still time," she said, looking at the clock. It was 4 p.m. here, 5 p.m. there. "It's not even dinner time in the future."

"These people are old," he said. "Dinner was an hour ago."

"True," she said. There was a beat of silence, a stillness filled with the tension between them, with her own discomfort and shame. She was sure he heard it too.

"I finally finished stripping the deck today," she said.

"Damn," he said. "That's hot."

"It is pretty hot," she said. "I can't actually believe I finished it."

"You can literally do anything," he said, and she laughed.

"I mean it," he added.

"So," she said. "I have to tell you something."

"Okay," he said.

"Last night," she said. "I went out with a new friend. This girl I met."

"Okay," he said again.

"We went to the bar," she said. "I had a couple of beers."

"Okay." He knew there was more to come. She swallowed. She was sure he could hear it.

"Some whiskey too."

"Okay," he said. His voice was patient. It wasn't angry.

"It sucked," she said. "I feel like shit."

"I'm sure you do."

"It wasn't the first time."

"How long?"

"A while. Pretty much since I got here. There was beer in the house. I didn't plan it. It just sort of—happened. But then I bought more. I started out with one a day. I thought I could stick to it. And then it kind of went off the rails."

"As it does," he said.

"As it does," she said with a sigh. She felt the weight of the lie lift off her chest, felt the tension in her shoulders loosen.

"Is there a meeting you could go to?"

She tensed back up. Stephen was always suggesting she go to a meeting. But then she felt something inside herself soften again, the rope wound tight around her neck uncoil. Maybe he was right. Maybe this was what it meant to surrender.

"I don't know," she said. "Maybe. There's this woman up here, Lou-Ann. Another friend. She's sober, and said she'd go with me sometime."

"Maybe you should do that," he said, then paused. "Are you okay?"

"I think so," she said. "Just—embarrassed. Mad at myself. I feel like a fucking failure."

"Sam," he said. "You're not a failure."

"I was so close to a year," she said.

"And you'll get there again."

"Yeah," she said. "Maybe."

"You will. Is there any alcohol left up there?"

"No. I dumped it all this morning. Everything."

"Good," he said.

"There's something else," she said.

"Okay."

"I've been..." She didn't know how to say it. "I guess I've been blacking out?" She said it as a question, because the truth was that she didn't know what was happening.

"Fuck," he said. "Okay. How often has this happened?"

"A few times now, I think. I don't really know. But it's different than before. It's weirder. It feels like a dream, but I'm sure it's actually happening. I wake up in the woods. Or by the lake. Somewhere I don't remember going. I just wake up there, like I sleepwalked or something."

"Jesus," he said. "I should come."

"No," she said. "It's okay. I'm okay. It's just a little scary."

"Sam," he said, and there was something in his voice—worry, most likely, but she heard it as judgment. She wanted to hang up but stayed on the line.

"Are you mad?" she asked.

"No," he said. "No, Sam. God. I'm not mad. I'm just worried about you."

"I know," she said. "I'm worried too. Last night was scary. Or this morning, I guess. I felt like a different person. That person I used to be, who didn't give a shit if I lived or died."

"I really think I should come," he said. "The school year's almost over anyway."

"No," she said. "I think—I think this is something I need to do on my own."

He was silent for a beat. She knew that more than anything he wanted to take care of her.

"You can't do everything on your own," he said. "It's okay to ask for help. To let me help. I'm here."

"I know," she said. "But this—whatever this is. I just feel like I need to face it alone."

She stood in the kitchen, her heart beating fast, waiting for a response.

"Okay," he said at last, resigned, the word a long exhale. "But will you please tell me if you need help? Can you promise me?"

Sam had never been good at asking for help. She was independent, she told herself. She didn't need anyone else. She'd been that way since she was a kid, when she'd learned she was essentially alone, that she'd always have to fend for herself. Everything she had to do in this life, she'd sworn back then, she'd do it on her own.

"Yes," she said. "I promise."

She wanted, more than anything, to believe herself.

Thirty-One

THE DAY WAS warm, and she drove with the windows down. She was on her way to the grocery store, and told herself she'd avoid the beer cooler and the spirits aisle. She would get coffee and milk, apples and eggs, a couple cans of tuna and a loaf of bread. She hadn't been eating much, despite all the work she was doing. It gave her the hard, hollow feeling she had chased when she was younger, her first disappearing act, when she tried to make her body as small as possible. When it felt as if her insides had been scooped out like a pumpkin, leaving only the hard exterior and nothing within. With the feeling came a memory—just a flash of an image, she and her mother carving jack-o'-lanterns at the kitchen table, newspaper spread beneath them, the stringy orange guts soaking through the sports section. As quickly as it came the image was gone.

When she got to town, she found cars lining Main Street, tents dotting the sidewalk. A string band was setting up outside the bait and tackle shop. It was, she realized, the annual art fair,

231

the event that marked the official start of summer in Boundary Pass. It must have been a Saturday, and it must have been June. The tourist season, whatever remained of it, would soon descend upon the town, and by the Fourth of July the place would come alive. The minigolf course and ice-cream shop would reopen, and every Friday a parade of SUVs would roll down Main Street, speedboats and jet skis hitched to their backs. The weekenders from Chicago—known locally as FIBs, or *fucking Illinois bastards*—always broke the no-wake laws, and the lakes would soon be humming like a massive swarm of city-dwelling mosquitoes.

She parked by the Beer Bar and walked down Main Street, stopping at stalls as she passed. Artists had once come from all over the state, more than a hundred tents packing Main Street and spilling down County M. But now there were only a dozen vendors or so, folks from closer by who didn't need to travel far. There was Indigenous beadwork and leatherwork and stained glass, paintings and photography, mostly of Northwoods landscapes, and every variety of wood carving one could imagine. Sam found herself at a folding table filled with little wooden animals. It was the seller she and her mom had always loved best, and every summer when Sam was young they had bought something from the woman who made them.

Sam's mother had once been a painter. She was good too, had enrolled in night classes at the community college, but dropped out when she had Sam. She tried to keep it up at first, but her studio became Sam's bedroom and her easel went to the basement, where it gathered dust. Letting go of that dream was something Sam was sure her mother regretted, though she'd never say so aloud. She was a woman who didn't believe in regret. When Sam was young, she blamed herself. As she grew up, she blamed her mother, who had hammered into Sam the importance of chasing her dreams. To never let anyone, or anything, get in the way of them. How could she have given up so easily on hers? Now that Sam was older, nearing the age her mother was when things got bad, she wished she could tell her that she understood now. That this, so often, is what women do. They have husbands, then kids—sometimes because they want them, sometimes because they're led to believe they should—and they put themselves last, behind the needs and desires and dreams of their family. They let go of their own.

"How much for this little guy?" she asked, holding a small walnut frog in her palm.

"Twenty," the woman said. She had a long white ponytail and dangly turquoise earrings, a yin-yang necklace on a leather cord, a tie-dyed T-shirt with UP NORTH printed across the chest. Like a relic from some other time, back when things were good. The woman smiled at Sam from her camp chair, a can of Coors in the cup holder. "Love that sweet peeper."

"Me too," Sam said. "I'll take him." She handed over the cash.

"Thanks much," the woman said, pocketing the cash and wrapping the frog in tissue paper. Her sun-leathered hands shook a little as she wrapped.

"My mom used to buy stuff from you every year," Sam said. "She collected the ducks."

The woman squinted at Sam, then nodded and smiled with stained teeth.

"Oh yeah, sure, I remember your mom," she said, her words long and slow, the *yeah* more like *yah,* the *sure* like a whirr, the *oh* stretched like a canvas. "Remember you too. Haven't seen ya in a few years though."

"We lost her a few years ago," Sam said, thinking not for the first time of the absurdity of the word *lost*. "I haven't been back in a while."

"Oh, I'm sorry to hear that, hon." The woman pressed the frog into Sam's hand and folded Sam's fingers around it, then patted Sam's hand with her own. "I could tell your mom was a good one."

"Yeah," Sam said. "She was."

Sam realized she'd slipped back into her own Midwestern drawl, those elongated vowels of her past spilling off her lips. Sometimes when she came home she code-switched intentionally, a kind of linguistic downshifting in order to better blend in. But now here it was, her old voice, speaking in the language of the land that made her, coming back unbidden—as if it, and she, had never left.

"You take good care now," the woman said, giving Sam's hand one last pat, and the small tenderness nearly made Sam weep. She hadn't cried in a long time, and now out of nowhere it was high tide in her chest, the waves threatening to break.

She choked back the ocean in her throat. "Will do," she said. "You too."

She wandered among the stalls, thinking about her mom. When Sam was young, they spent their Saturdays together, drawing on the living room floor. Sam would lie on her stomach on the shag carpet with her sketchbook open, mimicking her mom's movements. They'd listen to records and draw hands and birds and trees. Once, Sam's mother taught her how to draw a perfect circle, keeping her palm pressed to the paper. Sam's circle had turned out oblong, not perfect at all, but when they lifted their palms they were both blackened with charcoal.

In years past, the artist booths at the fair would have snaked alongside a variety of food vendors, a bustling beer tent, a small midway with rides for the kids. This year, there was just one grill going, manned by the local Lions Club, who served up burgers and brats, pulled cans of beer from a cooler rather than a brewer pouring from kegs. There were no rides, just a couple of sad-looking carnival games and no kids, the bored carnies looking at their phones as balloons remained unpopped and rubber ducks floated forlornly in a plastic kiddie pool.

Sam stopped at a painter's stall, was looking at a watercolor of a tree-lined lake when she heard her name. She turned and there was Gina, in a tank top, cut-off shorts, and aviator sunglasses, her legs long and tan, her hair golden in the sun. Like some glowing girl-god of summer. Sam, meanwhile, might have been a fish pulled from the lake in the painting, her guts flip-flopping wildly on a pier.

"Well, hey there, stranger," Gina said. "Fancy meeting you here."

"Hey," Sam managed, "it's good to see you." She meant it.

"Whatcha up to?" Gina asked.

"Oh you know, just taking in the local art scene," Sam said. "Join me?"

"Heck yeah," Gina said, and they walked together among the booths. At a screen-printing stand, Gina bought a sweatshirt with a pack of wolves on it, the Northern Lights glowing above them as they howled at the moon. They laughed as she put it on.

"It's perfect," Sam said. In the next booth over, they ran their fingers along the smooth polished pine of a hand-carved canoe paddle. The sound of a slide guitar floated up on the wind.

"Kinda sad this year," Sam said, gesturing at the quiet crowd.

"It's been like this the past few years," Gina said. "It's weird. It's so quiet here in the winter, and you get used to seeing the same people every summer. You look forward to it, without even realizing it. To see them again, catch up, hear about their lives, see how their kids have grown. It's like a big family reunion. And then one summer they don't come. They're just gone, and you never see them again."

Sam winced. "I know what that's like," she said.

"Oh shit," Gina said, stopping and turning to Sam. "I'm sorry."

"It's okay," Sam said. "Really. It's good to think about it sometimes. I've spent a lot of time trying not to."

"I get that," Gina said, and they kept walking. Gina's bare shoulder brushed Sam's. They walked to the coolers that held the musky and northern and bass, their gaping maws and giant teeth grinning up maniacally from the ice. Contest submissions would come in all summer, and the winner would be named in August at the Musky Fest, which officially closed out the season. The winner got their fish taxidermied by a local guy in the woods, a hermit with a bomb shelter who was known for his craft, specifically his preservation of the fishes' freakish grins.

"Bob the Muskellunge," Sam said, reading a handwritten placard below one of the fish. The fishermen always named their catches.

"They're so fucking creepy," Gina said. "Who would want that thing on their wall?"

"I don't know, man," Sam said. "Stuff of nightmares."

"I mean, I guess if you're into nightmares that's cool."

They both laughed. Sam smiled and looked at her feet, then felt Gina's fingers brush against hers. Sam let her fingers respond, wrap themselves around Gina's. The warmth from Gina's hand radiating up her arm, filling her whole body. Her skin was tingling, and she wanted badly to kiss her, right there in front of the musky. But she pulled her hand away, stuffed her fists in her pockets. Glanced over her shoulder, certain they were being watched. Convinced the whole town was watching.

Gina looked at her. "Why don't we blow this pop stand. Grab a beer?"

Sam wanted to go back to that dark bar, drink until she couldn't think about what else she wanted. Let her leg fall against Gina's, put her hand on Gina's thigh and squeeze, move her hand up higher beneath the bar, where no one could see. Lead her to the bathroom and press her up against the sink, kiss her hard, bite her throat, leave marks. The sudden violence of the desire shocked her. Pulse quickening, skin hot, not want but need. It felt primal in its urgency, beyond her control. She was ravenous.

She swallowed. "I literally want nothing else," she said, her voice cracking.

"So let's do it," Gina said, a grin spreading across her lips, mimicking the musky but far cuter. "You should let yourself have what you want."

Sam felt the heat in her neck, the hammering of her heart. "Maybe some other time?" she said. "I need to get some groceries, then get back to work."

"Okay," Gina said with a shrug. "Some other time then." She nodded toward the nightmare musky and their lunatic grins.

"See you in your dreams," Gina said, wiggling her eyebrows. Then she walked away.

Sam stood on the sidewalk and watched her leave. She stayed

there until her heart slowed down and her skin stopped buzzing, gripping her little tissue-paper-wrapped frog in one sweaty palm. The sick-looking fish grinned up at her, demented and strange and suspended in ice, telling her something she couldn't understand but somehow already knew.

Thirty-Two

◇◇◇◇◇◇◇◇◇◇◇

THERE WAS A banging on the door. It was morning, and the sound was loud—louder still, having shaken Sam awake, a half-sleep sound like some ghostly thunder. She sat up in bed and listened. The knocking continued, insistent and rhythmic. She pulled a sweater on over her tank top, threw on some sweatpants. She unlocked the bedroom door, then walked down the hall. It was early, and the cabin was still dark.

She paused in the kitchen, the knock and the sound of her pulse seeming to beat in time. She pulled a knife from a drawer. Her mother had never kept her knives sharp. She ran her finger over the blade, felt its dullness. But it could still break skin. She hid it behind her back, her fingers wrapped tight around the handle. She opened the door.

Gray morning light poured in. She saw the silhouette of a man's body before she saw his face.

"Irv?" she said, letting the air spool out of her lungs. Her father's old friend stood on the porch. He took his hat off in an old way that made Sam's heart catch again.

"Well hey there Sam," he said.

"Hi," Sam said, setting the knife down on the table behind her. "What's going on?" Irv's eyes went to the knife, then back to Sam.

"Very sorry to bother you," he said. "Hope I didn't scare you. I know it's early."

"No problem," Sam said, her pulse slowing. "Just a bit on edge lately. Want to come in?"

"Oh no," he said, putting up a hand, and Sam looked at the missing finger then looked quickly away. "Lots of work to do. Hauling up branches all over the preserve from the storm. Just wanted to check in, see if you need anything."

"I'm good," she said, wiping sleep from her eyes. "Thanks for checking, though."

"You got it," he said. "Listen—" He looked over his shoulder toward the road, twisted his hat in his hands. "Wanted to tell you. Found a deer this morning, in the ditch, just outside your place."

Sam's pulse picked up again.

"Shit," she said. "Did someone hit it?"

"Nah," he said. "Thing is—" He stopped, chewed his lip and looked up at the trees, then back at Sam.

"Thing is, Sam—it was gutted. Torn apart. Insides all pulled out."

Sam swallowed. "Jesus. What was it, you think?"

"Not sure," Irv said. "Never seen anything like it. Coulda been a coyote, I guess, but I never seen 'em make a mess of a meal like that."

Sam nodded, a slow creeping thought at the back of her brain, prickling around her skull. "A wolf, maybe? A cougar?"

Irv shook his head, shrugged a little.

"S'pose it coulda been a wolf. Some of them around. Not many, though. Cougars been gone a long time. Classified endangered years ago. Haven't been spotted up here in ages."

He chewed his lip some more.

"It was the state of the thing," he said, scratching his forehead, searching for the words. "Never seen anything like it, Sam. Whatever got it musta had some claws on it, that's for sure. Teeth, too. I don't know what did it, but it ain't like anything I ever seen."

Sam nodded. The thought, louder now, licked its way around her neck. She choked it back.

Irv looked her in the eyes, held her gaze.

"Got rid of the body," he said, securing his hat back on his head. "But wanted to tell you. Didn't want to scare you or anything, just—" He looked over his shoulder again. A flock of grackles lifted from the pines and rose up into the sky.

"Just be careful," he said. "Something prowling up here. You got a gun?"

"No," Sam said, feeling increasingly like an idiot in the woods without one.

"Know how to shoot?" Irv asked.

"Yeah," Sam said. "But it's been a while."

"Okay," Irv said. He reached into his belt and pulled out a revolver. "You take this."

He held it out to Sam. It was small and pretty, a nickel-plated six-shooter with a mother-of-pearl grip.

"I can't take that, Irv."

"Sure you can," he said, pressing it into her hands. "Consider it a loan. Hang onto it as long as you're here. I got plenty more, and you'll be safer with it. I'll feel better knowing you have it. Rest a little easier."

Sam regarded the gun in her hands. She had argued with her uncles about gun statistics, how a house was far less safe with one in it. The argument never worked, of course, and eventually she stopped having it. She closed her fingers around the gun, held it away from her body like it might go off. Irv reached into his pocket and pulled out a small box of bullets.

"It ain't much," he said, "but it'll do for now."

He placed the box in Sam's other hand.

"You practice," he said. "Put some cans up on one of them stumps and knock the rust off. Then head on into town and get yourself some more ammo at the hardware store."

Sam nodded. "Okay," she said. "Thanks."

"You got it. Wouldn't be right, you up here alone, unable to protect yourself." He paused. "Could be nothing. But you never know."

They stood for a moment in silence, the grackles making their strange, off-key sounds.

"Welp, best be going," Irv said. "You need anything, just holler."

"Thanks, Irv," Sam said. "I will."

"Okay then," he said, holding one hand up in a wave, what was once an index finger now just a stump, lopped off below the knuckle.

"Irv," she said. She paused. Afraid to ask, afraid of the answer. "The deer—"

"Yeah?"

"Was it a doe?"

He paused for a second, considering.

"Buck," he said. "Young one. Antlers just coming in. 'Bout the only thing left of the body I could make out."

She realized she'd been holding her breath as she let the air out.

"Okay. Thanks."

"You bet," he said. "Take good care now."

She watched her father's old friend turn to leave, a small wave of relief passing over her. But the thought of the gutted deer banged around in her brain, blaring like an alarm. She tried to shake it away. Irv made his way slowly down the drive, and Sam watched him. He walked with a hitch, a limp from some old injury. She stood on the porch with the gun in her hand, the box of bullets in the other. She realized she wanted him to stay.

That afternoon, she went to the garage and dragged a bag of empties into the yard. She opened the bag, the sick sweet stench of stale beer blooming into the air. She regretted buying bottles instead of cans. She thought of shattered glass on the ground, all those tiny shards. But she pulled six bottles from the bag, lined them up on a large sawed-off tree stump near the edge of the woods. She walked back toward the cabin, counting ten long paces. She picked up the gun and held it in her hands. Then she aimed, squinting into the sights.

She breathed like her uncles had taught her, a long time ago—slow and steady until her shoulders fell and her hands were loose. She pulled back the hammer and exhaled.

On her first round, she hit three of six. Each shot rang out, scattering birds in great black masses above the trees, echoing through the woods. She wore earplugs but still felt each shot, and the explosion of glass, in her teeth. She lined up six more bottles and reloaded. This time, she hit four. She set up six more, simultaneously grateful she hadn't gone to the dump and disgusted by the seemingly endless supply of targets. She'd apparently been drinking even more than she realized.

She took a deep breath and aimed. Felt her shoulders relax. Held the first bottle in the sights and exhaled slowly. She fired. One after the other, in a slow and steady rhythm, she pulled the trigger and watched the bottles explode, brown and green glass glinting in the sun. Six of six. She smiled.

She had always been a good shot. Her uncles had taught her when she was twelve. She refused to hunt with them, unable to stomach the dead deer they brought back in the beds of their trucks, those strong brown bodies bloody and bloated and stiff, their black eyes still open. But she loved to shoot. They took her out for target practice whenever she visited, letting her sneak sips from their cans of MGD in the woods behind her grandmother's house.

Deadeye, they'd called her, slugging her on the shoulder when she didn't miss a shot, the three of them drinking beers in the sun. She looked at the pistol in her hand, thought again of the guns her uncles had tried to give her. They were both lifelong bachelors, had no sons or nephews, and Sam was the closest they got to passing anything down. She hadn't seen them in years, and she missed them.

That night, she slept with the gun on the nightstand beside her. It was loaded. She lay in bed and looked at it in the dark, the moonlight slanting in just enough to make the metal glint. She fell asleep feeling both safer and more afraid. The thing she never told her uncles, whenever they'd offered her one of their pistols, was that it wasn't really the gun she was afraid of. The truth was that she was far more afraid of herself. She was afraid—and somehow she knew—that if she had a gun, she would eventually use it.

Thirty-Three

◇◇◇◇◇◇◇◇◇◇◇

THE NEXT MORNING, Gina called. Sam saw her name on the screen and almost let it go to voicemail, but picked up.

"Hey," Gina said. Her voice was low, and Sam felt dizzy. "Tonight? You, me, that jukebox?"

"Um," Sam said, "I'm kind of busy tonight."

"Tomorrow then?" Gina asked.

"Uh, tomorrow…" Sam started, and trailed, not sure how she would get out of it. She wanted to see Gina. But she couldn't drink again, wouldn't. "Tomorrow I'm actually busy too."

"What about Saturday?"

What day was it? Wednesday? Sam had no idea. Time seemed suspended, and she was never sure how much had passed.

"I just have a ton of work to do here," she said.

"So I'll help," Gina said. "What time should I come over?"

Sam stammered, incapable again of forming words.

"Or not?" Gina said. "I understand if you just need to be alone."

"Yeah," Sam said. "I think maybe I do need that right

now?" It was a question, and she hated herself for talking like this—uncertain, tenuous, leaving a gaping hole of an opening.

"No problem," Gina said. She sounded cool, but Sam was sure she also heard some disappointment. Her heart was beating so hard she swore Gina could hear it on the other end. "If you change your mind, you know where to find me."

She hung up before Sam could answer.

"Fuck," Sam said aloud. She liked Gina. She genuinely liked her, and wanted her to come over. Maybe they could be friends, she thought. *Maybe I can be good.* She called her back.

"I changed my mind," she said.

Gina laughed. "How's this afternoon? I can be there at three."

"Sure," Sam said. "Any chance you could bring a pipe clamp? Three-quarter inch." There was a small leak in the basement that needed fixing.

"You got it," Gina said. "See you soon."

I can be good, Sam thought, the phone still in her hand. *I will be good.*

Gina showed up at 3:15. Sam had replaced the last rotten deck board that morning. It was finally ready to be stained. She'd taken a shower, pulled on her least dirty pair of jeans. She picked a T-shirt from a pile and sniffed the armpits. Not great but passable. She'd have to get to the laundromat soon, the Big Fish Wash 'N Fold in town. Her pits were always a little musky these days—she'd run out of deodorant and hadn't replaced it. She'd scrubbed extra hard today, with the diminishing sliver of Dial, and now she smelled like her father. Her hair was still wet when Gina arrived.

"I come bearing gifts," Gina said, holding up the clamp in one hand and a six-pack in the other. Sam felt a fast wave of nausea roll through her.

"Thanks," Sam said, opening the screen door and letting Gina inside. She took the clamp and put the beer in the fridge but didn't offer one.

"Nice place you got here," Gina said, looking around. Sam had finally cleaned the kitchen, sort of, and the afternoon light made the place glow golden. It felt habitable again, like a normal person lived inside it rather than some kind of feral forest hermit.

"You want the tour?" Sam said.

"You know I do," Gina said, a sly smile spreading across her face, and Sam found herself looking at Gina's lips, that gap between her teeth.

This is a terrible idea, Sam thought.

"Follow me," she said.

There wasn't much to show, but Sam showed Gina everything—the two bedrooms, the bathroom, her parents' collection of Northwoods-themed trinkets. When they stood together at the doorway to her bedroom, Sam felt the swell of heat in her stomach. There was a pile of clothes on the floor, a few water glasses on the nightstand, and the bed was unmade. She felt Gina next to her, felt the warmth of her skin so close. Sam chewed a hangnail on her thumb, tore it off with her teeth.

"Where the magic happens?" Gina said with a grin. Sam gripped her throbbing thumb in her fist.

"Let me show you the basement," she said. "That's where the magic really happens."

Gina laughed. They walked carefully down the narrow steps, Sam in the lead and Gina following so close behind Sam could feel her breath.

Sam pulled the chain and the bare bulb burned, illuminating her father's old workbench, the walls lined with tools.

"Behold," Sam said. "My office."

"Impressive," Gina said. She picked up a birdfeeder that Sam's grandfather had built, turned it over in her hands and inspected its corners and grooves.

"Nice work," she said.

"Thanks," Sam said, taking it from her and setting it back down with a row of others. She suddenly felt protective. "My grandfather made it."

Gina nodded and walked around the room, picking up tools and putting them back on their hooks. She ran her fingers along the legs of the rubber waders that hung on the wall.

"Creepy," she said, and Sam laughed, relaxing a little.

"Yeah," Sam said, joining her by the strange torso-less body. "My dad used to wear them to help put in the docks in the summer and take them out in the winter. When I was a kid I'd go down to the lake and he'd show me how to do it, then chase me out of the water like some kind of sea creature."

"Sounds like a good dad," Gina said.

"He was," Sam said. "He is. The best." She wanted to say more, felt the need to talk about both her parents, how much she missed them. As usual, she swallowed the need.

"Now when I come down here, they scare the shit out of me," she said instead, grabbing a rubber leg and waggling it. "Literally every time I think there's a demon hanging on the wall."

Gina laughed, and continued her inspection, picking up a power drill and grinning. Sam rolled up an open bag of corn, embarrassed about her deer-feeding habit, wondered if Gina's mother had told her Sam's secret. The air in the room felt tight, and the warmth Sam had felt a moment before was quickly turning to heat.

"Do you want to go outside?" she said. She sucked the blood from her thumb and put her hands in her pockets. "See the irises I planted?"

She had planted them for her mother, and she wanted someone to know.

Gina turned from a row of screwdrivers to face Sam.

"Not really," Gina said, walking toward her. She closed the distance between them and stood in front of Sam. She reached out and slid two fingers into the belt loops of Sam's jeans, pulling her closer. "I'd rather stay here."

Sam's heart was hammering, and the waves of warmth rushed over her body in quick succession. Gina was so close she could feel the warmth radiating off her skin, felt the downy blond hair on Gina's arms brush against her own. She swallowed, felt desperate for a drink of water. It had been so long since she'd wanted someone.

Gina pushed her gently, until Sam's back was pressed against the wall. She slid one finger out of a belt loop and along the lip of Sam's jeans. The tip of one finger brushed Sam's stomach. She shuddered.

Gina leaned closer to Sam, their hips nearly touching. A current, like a shock, bounced fast and bright between them.

"Why don't we stay here?" Gina said, and then pushed herself into Sam, the hardness of their hips pressed together. Sam's arms had been hanging dumbly at her sides—*If I don't touch her, maybe this won't happen*, she thought—but she brought them up to Gina's hips, powered by some external force, and rested them on the sharp shelf of her. Then she dug her fingers in, pulled her closer.

When Gina kissed her, it felt as if Sam was falling from the tops of the trees, plummeting toward water. It made her think of parasailing as a teenager at youth-group summer camp, zip-lining into a lake somewhere while a bunch of kids told her to have faith in God as she let go. The feeling was terrifying, and thrilling, and she hadn't felt it in a long time. She felt it here, now, as Gina kissed her, her lips warm and soft, her tongue moving over Sam's. She wanted to keep this feeling forever, keep sailing down the zip line but never touch the water.

Gina pressed Sam harder against the wall. The concrete dug into her back, scraping skin through her shirt. Gina unbuttoned Sam's jeans, then slid her fingers down, beneath her underwear, until they reached the crest of her. One tip of a finger pressed there, soft and light and slow. Sam pushed her hips against Gina's hand, and her finger went down, and then deeper. Soon Gina was inside her, one finger then two, pressing in exactly the right spot. Sam closed her eyes tight until the dark was sparkling, and Gina's lips were on her neck, and Sam's knees were buckling.

"Please," Sam whispered, not sure what she was asking for, but in her own voice she heard a plea, a prayer, a sound somewhere between desperation and despair.

When Sam came, her vision went dark. Her knees collapsed beneath her and she knelt on the floor. Gina fell with her, then unbuckled her belt. She pushed Sam down so she was sitting on the floor, then straddled Sam's hips.

"My turn," she said, and she pushed her pelvis into Sam's. She pressed her lips to Sam's clavicle, ran her hands down the slight curve of Sam's hips. Sam held Gina by the waist, digging her fingers into flesh, and she felt something take over—something instinctual, something long buried—a rush of hunger, that need to devour. She flipped Gina around and her body was something outside herself, something desperate, grasping and biting at flesh, and the words *This is my body, given for you* flashed through her brain, and then *I could swallow you whole,* and Gina's body writhed and shook beneath her, and she heard no sound but the rush of want, like white noise in her brain, and she closed her eyes until her vision began to spark once more, before fading again to black.

When it was over, Gina kissed Sam on her neck, and then her cheek, and Sam walked her out, watched her get on her bike and ride away. When she was gone, Sam went back down to the basement. She sat down on the floor, the cool damp of cement soothing against the heat of her skin. She closed her eyes, and leaned against the wall, and felt everything inside her body leave her. It flowed out of her like a river, like an ocean's tide, this vessel a broken-down ship, carried away. It was a feeling her body remembered. Like riding a bike, like the smell of fresh-cut grass, like fireflies blinking above a yard at dusk—something that had been there her whole life, that lived inside her. It was as if her central nervous system was shutting down, like a machine—all functions turning off one by one, leaving something dark and empty: a void, a vastness, the hum of a clicked-off tube TV, crackling static. She felt nothing. She was nothing. She was empty, no bones or organs or heart—only a carapace, the shell of something newly shed. She was blank, vacant, alone. And as darkness fell around her, it felt like coming home.

Thirty-Four

SHE LOOKS INTO the trees, their arms reaching out and up as if in praise. She walks deep into the woods until she finds a clearing, and it's as if she's walked into church—the arched wooden doors flung open, the music from the organ loud, rising from the pipes and filling the vaulted room with sound. The sunlight through stained glass, illuminating saints carved in color, golden halos around their heads, slants of golden light suspending dust and smoke from incense in the air. The sound is golden too. She feels the hum in her body, in her bones, reverberating in her skin. And she knows, somehow, that she is this light. She is this sound. She is this place, holy and home. She feels as if she's been here before, as if she's returned after a long time away. The light gets brighter, and the sound gets louder. She can taste it on her tongue and swallows it, that golden sound in her throat, in her stomach, and she is full.

There is something here with her—a sound like voices, like singing, a choir. The sound does not frighten her. It feels like communion. Like renewal, rebirth. Like taking the body and blood on a Sunday, beginning again. And she remembers a line from a poem that she read a long time ago. *I am here / Or there, or elsewhere. In my beginning.* She remembers knowing that it meant something then, and it would mean something again. And here, in this forest cathedral, she knows the answer. She looks up into the branches, and the trees are singing, and they hold her, and she says the words aloud. She repeats them like the refrain of a song, like a hymn. The words from her lips, a river of sound. She gives them like an offering. She says them like a prayer.

Thirty-Five

◇◇◇◇◇◇◇◇◇◇

LONG AGO, THE memory had vanished. But here it was, summoned from some dark depth of her, the shards of a shattered mirror unbroken, falling back together in reverse, remaking an image whole. And in that mirror, her own forgotten reflection.

She was thirteen. It was Halloween. Their favorite holiday. Each year, they made new decorations by hand—a graveyard of Styrofoam tombstones, a family of skeletons hanging from trees and twisted into strange tableaus. Sticky cotton cobwebs stretched from floor to ceiling, dotted with small plastic spiders. They'd spend weeks decorating, transforming their house into a haunted one. They made their costumes by hand too, a mother at the sewing machine and a daughter beside her, cutting eyeholes and gluing fake fur. And each year, on Halloween night, they'd get ready together, standing side by side in the bathroom mirror, putting on their masks.

But that year, something was wrong. When she got off the school bus and opened the front door, something felt different. There was some unnamable energy in the air, like something in the house had shifted. It felt like coming home after being on vacation—the house empty, the windows shut tight and the air stale; a foreign smell, a strangeness in it. Like it was someone else's house. Like someone else had been there.

She stood in the doorway, afraid to step inside. There was a plastic skull hanging on the door where a knocker might be, a cheap motion-sensor thing that played haunted-house sounds when trick-or-treaters rang the bell. She switched it on, waved a hand in front of it. A witch's cackle, a ghostly moan, a wolf howling. The long, slow creak of a door, opening to some house of horrors. As she held her own front door open, her heart began to pound.

"Hello?" she called. Usually, if her mother wasn't working the late shift, she would call back from the kitchen, where she was making dinner, or from the basement where she might be folding towels. But no one answered.

She stepped inside and closed the door behind her, the muffled electronic sound of a mummy or a zombie or some other undead thing lowing from the plastic skull. The door latch clicked and it felt permanent, like she was being locked inside. Rather than kicking off her shoes, as she had done every day without a thought, she kept them on.

"I'm home!" she yelled. But there was only silence.

She walked upstairs, her sneakers sinking in the yellow shag carpet.

At the top of the stairs, she could see into the kitchen. There was something in a pot on the stove, and she could tell it was burning.

"Mom?" she called. Silence, still.

She went to the stove. A pot of tomato soup was boiling, and the viscous red stuff had burned to the edges. In a skillet were two grilled cheese sandwiches, burnt to black. She turned the burners off.

"Mom? Hello?"

She walked down the hallway and checked the bedrooms, but they were empty. Her pulse slammed around in her chest. She walked back down the hall and paused at the top of the stairs. The house was a split-level—the kind built in the sixties, ubiquitous in the neighborhood—with a single finished floor and a short row of stairs leading to the basement. There, a sprawling maze of dark, unfinished rooms, exposed beams and concrete, and one in-progress wall of wood paneling that would never be completed. Over time it would warp at the edges and peel away, bowing out into the room like some kind of suburban funhouse.

She squinted into the dark then walked downstairs, one slow step at a time.

Outside, the last shreds of daylight were fading. Soon it would be night, and the neighborhood kids would spill shrieking into the streets. The basement was black. She pulled the chain from a bare bulb on the ceiling and light flooded the room. She peered between the beams into dark corners, the light glaring off the boards in a way that made the whole room seem skeletal. She was terrified of the basement. There were so many shadows.

She walked slowly to the laundry room. The washer and dryer were silent. There was a bathroom in the basement, really just a toilet and a sink behind a thin plywood door. The door was closed. Sam knocked.

"Mom?" she said, pressing her ear to the door. "Are you in there?"

Nothing. She knocked again.

"Mom?"

She put her hand on the doorknob, and heard a sound behind

the door. It was muffled and low. A groan, ghostly, like something from the skull on the front door.

She turned the knob. It stuck, as it always did, the plywood warped from the humidity of the basement. She pushed hard, and still the door didn't budge. She stepped back, then threw the weight of her body into it, shoulder first. The door burst open.

Her mother was there, on the floor, her body curled around the toilet, motionless. Sam was sure her mother was dead. She knelt beside her, put a hand on her shoulder.

"Mom?" she said, shaking her. "Mom, are you okay?"

Her mother groaned. That low sound again, one Sam had never heard her mother make. Almost a growl, almost inhuman. Sam rolled her mother over. She already had her face paint on. She was going as a witch that year, and the thick green paint was clumped on her skin, collecting at the corners of her mouth in crusts. Her purple eye shadow was caked, mascara running down her cheeks in dried rivers. Sam jumped back.

"Mom," she said, "what's wrong?"

Her mother blinked, then slowly sat up, a zombie rising from the dead. Sam stepped farther back, terrified.

"Nothing," her mother said, and it was a voice Sam didn't know. Slow and garbled, a monster's voice. A voice like the girl in *The Exorcist*, terrible and possessed. A voice she would come to know well.

"What happened?" Sam said, crouching closer, touching her mother's arm.

"Nothing," she said again, licking her lips. They were cracked and dry, and her tongue ran slowly along the splits. "I'm fine." Her voice sounded like a tape played at half-speed. Sam helped her to her feet.

"Are you sick?" she asked.

"Yes," her mother said, steadying herself with a hand on the sink.

"Okay, let's get you to bed," Sam said. It was something her mother had said to her hundreds of times.

"No," her mother said, swatting at Sam in slow motion. The word came out like a shiver, a tremor that Sam watched run through her mother's whole body. Sam shivered along with it, suddenly cold.

"We have to get ready," her mother said, the words slurred and slow.

Sam swallowed. She smelled something, sick and sweet, wend its way out of her mother's mouth. Sam covered her nose, afraid she might catch whatever sickness her mother had.

Her mother stood with her hands on the sink. Then she stumbled out of the bathroom, Sam following close behind. She started up the stairs but tripped, stumbled, nearly fell. Sam grabbed her arm, helped her up the stairs. Outside, it was dark, and soon the doorbell would start ringing. The porch light was off, the jack-o'-lanterns they'd carved still unlit. She thought about flipping the light on, but she kept it off.

"Maybe you should lie down?" Sam asked. Her mother stood at the black mouth of the hallway and nodded. Sam held her by the arm, walked her down the long black corridor to her bedroom. She pulled the covers back and helped her mother into bed. Then she tucked her in and brought her a plastic cup of water from the bathroom sink.

"Drink this," she said, holding the cup to her mother's lips. Her mother swatted it away. Sam put the cup on the nightstand, and pulled the covers up to her mother's chin, like her mother had done for Sam every night since she could remember. Sam could hear the first trick-or-treaters now, their voices rising in the dark streets.

Her mother closed her eyes, her mouth open. The smell came again, and Sam held her breath. She waited there, no idea what to do. She could call her father at work, but he was probably on his way home already. She closed the bedroom door and stood in the hall, paralyzed with fear. She had always been terrified of the hallway, certain it was haunted. Her whole childhood, it would seem to Sam later, had been one long ghost story. But standing there in the dark, the fear took on a new shape. It was more real, more tangible, than it had ever been. It coiled around her.

She walked to the kitchen, flipped on the lights. She grabbed one of the burnt grilled cheese sandwiches from the skillet and put it on a paper plate. She poured herself a bowl of cold tomato soup. The shrieks of the children outside grew louder, a chorus of ghoulish joy.

She looked at the clock. Her dad should have been home by now. She wondered if she should call the doctor but thought better of it. Something about it all felt wrong. She knew, somehow, that whatever was happening, she couldn't tell anyone. She knew it was a secret. And it was one she would keep, long after she would learn the truth about what was wrong, long after she had a name for the sickness. All of it a secret she would keep for the rest of her life.

There were bags of candy on the counter, still unopened. She decided she wouldn't go trick-or-treating. She was too old for it anyway. Someone had to stay, give candy to the kids. She would put on her costume—she was going as a werewolf this year—but it would be the last time. She would stand in the bathroom mirror alone and stick fake fur to her skin. She'd peel adhesive off the pieces she'd cut and press patches of it to her chest, to the tops of her hands, to the space between her first two knuckles. She would slide a finger over the fur, petting it, smoothing it into place, liking the feel of it. She would put a set of plastic fangs in her mouth, press black stick-on claws to her fingernails. Finally, she would put on her mask. She'd look at herself in the mirror, at the mask she'd worked so hard to make, her eyes dark behind hand-cut holes. Though her hands trembled, she would feel safer inside the mask, in the fur that covered her body like a coat. She'd summon something brave inside her then, curl her clawed fingers, bare her teeth in the mirror and growl.

Soon, she would open the front door. The plastic skull would warble its ghost moans and monster howls, and she would smile at the kids and compliment their costumes, acting frightened of their teeth and claws, the dark empty sockets of their eyes. She would be glad for her own mask, so the kids couldn't see the actual fear she was wearing, how her face had gone pale with it. She would smile instead, a mask she'd learn to wear for good, and hand out candy, wish the kids a happy Halloween. When her friends came over, begging her to come out, she would tell them she couldn't this year, her parents were working. She would learn, that night, how to lie.

And soon there would be more nights like these—nights made of terror, when Sam would walk to the front door of her house and freeze, her body trembling at the threshold, never knowing what was waiting. And there would come a night when Sam, at sixteen, would come home to find her mother kneeling on her bedroom floor, the barrel of a gun in her mouth; when Sam would wrestle it from her mother's hands, then hold it in her own, and point it at her mother's head; when she would say, *Is this what you want?* and her mother would say, *Yes, please do it;* and Sam would toss the gun to the ground and say, *Do it yourself,* and walk back down the dark hallway, which no longer scared her, and wait to hear a shot—but would hear only silence, a sound of both relief and regret. When her once-happy family would fall into a well of that silence, would drown together in it and never resurface. When her house would become haunted by the people still alive inside it. When Sam would stop coming home, when she would stay out late and drink with boys she barely knew, get drunk enough to let them do whatever they wanted to her, and feel nothing at all. When she would drive home drunk and wake up in her bed remembering nothing. When she, like her mother, would change. When she would learn how to destroy herself. When she would start to disappear. When she would become, at last, the very thing that haunted her.

But before all that—on that first night, on the last Halloween, as the screams of childhood monsters rose up from dark suburban streets—Sam, still a girl, and not yet the thing she would become, sat at the kitchen table and waited, and ate her dinner alone.

Thirty-Six

◇◇◇◇◇◇◇◇◇◇

A SUMMER EVENING, sometime in late June. Long ago she lost track of the days, the weeks. Time has wrought and wrung itself out, spread thin and circular and endless like some kind of void, swirling and dark, even on a cloudless day like this one, even at this golden hour, the sun holding on just enough to cast a glow—the kind that makes the forest appear to be on fire.

She doesn't know how long she's been here, in these far northern woods. There are moments like this one, there are whole stretches of time, when she wonders if she's ever been anywhere else. When she is certain she's been here forever.

She sits on the porch, the sun dipping below the trees, the pink-yellow light turning blue. Around her, the nightjars sing and trill. She hears the music and hums along.

She is waiting for something to come. She is certain it's coming. Usually, at this time of day, near dusk, the crickets and peepers would start chirping, filling the forest with sound. But tonight, they are silent. The doe would come soon too, showing up at the trough for her dinner, but she will not come tonight. It's something else that comes, that keeps the other animals away. A man, perhaps, the strange one who showed up at her door, who's been here more than once. Perhaps a group of men, the ones from the hardware store or the bar, who had craned their necks as she passed, who had uttered violent words under beer-soaked breath. The men who will, if given the chance, always choose to hurt her.

Or maybe it's not a man at all. Maybe it's something else. Maybe an animal, some beast of the woods, some monster. Whatever gutted the deer, its feet light upon the earth as it slinks through the trees and edges closer, teeth sharp and jaws open, ready to kill.

She doesn't know what's coming. Only that it will be here soon.

Around her, night is falling. The song of the woods has gone silent. Even the whip-poor-will, whose lonesome evening call she's learned by heart, has quieted. There is only that soft whisper in the trees, in the branches, bending and bowing but never breaking, kept fast and firm by the bodies that hold them.

And here, on this porch, is a woman, or at least what used to be. Now, perhaps, she is something else. Something these woods have made from her flesh, the shell of something once named *woman* shed like snakeskin on the ground beneath her. Perhaps what has always existed beneath that shell of skin: the bones and flesh of something new. And in this new form—or perhaps this form that always was, beneath the body she wore, the costume she put on—she is neither woman nor man, neither human nor animal. She is something in between. She is, perhaps, all of these things at once.

Whatever she is, she feels life beating inside her skin, far below the dead cells and tissue, in her organs, wending along the rivers of her blood. It is a new feeling, a new life. She is alone, and alert, and she is held in a kind of dream, and she is more awake than she has ever been.

In one hand she holds a bottle. In the other, a gun. Both objects rest on bare thighs, parts of her she no longer recognizes but knows just the same. No longer soft and wide, spread across the surface of a chair, but narrow and hard, covered in a coat of hair. Her whole body a strange new shape. Hard in places it once was soft, straight where once was curve. New muscles have bloomed—small mountains of shoulder, new ropes in her neck, the sharp slant of calf, veins running up forearms in bulging blue rivers—their ridges rippling. Even her hands, which have always been strong, are stronger now, hair on knuckles where the skin was once smooth. These hands are callused and capable, tools built not just for work but more—something primeval, animal, bordering on the edge of violence and care. Hands that could both protect and kill.

It is a body both foreign and familiar. In it, she is still and silent and solid as the trees, the form she was always meant to be. In it she is powerful—like she was when she was a child, invincible in her skin. In this body, she is home. In this body, at last, she is alive.

She sits on the porch, new body poised. Beneath bare feet, her toes sink into the boards. The rot is back. It's spreading, she knows, through the wood. Soon the whole deck will be sick. The rot will work its way into the house; the walls and the floors will fester with death. But she will no longer try to fix it. She has more important work to do, in the time she has left.

And then, ear twitching, she hears them: footsteps, on the road, in the woods, all around her. A body or bodies approaching. She hears breath, steady and deep. Man or beast, she does not know, but she is certain it's something that hunts her. She has heard such things before, on evenings such as this, the summer sun dipping low, darkness falling. She has known this shift of night, this disturbance of silence. She has known this breath, these footfalls on leaves. She has sat like this before, still and silent and waiting.

But this time, she is not afraid. This time, she is ready. This time, she will not falter or flinch. This time, she will not run. This time, she will do something she has never done before—she will stay and fight. This time, she is certain, she will survive.

In the morning, she wakes. The sun is high and the birds are singing, the darkness of night burned away. She is no longer on the porch, but somewhere deep within the woods. She sits up and her body is a bright bolt of pain. Her head spins, the trees around her tilting like a theme-park ride. She puts her hands on the ground to steady herself. She looks down at those hands. Sees what looks like dirt beneath her fingernails. She looks closer, brings one hand to her face. Without thinking, she presses two fingers to her lips, then puts them in her mouth. Blood.

In an instant, a flash of memory. A dark night, a long time ago. A stairwell, a basement. A green couch, a concrete floor, a man standing above her in the dark. Holding her down, his weight against her body. And her fingernails clawing at skin, digging into his face and neck. Drawing blood, bright-red lines on flesh. And running, and waking, somewhere deep in the woods. Not these woods; somewhere else. And walking home, at dawn, body aching. Dirt on knees, bruises on thighs. Blood dried brown beneath fingernails.

And then, as quickly as it comes, the memory is gone. The

black curtain of her brain has fallen again. And she is here, in these woods, and it is morning. And then she sees something else glinting on the ground. The gun, its silver barrel gleaming in the morning light. There is no one else around her—no trace of animal or man, no body on the ground beside her, where she expects it to be, where some shadow of memory recalls something approaching, something running, shots ringing out in the night. There is nothing here but the birds and the trees, this body of a thing once called woman.

She picks up the gun. It is cold and damp with dew. She clicks open the chamber, finds it is empty.

Thirty-Seven

◇◇◇◇◇◇◇◇◇◇◇◇

"IT'S A FAMILY disease," Lou-Ann said.

Sam looked out the window. She didn't want to talk about it. They were in Lou-Ann's car, and the sun was high and bright. Sam had called Lou-Ann that morning, after she woke up in the woods, a gun at her side, no memory of how she got there. She hadn't been drinking, she told Lou-Ann on the phone, she was certain she hadn't. But she no longer knew what was real or a dream, what was truth or a lie. The lines had all gone blurry, indistinct and shifting and dissolving, like the edge of the woods at dusk, as night falls, when the light plays its best tricks.

She had walked back to the cabin, barefoot. When she stepped into the clearing, she heard the glass before she felt it, slicing into the soft arch of her foot. She plucked the shard of brown glass from her skin and watched the blood bloom, though she felt no pain. She walked to the porch and up the stairs. All the boards were solid, no rot to be found. But she remembered the wood beneath her feet, the black fingers of disease, reaching. She could still feel the softness and give, like any second she might fall through.

"I think I need to get out of the house," she had told Lou-Ann on the phone. Lou-Ann asked Sam if she was in danger, and Sam said no, but the truth was that she wasn't so sure.

"Do you want to go to a meeting?" Lou-Ann had asked.

"No," Sam said. "I just don't want to be alone."

"Copy that," Lou-Ann said. "Breakfast then. I'll pick you up soon."

"Thanks," Sam said. She had ended the call but kept the phone in her hand. She'd thought about calling Stephen, but didn't know how to explain what had happened. What was happening. The last thing she remembered was Gina—her hips, her mouth, their bodies pressed together. She'd reached behind her, under her shirt, felt the scrapes from the wall on her back.

She put a Band-Aid on her foot and crawled into bed but sat up, afraid to lie down, dead tired but afraid to sleep. Afraid of what might come in her dreams. The gun lay on her bedside table, its chamber empty. She got up, took two aspirin, made a pot of coffee, and waited.

When Lou-Ann came to the door, Sam was in the kitchen, on her third cup and wearing the clothes she'd had on the day before. Her hands were shaking.

"You look like hell," Lou-Ann said, pulling the screen door open.

"Feel like it too," Sam said. "Just need some food. I'll be okay." And Lou-Ann had put her arm around Sam and walked her to the car.

Now they drove, with the windows down, Sam's head throbbing and stomach sour.

"So," Lou-Ann said, "how long's it been in yours?"

"What?"

"The drink. How many generations?"

A familiar tightness curled around Sam's body, her shoulders hunched and hands clenched. She began to build a defense in her head, the words like muscle memory—*I wasn't drinking, I swear. Just a little sick today.* All the things she'd always said, so many times before, as she curled up on the cold tile of a bathroom floor, as she stirred Pedialyte into her water at work. But this time, something made her stop. The snake of the lie that had coiled itself around her neck for so long at last released its grip. She sighed.

"I don't know," she said at last. "At least two. Three, I guess, if you count me."

"We count you," Lou-Ann said. She shifted the Subaru into fourth, gravel crunching beneath the tires as they passed through the tunnel of trees. "Me, it was there as long as I remember. My parents, grandparents. Grew up hearing stories about my great-grandfather, who saw ghosts in whiskey, thought he saw God. Reason they call them spirits, he used to say. Got converted by some Jesus cult up here, who promised God would bring rain, make the crops grow. He was a farmer back then, like so many of our folks, after the Dawes Act."

Sam thought of her own grandparents, and the great-grandparents she didn't know, the farmers with too many children and never enough food, especially in seasons of drought. It was a life Sam couldn't imagine. She considered how much worse Lou-Ann's family must have had it.

"The big trick of it," Lou-Ann said, "was that you can't grow shit up here. Government talked a big game about us owning land, having our own crops. But the climate's too cold, soil's no good. The trees block out the sun. Nothing thrives. So the family starved, we lost some folks."

Lou-Ann paused, eyes narrowed at the road. "But my great-grandfather—well, he kept on working the land, kept on believing. Said it was part of God's plan. Heard it straight from God's throat, he swore, but only when he was shit-faced. He died like my father—dirt poor and drunk, his organs shot to hell."

"God," Sam said.

"Exactly," Lou-Ann said. *"God."*

They pulled out of the woods and onto the highway, and she threw the car into fifth. Sam felt the gravel-road vibrations in her teeth subside as they sailed along the blacktop, leaving a pleasant humming in her jaw. The windows down, the cool morning air rushing in. It felt good, and woke Sam up some, quelled the waves of nausea that pitched in her guts. She still couldn't remember drinking the night before, but the feeling of a hangover was unmistakable.

"What happened after your great-grandfather died?" Sam asked.

"They sold the land to some lumber company. Then my grandfather went to work for them. He was a drunk too, of course. But I remember the stories he used to tell, about cutting down trees. Said there was wisdom in trees. That they feel pain. I never forgot that. Said he'd drive the saw into their trunks and, by God, he could hear them screaming as they fell."

"Jesus," Sam said.

Lou-Ann glanced sideways at Sam with a half smile. "Can't help but notice you keep invoking the holy."

"Old habits die hard," Sam said.

"Ain't that the truth," Lou-Ann said. They drove a while in

silence, listening to the tires on the road, the wind in the trees. Sam thought about the folktales she'd heard growing up, about Paul Bunyan and Babe the Blue Ox. She thought about the lumberjack festivals she went to as a kid, watching men in Buffalo check flannel shirts cut down trees, the sawed-off disk of a pine stump she kept on her bookshelf, signed by one of the jacks in Sharpie. She had counted its rings, the old trick that told a tree's age, but had never considered that it might have felt pain. And those men had been heroes, not part of an industry that displaced people and wiped out old-growth forest, endangering trees like the hemlock.

"My grandmother," Sam said, her eyes closed, wincing against the headache. "She talked to trees too. Same as my mother. Said trees and animals had souls purer than any human's. Both of them were happier when they were outside, walking in the trees or working in their gardens, talking to the birds, no one else around."

Lou-Ann nodded, keeping her eyes on the road.

"Sometimes I think I'm a lot like them," Sam said. "In more ways than I'd like to admit."

"It's a funny thing, inheritance," Lou-Ann said. "It's easy to focus on the bad, but of course we get the good too. For a long time, I rejected the idea that things are passed down, or that they have to be. I was stubborn. Told myself I was my own person. That I could make my own decisions, battle my own demons. Took me a long time to realize that those demons were written in my blood, just like everything else. That they were born in me. And as much as I tried, I couldn't cast them out on my own."

Sam rested her elbow on the window, held her throbbing head in her hand.

"Yeah," she said, "I have trouble with that too."

"Turns out," Lou-Ann said, "when you inherit generations of other shit, when you're never sure what's coming or what might be taken away…well. Booze is a great way to smooth out the edges. Quiet that fear, kill the pain. Even when it's exactly what killed all them who came before, one way or another."

Sam nodded.

"Problem is, the demons are still there," Lou-Ann continued. "You carry them around with you your whole life and can never cast them out entirely."

She drummed her fingers on the wheel. "But you can learn to fight the fuckers."

Sam laughed. "I thought fighting was the opposite of what they tell you at the meetings. Thought you had to give yourself up to them."

"Well sure, in a sense," Lou-Ann said. "But there's power in letting go."

Sam thought about how exhausted she always felt, like every day, every waking moment, was a struggle. That to drink was to let go—of the tension, the anxiety, the despair. Of the way the world seemed to sit on her shoulders and neck, weighing her down. The feeling of being so tightly wound she might shatter. That to surrender to the desire, and then to numbness, was the only time she ever felt truly calm, maybe even happy. Like what they always talked about in church: living in the light of God's love. The sublime.

Sometimes, in the Al-Anon meetings she went to in New York, she listened to this idea of giving yourself up to your higher power, an idea she always hated—not just because she no longer believed in God, but because she hated the idea of ceding control. She was in charge of her life, she thought, sitting on those metal folding chairs in musty basements, defiant, looking around the room at all the sad sacks, crying and talking about the same shit every week, thinking: *I'm not like you people. You people are weak. I am not weak.*

She felt the hum of the road in her body, in her teeth.

"Maybe surrender," Lou-Ann said at last, "is another kind of fight."

Back in New York, the first and only time Sam spoke at an Al-Anon meeting, when she opened her mouth all the words she'd never said aloud, all the secrets she'd kept, poured out of her. For those few minutes, she felt relief in breaking the silence. She cried in a way she never had before—hard, guttural, unable to finish her words. She never spoke at a meeting again.

That meeting was held at a YMCA on the Lower East Side, a part of the city in which she'd spent so many years drinking. Where she would duck into a small, dark club and see music for five bucks, drink rail whiskey and nod along to the band, letting the bass pound through her body along with the buzz. More often than not, she left those meetings and went directly to a bar. One night, she walked out into the busy Friday-night hum of Delancey, then turned down Ludlow and stopped into the Local, one of her favorite dives. She sat down at the sticky bar and ordered a whiskey. The bartender, a cute butch lesbian with shaggy hair and blue eyes and known for generous pours, slid the glass over to Sam and smiled. Sam drank, fast, and ordered another. As the bartender poured, Sam glanced down the bar. Sitting a few seats away was a woman from the meeting. Sam felt a brief bloom of shame work its way up her neck but was already too buzzed to care. When the second drink came, she made eye contact with the woman, smiled, and raised her glass. The woman did the same.

Back then, Sam believed drinking was her lot in life, her legacy. There was something romantic about it—the narrative of the cursed, the fuck-up who felt the pain of the world so sharply she needed something to staunch the wound. She wore that story around, a chip on her shoulder, some tragic mythology. In her sober months, things felt a little less fated. For a while, things made more sense. She welcomed the way the air felt in her lungs, cleaner. She slept a little better. She was grateful every day she didn't wake up hungover. But it was never easy. The desire was always there. She knew, somewhere beneath all those new clean feelings, it never really left her. It was in her blood, and it always won.

And sometimes, in the moment when she let it, she wondered if those people at the meetings had it all wrong. If alcohol itself was actually her higher power, her God: the thing that, like Lou-Ann's grandfather, like her own mother and grandmother, maybe, helped her access something beyond the limits of consciousness, that lurked in the dark and liminal places, beyond what could be seen in the light of day—something that lived only in the spirit world, maybe even something sublime. She'd known of people doing peyote in the mountains, drinking ayahuasca or eating magic mushrooms or tripping on acid, and unlocking some secret meaning of life, maybe even meeting God. She also knew, on some level, that this kind of thinking was a trap—the devil itself playing tricks. But sometimes, she couldn't help but believe it.

*   *   *

When they got to town, Sam and Lou-Ann went to the Big Bear diner. It was a place where ruddy old regulars who knew everyone in town sat on vinyl stools at the counter, drinking coffee and talking to the waitresses, a mix of younger and older women who might have spent their entire lives up here. Or maybe, like Sam, they had run away from something too.

They sat in a booth by the window, which looked out into the woods. The Formica table housed red and yellow bottles of ketchup and mustard, a glass silo of sugar, a metal basket of individual butters and jam. The waitress—an old woman, no more than five feet tall, whose body was bent into the shape of a question mark—took their order and brought the food fast, multiple plates balanced on her arms. Sam ordered two eggs, sunny-side up, with bacon and sausage, home fries and toast, a short stack of buttermilk pancakes. No tofu scrambles here, she'd thought as she held the laminated menu, no tempeh bacon or quinoa bowls. She couldn't remember the last time she'd had real bacon. She grabbed the syrup pitcher and poured. Growing up, her family had bought only Mrs. Butterworth's, but this was the real stuff—golden brown, the color of bourbon, tapped from local trees. She drenched the pancakes, then shoveled huge dripping forkfuls into her mouth. She drank two glasses of orange juice, and the waitress kept the coffee coming.

"So," Lou-Ann said, taking a sip of her coffee, "how you doing?"

Sam shrugged and sopped up some yolk with a triangle of toast. She felt like she hadn't eaten in months, like she could eat forever and never get full. She felt a string of yolk dribble down her chin.

"I'm not sure," she said, not looking up from her plate. She wiped her chin with the back of her hand. "I guess I scared myself a little."

"Been there," Lou-Ann said. "That's how I found my first meeting up here." She watched Sam eat, with a look of either amusement or horror, maybe a little of both, like watching a child or a dog eat. Then she took a respectable human-sized bite of her own breakfast.

"Honestly I'm surprised they even have meetings up here," Sam said, her mouth full.

"Yeah," Lou-Ann said with a laugh, "attendance is slim. Just a few regulars, others come and go. I'd wager most everyone up here's got a problem, but only a few of 'em know it."

Sam huffed out a laugh, then shoved a last massive bite of pancake into her mouth.

"That seems right," she said as she chewed. She grabbed a packet of butter and a packet of grape jelly and spread them over her last piece of toast.

"But those folks who show up," Lou-Ann said, "they keep me going some days." She set down her fork, and Sam wondered not for the first time how people could do that: approach food, or booze, with such restraint when it was placed in front of them, rather than consuming as much as possible, all at once. Lou-Ann wrapped both hands around her mug. "It's good to have people here. Gets quiet. And quiet can be our best friend and our worst enemy at once."

Sam nodded. She swallowed hard, chased it with coffee.

"Can I tell you something?" Sam said.

"Of course," Lou-Ann said. "You can tell me anything."

"I've—" she started, trying at first to find the right words, then deciding to say it as plainly as she could. She exhaled. "I've been seeing things. Weird things. And I feel like something's been happening to me. Some kind of change. Like—a shifting."

Lou-Ann looked at Sam and nodded, prompting her to continue.

"I've been talking to this deer," Sam said. "A doe. She comes to the feeder at dawn and dusk. She talks to me, and I talk back."

Lou-Ann nodded again.

"And my body," Sam said, the words pouring out of her now in a rush. "It's changing too. It's like I'm turning into something else. I can see the physical changes, but it goes deeper than that. I can actually *feel* it, inside me—like something is opening up, or making its way out. I don't know. But I keep waking up in the woods, and I can't remember how I got there. And at first I thought I was just blacking out. I felt hungover afterward. But now, when it happens, I feel different somehow. Like, more awake. More alive inside myself."

"What else do you feel?" Lou-Ann asked.

"Like, everything all at once, and it's all so much sharper. The light, the sound. And sometimes I could swear I'm being followed, but other times it's like I'm chasing something. And I have no idea if any of this is real or a dream. But it feels so real."

She paused, tapped a finger on the lip of her cup.

"Also," she said, "I don't even know how to say it. There's this feeling like—return. Like this has all happened before. Like I'm coming home. This is all totally insane, right?"

"Maybe." Lou-Ann shrugged. "Maybe not." She tapped her own empty cup, spun it slowly on the table. "What do you think is happening?"

Sam shook her head. "I have no idea," she said. But as she said it, she looked out the window and into the trees. A thought began to emerge in her mind. A story, or at least a few threads of it. She grasped at the threads, but they were slippery like silk. She pulled up nothing.

"What is it?" Lou-Ann asked.

"I don't know," Sam said. She closed her eyes, reached again for the threads. They fluttered in the dark, and she grabbed at them. This time, she took hold of something.

"There was a story," she said. "That my grandmother told me."

Lou-Ann waited. Sam kept her eyes closed.

"It was some Celtic myth, I think. About a woman. Or—she was part woman, part deer." She closed her eyes tighter, strange images shimmering against the backs of her eyelids.

"It was a woman who could shapeshift into a doe."

She tried to remember more—the name of the woman, the details of the story—but when she peered into the cave of her memory, she saw something else instead. Some shadowy thing, hunched in a corner, peering back at her from the dark. She opened her eyes.

"Sounds a little like the Deer Woman," Lou-Ann said.

Sam blinked, nodded. She was pretty sure she'd read about the Deer Woman not long before, while paging through a book at the cabin one night. *Weird and Wild Northwoods,* or something like that. Her mother had collected books of legend and lore, the more eldritch and cryptid the better. That night, several whiskeys deep, Sam had pulled the book from the shelf and read while she drank, words swimming across the page. She'd found the Deer Woman there, alongside Sasquatch and the chupacabra, the hodag and the Beast of Bray Road. But the details were hazy. She told Lou-Ann this.

"Sounds about right," Lou-Ann said, rolling her eyes. "I know those books. White people love the Deer Woman. But it was a story my grandmother told me too. Just the kind of story you tell kids, I guess. But I always got the sense she believed it."

The waitress came over and refilled their coffees. Sam was starting to shake from the caffeine, but she didn't care. Despite having nearly cleared her plate, she was still somehow hungry. She felt the desire, vast and rapacious, to fill her body with everything—to eat the entire contents of the kitchen, the diner, the whole town. She drank more coffee to try to squelch it, the liquid scalding her tongue. She relished the burn.

"In any case," Lou-Ann said as the waitress shuffled away, "I think there's a lot of stories like that. About a woman who's more than she seems."

"I wish I could remember the rest of it," Sam said. "Or what it meant."

"Well, the Deer Woman anyway, she's a figure of fertility, the maternal. Love and protection and care. But she's also something else. Something dangerous, vengeful. A killer."

"A killer of what?" Sam asked.

"Men," Lou-Ann said simply. "And, in some versions of the story, drunks."

"Huh," Sam grunted, then shoved the last of the bacon into her mouth. She thought for a second of raw meat, of the pig who was killed to make it. But she chased the thought away.

"What's the moral of the story?" she asked, wiping grease from her lips.

"There is none," Lou-Ann said with a shrug. "I'm not one to deal in morality. It's just a story." She looked at the steam from her cup, watched it curl into the space between them. Then she looked back at Sam and sighed.

"But I guess if I had to tell you what it's about, I'd say it's a story about the different shapes a woman, and maybe a mother, can take. About the wilder things she can be. How she belongs more to the natural world than the one made by men—and if given the chance, she'll leave the world of men and return to the world in which she belongs."

Sam nodded, chewed the inside of her cheek until she tasted blood. It comingled with the bacon and made her think again of flesh.

Lou-Ann set down her mug, but kept her hands wrapped around it. She looked at Sam and held her gaze, as if searching for something. Then she spoke again.

"But there's another story," she said. "One I can't help but think of when I hear what you've been experiencing."

"Okay," Sam said, afraid of what was coming but sure somehow she needed to hear it.

Lou-Ann didn't speak right away. She looked out the window, where the evergreens stood tall around them. She sighed again, and it was a tired sound. Then, at last, she spoke.

"The windigo," she said. "Ever heard that one?"

Sam considered it. "Maybe," she said.

"Maybe in that book of yours," Lou-Ann said, one eyebrow raised. "White people love the windigo too. Even though they usually miss the point. Anyway, in some versions of the story, it's a creature of the woods, and of winter—a kind of monster. In others, it's a spirit that possesses you. Or a kind of psychosis, or both."

Sam nodded, thinking of the hodag—that mythical, murderous beast of the Northwoods, with horns and claws and fangs, which, according to the legend she grew up hearing, was a reincarnation of all the animals that had been killed before it.

"Whatever form it takes," Lou-Ann went on, "the windigo is driven by hunger. Hunger is this energy, this evil. This need to devour everything. It compels the creature, or the person it inhabits. And that creature, or that person, whatever it is—it eats."

"I'm not totally sure I want to know what it eats," Sam said, and Lou-Ann cracked a smile.

"You don't. But I'm telling you anyway." She looked out at the trees again before turning back toward Sam.

"The windigo eats people," she said. "It stalks its prey out there in the woods, and then it feeds. Or it causes the person it possesses to become a cannibal. Either way, its appetite is endless. Insatiable. Every time it eats, it grows. So it can never be filled."

Sam thought of Jeffrey Dahmer, who had stalked her state when she was young, kept body parts in his freezer and ate them. Maybe he was possessed by a windigo, she thought with a shudder. She thought again of the shadowy thing lurking in the recesses of her mind. She was suddenly very cold.

"In most interpretations," Lou-Ann continued, "it takes a mostly human form, but terrible. Emaciated, ash-gray skin, everything sunken. But in others, it has claws and fangs, eyes that glow in the dark. And, sometimes, antlers. It's like part animal, part man, part monster."

"Sounds cute," Sam said, attempting to dispel the feeling crawling around inside her.

"Super cute," Lou-Ann said. "Mostly, I think the more monstrous interpretations are white-people additions, to make the thing more frightening. As if a ravenous human woods cannibal possessed by unspeakable evil wasn't terrifying enough."

Sam laughed, but folded her arms around herself.

"Anyway," Lou-Ann said, "stories change over time. Some people tell this one to talk about colonialism, but it's older than that. Really I think it's about destruction of all kinds. Of people, of the land. But both stories, I think, are about the evils, and the appetites, of men."

It was then that the memory came to Sam. The spectral thing that had curled itself up in the shadows, pressed against the story her grandmother had told. Long buried there, it burst forth now from that dark corridor of her mind, into the light, fully formed.

An autumn day in her grandmother's kitchen. A clear sky and a chill in the air. The leaves on the trees bright yellow and red, the sun slanting in through the windows. And Sam, still small, sitting at the table, watching cardinals at the feeder and waiting on her own lunch. The heat was on, the radiators hissing. It was late fall, when things were still fighting to stay alive, before the first snow came.

There was a cast-iron skillet sizzling on the stove, meat frying in oil. It was venison, a deer her uncles had shot and processed—hung and skinned, butchered and deboned—and which her grandmother was now preparing. The same ritual their family repeated, and in no small part had survived on, for years.

When the meat was done, her grandmother sliced it up and slid it onto their plates. Next to Sam's plate, a glass of milk; next to her grandmother's, a beer. Sam looked at the fatty, wobbling thing on her plate. She'd eaten her fair share of venison but had never seen a cut of meat like this. It was thick and viscous, with a slimy sheen. She felt sick at the sight of it.

"It's the heart," her grandmother said, slicing her knife through the piece on her plate. "If you're going to kill an animal, you best use every part of it."

Her grandmother took a bite, chewed with her few remaining teeth.

"Go ahead," she said, her mouth full, nodding at Sam's plate.

Sam picked up her knife and made a small, slow cut, watching a clean line break open, revealing the slick pink meat inside. She stabbed a piece with her fork, lifted it to her lips, and chewed. She worked the soft, buttery meat between her teeth for what seemed like an eternity, prolonging the inevitable, trying not to gag. Then, at last, she swallowed.

"There you go," her grandmother said with a toothless grin, pointing her fork at Sam. "Now the deer's a part of you. It's a part of me, too."

Sam had been terrified. Certain the deer would come alive inside her. Every so often, in the days and weeks to follow, she would be convinced she could hear the deer heart beating, like that Edgar Allan Poe story she'd read in school. She'd press her hand to her chest and feel a pulse, not knowing whether it was hers or the deer's, wonder if maybe they'd become one and the same. And for a long time after that day, the thought of the organ sliding down her gullet and staying there, beating blood and alive inside her body, would stop her from eating any meat at all. Until, like most of her memories, it had faded away and was eventually gone.

But that day, Sam had looked at her grandmother, who believed in finishing the food that was given to you and leaving nothing behind. She held the knife in her small trembling hand, cut another piece of the heart, and ate until she cleaned her plate.

At the diner, Sam looked down at the empty plate in front of her, streaks of bacon fat and crusted yellow egg yolk the only remnants of her breakfast. Her stomach churned, and she choked back the desire to vomit. She looked up at Lou-Ann, who was looking at Sam.

"All these stories," Lou-Ann said. "One other thing they have in common, I think, is that they're about transformation. About becoming someone—or something—else. Or, maybe, something we've always been."

Sam tried to swallow, her throat dry. She reached for her water, took a long drink. Her skin was buzzing, her ears ringing. The diner was beginning to tilt around her. Lou-Ann kept her eyes on Sam.

"So," she said. "I suppose the question is, what is it you're becoming?"

Thirty-Eight

LATER THAT DAY, after Lou-Ann dropped her off, Sam walked to the lake. The woods were in full bloom now, the leaves of the hardwoods having turned from the yellow-green of spring to the Kelly green of summer. She stood on the dock and looked out at the water, watched the reflection of clouds ripple across the surface.

Out in the middle of the lake, two loons swam side by side. Every so often they'd call out, their songs strange and haunting and otherworldly, and Sam wondered what they were saying. When she was young, she and her mother would talk to the loons, call to them and see if they'd call back. When they did, Sam was convinced she had the ability, like her mom, and like her grandmother, to communicate with animals. They both talked to the birds, as they filled the feeders with suet and jam. They talked to stray cats, like those who gathered in packs and mewled at her grandmother's back door until she threw them scraps of meat, filled a small bowl with milk. Once, Sam spent a summer with her grandmother at the farm, and every day they fed the birds and cats together. Sam would try to pet the cats, their fast feral bodies covered in burrs, but they would always run away. They came right up to her grandmother, though. She'd sit down on the porch and the cats would rub against her legs. Sometimes the runts would even jump onto her lap, and she would pick the burrs off their backs.

"They gotta learn to trust you," her grandmother had said, as she scratched the neck of one particularly matted-looking tabby.

"Do you think they will?" Sam asked. She sat on the ledge of the porch, skinny legs swinging.

"Sure they will," her grandmother said. "I told your mom the same thing once, when she was a girl. And look at her now. She has whole conversations with the critters."

Sam had laughed, because it was true. As she got older, Sam always thought of herself as far more practical than her mother and grandmother, who believed in God but acted far more witchy than the standard Midwestern Catholic. She always said she was more like her dad, and her grandfather: those hard-working men who didn't allow themselves to think about sentimental things, who didn't have time for the supernatural. But she always held on to this thing about animals, and deep down suspected she had inherited the ability to speak to them too. It was silly, she knew, but she believed it anyway.

Sam took off her shoes and sat on the dock, put her feet in the water. It was cold and shallow, and she could see minnows swimming in packs. Ahead of her, near the shoreline in a tall patch of reeds, a fish jumped, the silver flash of its body breaking the surface in an arc, catching the sun before slipping below the water again, leaving a circle of ripples in its wake.

Sam rolled her pants to her knees and slipped into the water, felt the cold lick her shins. She dug her feet into the sandy floor, pebbles and rocks and reeds between her toes. She waded out until the water hit her knees, soaking her jeans. In the rainy season, the water would be waist-deep here. Soon there would be more thunderstorms. Then, soon enough, would come snow. Feet of it at a time, drifting up over the frozen lake, up the walls of the cabin, a blizzard blocking the roads for days. She would have to get more kerosene, more matches and lighters. She'd chop more wood to keep the fire lit. Maybe eventually she'd get a generator.

When Sam first arrived in the woods, she was afraid. Of storms, of power loss, of things she heard in the night and the images that ran through her head—of men and beasts and shadows in the trees, something breaking through her door. She didn't sleep much then, a slow crawl of terror working its way up her neck as she lay in bed, the covers pulled up to her chin.

Now, she slept well. Most nights, she wasn't afraid. She remembered the last time, waking up to the sound of footsteps in the woods. But since then, she had listened to the forest at night and heard in those footsteps not bloodthirsty bodies lurching toward her in the dark, but opossums and raccoons and deer, maybe even a black bear and her cubs. She heard the world of night all around her, and it felt like comfort. She let the choir sing her to sleep.

She walked back to shore, up the small rocky beach. She kept her shoes off and carried them as she walked back home. Above her, the trees bent inward, wrapped around her and protecting her from harm. As she walked, bare feet against the gravel, she wondered if she could ever go back to New York. The thought of it made her chest go tight. To live in the city again, in her corner of Brooklyn—where there were no trees, no grass, no quiet; where the only water was the East River and Newtown Creek, a superfund site that led to the sewage treatment plant; where the air in summer stank of hot garbage—now felt absurd. Why would she ever choose that over this? She'd been in the city so long she'd forgotten about this place—where the world breathed and flourished and thrived. Where its creatures weren't just surviving, but alive.

She stopped in the middle of the road.

"I can't go back," she said aloud. The words felt strange, but certain. She closed her eyes and listened to the trees. To the birds and the wind in the leaves. "This is where I belong."

She walked back to the cabin feeling lighter. When she climbed the porch stairs, she saw something hanging on the handle of the door. It was a small pouch, made from a large green maple leaf and tied closed with a few long blades of grass. She opened the pouch and peered inside. The scent of honeysuckle and lavender, something earthy too. A touch of ginger, maybe clove? It was tea, wild and dried. The smell reminded her of the kind her mother made for her when she was a kid, whenever she had an upset stomach.

A magic remedy, she called it. *An antidote. To cure the bad things inside you.*

She held the pouch in her hand, looked around her into the woods. She stood still and silent, waiting for a body to emerge. But no one came. She looked up into the trees, saw a cluster of crows perched together on the high branches of an oak. *A murder,* she thought. And she remembered something her mother once told her—that if you feed the crows, they'll leave you gifts. They brought her gifts all the time, her mother said. Little tokens of appreciation. When Sam was young, she believed this story, like she believed everything her mother said, like she believed in magic, maybe even God. But as she got older, she figured it was just one of her mother's superstitions, or maybe hallucinations.

No magic, just the stories of a disintegrating brain, of a reality that had become so twisted she believed them.

But there were always twigs and flowers and rocks on the windowsill in the kitchen, the gifts her mother said the crows had left her, an altar she kept to the wild. Sam kept altars like this too—little tokens she collected from wherever she'd gone, to keep her connected to the world.

She gripped the pouch in her fist. The wind blew lightly in the trees, sending the crows aloft, a great black mass rising up to the sky.

Thirty-Nine

◇◇◇◇◇◇◇◇◇◇

THERE WAS A message on her phone. It was Stephen. She didn't know how long it had been since they last spoke. She looked at the unread message, her finger hovering over the tiny trash can icon. Then she pressed play.

"Hey," his voice said, and it sounded far away. "Just checking in. I know you're busy, and I know you've got a lot on your mind. But I'm thinking of you, and I love you. And I guess I just wanted to say that."

There was a pause, a muffled sound in the background that might have been the cat, or the couple across the hall, who did a lot of fighting. The walls of their building were paper-thin, and the neighbors had certainly heard their fair share of Sam and Stephen's fights too. It was like some unspoken New York code, to pretend you couldn't hear all the things that went on behind shared walls. You kept each other's secrets.

"Call me back when you can," Stephen said. And for a second it felt like he was on the line with her, like they were talking, and everything would be fine. But she heard something else in the silence. An energy she'd come to recognize over the years, buzzing around, slamming back and forth like a pinball machine. A silence that meant he had more to say. He exhaled instead, breaking his own silence.

"I miss you," he said. And then the line was dead.

Sam stood in the kitchen with the phone in her hand. There was another missed call, another voice message. Gina. She hesitated, then pressed play.

"Well hey there," Gina said. "Just thought I'd call to say hi and tell you I had a great time the other day. Let's do it again sometime?"

Sam hung up before the message ended, her guts in her throat. It was a feeling that reminded her of chugging up a roller coaster, like when she'd gone to Six Flags as a kid, the rickety car making its slow crawl up the interminable arc of the American Eagle. She'd heard a rumor that a kid had died on the ride the previous summer—that his seatbelt had broken and he'd been launched from the car, gotten mangled in the beams. When the car stopped at the top of the ride, the wooden tracks creaking in the wind, she held the rail so tight her fingernails dug into her palms, making them bleed. She was suspended there, in time and terror. And as the car tipped over the edge, before it would speed straight down to the earth, she felt her brain lift itself out of her body. That was the first time she felt it: like her mind was escaping the confines of her flesh, of fear, and flying far away. She watched her body fall.

She watched her body the same way now, standing in the kitchen with the phone in her hand. But she wasn't there.

Over the years, Sam had fought the urge to leave. To stay in the room during an argument with Stephen, to not leave the apartment and slam the door and walk away. She fought to stay inside her body, to remain present in each moment as it passed. Most of all, she fought the desire to disappear the best way she knew how.

She thought of all the ways drinking had taken her away—how it turned down the dial until she eventually turned off completely. She thought of all the memories she'd lost. All the plans she'd canceled and the time she'd missed with friends. All the nights she'd spent on bathroom floors and all the days that followed, stripped away, curled up and shivering in bed, the question that played on repeat once again:

Why do I keep doing this to myself?

As if it was a choice. As if, when someone bought another round of shots, or refilled her glass of wine, or cracked open another beer and pressed it into her hand, she had the power to hear that question—*One more?*—and shake her head and smile, like so many other people seemed to do, and say, "I'm good," or "I'm okay," or, simply, "No."

The answer had always been yes.

For so long, Sam had told herself, *I'm not like them. It's not a problem. I'm not a victim. I'm not like them. I'm not like them. I'm not like them.*

Even when, at fourteen, she felt the first longing for obliteration—when she got drunk for the first time and knew it was a feeling she would seek for the rest of her life. Even before then, when she found her mother on the floor and knew, somehow, she would one day find herself there too. And even farther back still, when she was just kid, on the farm with her grandmother in summer, when she woke one night to a noise.

The farmhouse was a big, rambling place that was haunted, her grandmother said, by a woman who had hung herself in the attic. At night you could hear her in the walls. There were three floors, and Sam slept in her mother's old room, on the third floor—*the cold floor*, she and her cousins called it, for the drafts that came down from the attic. That night, she woke up to a sound, afraid it was the woman in the attic. She snuck down the stairwell, which they called the nightmare stairs, the entire corridor painted a dark and unsettling shade of blue. The stairs creaked beneath her feet. It was freezing. She stopped at the door on the landing, and slowly pushed it open. She heard the muffled sound of the TV and thought she might sneak in and curl up with her aunt, who liked to fall asleep on the couch with a horror movie on, like *Silver Bullet* or *The Lost Boys*. But Sam, who was eight that summer, parted the old pocket doors and saw her grandmother instead, splayed out on the recliner, an empty bottle of whiskey on the floor. Her mouth hung wide, hair a mess, legs bent at weird angles. If she hadn't been snoring, she might have been dead. What struck Sam most about the scene was not just the horror of it, but that her grandmother—the strongest woman Sam knew, who could pop the top of a jar better than any man, who could carry three kids in her arms like nothing—looked so small.

She pulled the door closed. She climbed back up the nightmare stairs and got into bed, pulled the covers over her head. She lay there, shivering, then leaned over the side of the bed and threw up. She knew she should clean it up but didn't; she just stayed there, paralyzed by a terror she didn't understand. She left the vomit to dry, and it worked its way into the carpet. She closed her eyes, tried to will the image of the vomit, of her grandmother, out of her head. *Maybe I can make it go away*, she thought. *Maybe it was a dream. Maybe it never happened at all.*

When she woke in the morning, she scrubbed the vomit with an old bath towel and threw it in the trash, but it left a stain in the carpet. Soon, the memory of the vomit, and of her grandmother, would be gone, and it wouldn't come back until now, thirty years later. But whenever she stayed with her grandmother, and slept in her mother's old room, she would jump over the stain in the carpet. When she got in and out of bed, she would leap over the spot. She thought of it that way too—*the spot*—though she didn't know what had caused it, or how long it had been there. She only knew she could never let her feet touch it. If she did, she was certain, something terrible would happen.

Forty

◇◇◇◇◇◇◇◇◇◇◇◇

THE PHONE RANG. Sam was outside, staining the deck. She felt good. She'd gotten up early, had gone for a run, had even made some eggs. Then she got to work. Using the new roller and brush, she painted—slowly and methodically, taking care to stain evenly, to get every crevice and crack. She ran the brush along the wood, watched it transform before her—brighter, more vibrant, alive. She finished the railing, and next up were the boards and the stairs. Soon the deck would look like new. She surveyed her work, pleased with the progress she'd finally made, the golden red of the stain gleaming in the sun.

She picked up the phone. It was Stephen. She had three bars of service, the connection clear.

"Hi," she said, genuinely happy to hear from him. She hadn't heard his voice in a while.

"Hey."

"How are you?" she said.

"I'm okay," he said. "You?"

"I'm good," she said. "Staining the deck."

"You're almost there," he said. "Nice work."

"Thanks," she said. She wanted to tell him about the project, how good she felt. She wanted to tell him all of it, let him know, in her way, that she was getting better. That she would be okay, and they would be too.

He cut her off before she was able to say any of it.

"Sam, we need to talk."

A fast wave of panic passed through her body. She could count on one hand the number of times Stephen had said those words in their decade together.

"Okay," she said.

"I've been doing a lot of thinking," Stephen started. "I mean, I've had a lot of time to do it. I've had nothing but time, turns out."

"Okay," she said again.

"And I just think—" he began, "I think I need something else."

"Something else?" Sam said. "What do you mean?" Her heart was pounding in her temples, in her chest, in her fingers. The sun was high and hot. She was thirsty.

"I need to see what else is out there," he said. "Who else is out there."

"Wait, what?" she said. "Are you leaving me?"

On the other end of the line, he sighed.

"I think so, yeah," he said.

Sam was silent. No words would come. She tried breathing, but the breath didn't come either. Her pulse—somewhere in her body, she could no longer place it—crashed around like a caged animal. The world was spinning, the trees seeming to grow larger and then shrink again, like the entire forest was a giant pair of lungs, breathing for her.

"Sam," he said, his voice a world away. "I'm sorry. But I've felt alone for a long time. I feel like, even before you left, you were gone."

"Stephen," she said, choking out his name. It was some other voice, not hers. "Please."

"I've already made up my mind, Sam. I think you should stay out there, and I'll stay here, and we'll go our separate ways."

A wave of heat crept up in her neck and snaked behind her eyes. That slow coiled thing working its way up her throat. He was leaving her, just like that. Just like she always knew he would. Just like everyone did.

"I'm sorry," Stephen said.

The creature coiled tighter, ready to burst from her throat. She knew, somewhere inside herself, that he was right. That she should let him go. But she would not be left. Not ever again.

"I see," she said, the creature hissing. She stood on her partially stained deck, gripped the phone tight, her other hand balled into a fist.

"Sam," he said, calmly. The angrier she got, the calmer he always became. She hated it. She remained silent, wielding it like a weapon. She was afraid of her own rage, afraid of what would happen if she opened her mouth, let it emerge from her body like the creature she knew it to be—violent, brutal, willing to destroy whatever summoned it.

This is how she always knew it would happen. He had decided he wanted something Sam could never be: a normal woman who wanted normal woman things, like marriage and kids, a normal little life. Sam had promised herself she would never be anyone's wife, would never be a mother. This line, she swore, would end with her. Whatever she'd inherited would get buried in the ground, burned down and scattered among the trees with her ashes. But he had told her many times that he chose her. That their life together was all that mattered. And she believed him. How stupid, she thought now, to ever believe anyone.

"I don't know what I want exactly," he said. "But I know I want a family. To feel like I'm part of a family. To be with someone who wants to be with me."

She wanted to punch a wall until her hand broke. Get in the truck and press the accelerator down hard, drive headlong into a tree, or the lake, feel the glass and metal smash around her, feel the pressure of the water pull her under. She hated him for making her feel this way, turning the anger inward, wanting to harm herself. She hated herself for believing him.

She'd been lied to her whole life. She'd lived in a family of liars, of perpetual deniers. She knew how to watch a lie unfold, fully formed, from your own lips, a creature with a life all its own. She knew how it felt to see something clear as day and then be told you didn't. To be told this so often you stopped trusting your instincts, started to wonder if maybe you imagined it, if it was all a dream. Maybe you were just losing your mind, like you always knew you would.

"I can't believe you're doing this," she said. The rage, which for a moment she had swallowed, had worked its way back up her throat. "But of course I can believe it. You're just like everyone else on the planet. Just like everyone else who lies, who leaves."

Stephen said nothing. Sam got mean when she fought. She hated this too. But cruelty, she knew, was a way to turn that inward-facing rage into a weapon. To destroy him instead of herself.

"You lied to me," she said.

"I didn't lie," he said. "I never lied. There was a time when you were all I needed. I meant that. But you put up all these walls. You stopped letting me in. And then you just left. No telling me how long you'd be gone, when you'd be back, if you were even coming back. And then you stopped calling. I was so worried, Sam, not even sure if you were alive or dead. You were just—gone."

He took a breath.

"But honestly, you've been gone a lot longer than that. You've been gone a long time. Sometimes it feels like you were never even here at all."

At a different time, in a different life, she would have kept fighting. But she knew he was right. The truth of it struck her like a tree cracking in half and falling in the woods. Sudden and massive, echoing around her. Her whole life had been made of leavings, and at some point, she had convinced herself she would never get attached. But the truth was that she held on. She clung and clawed onto whatever was in front of her, attempting to keep it. She had bound herself to Stephen—held on to him as tightly as she could, even as she slipped away.

For a moment neither of them said anything. She could fight. She could beg him to stay. She could struggle, as she always had, to wrangle and wrest the situation like a shot buck, mortally wounded but that wouldn't quite die, in an attempt to subdue it. But she wouldn't. She felt her body unfold from itself, felt the tightness in her chest dissolve. She wouldn't hold on. For perhaps the first time in her life, she would let go.

"Okay," she said. The word came out in a sigh, and the birds kept singing. The sun was still high and bright. Here in the woods, the world was not ending. Life was going on, and would continue to go on. She felt her body begin to dissolve into the forest. They were a single organism, she and the trees.

"Okay?" Stephen said.

"Okay," she said. And was there anything else to say? If there was, she didn't know it. He wanted to go, and she would let him. "Take good care of the Monster."

"But she's yours," he said. "Your familiar."

"She doesn't belong to me," she said. "Nothing is ever ours."

He said nothing. Had expected her to fight. But her body was empty of feeling. What had burned just seconds before—what had felt like it would burn her alive, torch the whole forest—was turning to something cold, something solid and unbreakable.

"Take care of yourself too," she said, and she was already miles away. There would be grief later, maybe, but for now there was nothing.

"I love you," he said.

"Okay," she said.

"Sam," Stephen said. Somewhere deep below the ice spreading fast across the lake of her, she wanted to tell him that she loved him too. She wanted him to tell her they would be together forever. That they would build the life they'd always talked about, the one they spent so many Sunday mornings in bed planning. She wanted nothing more, and she almost told him so.

Instead she said, "I should go."

And she hung up before he could say anything else.

In a tall Scotch pine, a squirrel scrambled up the trunk. In a birch, its white bark bright in the sun, a chickadee hopped from branch to branch. Somewhere, in the deeper woods, was the doe.

Sam closed her eyes, felt the sun on her skin. She was alone again, as she had always been and always would be. But all around her there was life—steady and constant and wild. And she was part of it. Maybe it was all she ever had.

When she turned to go inside, she saw it: a small pile of rocks and sticks, a few strips of birch bark, half a walnut husk. A sparkling piece of pink quartzite, a smooth black stone made round by water. A tiny piece of driftwood, a seed pod, a delicate white bird bone. The collection of treasures sat in a neat heap on the windowsill. She looked up into the trees, and perched upon a high branch of pine was a single crow. It was a gift, she knew. Maybe even an altar.

Forty-One

◇◇◇◇◇◇◇◇◇◇

IT WASN'T AS if she decided to go. It wasn't as if she had a choice. It was, instead, as if the choice had already been made for her—that it was written in the stars, or the trees, like fate or destiny or God's will, if you believed in that sort of thing. She grabbed her keys off the counter and left without locking the door. She got in the truck and drove, the late-afternoon sun in her eyes as she hit the highway, that golden light flickering between the trees. She pushed the truck up to sixty, then seventy, heard the old engine growl. The speed limit was fifty-five, but most folks drove slow. It was too risky, with the rutting packs of deer, and their young families, leaping into the road. She pressed the accelerator harder. It touched the floor. The windows were down and the radio was up, "Night Moves" by Bob Seger. One of her mother's favorites. After her mother disappeared, Sam went home to stay with her dad for a while, and she took a bunch of their vinyl. Her dad said he couldn't have it around anymore. So she took the Seger and Dylan and Jackson Browne, *Rumors* and *Harvest* and *Hotel California*, *Revolver* and *Rubber Soul.* She and Stephen played them on their stereo in Brooklyn, with the vintage speakers they'd found at a thrift shop. Back when they drank, they'd get a little tipsy, then lie on the floor and listen. Sometimes they'd dance, the windows open in the winter—the radiators hot and hissing—the curtains open. They could see inside their neighbors' apartments, knew the neighbors could see them too. But they didn't care. Their bodies buzzing, they swayed together on an old rug that had once been nice and had since been shredded by the cat, who watched them from her chair by the window.

Sam switched the radio off, heard only the sounds of the woods and the road and the wind.

When she got to the grocery store, she grabbed a bottle of bourbon and a six-pack. She planned to head straight home, where she could drink herself to oblivion, alone on the porch, maybe build a bonfire and take off all her clothes and howl at the moon or something. Rid herself of this feeling, of this world—of humans and love and heartbreak—and return to the world of the woods. And this, she told herself, would be the last time. The last binge, the final purge. A real cleansing, a new beginning.

But as she drove back toward the cabin, dusk drawing near, she saw the neon sign of the Beer Bar flickering on. Like a beacon, a lighthouse beam oscillating in the fog, and she a ship alone at sea; like the flashing red light of the fire tower in the state park not far from where she grew up, which she could see blinking from her bedroom window at night. A sound like her mother's voice at sunset in the summer, calling her home.

Once more, she thought. For old times' sake. A final, ritual goodbye.

She pulled into the lot, lined with Harleys. She didn't know what day it was, but it was without question happy hour. She parked the truck and left the windows down. She hooked her keys on her belt loop and stepped inside, the heads of the regulars swiveling. She grabbed a stool at the bar.

"What'll it be?" the bartender asked, slapping a coaster down. It was the same woman from the night with Gina, with blond hair, blue eyeliner, and a Motörhead shirt.

"Shot of whiskey and a beer," Sam said.

Just this one, she thought. Then she'd be on her way.

"You got it," the woman said. She poured a shot of rail whiskey and turned to the taps, tilted a pint glass and poured the golden ale. She set both glasses down in front of Sam, the pint carrying with it a perfect foamy head, an inch thick. Sam smiled.

"Good pour," she said.

"You know it," the bartender said, and gave her a wink before turning away.

Sam looked at the glasses before her, the amber of the whiskey and the gold of the beer. She thought of the devil on her shoulder, the monkey on her back, all the names this thing had been given, all the ways it stayed with her, all the times she'd fought it and all the times it had won. All the ways, despite how hard she tried to turn away, it always called her back.

She heard the music from the jukebox, the game on the TV, the voices and laughter that filled the room, the light sounds of people who didn't carry this burden. Or maybe they all did. Maybe, inside this place, they were all the same. All of them fated, all of them fucked.

She picked up the shot and took it all down. She took a drink of beer. It hit her fast. She wasn't sure when she'd eaten last, but the feeling was sudden and sharp, and then it was soft, spreading in a slow wave through her body. Her skin tingled, that blush of warmth in her neck.

"'Nother round?" the bartender called. Sam looked down at her beer glass, which was somehow nearly empty. At the other end of the bar, one of the Harley guys smiled at Sam, and Sam smiled back. Harley dudes were the nicest dudes. They got a bad rap, not least in small towns like the one she'd grown up in; got called sinners and Satanists as they roared through town, their engines growling, disturbing the nice, quiet people in their nice, quiet houses. They'd stop for lunch and a beer at the bar where Sam worked, and she knew even then, at seventeen, that the Harley guys were far kinder than the townies who called themselves Christians.

One more won't hurt, she thought.

"Please," Sam said, polishing off the beer. She thought of her bartending days in college, when she hung out in dive bars after her shifts, where she and the strangers she called her friends would drink and smoke and shoot pool and talk shit. In a way, it was where Sam had always felt most comfortable. She wondered what had happened to those guys, if they were still hanging out in those places, still drinking the same whiskey Cokes, talking the same shit.

The shot and beer appeared before her. She raised the smaller glass in the air, then brought it to her lips. She felt the fire in her throat, felt it fill up her chest. The best kind of burning. She thought then, as she often did when teetering on that fuzzy, dreamlike edge, of something she'd read once, long ago, that had lodged itself into the blank back rooms of her memory. This time, surging up out of nowhere, a word:

Pharmakon. She mouthed it to herself. A contronym: a word that possesses two opposite meanings. From the Greek: *both poison and remedy.*

She smiled. *Good brain,* she thought. *I haven't killed you yet.*

She took a drink. She was warm, and solidly buzzed now, and the pain of the day, of Stephen, of everything, was fading. Replacing it was want, the whisper of a voice inside her getting louder, clearing its throat. *To the hilt,* it said. *To oblivion.*

The bartender poured another shot. Sam raised it.

"To the men and women I've loved before," she said, and she said it loud, and she drank the shot down, her belly full of fire. Then she heard a voice. A sound, really, just a single word. She felt it before she heard it. Sensed the sneer of it snaking like smoke from some stranger's lips and down the length of the bar, curling into her ear.

Faggot.

It was a man's voice, deep and jagged, followed by a low rolling boil of laughter.

Sam had been called this word before, but the sound of it still shocked her. She looked down at the Harley guys at the other end of the bar, watching the baseball game. She looked around the room, saw groups of men hunched around tables, men playing darts and pool, men laughing and pouring back beers, handguns tucked into belts. It could have been any one of them. She'd heard it, clear as day, but no one else had seemed to. A tightness spread across her chest, a slow crawl at the base of her skull. But no—she would not be afraid. She turned back to the bartender and responded the best way she knew how.

"Keep 'em coming," she said, her jaw set tight. And the bartender poured.

She drank until the tightness went soft, until the room swam, until the sound of the voices around her swelled together as if underwater. She let her arms and legs go limp, let herself be swallowed, pulled beneath the waves. She felt herself sinking, slow and solid like a stone, the laughter and the lights and the jukebox pulling her down. She liked the pressure there, underneath. She liked the weight. She wanted it to press her to the sandy bottom of this lake, hold her there forever, never let her back up for air.

She staggered out of the bar and into the night. The air was crisp, the blue-black sky painted with stars. She looked up. She could see the white smear of the Milky Way, and all at once she remembered the constellations she had known as a kid. The ones she had forgotten, that her mother had taught her, that she had stopped seeing as an adult: Ursa Major, the bear, its body built from the Big Dipper. Canis Major, the wolf, guided by Sirius, the brightest star in the sky, dead center in his chest. And Orion, of course, his body building up and out of his belt. The hunter. In Sanskrit, she'd once read, and again the memory came in a flash, unlocking itself from the abyss of her brain: *mriga*— the deer.

The stars were swimming, spinning around her in fast circles of light. She put her hand on the porch railing and held on, trying to steady herself. She took a deep breath, and then another, the sweetness of whiskey and beer filling up her nose and lungs, along with the cool night air. Woodsmoke, maple, white pine, birch. She stepped carefully toward the stairs, fumbling with the keys on her belt loop, her fingers slow as her steps.

"Y'all right?" a man's voice said. Sam turned, saw the red cherry of a cigarette light up against the night. The shape of a man in a rocking chair in one corner of the porch, just beyond reach of the light. She remembered the voice of the man in the bar. She couldn't tell who it had been, couldn't tell if this was an enemy or friend. That was how it went with men.

"I'm okay," Sam said. "But I could use one of those."

She heard the chair creak, then watched the man lean forward slowly, the halo of yellow porch light illuminating his face. It was one of the Harley guys, big and bearded, the one who had smiled at her. He handed her a cigarette. She stepped toward him and took it, accepted a light from the flame of a Zippo, cupped in his big hands. This act, of giving someone a light—two heads leaned in close against the cold, taking the gift of flame from a stranger's hands—had always struck Sam as so intimate, an act of trust and kinship. How many sidewalks had she done this on, in Brooklyn and back home, with friends, with Stephen, with strangers, outside bars at night? How many other people in the world had shared this same small act?

"Thanks," she said, inhaling deep. She loved the way a cigarette hit after a night of drinking, the sharpness in her lungs, the way it somehow both clarified the night and made her head spin even more.

She stood in silence with the man, the two of them smoking, looking up at the stars. The sky was still spinning, but the smoke slowed it down. After a while the man rose slowly, the chair creaking under his weight. He put a hand, for a second, on Sam's shoulder.

"Take care of yourself out there," he said.

"I will," she said, relaxing a bit.

"I don't know you," he said, his hand still on her shoulder. "But I promise this will pass."

Sam smiled and looked at the man. His eyes were light, deep wrinkles at the corners. His beard was full and gray, but looked like it had once been red. She felt like she knew him.

"Thanks," she said.

He nodded, and turned, and walked back into the bar, a second or two of sound pouring out through the door—laughter, the clinking of ice, a song on the jukebox she used to know—and then silence again as the door closed. She finished her cigarette and stubbed it out, dropped it in a rusty coffee can that served as an ashtray. She stood on the porch of the bar a minute more, looking up at the stars, breathing in the night. And this is the last thing she would remember.

She wouldn't remember getting into the truck. She wouldn't remember trying three times to put the key in the ignition, stabbing at it stupidly until she got it. She wouldn't remember starting the engine, or turning the radio on, turning it up loud. She wouldn't remember the windows down, sitting in the lot with the engine running. She wouldn't remember opening the glove box, pulling out the gun. She wouldn't remember holding it in her hands, running her thumb over the pearl handle. She wouldn't remember thinking of her mother, on the bedroom floor, her lips around a barrel like this one. She wouldn't remember closing her eyes, clicking the safety off, and pressing the gun to her own lips. She wouldn't remember the steel, so cold on her tongue, or the way the night air seemed to rush in all at once through the windows, the porch light of the bar flickering. She wouldn't remember thinking, *Not this, not like this,* and taking the gun out of her mouth.

She wouldn't remember pulling out of the lot, the truck's tires kicking up gravel. She wouldn't remember the sound of the road, of the night, of the wind in the trees as they rushed past. She wouldn't remember closing one eye to see a single yellow line, and then closing them both, pressing the accelerator to the floor. She wouldn't remember keeping her eyes closed, long after she knew she should open them.

She wouldn't remember the deer—a doe—stepping into the road, just as she opened her eyes. She wouldn't remember swerving or slamming the brakes. She wouldn't remember the doe's body, slender and strong, as it hit the hood. She wouldn't remember the sickening thud, the shattering glass. She wouldn't remember the truck rolling over—once, twice, three times—spinning in slow motion, like a tape being slowed down, like a scene from a movie played back in half-time, like a dream. She wouldn't remember the crush of glass and metal, or the way the back window popped, as if blown out by a storm. She wouldn't remember the end—one slow, final crunch, as the truck hit a massive, towering pine.

She wouldn't remember the sound: high and sharp and loud, filling up the truck and her body and the whole night. A sound like screaming, whether human or animal or earth, whether it came from her or the deer or the wind or the tree as she struck it. She wouldn't remember the silence that followed, the night around her calm, the wind dying down, the crickets and peepers still, leaving only the ticking of an engine, her vision fading to black.

Forty-Two

◇◇◇◇◇◇◇◇◇◇

SHE WOKE UP deep in the woods, in the dark heart of the forest. Far away from the road, far away from humans. Somewhere safe. The trees dense on all sides, holding her. She could hear the woods breathing, one great body beating along with her own.

The night was a solid black wall, but somehow she could see. Shards of sky peeked in through the trees. But there were no stars, no moonlight. She was curled up on a bed of pine needles. She wore no clothes, but she wasn't cold—something inside her was humming, keeping her warm. She felt it in her chest and lungs, covering her like a blanket, holding her like the flames of a bonfire.

Beside her lay the doe, eyes closed, breathing. And next to the doe, curled up in a tiny red-brown ball of fuzz, a fawn.

"Thank God," Sam said aloud, though she hadn't thanked God, or believed in God, for a very long time, since she was a girl—or whatever it was she had been back then. But as she said it, she believed it.

The doe opened her eyes.

"Hello," she said, her voice low, her head tucked between her two front legs. It was how Sam's cat slept sometimes.

"I dreamed you were dead," Sam said. "I dreamed I killed you."

She sat up and looked at the doe, then the fawn. The last thing she remembered was leaving the bar, the night sky spinning. But now, somehow, she felt fine. Her head was clear, the world was still. It seemed all wrong, after how much she'd had to drink. She didn't even know how much. She had lost count, stopped keeping track, like she used to. Maybe she was still drunk. But how had she gotten here, so deep in the woods? She did a quick scan of her body, her bare limbs. No cuts, no scratches, no bruises, no blood. No sweet remnant of whiskey on her tongue, no stale reminder of cigarette smoke. No pain.

The doe lifted her head. Beside her, the fawn slept soundly, her small brown body rising and falling gently with each breath.

"I'm just fine," the doe said, her voice soft. "We're fine."

The doe was calmer than Sam had ever seen her—no longer held taut by the constant tension that kept her twitching, whatever sent her bounding fast into the woods.

"You should go now, though," the doe said. Her eyes were kind, full of something that reminded Sam of when she was young. "You have a lot to do."

"What do you mean?" Sam said. She searched for her shirt, her jeans, her boots, something, but found nothing. She ran a hand down one bare arm, both her legs. The hair on her body was thicker than it had ever been. She felt warm and safe beneath it.

"I mean it's time to go," the doe said.

"I don't understand," Sam said. "Go where?"

"I think you know," the doe said. Her eyes, bright and clear, seemed almost human.

"I don't—" Sam started.

"You do," the doe said. She got to her feet and stepped closer to Sam, then looked directly at her, holding her gaze. Then, for just a second, the doe pushed her forehead into Sam's chest. She was warm, and soft, and strong, and Sam's body filled with something she couldn't name. She put a hand on the doe's head, held her. Then the doe pulled away.

"It's been good to know you," she said.

"Maybe we'll see each other again?" Sam asked.

"Maybe," the doe said. "You never know. What I can tell you is that if you think of me, I'll be around. Just listen to the trees."

These last words were something Sam had heard before. Something she had forgotten.

The last time Sam saw her mother, they were standing at the edge of the woods—these woods—feeding the deer and the birds. Her mother was talking strangely by then, whispering to the trees, slurring words no one could understand. She'd go for walks and be gone for hours, sometimes entire days, and come back covered in mud. She stopped showering, let her hair grow long. She stopped brushing it too, and it became more like a mane, matted and wild, dotted with leaves and twigs that Sam would pluck out without her mother even noticing. It was as if her mother had gone feral. She said this to Stephen sometimes, trying to make a joke of it, but there was no better word. She seemed to be transforming, becoming some kind of creature, neither human nor animal, or maybe both. The woods seemed to be speaking to her, and she seemed to be speaking back. She seemed to reside in a world no one could see or hear but her.

But in that moment at the edge of the woods, her mother's words had been clear. She looked at Sam, and her eyes were clear too. Not cloudy or bloodshot, as they had perpetually become, but a startling shade of green. It had shocked Sam, to see her mother again. To see the woman she had once known and loved, who she had once dreamed of becoming, standing there in front of her, for the first time in years.

She smiled and took Sam's hand. And Sam had known then that she was leaving.

Now, Sam looked at the doe and the doe looked at her. Her eyes were bright.

"Wait," Sam said. "I never asked you your name."

"You know it," the doe said.

Sam shook her head. "I don't," she said. But the doe only smiled.

"You do," she said. Then she turned, and nudged her sleeping fawn awake. The fawn stood, stumbling on stick legs. They turned and walked together, deeper into the woods, the soft crunch of leaves beneath their feet. And then they were gone.

When she woke again she was in the ditch. The truck was smashed against a pine tree, its hood accordioned and the glass blown out. But it was upright, and she was somehow alive. She knew she shouldn't be. She hadn't been wearing a seatbelt. She sat up in the leaves, her head pounding, a sharp ache in her back and neck. She was fully clothed, but freezing in a T-shirt. She inspected her bare arms, which were covered in cuts. Blood had dried in a river down her shoulder, along the softest part of her forearm and wrist. She tried to stand up but fell, then crawled on her hands and knees toward the truck. Maybe it would still run. Maybe she could drive home.

The first threads of morning crept into the sky; the woods and the road were quiet. But there was no wind, no birdsong, no sound like water in the trees. Just stillness, strange and silent.

As she neared the truck, she saw it—a body, brown and soft and strong, somehow smaller than it had seemed before, splayed wide atop the hood. Her mouth was open, and Sam could see her teeth. Her fur was matted with blood. Her eyes were closed.

Sam approached slowly. She reached out a hand and touched the doe's front leg. When she didn't move, Sam laid her hand on the doe's back. She was still warm, but she wasn't breathing. Sam stood still, her hand on the doe's body, her own breath spilling in small clouds into cold air. She kept expecting the doe to wake up, hoping desperately she might open her eyes.

"I'm sorry," Sam said, her hand still resting on the doe's body. "I'm so sorry."

She let her arm fall to her side. A great wave of grief, sudden and massive, surged up inside her. It pitched like waves on the lake in a storm, made her knees buckle beneath her. She fell to the ground. She did not cry. What came out of her instead was a sound—deep and guttural, an animal sound, erupting not from her lungs, it seemed, but from her stomach—from somewhere deep within her. It was a lowing sound—a cry, a howl, a sound that racked her whole body as it was released, then carried up into the trees, shaking the branches above her, making the tops of the pines dance and bend. It was a wild sound—a sound like an exorcism, like all the horror movies she'd ever seen, when a priest attempted to summon some kind of demon from its host. The final scene, the last transformation, teetering on some threshold—when the thing within would be ejected from the body it inhabited or it would stay inside forever.

She let the sound pour out of her until she was empty, until the last echo was gone, and there was nothing left but silence.

At last she stood, her body covered in blood and dirt. She lifted the doe off the truck and carried her deep into the woods, then laid her down on the forest floor. She crouched above the doe's body as the wind returned to the trees, as the crickets and peepers began to sing again, as the choir of night came back to life, one last gasp before dawn, and birdsong, would replace it. She said a prayer.

Keep her safe, she said to the trees. And the trees heard her.

Hold her. Please don't let her go.

And the trees responded in song—the woods a chorus, the forest a hymn. They sang a dirge as she dug a grave with her hands, as she held the doe's soft body in her arms, then lowered her into the ground. As she filled the grave with dirt, covering the body with pine needles and leaves. They sang as she said goodbye.

She walked back through the woods until she found the road. She followed the tunnel of birch and pine as the sun began to rise, and walked the long miles toward home.

Forty-Three

◇◇◇◇◇◇◇◇◇◇◇◇

WHEN SAM REACHED the circle of trees, it seemed like some holy opening. The sky was pink and orange and bright. She walked up the gravel drive and took off her shirt. She peeled off her sports bra, unbuckled her belt, took off her jeans and underwear. She threw her clothes, stiff and sticky with beer and smoke and sweat and blood, into the fire pit. She walked to the garage, found the lighter and fluid. She grabbed a few logs from the woodpile and walked back to the pit, then stacked them like she'd learned when she was young, placing them atop the kindling—the leaves and sticks she tossed in every day as she worked in the yard. She doused it all with fluid. Then she set it on fire.

A massive ball of flame, bright and fast, engulfed her clothes and the sticks and the pile of dead leaves. It caught the dry wood fast and Sam stood close, let the flames lick her skin, singe the hair on her legs. *Burn the booze, burn the bar. Burn the truck and the doe. Burn it all to the ground.* She winced at the thought of the doe—how her legs were splayed across the hood, how her mouth had hung open. Where was her fawn? Had she been watching from the woods? Did she see it happen, watch her mother die painfully and brutally and alone, just as she would be left?

Sam shook the thought away, squeezed more lighter fluid from the bottle, watched the flames get higher and brighter. The birds were singing, somewhere far above the fire. She stepped closer.

There's a clean feeling that comes with being burned. She felt it not just in her skin but beneath it, in her bones and teeth. It felt like shaving her legs dry as a teenager, in the mornings before school, running her fingers along them afterward, bare and open, stinging and raw. The thick black hairs would sprout back up in a matter of hours, just like the ones on her father's jaw, a coarse dark layer where the skin had been smooth. Sam had hated this as a kid, and even as an adult. She'd battled her body for most of her life.

But now, she knew, she would stop fighting. The hair being burned now would grow back new, thicker and darker than ever before, and she would let it. She would watch it grow long on her legs, under her arms, sprouting between her eyebrows, on her jaw and neck and chest, above her upper lip. She would allow her body to take its natural shape, dark and wild like the forest, like the trees and the beasts within them. Shed her old life like a skin, like a winter coat, and see what new life might grow back.

She stood next to the fire, the heat filling her up. She felt it in her lungs, in her head, in her skin. She wanted to swallow it, to be swallowed. She thought of something she'd once seen in the Arizona desert, where people threw pictures of those they'd lost, objects belonging to the dead, into a great metal urn, which was hoisted onto a stage by a crane, then set ablaze. People jumped and danced and cheered, watching the memories of their friends, lovers, and families go up in flames, dancing while they burned. She breathed in the smoke. She breathed in the flames.

Let it all burn, she said to the trees. *Make me new.*

Forty-Four

"HELLO?" THE VOICE on the line was low, still half asleep.

Sam glanced at the clock on the stove. It was only 6 a.m. After the fire died, when her clothes were burned to ash and her whole body was raw and red, she had hunted around in the yard and eventually found her phone. It was damp with dew, the screen shattered into a spider web. For a moment she was afraid it wouldn't turn on. But it had, its battery in the red, and she stood in the yard in the early-morning sun, her bare skin pulsing with the ghost of the fire, grateful to see one lone bar of signal on the screen.

"Hi," she said. "I'm really sorry to be calling so early. Did I wake you up?"

"Nope," the voice said. "Early riser. Are you okay?"

"I think—" she said, and she stammered it. "I think I need some help."

"I'll be over in twenty. Okay? Will you be all right until then?"

"Yeah," she said. "I'll be all right."

"Okay. I'll be right there. Just hold on."

Lou-Ann arrived fifteen minutes later. She wore an old sweat-shirt over grass-stained jeans, sneakers that had once been white. Her salt-and-pepper hair was pulled back into a low ponytail. She opened the screen door and stepped inside.

Sam had showered, keeping the water cold against her skin, but it had hurt anyway. She'd gently cleaned the cuts and scrapes on her arms. She had a few bruises blooming too, on her shoulder and forehead and wrist. It was a miracle she wasn't more badly hurt. She had pulled on a pair of jeans, the denim painful against her skin, and one of her father's old sweatshirts. It was huge on her, even though her father had not been a large man. There had been a period, in the early nineties, when things had been good in their little family, at least as far as young Sam could see. They ate well in those years, and in photos her father had gotten thick. In a family portrait they'd taken at church, they looked happy.

Those days hadn't lasted long. Still, Sam's parents had given her everything, even when they had very little. She thought that this, in the end, was what it meant to be a parent: giving away everything you have in order for your children to survive, even if it kills you.

Sam pulled the sleeves of the sweatshirt over her hands. Lou-Ann stepped toward Sam and wrapped her arms around her. Sam let herself be held, despite the pain of fabric on her skin. She held on tight, for what felt like a long time. She felt her body go soft. She buried her face in Lou-Ann's shoulder and cried.

"Let's go," the older woman said, pulling away a little but keeping Sam steadied, her hands firm on Sam's shoulders. She nodded, then followed the woman out the door.

※　　※　　※

In the church basement, Sam clutched a Styrofoam cup of coffee and fidgeted in a small metal chair. Her skin pulsed hot beneath her clothes. Lou-Ann sat next to her, close, and they listened to stories—some Sam had heard before, others she hadn't. There were five other people in the room, which seemed like a lot. They were worlds away from the packed rooms of New York, where community center staff had to bring in extra chairs and the circles were sometimes three rows deep. Up here in the woods, where most people didn't acknowledge their problems, let alone talk about them, these five people seemed to Sam a small miracle.

Most of them were older men and women, with grizzled faces and hardened hands, people who looked like they'd spent their lives working: contractors, plumbers, lumberjacks; maybe they worked at the casino or the hardware store, maybe they ran a lodge or tended bar. As they spoke, Sam crossed her legs and uncrossed them, picked small divots in the rim of her cup as the coffee went cold. She stayed silent, unable to bring herself to say anything. She was alive, and she was here, and that was good enough for now.

That afternoon, after breakfast at the Big Bear, Sam and Lou-Ann walked to the lake. They sat on the dock, their shoes off and feet in the water. They talked, watching canoes and small fishing boats trundle along the shoreline. The season was picking up.

"What's it like," Sam asked, keeping her eyes on the water, "living up here for good? Do you ever get lonely?"

"You know," Lou-Ann said, looking out at the water, "I don't really get lonely anymore. I used to, but not anymore."

The sun was out, the wind was low. Soon the woods would be busier, tourists ripping around on speedboats and ATVs, setting off fireworks. You could get the big illegal kind—the Black Cats and M-80s and Screamers—at a tent just off the highway. Sam hated fireworks, hated the Fourth of July, hated the rich people from the suburbs who came up with their broods of children who made so much noise, their disruption of the stillness like a violence against this place, explosions punctuating the night sky like gunfire. But she knew the place depended on them too, was hopeful this season might be a good one. For now, though, it was still pretty quiet.

Maybe Sam would get a job. There was the lodge a few miles away, on Lynx Lake, that almost always had a Help Wanted sign in the window, despite business being slow. They usually hired high school boys in the summer who could fix things, do the landscaping, catch some perch for the Friday fish fries. Sam could do that. She'd stop in next week and apply. They were selling the place too. The owners were an old couple her parents used to know, and it had been on the market for years. Like they were just waiting for the right person to come along. Sam knew how that went—not wanting to let go, holding on to something too long. Maybe, if she saved enough money, she could buy it, fix it up, run it herself.

"I mean, look at this place," Lou-Ann said. She nodded toward the lake, toward the trees. "It's hard to be lonely in heaven."

"I guess so," Sam said.

"Plus," Lou-Ann said, leaning gently into Sam, their shoulders touching, "you ain't alone. You got me."

She looked at Sam and smiled, and Sam smiled back.

"You call any time you want, kid," Lou-Ann said, looking back out at the lake. "I'll keep the phone on the hook for you."

Out toward the far shore, two loons were gliding together across the water, cutting a gentle V behind them. Sam thought of Stephen. She had once believed they'd be like those birds, traveling side by side the rest of their lives. But she'd never be able to love him like he deserved to be loved. She wondered if she'd ever be able to love anyone right, if she'd ever be able to stay with someone forever. She missed him.

Lou-Ann walked Sam home. As they got closer, Sam stopped at the corner lot, just down the road from her place. The house was set far back in the woods, up a long sloping hill. It was covered in overgrown weeds and fallen branches, the forest closed thick around it. But through a break in the trees, she saw the wooden planks of its walls, gray from years of snow and rain. Most of the windows were blown out, the porch cracked in half and collapsed, the roof caved in where a tree had split it open. Why she'd never looked closer, she didn't know.

"Lou-Ann," Sam said. Lou-Ann stopped beside her. "Have you seen a man around here lately, living in this place? Younger guy, burly, reddish-brown hair?"

Lou-Ann frowned. She looked at Sam, then back at the cabin. She shook her head.

"Far as I know, no one's been here for years. Folks who owned it passed over a decade ago. The son was supposed to come up, take it over, stay. But that was before."

"Before what?" Sam asked. Lou-Ann looked at her, lips pressed into a straight line.

"Hell of a thing," she said. "He did come up, few years back. Started working on the place. Thought he was going to stay. But he was—he wasn't well."

Lou-Ann paused, ran a hand through tall roadside weeds beside her. "Had it in him too, I suspect."

Sam nodded. "What happened to him?"

"Well," Lou-Ann said, "some folks said they saw him at the Beer Bar one night, getting pretty well lit. Then, I guess, he got in his truck and drove back home—"

Lou-Ann paused. Sam looked at her.

"They found his truck," Lou-Ann said, "but no one ever saw him again."

Sam swallowed hard. "What was his name?" she asked.

"Daniel." Lou-Ann paused. "Danny."

Sam stepped closer to the property. The wind kicked up, she was sure of it, clearing a path through the weeds.

"Real shame," Lou-Ann said. "Nice people. Was a nice place once too. But these woods—" She paused, then shook her head. "Sometimes they take you."

On the north side of the house, part of the stone chimney rising from the foundation had crumbled. It reminded Sam of the steeple of her childhood church, climbing up into the trees, reaching toward heaven. As a kid, she always feared it would fall.

"Danny," Sam said aloud, and shivered. She wondered if she'd even seen Danny at all, or if, like so many things she'd seen up here, he had been some kind of shadow—of a life that might have been, or might still be. She looked at the house, which had once been someone's home. She looked at the chimney, and up at the trees.

Lou-Ann put a hand on Sam's shoulder. Then she led Sam down the road to her own driveway. They walked in silence, then stood at the mouth of the path, looking up at the cabin.

"You know," Lou-Ann said, "I've been thinking about you, and this place. I've been thinking about its name."

Sam nodded, but said nothing, kept her eyes on the cabin alongside Lou-Ann.

"Do you know there's a language of flowers? That each flower and plant means something in that language?"

Sam nodded again. She had heard this before but wasn't sure where. There was a strange feeling curling around her, like she knew what was coming.

"Yup," Lou-Ann said, keeping her eyes on the cabin. "It's often attributed to Victorian England. But of course it's a language much older than that. Ancient, really. Floriography. A way to communicate through plants."

Sam waited. Lou-Ann continued.

"And in the language of flowers, do you know what *hemlock* means?"

"No," she managed, though she suspected she did.

Lou-Ann turned to Sam, looked her in the eyes. *"You will be my death."*

Sam looked back at the cabin. The trees were bending in around it, blocking out the sun. There was a chill in the air. She shivered again.

"Maybe I should consider a name change," she said. Lou-Ann cracked a little laugh, and the moment loosened its grip.

"Nah," she said. "Just remember that. There's life and death in everything. Light and dark. We hold both at once."

Sam nodded. She felt at once repelled by and pulled toward the cabin. She wanted to turn away, but felt it calling her.

"You'll be okay," Lou-Ann said. "I know you will."

She hugged Sam then, and Sam thanked her, and they said goodbye. The older woman turned down the road and Sam walked up the drive. She stood outside the cabin, which was in far better shape than it had been when she'd found it. She surveyed the work she'd done, thought of all the work she had yet to do. She would stay as long as it took.

She went inside and walked down the dark hallway to her parents' bedroom. She had kept the door shut. Now she stood outside it, on the threshold of whatever lay beyond. For a moment,
she found herself thinking of the cabin's name, of words that
possess more than one meaning. She remembered a word she'd
learned growing up, in her small Scandinavian town—a word
that came to her now, standing in the dark before this bedroom
door, summoned in this shadowed passage as if by a spell.

Dyr. From the Old Norse, a word that means both wicked
and dear. A word like *dire,* and like *deer*—a word that warns of
disaster and horror; a word that means animal, brute, or beast.

She put her hand on the doorknob and turned.

Inside the bedroom, there was no darkness. The sun was
bright. It came in through the windows in warm slants of gold.
Sam stepped into the room, the log walls her father had laid
glowing the color of honey. She felt her blood beating in her temples, her vision start to sparkle and blur. Her brain began to tilt,
then seemed to lift from her body, floating toward the ceiling.
She pressed her hand to the wall and closed her eyes.

Then she tore the room apart.

She ripped blankets off the bed, broke open the closet doors
and wrenched every shirt off its hanger. Sweatshirts and flannels
flew to the floor, plastic hangers snapping. She turned over boxes
of records and books, threw her mother's paintbrushes against
the wall, willing them to shatter.

Her body was not her own. Or maybe it was hers for the first
time. She felt more animal than human—she was the beast that
lived in the woods, a thing made of hunger who stalked its prey
and gutted it. She was the bear that crashed through screen doors,
taking what it needed to feed its own. She was the bird and the

squirrel, the branches of the tree upon which they landed. She was the deer, a creature fueled by survival.

In the back of the closet, she found a shoebox. She stood in the darkness, body humming, lungs heaving. She held the box in her hands. Then she opened it.

Inside, there were faded photos and a collection of trinkets—stones and feathers and figurines—and beneath them, a small hardcover book. She sat on the floor, cradling the box in her hands. Her breath slowed; her brain began to swim back inside her body. She set the box on the floor and picked up the book, wiped the dust from its cover. The title—*Celtic Mythology*—was stamped in delicate gold leaf. She opened the book to where a ribbon marked the page, and read the entry.

Cailleach Bhéara, or Cailleach: Also known as the Divine Hag, the Queen of Winter, or the Old Woman of Beare. She is the creator of the northern Winterland, and is associated with horned beasts. According to Irish legend, she lives off the coast of the Beara Peninsula, on a remote island called the Land of the Dead. To avoid capture from predators she takes the form of a deer, and is often seen herding other deer to safety. A protector of women and the land, she is sometimes thought to be connected to the Greek myth of the Ceryneian hind, a creature who took the form of a massive doe, or female deer, with the golden antlers of a stag. A creature swift of foot, with a dappled coat and golden hooves and which breathed fire, it lived in the boreal forest. (See: *Boreas,* god of the North Wind; See: *Hyperboreans,* "beyond boreas," a mythical people who lived beyond the North

Wind, in the wilderness past the edge of the known world.)

Cailleach. She said the name aloud, remembered the shape of the word in her mouth, heard her grandmother's voice as she told the story. She set the book down. She rifled through the box. An acorn, a pine cone, a piece of pink quartz. A photo of Sam, her mother, and her grandmother, hiking in the woods. At the bottom of the box, she found a journal. It was old, and small, its cover soft and weathered. Most of the pages had been torn out, but tucked inside was an envelope. Sam's name was scrawled on the front, in a familiar hand. She held the envelope, hands trembling, then slid a finger beneath the seal and opened it. Inside was a letter. The handwriting was shaky, barely legible. She willed herself to read it.

I'm sorry, Sam, the letter began. *I never planned for this. I always thought life would be different—for you, for me, for all of us. But I know now that some things are fated. There are things we can't control. And at some point, we have to stop fighting whatever is in us, and let go. We must listen to the woods, to the animals and the birds and the trees, and they'll tell us where we need to be. I hope that when the time comes, you can listen too. My daughter, You're a part of me, and I'm a part of you. And we're all a part of everything. Please don't forget that. But it's time for me to go. Remember what I said about the trees. Listen to them, and they'll tell you too. You'll hear them, and in them you'll hear me, and you'll know when it's time for you.*

Sam knelt on the floor, hands trembling, gripping the letter. She read the next line, the last line, and then read it again, trying to make sense of the words. They swam with the room around her, tilting and spilling off the page. She watched them move over her hands, crawling up her arms like insects, working their way inside her skin, burrowing. She felt them, alive and buzzing in her blood.

I love you, they said. *We'll be waiting.*

Forty-Five

◇◇◇◇◇◇◇◇◇◇◇

SHE MADE A pot of coffee. Took a cup and the journal to the porch and sat in the sun. She turned to a clean page and wrote three letters of her own. One was to Gina, apologizing for disappearing, explaining everything as best she could. Maybe they'd be friends, she thought, maybe eventually something more. What she needed, for now, was to be alone. Fully, for real, maybe for the first time in her life. *I like you*, Sam wrote, *and I think it might be nice to be in each other's lives, someday, if you're open to that. In whatever form feels best.* As she wrote it, she felt something like hope.

She wrote to her dad, telling him all the things she had always wanted to say but had never known how. That she loved him, that she was proud of him. That she saw so much of him in herself, and more of it every day. That it was never too late to start over, become something new. She told him she'd visit more often. She told him to take care of himself.

Then she wrote to Stephen. Over their decade together, Stephen had written Sam many letters—from small, silly notes on yellow Post-Its to pages-long odes. Sam had kept them all, and if she ever went back to New York to move out of their apartment, the box that held them would be one of the only things she'd keep.

Until now, she hadn't written him any letters. To write something down, she knew, to put words in ink on paper, was to give something of herself away, to say something permanent that could be kept, and couldn't be taken back.

Sam had lived most of her life believing everything was temporary. That people would leave—either by choice or by death or in other ways, whether of the brain's volition or by some weapon with which you broke it. That in the end she would always be alone, as everyone essentially was. At some point, this story had become her own mythology. It was the story she told herself, and the one she believed. A self-fulfilling prophecy, a story made real by her action and inaction, by her silence, by the walls she'd been building around herself since she was a kid, when her parents had disappeared, in their own ways. When she started disappearing too. It was a story that lived inside her—passed down, inherited, like her skin and her hair and her green eyes. Stephen had left, but the truth was that she'd left a long time ago. It was just as he said—maybe she'd never really been there at all.

She wrote him all of this. Her hands shook. Her fingers were numb. The ink was running dry. She shook the pen, and she wrote and wrote, filling page after page in the journal—her mother's journal, with so many pages still empty. She told him everything she should have told him before. She wrote down all the lies she'd told, all the ways she'd hidden. She told him all the good she remembered, too, all the things she would miss: mornings in bed in Brooklyn, the cat curled up between them; reading the paper and drinking coffee under the covers, that slant of sunlight coming in through the window. Walking around their neighborhood on summer nights. Reading on the fire escape. Playing records in their living room and dancing. Making dinner in their tiny kitchen, the Monster circling like a furry little vulture at their feet.

She told him that she loved him, that she missed him, that she couldn't imagine her life without him. Everything she wrote, for once, was true.

She knew he was better off without her. That he would find someone else who could love him better than she could. Maybe he'd have a little family. She wanted him to have that, to have everything he'd always wanted and that she could never give. She wanted, more than anything, for him to be happy. She wrote this to him too.

She tore the pages out of the notebook, found envelopes in the junk drawer, and folded the letters inside. She licked and sealed them closed. She found a book of stamps—old and yellowed and not enough postage—and pressed three to each letter. She addressed the envelopes in a shaky hand, sending one to the hardware store, one to her childhood home, and writing down her own address in Brooklyn one last time.

Her head ached and her heart raced. The hangover was hitting hard. Maybe it would be her last. Maybe today would be the first day of one day at a time. Maybe she'd go back to that church basement with Lou-Ann, and maybe she'd keep going.

Or maybe she wouldn't. Either way, the rest of her life was waiting.

She swallowed two aspirin, grabbed the letters, and stepped out the door. She left her keys and her phone on the counter, left the cabin unlocked, and stepped into the sun.

She would walk the long miles to the grocery store and mail the letters. She would stop at the mechanic's shop and have them tow her father's truck, still smashed against the tree, beyond repair, bearing the reminder of what she'd done—bearing her whole life in the twisted metal, in the dried blood on the hood and the fur in the fender. She would have to walk past it on her way, and she would force herself to look.

But before she set off, she would walk around to the side of the cabin. She would see the irises she had planted, already in bloom, their purple flowers reaching toward the sun. She would remember what the doe had told her, what her mother had told her. She would walk past the feeder in the front yard, reminding herself to refill it. Then she would walk on, her shoes crunching against gravel. She would be tired, and her whole body would ache, but she would keep going.

Eventually, the pain would fade. The feeling in her fingers would return. She would feel a little better each day. Eventually, she would not be sick. She would let the hair on her body grow long, covering her skin like a coat. She would get strong again, stronger than she'd ever been. She would run in the woods and never get tired. She would swim in the lakes without stopping. Out of the ashes of this body a whole new creature would emerge—a better version of itself, a brand-new form. She would be alive. She would be awake. She would not be afraid.

But before all that, she would walk those miles to town and think of her family. She would remember days when she was young, when her parents were still young too, and the summers they spent in the Northwoods together. She would think of the fires they built, the fish they caught, the walks they took in the trees. She would remember winters, the silence of new snowfall. She would remember one winter when she was a girl, taking a walk alone, and spotting a deer bedded down in the forest—a doe, curled up in a burrow under the trees, and next to her, a fawn. They watched each other, held in a moment that seemed to last forever.

She would remember her father next to her in the fishing boat at dawn. She would remember the three of them sitting around the fire, roasting marshmallows as the flames shot high into the circle of trees, her mother telling ghost stories as night fell, the last shreds of daylight letting go. She would remember her parents tucking her in, the windows of the cabin open wide, and falling asleep to the sound of crickets and peepers, the barred owl, a pack of coyotes singing into the night, and feeling so safe, so held, her whole life stretched out before her, seemingly endless, like the light in summer.

And she would remember hiking in the woods with her mother, and her grandmother, the women teaching the girl how to spot cardinals and finches and sparrows; to tell the difference between a grackle and a crow, a spruce and a fir. To identify the mushrooms and berries and herbs and flowers that could be dried and turned into tea, and those that would kill you. To bend the needles of a pine tree and smell the sap, to place your hand on its trunk and know whether it was healthy or dying, having contracted a borer or some invisible disease, or whether its time had simply come. To stop in the woods and listen—to the trees, to the wind, to all the things the forest was saying.

Listen, the women told her, *and you'll hear it.*

She would remember believing so fully in their words, in what they could see and hear. Like magic, like ghosts, maybe even like God, she believed in them. She'd been so afraid, in so many ways, of becoming these women. She didn't know if she was even a woman anymore—if she was man or beast or both—but she knew, in the end, she was just like them, these women who raised her. Hard and soft in the same ways, monstrous and beautiful.

She would walk those miles alone, and she would listen to the trees, the way the wind in the pines rushed like water. She would hear the music of the woods, like a song she once sang in church, feeling the harmonies of the hymn in her body, vibrating in her skin, rising up and filling the cathedral with sound. She would say thank you, and she would say it aloud. Maybe she would even pray. To the trees, to this place that had made her. A place she'd left for a while, and to which she'd finally returned. She would mail the letters, and then she would walk back the way she came.

But this time, she would not take the road. She would turn, instead, into the woods, into that holy opening that called her. She would listen to the sound, and she would follow it. She would walk until the sound got closer, until it rose up around her like a choir. She would walk until her body disappeared into the trees, and she would know, at last, that she was home.

Acknowledgments

I DIDN'T PLAN to write this novel so much as it emerged, unbidden, and rather like the doe—weird, willful, sometimes a total pain, entirely insistent upon survival. It's been a long, strange path, one that forged itself through the woods as I followed, fighting black flies and brambles and old ghosts, beginning to understand the edict I repeat to my students—*Trust the process*—in a whole new light. Most of that time was spent toiling alone, at several desks across several states: from a cabin in the Wisconsin Northwoods to my apartment in Greenpoint, Brooklyn; from North Carolina to Ohio and back again. But as is always true of making a book, amid all that solo struggle, so many people helped along the way. Here I offer my deepest thanks.

To my literary agent dream team, Marya Spence and Mackenzie Williams at Janklow & Nesbit, for finding this book when I feared it was lost, then bringing it home. For your brilliance, belief, advocacy, vision, and style. Triple M forever.

To Michael Taeckens, literary matchmaker extraordinaire, who introduced us.

To my editor, the inimitable Vivian Lee, for understanding this story fundamentally, for taking it on, and for making it so much better. To the excellent team at Little, Brown for bringing this book to life, including but not limited to: Morgan Wu, Karen Landry, Albert LaFarge, Jeffrey Gantz (for all the bird fact-checks!), and Keith Hayes, for the cover of my creepiest dreams.

To Adriann Ranta Zurhellen for insight and advice across all those early drafts.

To Jami Attenberg's #1000wordsofsummer for getting me started. To Matt Bell, who helped me *Refuse to Be Done.*

To Margy and Ed Campion for giving me a room of my own, several times over.

To the people, places, and creatures of the Northwoods, specifically the Chequamegon-Nicolet National Forest, where this book was born and whose DNA lives in these pages. To the town of Boulder Junction, and to Cherie Sanderson and the staff of the Boulder Junction Public Library, for helping me find *Woodswoman* by Anne LaBastille and for inviting me back. To Ross' Teal Lake Lodge, home of the original Hemlock. To all the lakeside bars and Friday fish fries. To the Lac du Flambeau, Ojibwe Nation, and all First Nations people of northern Wisconsin who called this land home long before it was ever called the Northwoods.

To the good folks at the following institutions, where, alongside building a career as a teacher, I've been able to work on this book and carve out the shape of my life as a writer: Sarah Lawrence College's MFA program and Writing Institute, Kenyon College and the Kenyon Review Writers Workshops, Vermont College of Fine Arts, Denison University, and finally the University of North Carolina—for bringing me to Chapel Hill as the 2020–2021 Kenan Visiting Writer to complete the first draft, then bringing me back to finish it. Special thanks to the Margaret R. Shuping Fellowship for continued support, and to my creative writing colleagues for the friendship, laughter, long talks, fake beers, and walks in the woods.

To the Black Swan Event crew, my writing community still. To Melissa Febos for being the person I call. To T Kira Madden for writing and reading alongside me. To Vijay Seshadri, who told me this was my vocation. To Jo Ann Beard, who taught me that genre is a construct.

To my students, who teach me always, who keep me going, who remind me that this practice is sacred. Keep the incense burning.

To the queer writers who came before and those yet to come. To the educators, librarians, booksellers, and organizations who continue to teach, lend, and promote books by queer and trans authors in the face of book bans and anti-LGBTQ+ legislation that threaten both free speech and queer lives.

To Beth Binhammer for helping me find a way through the darkest forests.

To my Wisconsin family, both biological and chosen, for your love and support, and all those trips Up North.

To Grandma Mary—I wish you could have read this one. I think you would have liked it.

To my mom, Becky Faliveno, who taught me how to take care of (and talk to) plants and animals, how to listen to the trees, the glory of a walk in the woods, and how to draw a perfect circle. To my dad, Bob Faliveno, who taught me how to fish, the importance of a strong cup of coffee on a quiet morning, and everything I know about refinishing a deck (and who fact-checked my work around it). To both my parents, who took me to the

Northwoods and taught me to love it, who showed me all the creature features and let me read all the Stephen King, who made this story, and this whole life, possible.

To the best black cat, Molly, the inspiration for Monster and my own sweet familiar.

To John, my first reader and best friend, for reading this book again and again, for seeing it, and me, so fully, and for keeping the Saunders meter pointed forward. For always making space for me to write, for following me across so many state lines, and, at last, for landing in our own little circle of trees.

To Paul, who loved the Northwoods, and who told me just before he died that I was a novelist. You were the first person to call me that and the first to believe it. I know you needed to go, but I wish you could have stayed.

To those who have struggled, or still struggle, with substance abuse and addiction, mental illness, self-harm, or suicide, and to those who have loved or lost someone who has. There's light beyond the darkness of these woods. I hope you find it. I hope you hold on until you do.

About the Author

MELISSA FALIVENO IS the author of the essay collection *Tomboy-land*, named a Best Book of 2020 by NPR; New York Public Library; *O, The Oprah Magazine*; and *Electric Literature*, and the recipient of a 2021 Outstanding Achievement Award from the Wisconsin Library Association. Her writing has appeared in *Esquire*, the *Paris Review*, the *Kenyon Review*, *Literary Hub*, *Prairie Schooner*, *Brevity*, and the *Brooklyn Rail*, among others, and in the anthologies *Sex and the Single Woman* and the forthcoming *Hit Repeat Until I Hate Music*. Born and raised in small-town Wisconsin and a longtime resident of Greenpoint, Brooklyn, she is an assistant professor of creative writing at the University of North Carolina and lives in the woods outside Chapel Hill.

RAISING READERS
Books Build Bright Futures

Thank you for reading this book and for being a reader of books in general. We are so grateful to share being part of a community of readers with you, and we hope you will join us in passing our love of books on to the next generation of readers.

Did you know that reading for enjoyment is the single biggest predictor of a child's future happiness and success?

More than family circumstances, parents' educational background, or income, reading impacts a child's future academic performance, emotional well-being, communication skills, economic security, ambition, and happiness.

Studies show that kids reading for enjoyment in the US is in rapid decline:

- In 2012, 53% of 9-year-olds read almost every day. Just 10 years later, in 2022, the number had fallen to 39%.
- In 2012, 27% of 13-year-olds read for fun daily. By 2023, that number was just 14%.

Together, we can commit to **Raising Readers** and change this trend. How?

- Read to children in your life daily.
- Model reading as a fun activity.
- Reduce screen time.
- Start a family, school, or community book club.
- Visit bookstores and libraries regularly.
- Listen to audiobooks.
- Read the book before you see the movie.
- Encourage your child to read aloud to a pet or stuffed animal.
- Give books as gifts.
- Donate books to families and communities in need.

BOB1217

Books build bright futures, and **Raising Readers** is our shared responsibility.

For more information, visit **JoinRaisingReaders.com**

Sources: National Endowment for the Arts, National Assessment of Educational Progress, WorldBookDay.org, Nielsen BookData's 2023 "Understanding the Children's Book Consumer"